Hold
Love
Strong

Hold
Love
Strong

A novel

MATTHEW AARON GOODMAN

A TOUCHSTONE BOOK
Published by Simon & Schuster
New York   London   Toronto   Sydney

Touchstone
A Division of Simon & Schuster, Inc.
1230 Avenue of the Americas
New York, NY 10020

First Touchstone trade paperback edition March 2010

TOUCHSTONE and colophon are registered trademarks of Simon & Schuster, Inc.

For information about special discounts for bulk purchases, please contact
Simon & Schuster Special Sales at 1-866-506-1949 or business@simonandschuster.com.

The Simon & Schuster Speakers Bureau can bring authors to your
live event. For more information or to book an event contact the
Simon & Schuster Speakers Bureau at 1-866-248-3049 or visit our
website at www.simonspeakers.com.

Designed by Claudia Martinez

Manufactured in the United States of America

3   5   7   9   10   8   6   4   2

Library of Congress Cataloging-in-Publication Data
Goodman, Matthew Aaron
Hold love strong: a novel /
Matthew Aaron Goodman.
p. cm.
1. African American young men—Fiction. 2. African American families—Fiction.
3. Poor families—Fiction. 4. Drug addiction—Fiction. 5. Low-income housing—Fiction.
6. Queens (New York, N.Y.)—Fiction. 7. Domestic fiction. I. Title.
PS3607. 0586H65   2009
813'.6—dc22   2008030677

ISBN 978-1-4165-6203-0
ISBN 978-1-4165-6204-7 (pbk)
ISBN 978-1-4165-6222-1 (ebook)

For my father and his;
For my mother and hers;
For Nadia;
For my brothers,
And their brothers,
My brothers, my brothers . . .

COMPOSITION

If I am not for myself,
Who will be for me?

If I am only for myself,
What am I?

If not now,
When?

—HILLEL

BAR 1

Hold Love Strong

I

The first pain came at noon but she didn't tell anybody about it. My mother was thirteen and she went about the afternoon being every part of such a precarious age. She watched TV. She popped pimples and studied her face in the bathroom mirror. She listened to the radio, sang along with songs, and laughed along with the afternoon DJs. She wrote in her diary. *I still can't Beleve! I'm pregnant,* she scribbled in bulbous letters that began and ended in curls. *I can't beleve my belly is soooo big!* At five, she took a nap and awoke three hours later, home alone and in a wet bed. She thought it was pee, balled the sheets, put them in the trash, and told herself she was disgusting. Then it was midnight and the pain became a fiery Cinderella banging to flee her guts. Still, she ignored it. Twenty minutes later, another pain came like the previous one but angrier, and so along with the banging it tore at her, buckled her knees, and left her coiled and crying on the floor. She had to do something. She had to find an answer; or something to distract her from the increasing frequency of such mercilessness; or some kind of pliers to rip and wrench the pain out of her. She went to her best friend Cherrie's apartment one floor below ours. It was a Friday night and she knew Cherrie would be awake watching TV.

"It's just gas," Cherrie decided, pouring my mother a glass of ginger ale in the kitchen. "What you eat?"

"Some Ring Dings and a bag of Doritos," said my mother.

"A whole bag, damn!" Cherrie forced her surprise to fit into a whisper because her mother was asleep in one room, her big sister Candy was asleep in the other, and the walls in the apartment, like the walls in every Ever Park Project apartment, amplified even the slightest sound.

Although Cherrie had a way of convincing my mother that what was major was minor, and although my mother hoped that what was going on inside her was something trivial and unholy, she was still just thirteen, so she was scared, maybe even desperate.

"Should I call James?" she asked.

The year was 1982. There were no cell phones or pagers so there was no way to get in touch with people unless you knew where they were or left a message where they would soon arrive. My grandmother and my mother's sister, my Aunt Rhonda, would have been my mother's first and second choices, but they had taken my Uncle Roosevelt and my cousins Donnel and Eric to see *E.T.*, so there was no way of speaking to them, and calling where they would arrive meant calling where she had just left. As for James, he was my father. That is, James Llewelyn Arthur sowed the seed that became me. He was twenty. The last time my mother and he spoke they fought over a retractable Bic pen. He wanted it. She wouldn't give it to him. He punched her breast. She stabbed him in the leg with it. That was the previous week. Since then he was gone and never found; never found a phone; never found another pen and paper to write a letter; never found two twigs to rub together to make a small fire so a smoke signal would drift into the sky and prove he knew we were alive.

"James?" said Cherrie, wiping her mouth after swigging straight from the two-liter bottle of ginger ale. "What's he gonna do?"

Although the answer could only be nothing, my mother used Cherrie's phone to call James. Of course, there was no James to speak to. He was out said his grandmother, an old woman with a wobbly, frayed voice who was too lonely to even wonder, let alone ask, why my mother was calling so late. "You know," she said, "come to think, I ain't seen him since yesterday. I hope he comes home tonight."

"Tell him Angela called," blurted my mother.

"Who?"

"Angela."

"OK, Angela, that's such a pretty name. I once had a dear friend named Anita. That's a pretty name too."

"Tell him I need to see him, that it's real, real important. Tell him to call as soon as he comes in. It don't matter what time it is."

"He has your phone number?"

"Yeah," my mother answered, trying to sound confident yet wondering if he remembered it.

Because my mother hadn't left a note nor trace of where she went and why she left, she and Cherrie ascended the stairs from the third floor to the fourth floor and returned to my grandma's apartment. There, they sat on the plaid, mustard-colored couch and watched TV as if late night reruns of the Three Stooges could refute my mother's pregnancy and pains and transport them to who they should have been at this time in their lives, nascent teenage girls just beyond the loss of their last baby teeth, confidantes whose essential aims had yet to be developed and so needed to be discussed in that mighty gabbing and giggling best thirteen-year-old girlfriends do when awake after midnight.

Just as suddenly as each pain before, another crash tried to split my mother in half. She slammed herself into the back of the couch, and breathed so hard and fast snot flew from her nose.

"What's it feel like?" asked Cherrie, touching my mother's round belly with both hands.

"God damn, fuck!" said my mother, sweating and shaking her head no. "It's like I got lightning inside me."

When the pain dissipated, Cherrie got my mother a glass of water from the kitchen. Then there was the sound of keys opening the door, a click and clack and then two clacks more. Locks were being unlocked. Someone was about to be home.

"Ma!" my mother shouted as if she had fallen down a dark hole and feared she would never be found. "Momma!"

But it wasn't my grandma. The door opened and my Aunt Rhonda walked in holding Eric in her arms, his legs dangling around her waist as he slept with his head burrowed in the crook of her neck. Eric was two and he was afflicted with a particular idiosyncrasy that made him somewhat of a spectacle. He was born with Sjögren's syndrome so he could howl and shout, and he could screech and scream until every vein in his head seemed as if it might explode, but he could not cry. Never. Not once had there ever been nor would there ever be a tear in or falling from his eyes.

"Sorry we so late," my Aunt Rhonda said, taking her keys out of the door so not yet looking at my mother. "The first movie was sold out, so we had to see the later one."

My Aunt Rhonda was seventeen. She was five foot three inches tall, one hundred and ten peanut-butter-brown pounds of a young woman, and the extreme of the lesson my mother was learning. That is, she only knew loving herself through seeking, finding, and being hurt by men who did not love themselves nor comprehend the value of being someone cherished. She said hello to Cherrie. Then she looked at my mother and her eyes got stuck.

"Jelly, what's wrong?" she asked, calling my mother by the nickname she had given her when she was a little girl.

"She got gas," said Cherrie. "I made her drink some ginger ale. She'll be all right soon."

"See," my Aunt Rhonda scolded. "I told you to stop fucking with all that junk food."

Through the open door my Uncle Roosevelt strode into the apartment, dragging my Aunt Rhonda's eldest son, my cousin, weary-eyed, half-asleep four-year-old Donnel by the hand behind him.

"Damn, Jelly," Roosevelt said. "Why you look so crazy?"

My Uncle Roosevelt was an amber-skinned, narrow-eyed, gangly nine-year-old who already owned the kingly disposition only the world's most blessed men approach possessing. His grace was astounding. No season, situation; no rage, pain, or suffering touched him. He let go of Donnel's hand, crossed in front of my Aunt Rhonda, and came to the couch.

"How's the baby?" he asked.

"Where's Ma?" my mother said.

"She's coming," my Aunt Rhonda answered. "She got stuck talking to Mr. Goines outside."

"He loves her," added my Uncle Roosevelt, stating what everyone knew to be truth.

He leaned over my mother and put his ear against her belly. Suddenly my mother winced and moaned and was racked with a wave of pain that made her nostrils flare, lips quiver, and her body shudder as if her ribs were pounding her organs to pieces. My Aunt Rhonda ran to her, seamlessly handing Eric to my Uncle Roosevelt, who cocked his hip, set Eric upon it, and tucked the boy's head beneath his chin without waking him.

"Jelly," said Rhonda wiping the sweat from my mother's forehead with her hand. "Jelly, your water break?"

"I don't know," my mother moaned. "It just hurts."

When the contraction ended my Aunt Rhonda told Cherrie to call an ambulance.

"No," said my mother.

"What you mean, 'No'?" my Aunt Rhonda asked. She stood tall, planted her hands on her hips, and looked down at my mother. "We got to get you to the hospital."

"James is gonna call," said my mother.

My Aunt Rhonda sucked her teeth and rolled her eyes as if making a red circle around an incorrect answer in the air. "Jelly, you about to burst!" she scolded. "We don't got time for James."

"I got time," said my mother.

My father was not the type of man who gave a damn or sacrificed in the name of what was necessary, just, and good. My mother was impulsive and headstrong. We were going to be a family is all she believed. That's it, that seventh-grade cusp of pubescent confusion, that dream trumped all truth. That conviction was her head and heart and the construction of her vital organs. James would come around. He would realize it was only a pen and she didn't mean to stab him. It was only a matter of time. They would raise me together. She paid no mind to my Aunt Rhonda's history, the other young histories pushing strollers in the neighborhood, nor what anyone warned her. James Llewelyn Arthur loved her infinity. That's what he told her just before the first times but never after, just before she gave him her virginity, just before the first time she gave him head, just before she let him go down on her, bury his lips, lick, lap, and spread the one part of her body she had never studied in the mirror nor had the courage to touch herself.

My grandma came into the apartment. "What are you all crazy or something?" she scolded. "Why is this door open?"

"Ma," my mother whimpered.

My grandma didn't speak. She didn't blink or breathe. A passionately constructed woman of only thirty, she swiftly studied the scene. She looked at my mother. She looked at Cherrie. She looked at Rhonda. All of my grandma's features possessed a depth and delicacy that made her and everything within ten feet of her beautiful. Her body and being were balance. Her arms were long and muscular as were her legs, fingers, neck, earlobes, and the length of time her laughter lasted.

"When was the last one?" she asked.

"Just before. Maybe not even two minutes," said my Aunt Rhonda. She slammed her eyes on Cherrie. "What I tell you? Shit, what the fuck I say?"

Cherrie sprinted into the kitchen, where our phone sat on the counter, and my grandma and my Aunt Rhonda led my mother into the bathroom because the couch was my grandma's first and only couch and even though she bought it used she refused for it to be ruined or even slightly stained by anyone or anything, even birth, no matter how divine an occasion it was.

"Mind your nephews!" my grandma told Roosevelt.

"I got them," he said, taking Donnel's hand, leading him and his wide eyes to sit on the couch, and then sitting beside him with Eric, still sleeping, balanced against him.

In the kitchen, Cherrie turned the rotary dial, held the phone to her ear, and listened. Nothing. She tapped the switch-hooks hoping that there was some kind of short, or that one of the buttons was stuck. Still, nothing. She slammed the phone into the cradle then picked it up and held it to her ear again. Nothing. She slammed the handset down.

"It's dead!" she cried out. There ain't even a dial tone!"

My grandma closed her eyes and cursed everything under her breath, Queens and the state of New York, the phone company and Ever Park, life, herself, America. The phone could have been dead for one of any number of reasons: the phone bill hadn't been paid; the phone company didn't do the proper upkeep; someone in our building cut a wire thinking splicing it would give them phone service.

"Go downstairs," shouted my grandma. "Don't act like you ain't got no sense! Use yours. And if that don't work go use a pay phone! Shit, Cherrie, don't just give up!"

Cherrie bolted out of our apartment like my grandma's voice was fire and the drum of Cherrie's heavy feet could be heard thumping down the stairs until she reached the third floor's door, which squealed when it opened then boomed when it closed.

In the bathroom, my grandma and my Aunt Rhonda helped my mother take off her clothes.

"My shirt too?" asked my mother.

"Shirt too," ordered my grandma. "Unless you got the money to pay for a new one if it gets bloody."

So off came my mother's shirt and for a moment my grandma, my aunt, and my mother just stood there, three proximate shades of black women, autumnal hues in a small, plain bathroom with white walls, a white porcelain sink, a white bathtub, and a white toilet with a broken black plastic seat. My grandma and my Aunt Rhonda looked at my mother, who, looking in the bathroom mirror, looked at herself as well. In addition to the disposition and body type of my grandma, my mother was the color of an old penny at the bottom of a wishing well. Equally, she reflected and absorbed sunshine, streetlights, and the hopes of those who wished upon her, then cast her off. Her eyes and lips, her nose, shoulders and breasts, even her thighs and hips were shaped like new leaves, full yet still timid, still approaching their eventual lustrous peak.

My grandma snatched the red bath towel from the back of the bathroom door and put it on the floor. "Here," she decided. "Lay down on this. And Rhonda, get behind and hold her. That baby is coming. I can feel it. We ain't got much time."

My mother lay down. The bathroom was so small her head crossed the threshold of its doorway. Behind my mother, on her knees, wrapping her arms around her and wedging her thighs against my mother's back, my Aunt Rhonda kneeled on the coarse, grey carpet of the living room. My grandma stepped into the bathtub. She hiked her skirt up over her knees, squatted, and put my mother's ankles on her shoulders.

"Lord have mercy," she said. "Lord have some motherfucking mercy on me."

My mother sweated, shivered, and writhed from the pain and the fright. Another contraction came and went. Then she cursed and screamed and told my grandma she didn't want to live no more.

"Jelly, shut your mouth!" demanded my grandma. "Stop thinking about yourself! You about to be a mother!"

On the couch, Donnel asked question after question and Eric awoke and hollered for my Aunt Rhonda. He reached for her. He fought to get out of my Uncle Roosevelt's arms. My uncle tried to keep them calm. He hushed them. He softly sang verses of spontaneously composed lullabies. He tried to remind my cousins about the movie they just saw, how ET had a magic finger and loved Reese's Pieces candy.

My mother quaked with another contraction and she moaned and rolled her head from side to side as if her neck and spine were suddenly severed. Then she stopped and looked down at the round mound of her belly, her eyes so wide it seemed she was surprised by the sight. She put her hands on it, and with her fingers spread as wide as they could stretch, my mother began to weep. But it was not weeping caused by physical pain, or by ignorance, or even a weeping caused by fear. My mother wept because although she was still a child she had enough sense to understand that she was not prepared to shape my life. She couldn't multiply or divide. She didn't know north, south, east, or west. She couldn't tell time on a regular clock. This is not to say she was dumb. In fact, my mother was brilliant, so smart she could remember all of the words in a song after hearing it just once. What my mother was then was the product of low expectations. She had been failed so she had failed. And yet, social promotion: she had just graduated the seventh grade.

But when she felt weak, when she felt hopeless and useless and begged my grandma to make the pain stop, to let her quit, my grandma said, *"No!"* My mother couldn't stop, not even if great God Almighty Himself said she could quit. And so, because my grandma was not the type of woman anyone could disregard, my mother pushed with her life. She clenched the air in her fists. She gritted her teeth. She closed her eyes so tightly she saw everything she'd ever wished to see, every mountain and ocean, every sandy beach, tropical waterfall; elephants and lions and giraffes in Africa; she saw Jesus, she shook President Reagan's hand; she saw the Statue of Liberty; herself with a car, a fur coat; a collie like Lassie; she saw herself as a movie star. Her toes curled. Her calves cramped. Her heart became a volcano bursting blood. She saw her dreams. She felt their temperature. She smelled them.

My grandma saw my head. She took it in her hands and pulled gently, but then, holding one hand up as if halting a train, she shouted: *"STOP!"*

Every muscle in my mother's body went limp. My umbilical cord was wrapped twice around my neck. My mother's pushing combined with my twisting and turning was killing me. I was being lynched and I was hanging myself. My face was the color of an electric blue bruise. One more push or pull, one more twist, and I was dead. My mother begged to understand what was happening.

"Momma," she said, propping herself on her elbows. "Momma, please."

"What's wrong?" asked Rhonda. "Ma, what is it?"

My grandma breathed deep. "Shh, both of you, let me think."

Outside of the bathroom, Eric stopped hollering, Donnel stopped asking questions, and my Uncle Roosevelt stopped hushing and singing lullabies. All of Ever Park, all of Queens went silent. Then, in through the door burst Cherrie.

"They coming!" she shouted. "A ambulance is on the way!"

My Aunt Rhonda looked over her shoulder at Cherrie, her eyes demanding silence.

Cherrie stopped in the middle of the living room. "What's going on?" Cherrie said, her voice a fraction of its preceding size.

In the bathroom, my grandma looked up at the ceiling. "God," she whispered. "Jesus. Somebody, please help me save this child."

My grandma took one deep breath, closed her eyes, and made the same prayer silently. Then she opened her eyes, gently held my head and slowly drew my shoulders free. She paused to think. What next? What could she possibly do? The umbilical cord was taut. She cupped her hand beneath me, breathed, then cautiously guiding me in an un-hurried somersault, she turned me upside down, freed my legs, and unwound the umbilical cord from my neck. My grandma saved me from that which fed and kept me for the first nine months of my life. She cleared my nostrils and mouth with her pinky. Then she wiped the blood from me with the palm of her hand.

"Roosevelt!" she called out. "Get me a knife! A sharp one. One of the ones with the wooden handles."

But it wasn't my uncle who brought my grandma the knife. It was Donnel. Like a miniature Mercury, he burst into the bathroom and held the knife out to her. Then he stood on his tiptoes and looked at the new life my grandma cradled to her chest.

"This your baby cousin," she said. She pushed me into his arms. "Now, hold love strong."

Donnel held me against his chest like a ball of loose yarn and my grandma cut my umbilical cord and left me the ugliest outie the world has ever seen. She washed me in the sink and handed me to my mother. And as my mother held me on the floor in the bathroom, as she wept and dealt with the awe of my making, Rhonda asked what my name should be because my mother had not yet been able to settle on one.

"Abraham," my grandma announced.

"Like the president?" Rhonda asked.

"No," said my grandma. "Like the old man in the Bible that God said was gonna be the father of a great people as numerous as the stars."

II

I'm one of hundreds; one of thousands; one of millions now and millions more to come; a project nigga, a beautiful project nigga through and through. I lived in Ever Park every day of my life; in a building of stacks, of bricks stacked upon bricks, people stacked upon people, the smell of adobo stacked upon the scent of frying chopped meat stacked upon a hungry baby screaming for food. I lived on a ladder, on one of the rungs between third and first world. I didn't care about people starving in Africa or Mexicans stuffed like sardines in the back of a truck just to get a chance at the American Dream. I didn't care about wars in other countries, apartheid in South Africa, feeding the world's poor, housing the world's homeless, or bringing freedom to every communist country. I hardly cared about slavery. I'm not saying I didn't know or think about those things. I'm not saying I was unsympathetic, impervious, uneducated. I was affected. I understood. But I also knew how people lived where I lived so I didn't need to go looking for struggle, pain, or a country of people who needed to be free, because that country, those Somalians, those Rwandans, those Iraqis were my people, my family in Ever, where men came home from prison desperate for the gentle touch of a woman, for a breast to rest their heads on, a neck to nuzzle into, for the sanctuary of a lover's voice whispering about the brightness of their future, how now there was nothing to stop them, nothing standing in their way then two weeks later these men found themselves missing the prison's hospitality, the three square meals a day, the library, and the fact that their misdeeds made them members of a world rather than unemployable pariahs. Where were they to go, brothers wanted to know. Back to Africa? Haiti? Jamaica? Puerto Rico? Trinidad? The Dominican Republic? And do what? Die dirt poor or in the midst of a civil war? Wasn't this America; wasn't this the greatest land of all great lands of opportunity? In Ever, we were three things: broken, desperate to leave, or soldiers in a war so impossible to win that everything we did, even blinking our eyes, even licking our lips, might be suicide.

Then crack hit. Then AIDS came right behind it. And who wasn't plucked and sucked dead either got high, wasted away one bloody sore at a time, or fought with all of their might just to exist, just to walk down the street, just to make love without being afraid of saliva and semen, just to share a can of soda, a straw, a spoonful of ice cream with a best friend, just to sleep with some semblance of restfulness and peace. How did AIDS spread? Where did crack come from? What, who, if anything and anyone, was safe? In Ever, brothers and sisters were fish and dying was the H, the 2, and the O of our lives. So what did we do? We did what anyone would do. We breathed in dying and lived in dying as if dying and the baggage that came with dying were normal, like everywhere in the world mama stole from grandma and sold her pussy in the stairwell to get high.

III

I was a statue, the type of infant whose stoic, tearless nature and irrevocable insomnia led my family to believe I was afflicted. I could be knocked down, dropped, shaken like a bottle of soda, even forgotten for hours at a time, yet still I would not burst, cry out, whimper; still I would not look upon the world with anything less than a wide, exacting stare. Over the course of the first two years of my life, all kinds of ailments, retardations, and deficiencies were prefaced with maybe and assigned to me. Maybe I was deaf. Maybe I was mute. Maybe too much water surrounded my brain. I didn't get enough air. I was blind, lacking the sense of touch. I was autistic, dyslexic, unable to make the connection between need and action, emotion and thought, heart and mind. When put down, when brought to the floor, when seated on the bus, when planted on a lap, I grew roots; I stayed. When put to bed, I lay on my back, my brown eyes round, unblinking, doll-like. When lifted and carried, I leaned back, made myself a weight greater than I actually was, pushed away from my embracer as if determined to attain a particular distance, freedom, a space that gave me enough room to look around, lay my eyes upon the people and environment enveloping, studying, tickling, prodding, and fussing over me.

When she was not doting over her newest truest true love, when she was not chasing after or being chased, flirting or playing coy, my Aunt Rhonda teased me, poked my belly, picked me up to sit me down again so she could study my stillness and have a laugh. When he was not playing basketball with friends, practicing his shooting form in the bathroom mirror, or dribbling a ball in the apartment, the hallway, on the roof, or up and down the stairs, my Uncle Roosevelt utilized me like an inanimate object. I was the stone he used to prop open a door, the broom he used to sweep the kitchen floor, a table he tried to balance things on, a shotgun he tucked under his arm, cocked and aimed. The doctors at the clinic had no time for me. I looked healthy, they said. My stool was normal. I didn't have a fever. *Take him home,* they said. My mother fretted over my lethargy, my aloofness, the distance I seemed predetermined to attain. She feared she did something to damage me during her pregnancy and her fear was so great she was positive she must have. Perhaps it was the cigarettes she'd smoked, the pulls from a joint. Perhaps it was her youth, that because she'd only menstruated a handful of times prior to my conception and without any semblance of regularity, I was damaged. Maybe she'd run around too much, chased, teased, laughed, and sobbed. Maybe she talked on the phone too loud. Maybe she watched too much TV. Maybe the various manifestations of her physical, emotional, spiritual, and intellectual immaturity pervaded me, infected me with the particulars of my nature.

My grandmother told her not to worry. She shrugged off all fears and doubts. She said I was Job; Jonah in the belly of the whale; Noah in his ark; Moses in the desert. It was my great patience that would help me overcome everything the world, this life, gave me.

Of course, my mother didn't believe her. She couldn't. She didn't have the capability. She was a teenager. How she felt, not facts or biblical stories, burned inside of her, mingled with her desire to dance and flirt and the fantasy that there was a brother who was her prince, who would soon arrive, ride into Ever on his horse, his magic carpet, in a car, a boat, a plane, and whisk her away, take us to a land where she was queen.

Yet, because she was the only parent of a black boy from the projects she also knew herself as the sole remaining partner of a creation that would not only outgrow her but also live in a land that, if it did not despise me, certainly made it difficult for my soul to achieve a human level of peace. Like any mother, she knew she could only protect me for so long, that her role as the center, the cause, and the solution of what occurred in my life was a fleeting post. The summation of these facts caused her to doubt herself, perhaps even hate herself. That she was already a mother at thirteen, and what motherhood meant for the remainder of her life, was often, if not always, too tremendous a weight for her to bear. So, although she did no greater wrong than what both my Aunt Rhonda and my grandma had done before her, having a child while still children themselves, my mother was fraught with self-abasement, and eventually, mortal defeat. In her diary, she cursed herself. She cried at night. She was ornery. She acted out, threw tantrums and doled out silent treatment as if extreme action would both reverse her life and provide her control over it. Some days she couldn't bring herself to pick me up, to hold me, to feed me or change my diaper. Sometimes she watched me sleep and considered ways to make me not hers. She could leave me outside, put me on the stoop of a church, leave me on the bus or train with a note. Maybe the pawnshop would take me. Maybe some rich white woman in Long Island needed a small, brown novelty. Maybe she could take me to an ocean, a river, lay me down, sail me away.

While my mother struggled with how tremendously my arrival into the world had changed her life, Donnel, encouraged by my grandmother, propelled by both curiosity and an already intact sense of paternal responsibility that belied his age, slowly assumed more and more responsibility over me. He loved to hold me, to feed me, to proclaim that I, Abraham, was his baby cousin. He, when my mother couldn't, owned my well-being. At the park, in the waiting room of the sulfurous city health clinic with the failing fluorescent lights, in the Laundromat, on the bus, through summer's hottest days, through autumn, winter, and spring, and when we went shopping along the avenue, Donnel carried me, moored me upon his narrow hip. According to my grandmother, never had a brother so young walked with such pride; never had a boy emanated a holy power of unconquerable manhood.

Donnel taught me how to speak. He taught me how to hold a bottle. He reveled in making me giggle and smile. And like a puppeteer, he taught me how to walk. He stood in front of me, held me by my hands and helped me balance, then walked backward as I walked forward. I moved where his hands, his eyes, his smile led me. I lifted and dragged my feet according to his desire. By the time he was five, Donnel, with limited supervision and later no supervision at all, determined if and when I soiled myself, then changed me, gently laid me on a kitchen chair or the couch or, when need be, utilizing the dexterity and balance only available to fearless children and great athletes, he changed my diapers in his arms, pressed me against his body, nestled me in the crux between his rib, arm, and abdomen.

The bond Donnel and I had, the bond he was unconsciously but purposefully building was, in its essence, the fundamental mooring and foundation of my family. We were not grandmother, daughters, sisters, or sons. We were not uncle, aunts, and cousins. We were brothers. Our love was unwavering, unflappable, greater than anything presented by the Bible, the Torah, and the Qur'an combined. That is, where we'd go, what would occur, what we lost and gained together, what we suffered and championed through, what we sometimes wished to recall and force ourselves to forget, our lives, the occasions and circumstances, were more than everything, more than forever, more than even the truth.

BAR 2

Ornithology

I

His nose boxed in, swollen and buckled like a jammed thumb, Lyndon Goines was a former amateur boxer who lied about being a Golden Gloves champion, a hard-working maintenance worker at the Queens Botanical Garden, and Ever Park's resident conversationalist, canvasser, activist, and organizer. Smelling like wet earth, he collected signatures on petitions then mailed them to city assemblymen, the mayor, congressional representatives, senators, the Supreme Court, and the president. He attended community and city council meetings clad in weathered three-piece suits. He'd step to the microphone, stomp his foot, and demand equality and justice. He wanted the potholes filled, the public streets paved flat and smooth like the streets in wealthy neighborhoods. He wanted the public library on Columbus Avenue, the only library within walking distance from Ever, to have the same amount of books as the smaller libraries in the exclusive white neighborhoods. He insisted that rather than putting new nets on the basketball rims in the park or funding basketball leagues and clinics, the city should allocate money to supply our public schools with the proper resources and implements, textbooks published post civil rights movement, microscopes for biology class, rulers, compasses, and protractors for math. He wanted each school to have adequate paper and pens. He wanted working water fountains with drinkable water and toilets that flushed. He wanted solar-powered scientific calculators and college prep classes for young brothers and sisters in high school. He wanted the music programs reinstated. He wanted art classes again. And how about horticulture? Get the kids to know what it means to couple with the earth. And the elevators in Ever Park? He wanted them fixed once and for all. He said if the city, the state, the country had enough money to blast men into outer space and wipe the green Statue of Liberty clean, then they could certainly equally provide for its brown citizenry.

Lyndon Goines wanted and his wanting was only equaled by one thing: his love for my grandma. He'd been in love with her since he first saw my grandma walking down the street, hips, he said, swaying like two apples clinging to a branch in the breeze. Never once did he doubt his love for her. But never once did he shout about it either. He was the type of humble southern man who had come north to do two things: fight in Madison Square Garden and find his queen. All he arrived with was this desire, a suitcase of belongings, his boxing gloves, and a wallet-sized photograph of his mother, who, when Mr. Goines took the picture out to show, he swore was named Beautiful Gorgeous Weeks before she married his father, Everett. She was the first grandchild of a freed slave, and so was his father. Lyndon Goines was the middle son of five boys, and just about as gentle as he was indefatigable. Once a week, he brought my grandmother various forms of plant life. He brought her tiny cactuses, bonsai trees, and flowers: tulips, poppies, ranunculas, orchids, lilies. From his gifts, I learned the names of flora born and blooming miles from Ever. Once he brought an African violet, a Venus flytrap, and an orchid that smelled like chocolate. But nothing, not one of his gifts, survived forever. Even the hardiest cactus he delivered eventually withered and bent at the stem. Still, the dying of a plant or my grandma's indifference never once caused Mr. Goines's love to wane. His heart was planted, rooted and green like an evergreen tree. Whenever he saw anybody in my family, he asked about my grandma. Then he suggested we put in a good word for him. We should tell my grandma to give him one chance, unhook the chain latch, let him and his punching-bag face in, just once, so he could sit in the kitchen, talk to her, watch my grandma's hips sway as she made her way between the stove, the sink, and the refrigerator. He swore he was a good man, a fine man. He'd even help with the dishes. But if she didn't believe it, if she wasn't ready, he said he had all of his life, forever to wait. He'd never been knocked out in a fight, never once stayed on the canvas. Sure, he'd lost. But he always lost by decision, in the middle of the ring, the referee holding his opponent's fist up.

So, every Christmas Mr. Goines showed up at our door with a Christmas tree. Every Valentine's Day: a dozen roses. Once, he arrived sweating and straining, his arms wrapped around a potted palm tree. And once, he showed up with birds.

My mother and my Aunt Rhonda were in the bathroom, leaning over the sink, squeezing their reflections into the small square mirror at the same time, hurrying to put on eyeliner, lip gloss, and mascara. Although they had each borne children, my mother and my Aunt Rhonda had the bodies of young, sexy sisters prepared to do nothing less than love. My mother was eighteen and the adolescence she had possessed and carried me within had become a bouquet she didn't know how to hold, present, nor take flattery for. The curves, the lush smile that made fireworks of her eyes, the way she threw her head back when she laughed and leaned forward when she sighed, all of the physicality that men cooed and fawned over, were like something sticky yet unable to be removed or washed away. So she tried to hide it. She hunched and slouched. She covered her mouth with one hand. She folded her arms over her chest when young men were near. My Aunt Rhonda was the opposite. She was twenty-two and determined to not just be loved but be worshipped by every brother who laid his eyes on her. Her face and body, although more than moderately attractive, were constructions of elongated ovals with no clear perimeters, so parts faded into others, her eyes into her cheeks, her jaw into her neck, her shoulders into her narrow back, her back into her hips, her hips disappearing into her thighs. She complained about her physical shape all the time, how her body was half the body of my mother's, how her breasts dropped if she didn't cinch the straps of her bra. Yet she wore the tightest clothes and carried herself as if at the end of her limbs and on top of her head were plumes of jeweled feathers. And around young men, she used the most suggestive language, licked her lips, cocked her hips, and pretended to be dumb.

Sometimes, after hours of cajoling, my Aunt Rhonda was able to get my mother to dress and, at least, attempt to act like her. And on the night Lyndon Goines arrived with birds in hand, my Aunt Rhonda had succeeded. So my Aunt Rhonda and my mother wore matching tight white pants, white heels, and royal blue blouses that squeezed their breasts and ended in frills at their waists. They had a date, the twins from the third floor, calm, cool Jamel and his antithesis Dave, otherwise known as Doo-Doo, the heavyset, pigeon-toed brother with a lazy eye and a perpetually runny nose who my Aunt Rhonda swore she was only spending time with because she was a good sister, and she wanted the best for my mom, and Jamel and Doo-Doo were a package deal. Like every man between the age of eighteen and forty who was either secure enough to disregard the fact that my mother had a child or ignorant about the degree to which my mother had had her heart broken, Jamel had a crush on my mother. But two things made him different than the others. First, every sister in Ever had a crush on Jamel, but because he wouldn't give them the time of day, they hated him, spread rumors that he was a homosexual, that his penis was so itsy bitsy there was no chance at being pleased. And second, none of the sisters' nastiness, none of their remarks or disapproval, or attempts to lure Jamel away from the despondency my mother dealt him, distracted him from what he wished for: one date with my mother. My Aunt Rhonda couldn't fathom what my mother's problem was. "You just like Momma," she'd huff on a nightly basis, her hands jammed on her hips. "You don't think any nigga is good enough!" But finally, my mother had given in. Finally, she had accepted Jamel's offer.

There was a knock on the door. Then there was another. My cousins and I sat on the couch, but we didn't move to answer it. We were watching cartoons, mesmerized by the TV, absorbing all of the heroism we could. Donnel was nine and he didn't respond to noise unless it was Eric or me interfering with his relationship with the TV, asking questions or breathing too heavily or sneezing or coughing. Eric was seven and at the beginning of his infatuation with drawing things he saw and things he swore he had once seen. He had a few old crayons and markers on his lap and some paper he'd taken from school and he was in the midst of drawing the characters in the cartoon. I, sitting forward, my legs dangling above the floor, was five and very much an imitator of Donnel and, to some degree, Eric. Thus, because they ignored the door, so did I.

A third knock came and my Aunt Rhonda hurried out of the bathroom, sure it was her and my mother's dates.

"You all don't hear that?" she scolded, sashaying across the room, placing one foot directly in front of the other, her hips slamming left and right, as if the person on the other side of the door could see her.

"Hear what?" said Donnel, his eyes trained on the TV.

"Boy," my Aunt Rhonda said, continuing to the door, "what I tell you before I started getting dressed?"

Although still a child, Donnel chose which questions he answered and which he ignored. So he was silent. My Aunt Rhonda stopped walking, put her hand on her hip, and waited if not for his answer then someone's. I was missing my two front teeth, and although I was too shy to smile and I covered my mouth with my hands when I couldn't stop myself from doing so, and although I recognized that everything I said sounded wet and whispery, I didn't yet understand that knowing an answer didn't require that I blurt it out. So I spoke.

"You said," I slurred. " 'Don't start noth'n.' "

Quickly, Donnel pinned his middle finger on his thumb, then snapped it free, flicking me in the middle of the forehead so hard the blow knocked me back on the couch and the pain caused me to squint. But I didn't hold my head with both hands or squirm as if desperate to get out from under it. I heard Eric laugh and swung my foot to kick him.

"That's enough," ordered my aunt.

With a long, swift stride to the couch, she yanked me upright. My eyes welled with tears. The middle of my forehead burned from the blow. Then my mother walked out of the bathroom and I swallowed, blinked, and sailed years away from pain. Even at the age of five, I was overcome by my mother's beauty when she let her beauty shine. She could transform herself, metamorphose from a gritty, testy sister who wore neither a smile nor a hint of being delicate to a being who exuded feminine glory.

"Abraham, sit right," she said.

I sat as tall as I could, for not only did my mother demand it, but, although I was only five, her being in love and making her angry were the thing I most wanted and the thing I never wanted to do. Maybe Jamel would be the one; maybe he would be my father.

My mother tugged at the bottom of her shirt. She shifted and squirmed. She hooked her thumbs in the top of her pants and pulled them up.

"This shit's tight as hell," she said.

My Aunt Rhonda quickly stepped to my mother. She fixed and re-positioned her clothes. Then she shifted my mother's breasts in balance and tried to smooth a ripple out of the back of her pants.

"You got panties on?" she asked.

"How you know?" said my mother.

"Cause I see the line," said my Aunt Rhonda. Then she pointed at the bedroom they shared with my grandma. "Take 'em off."

"What you mean?" my mother asked.

"Don't wear none." My Aunt Rhonda gave my mother a gentle push. "Hurry up. Go."

My mother left the room and my Aunt Rhonda went to the front door and with one hand on the knob and the other ready to unhook the latch, she watched my mother close the bedroom door. Then she looked at Donnel, Eric, and me.

"You ready?" she asked.

She took a moment more to assess her own beauty, pressed an easy smile across her face, and opened the door. But to the surprise of us all, it was not Jamel and Doo-Doo at the door. It was Mr. Goines. Dressed in a wrinkled brown suit, white shirt, and yellow paisley tie, he took one long step into the middle of the room holding a small birdcage covered with a soiled bath towel.

"Lovebirds," he said, pulling the towel from atop the cage. "Where is she?"

"She ain't here," said my Aunt Rhonda, still holding the door ajar.

The birds chirped and cheeped, and I leapt from the couch and ran to the cage Mr. Goines held, his arm extended high at his side.

"You got birds?" I asked.

The birds were radiant. Dusty green feathers covered their bodies. Sunset red was their face. Their eyes were small black pearls. Donnel and Eric hurried from the couch and stood beside me.

"What's their names?" Eric asked.

"They don't have names," Mr. Goines said.

"How do you got birds with no names?" said Donnel, peering into the cage like a child but sounding like the truculent young man he was bent on becoming.

"They're for your grandma to name," said Mr. Goines.

The bedroom door opened and my mother walked out. Mr. Goines looked up, studied her, and said: "You know, the older you get, the more I swear you your mother's twin."

Although she was always accepting of Mr. Goines, his gifts, his sudden arrivals, and the love he had for my grandma, the comment embarrassed my mother and she blushed, her penny-color skin swelling a warmer shade. She looked down and curled into herself a bit.

"Mr. Goines," she said. "What you doing here?"

"He's got birds," I announced.

"I see that." My mother smiled at me. She looked at Mr. Goines and a tumble of airy laughter rolled from her mouth.

"You giving Momma birds?" she asked.

"She know you're bringing them?" scolded my Aunt Rhonda, sounding jealous.

Mr. Goines thought for a moment. Then he shifted his eyes to my Aunt Rhonda. "With all due respect, I believe your mother is the type of woman who knows more than she knows."

My Aunt Rhonda jammed her hand on her hip and tilted her head incredulously. "What kind of crazy shit is that?" she asked. "Huh? Cause I know you ain't trying to make no sense saying some nonsense like that."

"It means that Momma ain't got to know to know," my mother answered. "She been around long enough to know birds in a cage was bound to happen."

"How can you tell one from the other?" I asked no one in particular.

"You ain't supposed to," said Donnel, his cheek brushing against the side of my face with each word he spoke.

"Why not?" I asked.

"Cause they birds," he said. "They meant to fly, not be here with us."

The birds stayed close together on the perch and although they looked fragile there was a fierceness to their unity, an inseparable inseparability. Donnel squeezed his finger through the bars of the cage to see how close he could come to touching the birds. The birds chirped. Then they flew back and forth in the cage, from one side of the bars to the other, stopping to hold on to each wall of bars before flying again, flapping until they came to rest together on the bars at the back of the cage. Donnel whistled to the birds. And I watched the birds pause, tilt their heads, and consider his song. I glanced over my shoulder at my mother. She smiled at me. I don't recall what I was thinking, but it was clear that whatever it was she understood so her empathy made me feel good. I turned my eyes back to the birds, then shifted them just enough to see Donnel purse his lips and whistle more. I couldn't whistle, both because I didn't know how and because my teeth were missing. But then, that didn't stop me from trying. I watched Donnel's lips for a moment more and listened to his airy tune. Then I turned my face to the birds again, took a deep breath, pursed my lips as best as I could, and breathed a gentle wind that joined Donnel's song as it crossed through the bars and ruffled the birds' feathers on the other side of the cage.

II

As a child, I was obsessed with flight. Sometimes, before I went to sleep, I'd lie beneath the sheets and pretend I was a bird, a cloud, an astronaut, a superhero with the super power of not speeding or soaring, but floating, drifting according to the whim of wind. When a plane passed over Ever, I'd stop whatever I was doing, stop playing, stop teasing, stop walking, stop talking, and look up. Later, when I became a teenager and I began to develop a sense of the world and where I was in it, and when I was feeling awry and no one was around to say *Nigga? What're you doing?* I threw things at planes that passed overhead. I threw anything that was near, anything I could snatch and heave: rocks and basketballs; bricks and books, chewing gum, pens, pencils, glass bottles; even spit; and when there was no object to be found, when I stood amidst nothing, I hurled fistfuls of emptiness, sometimes one after the other, sometimes at the same time.

I wasn't the only Icarus in Ever. Far from it. Percival, a dark-skinned brother whose angry disposition was lost the moment he spoke about his son Shakeem, taught Shakeem how to fold perfect paper airplanes, and together they spent Sunday mornings throwing their planes from their window and watching how far they sailed before landing on the concrete that surrounded Ever, the concrete courtyard—the cracked concrete parking lot, the concrete sidewalk that shrank in the winter, then swelled, heaved, and fractured more and more each summer. And Mr. Lucas, an old, gangly flutist from the fourth floor who had once lived in France, had a parrot named Charlie Parker that he never placed in a cage, so it flew, shat, and shelled peanuts wherever it wanted. And Tariq Abdullah, a stout, muscular, reckless blasphemer who'd become Muslim and grounded during his stay in Franklin Correctional Facility, fed the pigeons on the roof with saltines while pacing and reading aloud from the Qur'an. On the basketball court, brothers argued over who jumped higher, who had the greatest hang time; who flew. The best-looking women were fly. Everyone wanted Air Jordans. Crackheads got high. You smoked dope and got lifted. When I was sixteen, Anthony Roberson, an effeminate, bespectacled fifteen-year-old with a chipped front tooth and the best dance moves anyone in Ever had ever seen, spread his lithe arms like wings, ran as fast as he could, then hopped, skipped, pirouetted, and leapt from the roof of my building and screamed all the way down.

Then there was Tyrone Jackson, the Vietnam veteran who was first mocked, then, eventually, reverentially dubbed Lindbergh. A helicopter mechanic, Lindbergh served two tours fighting for democracy and freedom. Some said he had been the most handsome man in all of Queens before America dropped him in Da Nang and Lindbergh, a toothless loon with half a head of short, dry dreadlocks and a shopping cart full of miscellany, replaced him. Lindbergh collected cans and scrap metal and anything else he could sell to make an honest living. Seven days a week, rain or shine, oppressively humid, fiercely hot, and in the unbearably cold, he wore fatigues, a field jacket, and a black beret as he pushed his cart and scrounged through Dumpsters and garbage cans so much his hands were as hard as hooves and his fingers were talons. Everyone said Lindbergh was crazy. Some said he was lost. Some said he needed Jesus. Jehovah's Witnesses chased Lindbergh down and handed him flyers. Sometimes one of Ever's scratch-ticket addicts or Lotto fiends bought him a cup of coffee from the corner store and stood outside drinking coffee with him, sipping and saying this or that, trying to get Lindbergh to open up. Occasionally, someone offered Lindbergh a day's pay doing backbreaking labor, shoveling rubble, demolishing a decrepit building in the neighborhood with a crowbar, and occasionally he'd do it, hammering and shoveling all day without taking a moment's break. Some people said Lindbergh was a drunk, that his body pumped Night Train, not blood. Some said he was a junkie, that he jammed this or that into his arms and lungs. Some said he was broken. Most agreed that his soul had been stolen.

But none of it was true. Because before Lindbergh was anything—in fact, before Lindbergh was a soldier—he was an artist. He was a creator, an innovator, silently but radically forthright with regards to what he wished, what he deemed necessary for himself, his environment, and us, we, the people of Ever Park. The trash and miscellany Lindbergh couldn't sell, he bent, twisted, affixed, and built into helicopters. Hundreds of them. The size of small cars, the size of infants, small enough to rest in the palm of your hand. Helicopters from cans too crushed to be redeemable. Helicopters from plastic forks, bottle caps, and the spokes from bicycle wheels. Lindbergh built helicopters wherever the spirit moved him, in stairwells, in the park, perched on the backs of benches where pigeons sat impervious to the earthbound concoctions. Sometimes, I'd wake up and walk out of my building in the morning and there one would be, smack in the middle of the sidewalk, a four-foot psychedelic chopper with a working propeller made of mattress springs and detergent containers. Lindbergh's helicopters would sit there, randomly placed around Ever, until someone took them, children played with them until they broke, or the weather, the elements of the world, tore them apart.

Once Lindbergh gave a helicopter to my mother. It was built out of potato chip bags, sip-box straws, and garbage ties. I was six. She was nineteen. It was winter and we were waiting for the bus. We were on our way to the emergency room at the hospital because I had whooping cough and it kept me gasping and coughing up thick green phlegm all night. My coat was zipped to my chin. A knit hat was pulled over my eyebrows, and a thick red wool scarf was looped around my neck. I coughed, gagged, and gasped and everyone standing at the bus stop except my mother stepped away from me.

"Abraham," she scolded. "Cover your mouth. The whole world don't want what you got."

I coughed again and a wad of phlegm jumped from my lungs into my mouth.

"Spit," my mother demanded, peeling the plastic lid off of a paper coffee cup and holding it in front of my mouth.

I spit in the cup that was already half full of mucus and my mother put the plastic lid back on.

"They gonna see now," she huffed, simultaneously talking to herself and anyone who would listen. "Take my baby to the doctor and the man says he just got a little cold."

My mother stepped from the curb and stood in the middle of the street. She jammed her hands on her hips, glared down the empty road, the distance that was to produce the bus.

"Where's this motherfucker?" she shouted. "Fucking bus. Got my baby standing out in the cold!"

I coughed and hacked more and my mother looked for the bus three more times, each time getting angrier and more impatient, each time cursing the bus, the bus driver, the bus company, the doctor at the clinic.

"Shit," she said. "I bet you if we was in Africa, there'd be a mother-fucking bus! It might have no wheels and be pulled by some elephant, but there'd be a bus for us, that's for damn sure!"

My mother stepped back onto the curb. She snatched my hand. Then Lindbergh was suddenly at the bus stop, one hand gripping the front of his shopping cart as if he feared it might roll away, his other hand extended, offering a small helicopter to my mother as if it were a flower.

At first, my mother ignored him. She looked at him out of the corners of her eyes. She pushed a dismissive sigh out of her mouth. She looked at the brothers and sisters waiting for the bus with us. Then, when Lindbergh didn't leave and his hand holding the helicopter didn't drop, she gave in and took the gift from him.

"Thank you," she said.

Lindbergh was silent, emotionless. He left his empty hand extended as if he wanted something soft and simple back. I stood at my mother's side and looked at her. She studied the helicopter. Its propeller worked. Its doors opened. A miniature man made from a plastic spoon sat in the cockpit. Like my mother, I couldn't believe it. I wondered what would happen if my mother tossed the helicopter into the air. Would it fly or crash to the ground?

I looked at Lindbergh for an answer. He was a broken brother. His lips were chapped and their splits were caked with dry blood. His eyebrows were as knotted and mangy as his hair. And the whites of his eyes were not white nor even a pallid yellow or grey. They were a few shades lighter than the brown of his eyes so no matter the day's weather or temperature he always looked sodden, muddy. He looked back at me and we studied each other. He rolled his lips in and out of his mouth, over his toothless gums, and a couple of the cracks began to bleed a bit, fill with electric bright blood. In the name of human liberties and democracy, in the name of an equality he, we, and brothers throughout history were never provided, Lindbergh had killed and witnessed the killing of innocent people and it crushed him. His teeth rotted from it. His skin dried and flaked. Something precious had been ripped from his chest and all he had left was the paranoid guarding of the hole.

Just as suddenly as Lindbergh had arrived, the bus pulled up. My mother gave my hand a tug to let me know it was time for us to go. But before I moved, Lindbergh dropped his hand until it rested flat on my head. Then he squatted until our eyes were level.

"*Semper fi,*" he whispered, his voice a rusted metal chain dragged through a rusted metal slot. "*Semper fi.*"

Then with a groan and the creaking and cracking of his prematurely arthritic knees, Lindbergh stood, made eye contact with my mother for a moment, and apologetically backpedaled two steps. He walked away, pulling his rattling, squeaking shopping cart behind. I had no idea what *semper fi* meant. Although my mother knew it had something to do with the military, with being a soldier, neither did she. But the definition of the phrase didn't matter. Not to me, not then. What mattered then was when we sat down on the bus, my mother gave me the helicopter, and I played with it. I held it up to the bus window. I tapped its propeller with my finger to make it spin. I imagined I was a pilot, a soldier who, with every flick of finger against propeller, flew farther away from coughing and the grating, burning in my chest.

III

Night. The snow lay so flat and clean it seemed no one ever dreamed about what the world was. Beneath the pallid glow of streetlights and the spotlights that highlighted Ever, no trails marked where people walked. No laughter; no arguments, no one preached over the cacophony of a heated group debate; no young brother explained his superstitions and routine before rolling dice against the base of my building. No sounds from passing cars, no rumble of buses; no police sirens devouring the breath of everyone in Ever. Snow balanced on branches, telephone wires, along the rims of garbage drums, and flakes as big and drifting as feathers floated and spun in the whip of wind as they fell from the black sky.

I was eight years old, but I stared out of the window in our living room as if I were fifty and doing time for fifty more. I wore my PAL basketball jersey over a white T-shirt and my favorite black Adidas sweatpants with the three red stripes running along the outside of my legs. With my elbows on the windowsill, my cheeks pressed between the heels of my hands, I watched the path of a white flake until the flake was lost amidst the others, the swirling whiteness, and I had to choose another. I suffered from the stillness, the whiteness that had been forced upon Ever, that suppressed my youth, my joy, my ability to run about. This was death. Every flake killed me over again. The schedule I'd Scotch-taped on the refrigerator three months earlier said there was a championship basketball game at 6:00 p.m. and my team had made the championship. Now, because of the snow, it was cancelled. *Shit*, I thought, *damn this snow.*

All of the bruises I'd collected, the floor burns, all of the trash my friends and I had talked that week in school were for nothing. Didn't the world, didn't the sky, didn't God know how seriously we took this game; how much freedom it provided? I thought it couldn't be. I wouldn't let it be. I stared out of the window and hoped for heat, for a sudden fiery wind. I considered what I could do to reverse the state of the world. How could I excise the snow? How many matches would I need? How many lighters? If only I could wish a fire. I took no comfort in the fact that the game would be rescheduled. I took basketball, we took it, too seriously to have any game let alone our championship suspended. So I prayed against it. I hoped. But my hope did nothing. It was true. Inarguable. Ever was adorned, silenced, ravaged by white.

Behind me, lying head to foot and parallel on the couch, my mother and my Aunt Rhonda painted red nail polish on each other's toes.

"Abraham, no matter how bad you want it, that snow ain't gonna stop," my mother sighed.

"Shit," added my Aunt Rhonda. "It's supposed to be the worst snow-storm in history. A whiteout! That's what the news said."

"Well whatever the news say, I still got to go to work," my grandma shouted from the kitchen.

My grandma was already dressed for work. White pants, a white shirt, white shoes: she was a night orderly at Queens Hospital, a job she fought, prayed, and begged for for two years before they promoted her from the hospital's laundry room and gave her the chance, a job she loved, the calling she said she found after that night she helped my mother deliver me. She stood in front of the stove frying chopped meat and boiling spaghetti for dinner. She was nearing forty, so her grace was neither new nor negotiable, nor was it something she would deny, and it was not some banner she held or waved triumphantly. Rather, it was a buttress, like riggings of a ship, the cables and trusses of a suspension bridge. Adaptable, responsive, my grandma gave off an air of absorbency, a manner that indicated that weathering and holding everything was simply how she lived.

"I remember," she continued, pausing to make sure she had our attention. "One time it snowed so bad the news showed white folks skiing from Midtown all the way to Wall Street."

We were in a box, hemmed and penned in, ants in frozen milk. The walls of our living room were white. The ceiling was white. Above the window, where the ceiling and the top of the wall met, was the coffee-colored stain we sometimes claimed to look like things, as if it were a cloud in the sky. All around us, above our heads, in the walls, in the bathroom, and in the kitchen, pipes knocked and leaked. The belly of the electric heater we used to keep the apartment warm sparked and burned red. Just in front of it on the floor, Donnel and Eric played War with an old deck of cards. Eric threw down a jack. Donnel dropped an ace.

"I win," said Eric.

He reached for the cards. Donnel slapped his hand away.

"Nigga," he scolded. "How many times I got to tell you an ace beats everything?"

Outside in the snow a man jogged into the pale, yellow ring made by a streetlight. He stayed in the glow. He danced, fluttered, moved in circles. He dipped one shoulder then the other. He punched, jabbing and hooking then ducking as if punches were thrown back at him. He held his fists beneath his chin. He bobbed his head.

"It's Mr. Goines!" I shouted, turning to look at my cousins and my mother and aunt on the couch.

Mr. Goines was shadowboxing, sparring an invisible opponent who must have been twice his size and ten times as quick. He dodged. He dipped. He weaved. He pretended he was slugged in the face, pounded in the ribs. He wobbled, then backpedaled, then rope-a-doped off the invisible ropes that marked the perimeter of the pallid ring and punched back.

Donnel and Eric joined me at the window. Then, hurrying across the room on their heels so the fresh polish on their toes wouldn't smudge, my mother and my Aunt Rhonda arrived.

"Look at him," said my mother, pressing her face against the window above my head. "He's beating up the snow!"

"Ma," shouted my Aunt Rhonda, her voice an amalgamation of glee and mockery. "You got to see this! Hurry! Come look!"

"He's boxing!" added Donnel.

"I don't need to see that fool to know he's crazy," my grandma said, still standing at the stove.

But a moment later she amended her declaration. She huffed a breath of annoyance, turned the stove down, and came to the window. She watched Mr. Goines. And waiting for her opinion, I watched her. So I saw how the face she first brought to the window changed, and her eyes softened, bending from a cold, hard stare to an engrossed yet somewhat perplexed gaze, as if she was seeing a sight she appreciated but didn't trust.

"That man is touched," she decided. Then, as if she could no longer stand to watch, she ordered us to move, unlatched the window lock, and threw open the window.

"You a damn fool!" she shouted, leaning her head outside. "You know that, Lyndon Goines? You gonna catch pneumonia and die!"

Mr. Goines stopped punching and bouncing on the balls of his feet. Then he turned around, looked up to our window, and his hands fell to his sides.

"Gloria!" he called out, his shining smile introduced by the tumble of breath that carried my grandma's name. "How my birds doing?"

"They fine," said my grandma.

Then, as if suddenly recalling that Mr. Goines believed even the slightest interaction between them was flirtation, and he loved it, loved talking about it, telling anyone in Ever who would listen, my grandma slammed the window closed, spun around, and strode back into the kitchen.

"Pay that man no mind," she scolded. "And get away from that window. Don't give him no audience to act stupid in front of."

Standing in the snow and still looking up at our window, Mr. Goines's smile did the impossible, growing wider and gleaming more than it had just been glowing. Slowly he resumed bouncing on the balls of his feet. He made his hands fists and raised them above his head. He backpedaled a handful of steps and shadowboxed for a few moments, dipping and weaving and throwing a half-dozen stiff jabs. Then he turned and jogged out of the ring of pale light, disappearing into the darkness of Columbus Avenue and the falling snow.

My cousins returned to playing cards. My Aunt Rhonda and my mother returned to the couch and resumed painting each other's toenails.

Wondering where Mr. Goines went, and thinking he might soon and suddenly return, I stared out of the window. Then I went into the kitchen, planted my elbows on the counter, planted my chin in my hands, and watched the lovebirds in their cage. Their names were Lady and Man and only my grandma could tell them apart. It was too cold for them so they were puffed up, and their beaks were tucked into the feathers of their chests. I was bored, ornery, and looking for a place to aim the frustration gnawing on me, so I took a deep breath and blew it as hard as I could at Lady and Man, ruffling their feathers.

"Abraham, why you messing with those birds?" my grandma asked.

"Why do they got to stay in the cage?" I answered.

"Cause that's where they live."

"What happens if they want to get out?"

My grandma laughed. "Where they gonna go?"

"Wherever they want."

My grandma stirred the chopped meat in the pan. Steam rose around her hands. "They probably afraid anyway," she decided.

"Afraid of what?" I asked.

"You and your questions," she said. "Lady and Man ain't never been out of that cage. And besides, they lovebirds. All they need is each other."

"They need to be free," I decided.

My grandma stopped stirring the chopped meat and turned around to look at me.

"Abraham," she said in the gentle scolding tone she employed when she found something, an act, accusation, or statement, curious, "you saying my birds ain't free?"

Keys rattled at the door. The locks clacked, clicked. Then the door swung open and my Uncle Roosevelt and his girlfriend walked into the apartment. They were covered in snow. Their noses were running. Their eyes were watering from the cold. And their hands and arms were full of grocery bags of nonperishable items; boxes of sugary cereal, Cup-a-Soups, bags of potato chips, cheese puffs, pretzels, cans of fruit and vegetables, and a ten-pound bag of bird food.

"It's bad as all hell out there," my Uncle Roosevelt said, crossing the room toward the kitchen.

"Take off them shoes," ordered my grandma. "And your coats. You all is dropping snow all over the place. Now, you want something hot? How 'bout some hot chocolate?"

Like a brown version of Michelangelo's statue of David, my Uncle Roosevelt had bloomed into a holy statue of a man. He was tall, strong, and good-looking; symmetrical; the type of man who didn't have to wink, lick his lips, wear cologne, speak, or move around to be enticing. I idolized him. No. It was more. I wanted nothing else but to be him. And I wasn't alone with this wish. In Ever Park, every brother with a heartbeat and a last breath wanted to be him. He was our Michael Jordan, our Ever Park king. He was seventeen years old, six foot four inches tall, body made solely of bones and lean muscle. Everyone called him Nice. And so I called my uncle Nice too. But he didn't just epitomize the nickname. He expanded its definition. That is, the word *nice* only described what my Uncle Roosevelt did on the basketball court when he wasn't moving, when he paused, held the ball on his hip, and contemplated the game and the world around him. In Ever, no one had, ever could, or bothered dreaming about stopping my uncle on the basketball court. He scored with his left hand. He scored with his right. He scored with his eyes open, his eyes closed; in sneakers and boots, jeans and shorts; and sometimes, after he'd given in to my grandmother and gone with her to church or had to attend the funeral of another young brother, I'd seen him score in shoes, dress pants, a white shirt, and a tie. He was as ambidextrous as a left-handed man with two left hands, a right-handed man with two rights. The only time I ever saw my uncle stopped on the basketball court was when he stopped himself. Half of the time it was because he was bored with the game, and the other half of the time he called it quits so he could be with his girl, she who stood beside him in our apartment, tall and shapely, terra-cotta skin and rose lips, and with hips and shoulders that made it clear the sky was weightless upon her. Her given name was Tiffany, but Nice called her Luscious, so everyone in Ever called her Luscious too. When Luscious came to the court to watch Nice play, he celebrated her presence by dunking with his right hand, with his left hand, and with both hands every time he touched the ball. They loved each other; in fact, they loved each other so deeply that I never once saw them standing in the same place and not touching each other in some delicate manner, holding hands, linking pinkies, leaning on each other. Even when they were talking with different people and facing opposite directions they reached back, laid their hands on the small of each other's backs, dipped their fingers into each other's back pockets. Every time I saw them kiss, I stared. Every time I saw them embrace, I wondered what it felt like to disappear and be fortified at the same time.

Nice put down the grocery bags he carried. Then he took the bags from Luscious's arms, put them down, and gently plucked her gloves from her hands. He unwrapped the white scarf from around her neck, kissed the tip of her nose, and helped her out of her coat.

"You all need to stop that shit," said my Aunt Rhonda.

"Stop what?" asked Nice.

"That kissing in public shit."

"I kissed her nose."

"Yeah, well who knows what you'll start kissing next."

I walked out of the kitchen. "Ma," I said. "Can I go down to the park?"

My mother didn't acknowledge me, Nice and Luscious, Donnel and Eric, or what Rhonda said. She focused on painting the red polish on Rhonda's big toe as if there were nothing else in the world but her and that toe. She wanted what Luscious had: a man's love. But if she couldn't have such a thing then she wasn't going to fight it like Rhonda. But she would not witness it either. She would not recognize how absent it was.

Nice contemplated my eagerness and an empathatic smile eased across his face. "A, what you fall and bump your head?" he asked. "Shit, Lindbergh ain't even out in this weather."

"You went out," I snapped. "And we just saw Mr. Goines."

"That's cause I had to get groceries and make sure Luscious got here safely." Nice looked at my mother and aunt on the couch. "Goines is outside?"

"That nigga is crazy," decided my Aunt Rhonda. "He thinks cause Buster Douglas beat Tyson the other night he got a chance at being something. And don't be lying to the boy!"

"Who?" Nice asked.

"You," accused Rhonda. "Luscious lives on the second floor. She don't need you to pick her up. She could have walked her ass up here all alone."

"She came with me to the store," my uncle said, defending himself against my Aunt Rhonda's attack.

Luscious ignored Rhonda and wrapped her arms around Nice so he would ignore her too. "Baby," she said. "Which one is the new one?"

Nice glared one last moment at my Aunt Rhonda, then he sighed and smiled. He kissed Luscious's forehead.

"Over there," he said, pointing at the two-foot-tall trophy next to the TV.

My uncle's trophies lined all four walls, each glowing and topped with a golden figure or a basketball. Some were a foot tall. Some stood two and three feet. A few were as tall as me. There were plaques, certificates, and ribbons. He was an MVP. He was a champion. And there were more trophies in the room he, Donnel, Eric, and I shared. They cluttered the dresser. They filled the shelf in the closet. He had sneaker boxes filled with medals and letters from college coaches begging him to consider playing for them. He had college brochures, and college paraphernalia, and college pens, pencils, and pennants. Sometimes, I took one of the college brochures or players' guides the coaches sent him into the bathroom when I needed to use the toilet, and I'd sit there, my pants around my ankles, flipping through the pages, amazed at the contents of the glossy photos, the college students and their college lives. Coaches called nightly, and some called so often, I learned to recognize them by the sound of their voices just as they came to recognize me. *Oh, hello, Abraham,* they'd say. *I bet you play basketball too.* It seemed like every institution of higher education in America had a room, a jersey, a classroom, a professor, a tutor, and a plethora of salacious women just for my uncle. All he had to do was sit down, listen to what they had to say, and sign his name. Then he would be on TV, and win college championships, and be the MVP of tournaments and leagues. And then, with hard work, he would be a star in the NBA. He was a junior in high school. One day, everyone would wear Nice's jersey. He was going to make millions. It was his destiny. And that destiny, he swore, would take us out of Ever. And we believed him. He could do no wrong. He was king. My grandma did everything for him. She cooked him extra meals when he got hungry. She woke him as many times as he needed to be woken before he got out of bed to go to school. She found a way to buy him new clothes and she made my Aunt Rhonda and my mother do the same. Nice was royalty, blameless.

He picked up his newest trophy and showed it to Luscious. My grandma took the grocery bags into the kitchen.

"Forty-two points," she called out. "He was taking them to school! My baby couldn't be stopped! It was like Jesus come down from the sky and took control of Roosevelt's soul!"

There was a moment of silence. Then my grandma shouted: "Roosevelt, I don't see no milk!"

"Damn," he sighed, shaking his head. "I knew I forgot something!"

God gave Nice physical gifts, court vision, the body, dexterity, and the stamina of a perpetual dancer. Yet, when not on the basketball court, he blundered. He tripped over himself. He forgot things of great importance. He made impulsive decisions, jumped to conclusions, and was easy to lead astray. He was carefree and untouchable, but because he was also a dreamer, solely grounded in everything related to hope, he struggled to recognize the difference between real need and fleeting desire. Although I was a child I had no doubt Nice had remembered the milk up until the moment he thought about something he wanted and hoped to get, and then, puff, what he needed to get and do left his head. Hoping, wanting, and getting, that was my uncle. It made him a great basketball player. It caused him to be loved, to not have a single enemy in all of Queens. Occasionally, it made him steal things from corner stores, clothing stores, any establishment he deemed unworthy of patience or money. Sometimes Nice came home bragging about the slice of pizza he didn't pay for, the Chinese food he took and ran with. Sometimes he came home with the stolen article of clothing, the hat, the shirt, the jacket he wore.

Luscious reached up and touched the side of Nice's face. "Baby, didn't I ask you if your grandmother needed milk?"

Although he made many, every mistake Nice made exhausted him. He deflated. He was a perfectionist. It was yet another reason why he was so gifted on a basketball court. He practiced and practiced until everything was just right. His eyes softened. He laid them upon Luscious. He blinked. There was something more than his forgetfulness. He shifted his eyes to my grandma.

"There ain't no money left," he said.

My grandma walked out of the kitchen. "What you mean there ain't no more money?"

"I mean," said Nice, "all that stuff we got cost more than what you gave me. I had to tell 'em that I'd bring the rest of the money tomorrow."

My grandma put her hands on her hips. "Well, that's it," she said. "That's all the money I got."

"I swear to God," said Nice, "I swear one day, when I'm in the NBA ..."

My mother interrupted him. "Abraham, where's that money I gave you to get something to drink after your game?"

I reached into my pocket. Then, smiling, suddenly feeling joyous and proud instead of heartbroken, I pulled three dollars out of my pocket and held it up for everyone to see.

"Well, hurry up," Nice said, a smile and shine easing upon him. "Go get your coat."

It was us versus the world, us against the snow. I looked at my mother. "I can go?" I asked.

"Shit, you just bent on being as crazy as Goines, ain't you," she said.

Then she thought for a moment. I waited.

"So go ahead," she said, waving her hand at me dismissively. "Probably do your ass some good to see up close how serious all this snow is."

Before anything else was said, I raced into the bedroom and dressed as fast as I could. I put on my winter coat, my winter hat, gloves, and an old pair of sneakers. Then I ran out of the room to join Nice.

"Hold on!" said my grandma. "Stand together. The both of you."

Like two soldiers standing at attention, my uncle and I stood side by side.

"Now tell me. What you gonna get?" demanded my grandma.

"Milk," my uncle said.

My grandma shifted her eyes to me. "Abraham?"

"Milk," I said.

"Good," said my grandma. "I'm counting on you. Don't let your uncle forget."

I looked up at Nice. He looked down at me. "You got me?" he asked, holding his hand out for me to slap.

I slapped it. "Yeah."

We walked out of the apartment. Nice stopped, turned around, and locked all three locks with his key. Then we heard the chain latch clack and slide into place on the other side.

"Milk!" shouted my grandma one last time. "And don't keep Abraham out too long. You know how he starts coughing!"

Outside in the hallway, the walls were cinderblocks painted eggshell white. They were scrawled and scribbled on; graffiti, names and nicknames, declarations of existence. There were hearts with initials in them and sexually explicit drawings. *Fuck* was spelled wrong. Gangs and crews proclaimed they were the most powerful, the utmost, the killers of all killers who killed for nothing, for everything, no matter the time. Things were written in pen and crossed out with marker. There were bullet holes. A few spots were still spattered with blood. There was garbage, foil wrappers, plastic utensils, papers, balled-up napkins, soda cans, broken glass. There was a backpack, torn open, classroom handouts and quizzes spilling out. The floor was concrete, painted industrial grey, and covered with dust so dense it looked like ash coated the floor. It was cold. A wind rushed through.

Nice looked down at me. "You sure you're gonna be warm enough?"

I was so happy to be going outside I was sweating. I nodded.

Once again, the elevator was broken.

"Motherfucker," said Nice, pushing the button repeatedly. "Me and Luscious just took this bitch." He kicked the elevator's doors. "Fuck it. Let's go."

We walked to the stairwell and stopped in front of its door. It was exactly eighty-four steps from our floor to the bottom.

"You ready?" he asked.

I swallowed. The stairwell was always dark and cold and all of the lights were blown so I feared what we'd find, brothers and sisters desperate for a place to sit, be warm, hide. Someone might be urinating or getting high or crying or a young couple might be ravishing each other, sucking and licking and humping with the hope to lift and carry the other away. Someone might be waiting to rob the first person coming down the stairs. They might have a knife or a gun. They might be reckless, distressed. Too many horror stories came out of the stairwell. Too many sisters were raped or almost raped. Too many brothers got jumped, beaten with pipes and bricks, cut with box cutters, stabbed with screwdrivers.

Nice put his hand on the door, pushed it, and walked into the blackness of the stairwell. I followed and paid close attention to the sounds around us, listened more desperately than intently for clues and reasons to stop walking, run back, save Nice and me from bearing witness or, worse, being victimized. I wasn't a fighter, but I'd fight if I had to, if I was forced to by circumstances and threats against those I loved. I descended with my fists clenched. I squinted into the blackness as if narrowing my eyes would help me see. Luckily, there was nothing. No sound; no one. In fact, the only noise came from our footsteps, sticking to something like syrup on the steps between the second and third floor.

"A," Nice said, somehow sounding calm, his voice echoing through the stairwell. "Who were you gonna be tonight?"

The application of fantasy was how Nice survived, how he taught himself to play basketball and how, through watching and listening to him, I learned to play basketball as well. I couldn't just be Abraham Singleton. I wasn't enough. I was in Ever. I had to imagine myself as someone or something else for flight. So sometimes I was Michael Jordan. Sometimes I was Magic Johnson. I imagined I was the greatest, the strongest, the fastest, the highest leaper, the most courageous and clutch, and because I never made mention of it, because I never shared the notion with anyone, there was no one who could tell me no or prove that who I imagined was not who I was. So every time I played I chose a player and made the moves he made. I scowled like them, swaggered. But that night, that game, my first championship and chance to win a trophy, I'd planned something else. I'd decided to be the one champion, the one MVP, I knew.

"I was gonna do 'em like you," I said.

"Me?" Nice laughed. "What you gonna waste your time being me for?"

I thought for a moment, then said: "Cause you got all them trophies."

We made it to the bottom of the stairs. Nice pushed the door open. We crossed the dim, industrial green of the building lobby. We stopped at the entrance of our building, at the heavy steel door with the slim rectangular window fortified with chicken wire in its glass. We stared outside. All of the snow extinguished Ever, the bustling, ramshackle world we knew.

"So Goines was outside?" Nice asked.

"He was boxing," I said. "Punching the snow."

"Maybe one day Ma will give him a chance, you know," he said. He laughed a quick breath, then became serious. "Listen," he said. "Don't be me. Don't be no one but you. You understand?"

Nice pushed open the door and I followed him into the whiteness. I didn't understand. Why not be him? Wasn't he the greatest, a hero? If not be like him, then be like who? *Be you,* he said. What did that mean? Who was I? What could Abraham Singleton do?

The wind whipped snow against me and ripped my face left and right. I tucked my chin to my chest and kept my eyes on the back of Nice's legs. The snow was two feet deep. I pumped my arms and lifted my knees just to trudge through it. We crossed the snow-covered concrete courtyard, the parking lot, and the sidewalk. Then, when we reached Columbus Avenue, we made a left and walked down the middle of the street, past parked cars engulfed in snow, past streetlights and the circles of pallid yellow they cast upon the dusty blue darkness of fresh snowfall meeting its first night. Snow spilled, tumbled, and cast about each time I stepped. I thought about what Nice said, what he told me to do. Snow melted and dripped down my cheeks. We came to the basketball court and the twenty-foot chain-link fence that surrounded it. Nice walked up to the fence and stopped. Then reaching his hands up, he gripped the fence and gazed at the snow-covered court, the steel backboards, the steel rims with snow perched on them. We stood in silence for a few long moments. I looked at Nice and then at the court and then at Nice again. I wondered what he was thinking, what he hoped for.

"You figure out who you gonna be?" he asked.

"I'm gonna be you," I said.

He laughed. "Then who am I?"

I shrugged. "You you too."

"Just like that?" he said.

"Uh-huh."

"Ain't no one else you want to be?"

"Who else is there?" I asked.

Nice considered my question.

"I bet you three dollars I can make it from here," he said.

"We only got three dollars," I said.

"Good," he said. "Then I'm betting everything. I'm putting the house down."

Nice let go of the fence, stepped back, and blew on his hands. Then he dribbled an invisible basketball. He paused and put it on his hip. I knew what he was doing: his free-throw routine. I'd seen him do it and I'd imitated it thousands of times. He took a deep breath, exhaled, and I watched the air billow from his mouth.

"Ladies and gentlemen," he said, speaking as if he were an announcer. "Here we are. No time left on the clock. Score is tied. Good guys versus bad guys. Nice versus all the snow in the world. We need this to win."

Nice dribbled his invisible basketball again, twice with his right hand, twice with his left. Then he stopped and measured the rim through the rusted fence.

"Listen to the crowd try to distract him! Listen how loud they are, how much they're booing and shouting!" he announced.

He took a deep breath, in through his nose, out through his mouth. He bent his knees, brought the invisible ball to his waist, then slowly raised it above his head and shot, flicking his wrist, pushing the ball toward the rim with the tips of his fingers. And I watched it, the invisible ball soaring over the fence, floating through the falling snow, drifting across the fifty feet that separated us from the rim.

"It go in?" he asked me.

I looked through the fence at the rim. Everything was silent. I was just beginning to learn such silence could exist between two people, that despite proximity, people could be distant in their thoughts.

"Yeah," I said.

"Thank God," Nice said. "I ain't trying to go home with no milk again."

So we trudged through the snow, toward the only open corner store ten blocks away, engulfed in a world of white, obligated and determined to get what my grandma demanded. All the way there, inside the store, and all the way back, Nice told me about basketball, about him playing in college and the NBA and him having a big house where we all could live and cars and money and I felt the earth moving. I felt it spinning on its axis, slowly revolving around the sun.

"Between you and me," Nice said when we got back to our apartment and he unlocked the locks. "In a few years, we won't need to be getting no milk from the store. I'll buy a plane and a cow farm and some white farmer niggas milk those motherfuckers whenever we're thirsty."

BAR 3

Distant Lover

I

The heat in our building was broken, or rather deeply confused. Hot, dry air blasted into our apartment. And the phone was out. And the electricity was cut off too. So our apartment was dark. My grandmother had been let go from her job at Queens Hospital. They were making cutbacks. Layoffs. "Restructuring" is what my grandma said the hospital's administration called it. They started from the bottom. Everyone who needed the money most, everyone whose education and skill set made finding a good job a difficult test, everyone who was simultaneously just getting by and trying to provide their children a better opportunity than they had were fired first, the orderlies, the porters, and the security guards. Trickle-down economics.

My mother and I were in the kitchen, sitting at the table. She was slouched in a folding metal chair to my left and her bare feet rested across my thighs. I was doing my homework. It was June, the last weeks of school, and it was after midnight. Our only light came from the dozen prayer candles huddled in the middle of the table that my grand-mother bought at the dollar store and kept in the closet for just this sort of thing. There was Our Lady of Guadalupe, Saint Michael and Saint Lazarus, Saint Anthony and Saint Joseph, Saint Clare and a few Saint Judes, the patron saint of difficult cases. There was even a candle for the pope and another for Mother Teresa, although being that they were alive no one in my family knew why. I was small and skinny, so wispy the thin gold chain with my name on it that my grandma bought me for my seventh birthday hung like a stone around my neck and tapped the top of the table when I leaned forward over my homework and wrote my answers. I wore shorts and a tank top. I multiplied single digits and wrote spelling words five times each. My mother wore shorts and a red bathing-suit top. A wet dishtowel was draped across the back of her neck. She had headphones on and she alternated between watch-ing me and staring at the floor as she listened to the same song, Marvin Gaye's "Distant Lover," over and over again. Each time the song ended, she hit the stop button, the rewind button, and the play button on her Walkman. Then she settled into the song again, slouching deeper into the chair, disappearing in the four-minute sanctuary of the what and who of this distant love.

I focused intensely on my work, aiming to please her, aiming to make good on the promise I repeated so often it was not a promise but, quite simply, a fact. I would do well in school. A film of sweat covered every inch of my body and caused the underside of my legs to stick to the chair, my arms to stick to the table, and my hand to stick to my homework paper. My grandma was asleep in the bedroom she shared with my Aunt Rhonda and my mother and the ebb and flow of her snoring dragged my thoughts to her. Just like the previous night, and just like the night two weeks before when our electricity was first cut off, she had gone to sleep early. She had been out of work for four months. She had no prospects for a job. My Aunt Rhonda and my mother were looking for jobs, they met with their welfare case managers, and they were enrolled in a GED class, but the class was so overcrowded and so egregiously organized their progress was so slow they decided there was no sense in going. David Dinkins was the first black mayor of New York. *Ask your teachers what that means,* my grandma said before she went to sleep. *Ask them why folks is worse off now than we was before.*

All of the windows in the apartment were open so the sounds of the street, of traffic and music and the occasional laughter and shouting leapt into our apartment from below and bounced like rubber balls off the walls. Taking advantage of the darkness, my Aunt Rhonda lay on the couch in the living room, giggling and whispering things of an erotic nature in a coy tone to her new boyfriend, Beany, a diminutive twenty-year-old with the gentle, unassuming face of a boy who believed all he'd heard in church. Beany lived three doors down the hall with his mother, father, little sister, and their two cats, Geronimo and Sam. His mother and father were hardworking church people. His sister, Cecily, was a straight-A student. In fact, Beany had been a straight A student too, but in his mid-teens his aspirations changed and Beany became bent on being the baddest motherfucker in Queens. Fuck you was his disposition. From his vantage point, everyone was out to get him. But because Beany was small and because he didn't have the personal history or family structure to prove his courage or translate it into rage, and because his father was very much the master of his home, Beany, more than anything else, was bluster. I heard my Aunt Rhonda giggle and Beany beg please. Then I heard her say stop and it's too hot, then slap him and giggle again.

Our apartment door opened, and a pale river of light rolled into our apartment. Then the door closed and the darkness returned. Donnel was home. He mumbled a hello to my Aunt Rhonda then walked into the kitchen, a red brick in each hand.

"Where you been?" I asked.

"Stairs," he said, short of breath. "Up and down, from the basement to the roof."

Donnel wore grey sweatpants and a grey sweatshirt and although the kitchen was no brighter than dim, I could see that his collar was soaked with sweat. He was twelve. His body carried the must of a man who should be wearing deodorant and he was so lean the veins on the back of his hands looked like noodles hidden just beneath the surface of his cherrywood skin. He hated seeing my Aunt Rhonda with a man because he knew what the product of such a coupling was. Sooner or later, she'd be crying. Sooner or later, she'd be whirling in a fitful rage. Then she would be silent, lost, alone.

Donnel planted the bricks on the table and surveyed the kitchen, the bouquet of flowers Mr. Goines delivered the previous day that we'd pushed to the back of the table, the dishes in the sink, and the birdcage on the far corner of the counter, a moat of discarded seeds surrounding it. Inside the cage, the birds perched beside each other and tried to sleep through the heat, their beaks burrowed in their green chests. Donnel crossed the room, stuck his finger through the bars of the birdcage, and whistled a few high notes.

"How many times?" I asked.

"Twenty," he said.

"You crazy?" I said.

Proudly, he looked at me over his shoulder. "Why?"

"Cause it's hot."

"Nigga," he scolded. "Heat can't stop me."

That spring Donnel had been beat real bad. Jumped after school, a crew of young brothers split his lip, split his head, black-and-blued, and broke blood vessels in both of his eyes. He fought back though, and his hands were so swollen and battered they looked like he'd spent hours grating them against a rock wall. He couldn't grip or squeeze so he had to open bottles, bags, and cans of soda with his teeth for a week. Donnel must have thrown as many punches as he'd been dealt. Him against what I imagined to be hundreds, not one of whom he named. He refused to; refused to say why, refused tell anyone where it happened, when it happened, if he was alone or with friends. It didn't matter how many times we asked, or how many times I begged him to tell just me as we lay head to foot in bed at night.

The one thing he did say, the one thing he swore his life away on, is that it would never happen again. Never, he said. And it wouldn't happen to Eric or me. Never, he swore. Not once. No one would so much as think of breathing on us. He'd kill if he had to. With his bare hands. Bet on it, he said. He made up a workout program and followed it religiously to ready himself. He did push-ups and sit-ups, seemingly thousands at a time. He did pull-ups from crossing signs every time we came to a corner and the sign glowed *Don't walk*. He leaned our mattress against the wall and boxed it, pounding and pounding it until he was soaked in sweat. And he ran with the bricks; ran around the block, ran up and down the stairs.

Donnel came to the table and looked down at my schoolwork. He was in the seventh grade. Maybe he was passing his classes. Maybe he was failing. He didn't care, and although she swore she cared, although she asked him when she was going to see him doing homework and where his report cards were, my Aunt Rhonda was too concerned with what she wanted to truly care either. As far as she was concerned, Donnel was a man; what he wanted, if he really wanted it, he'd figure out how to get. The thing Donnel most wanted was for my Aunt Rhonda to be free from her desperate need for a man, and going to school had nothing to do with it. So Donnel either didn't go to school or went to school with a level of contentiousness that made teachers demand that he tell them who he thought he was.

"What you doing?" he asked, picking up my math homework and holding it so he could see it in the candlelight.

"Multiplication," I said. "I finished that already."

He studied my answers for a moment. Then he put the page down in front of me.

"What's six times six?" he asked.

I thought for a moment. "Thirty-six," I said.

He pointed at one of my answers. "You got thirty-two," he said. "Fix it."

I looked at the problem Donnel had identified. He was right. I erased the answer, blew the pieces of rubber eraser from the paper, and wrote thirty-six.

My mother pressed the stop button on her Walkman and took her headphones from her ears. "Donnel, let Abraham be," she scolded. "He's got schoolwork to finish."

Donnel ignored her. He tapped my shoulder. "Want to go swimming?" he asked.

"Swimming?" I said.

"In the pool," Donnel said.

"The city closes the pool when the sun goes down," snapped my mother. "You know that." She smacked my cheek with the back of her fingers to get my attention. "Can't you see he's fuck'n with you?" She tapped her hand on my homework. "C'mon, finish. I ain't got all night."

If there was one thing Donnel wasn't, it was a liar. He hated even the insinuation that he might be. He planted his hand on my homework and looked at my mother, his face and body taut, his eyes shining, black steel in the candlelight.

"Someone put a kid pool on the roof," he insisted.

My mother looked Donnel dead in the eyes and considered what he said. She was twenty-two, lonely, hot, and always willing to embrace an escape from life.

"The elevator working?" she asked.

"I heard it going up and down when I was in the stairs," Donnel said.

"You sure?" said my mother. "Cause I ain't try'n to get stuck."

"Who?" Donnel teased.

"Me," my mother said. "What? You gonna tell me I can't come?"

Donnel knew he'd won. He took his hand from my homework.

"And the water's clean?" my mother asked.

Donnel shrugged. "Looked clean to me."

My mother thought for a brief moment and I wondered what she considered. Maybe she reflected on the facts of her life, that she was without a job; that my grandma was out of work too; that my Uncle Roosevelt was out somewhere who knows where doing who knows what with Luscious; that my Aunt Rhonda was on the couch with Beany, cuddling and entertaining fantasies; that my grandma and Eric were asleep, deep in safe, dark worlds of dreams; and that there she was, in Ever, sitting in the almost dark, sweating in a kitchen as her son spelled simple words and solved simple math equations that didn't solve any of our problems.

She swung her legs off my lap, leaned forward, and tapped her hand on the table. "Abraham," she said. "Hurry up. Finish what you got."

My mother took a candle from the table and quickly disappeared into the bedroom she shared with my grandma and my Aunt Rhonda. Donnel took a candle and went into our room to change into shorts. I wrote the last spelling words as quickly as I could. Then Donnel came back into the kitchen for me.

"You ready?" he asked.

I finished writing. I put my pencil down. Then I stood in a rush.

"Put your shit away," Donnel ordered. "Put it in your bag. Don't be leaving it all out."

Hurrying, I put my homework into my school folder and stuffed it into my backpack. Then I took a candle and followed Donnel into the dark living room.

"Where you all going?" asked my Aunt Rhonda.

"To the roof," said Donnel, not even slightly shifting in the direction of his mother and Beany.

"How long you gonna be gone?" my Aunt Rhonda asked.

Donnel didn't answer. He unlocked the door and opened it as wide as he could. The room flooded with the pale glow of the hallway's light and Donnel swung around and looked at my Aunt Rhonda and Beany as if he might catch them committing a crime. My Aunt Rhonda was slouched against Beany and her hand disappeared somewhere in his lap. Quickly, she pulled it free and covered her eyes as if the light was not pallid but blinding.

"Donnel, damn!" she complained. "What're you doing?"

"Go on!" said Beany. He pulled away from my Aunt Rhonda. "Nigga, stop being stupid. Get out of here!"

Donnel held the candle just beneath his chin, his eyes on Beany. "Who you talking to?" he asked, his voice molten anger.

"*You*," said Beany.

"Nigga," Donnel began, but my Aunt Rhonda interrupted him.

"D," she said, "take your little angry ass wherever."

"Before you get hurt," Beany added.

Hurt? Donnel glared at Beany for a long, dangerous moment. I feared what he might say and its repercussions. Donnel had a tongue as sharp and wicked as arbitrary hate and raining razor blades. I'd seen him slice and dice and fillet brothers, name all of their deepest secrets, and then chastise them for bothering to keep them. He shifted his eyes to me. And although I was afraid, I tried to use my eyes to let him know that whatever happened, whatever he said and however Beany reacted, I had his back, that if Beany leapt from the couch and tried to kill him, I'd be there killing Beany more. Donnel swallowed then moved his eyes from me back to my Aunt Rhonda and Beany. I assumed he would speak, say something vicious. But he said nothing. Whatever my Aunt Rhonda wanted, whatever she believed she needed, Donnel always, somehow, found a way to rationalize and give in to. He blew out his candle, put it on the floor, and called for my mother.

"Jelly," he said. "You coming?"

"Meet you up there," my mother called back from the bedroom.

Donnel turned around and walked into the hallway light. Blowing out my candle, putting it down, and holding my breath as best as I could, trying not to breathe in the stale stench of hot piss that bloomed in the elevator and lived in the hall, I followed him. We took the elevator up to the top floor. Donnel muttered about how he would kill Beany if he did anything to my Aunt Rhonda. I told him that I had his back and that I hated Beany too.

"Serious," Donnel said, leaning against the back of the elevator and glaring at its steel door. "Nigga is crazy if he thinks I'm gonna do nothing the second he hurts her."

We reached the top floor and the elevator door squelched and groaned open. We climbed the flight of stairs to the roof. Donnel shouldered open the door and I followed him. And then, there it was: a pale blue plastic kid pool sitting between the blackness of the sky and the blackness of the tarred roof.

"I told you," Donnel said.

We walked to the pool and stopped at its edge. It was filled with water.

"Is it warm?" I whispered as if the night were a baby I was afraid to wake.

Donnel bent down and put his hand in it. "Perfect," he said.

Behind us the door to the stairs swung open and out walked my mother followed by my grandma.

"So I see how it is," said my grandma, her voice deep and craggy from sleep. "You all taking a vacation without me."

"You was sleeping!" I said, excitement making my voice loud.

"So?" said my grandma.

Donnel peeled his sweatshirt off, dropped it, kicked off his sneakers, and stepped into the water.

"Look at you," said my mother, teasing him as she and my grandma came to the edge of the pool. "Donnel, you so skinny I can see your heart beating."

"My heart?" said Donnel. Standing in the middle of the pool, the water just below his knees, he curled his fist to his chest, flexed his bicep, and gave the tight little mound a kiss. "What you know about this?"

"I know it ain't shit," my mother laughed.

"It looks like you got an itty bitty egg under your skin," I teased.

Donnel splashed water at me. "Nigga," he said. "What're you talking about? Go ahead and lift your shirt. C'mon. Let's see that nasty ole' outie of yours."

My outie button was the subject of most of the harassment I received from my cousins and everyone else our age who had either seen me shirtless themselves or had heard about my belly button, the tiny, limp fist that stuck out an inch and made it seem like I had a nipple in the middle of my stomach if my T-shirt was too tight. I was embarrassed by it. Sometimes I pulled on it and pushed it in and held it there, like I was plugging the hole in a dam, hoping it would stay in. Sometimes I pondered how much it would hurt if I cut it off.

"Donnel," scolded my grandma. "You know I made that belly button with the help of great God Almighty. That right there ain't a defect. It's what . . . He told me to do."

My grandma wore a pair of my uncle's basketball shorts and one of his basketball T-shirts.

"And Donnel," she continued, "don't go pretending you didn't have no hand in it either. You was right there too. So maybe you was holding Abraham too tight. Or maybe you wasn't holding him tight enough. You know, you didn't have none of those muscles you got now back then."

Donnel's body was goldened by the reflection of the moon in the pool, the lights of Ever Park and Queens, and those lights way off in the distance, the electric ivory that was Manhattan. "I remember," he said. "A is lucky to be alive."

Donnel looked at me and smiled. Then he splashed water at me and clapped and laughed as I squinted and blinked and hastily wiped the water from my face. I kicked my sneakers off and stepped into the pool. Then Donnel and I urged and teased my mother and grandma until they joined us.

"Don't splash," my grandma scolded, holding the edge of the pool as she stepped over it to join us. "I don't want my hair to get wet."

We squatted and sat down in the water and our legs touched in the middle of the pool. The kid pool was the first pool I'd ever been in that wasn't packed with people on a hot summer day, brimming with children splashing and peeing and seeing who could hold their breaths longer; with teenagers ogling and wrestling each other; with mothers holding infants. I was conditioned to be one of many, to be of the masses; to be crammed in and to call such conditions relief; to know crowds as home. My mother, grandma, and Donnel whispered and cursed Ever, how strange it was that when the heat was broken the elevator ran smoothly. Donnel talked like an adult, like he was husband and they were his wives. He could do that. He had an ability to speak in the manner and on the terms of those he was with. I half listened and looked up at the sky, watched the lights of airplanes blink through the blackness, wondering who went where.

"You all right?" asked Donnel, flicking water on my face and shifting attention to me.

"Yeah," I said, meeting his eyes. "Why?"

He shifted his eyes to my mother and laughed a tumble of breath. "A can be so quiet, can't he?"

"He always been that way," my grandma said.

My mother reached over to me, pressed, then slid her wet hand down my ear, my cheek, and along the line of my jaw. "Mister Man," she said, calling me by the name she used for me when she wished to tell me how much she loved me but either chose not to or could not say the words.

Donnel spun himself around in the pool, hooked his legs over its plastic wall, and leaned backward into the water. He floated on his back, his arms at his sides, his head in the middle of the pool. The only sound was the waves made by Donnel's movement, the water lapping against our bodies and the walls of the pool.

"Look at the moon," he said, talking louder than necessary because his ears were submerged in the water.

The moon was nearly full, like someone had punched a hole in the black night and there was white on the other side. My mother laid her arms along the edge of the pool, leaned back, and looked up.

"Sometimes, don't it look so close you can touch it?" she asked.

Donnel turned to his side and splashed water at me. "Lay on your back," he said. "It's nice. There's nothing to be scared of."

"Who said I'm scared," I snapped.

Donnel lifted his legs from the edge, turned, and quickly sat on his knees.

"Here," he said, laying his hands on the surface of the water. "Lean back. I got you. Lean back and put your feet up."

"You gonna pull your hands away," I said.

"I got you," he said. "Trust me."

I turned around, bent my knees over the lip of the pool, and looked over my shoulder at Donnel.

"Come on," he said. "Sometime before I'm dead."

I leaned and lowered myself until I felt the tips of Donnel's fingers, then the flat of his hands against my back. Slowly, he lowered me.

"Abraham," my grandma laughed. "Open your eyes!"

"They're open," I said.

"Then open them wider," Donnel ordered.

I opened my eyes as wide as I could.

"And breathe," he said.

I breathed. The surface of the water hovered an inch from the corner of my eyes, two inches from the sides of my nostrils, and half an inch from the corners of my lips. My ears were under water. All sound was muffled. It was wonderful. Peace.

"All right," Donnel said. "I'm gonna let go."

I felt his hands leave my body. Then the water rippled against my skin when he returned to lying on his back.

"Imagine doing this in the ocean," he announced, making sure to speak loud enough for me to hear.

"What if you got tired?" I shouted back.

"Then you climb onto your boat," he answered.

"Who's got a boat?" laughed my grandma.

"In the ocean," Donnel said, "you can have whatever you want. A, what you want?"

I thought for a moment. I wanted whatever he wanted, whatever he needed.

"I don't know," I said. "What you want?"

"Who?" he said.

"You," scolded my mother. "Unless you see some other skinny nigga in the pool."

"All I see is the sky," Donnel said. "There could be thousands of niggas in this water for all I know."

"So what you want?" I asked again.

"A boat for one thing," said Donnel. Then after a brief pause he added: "And a trumpet."

"A trumpet?" my grandma said.

"If I had a trumpet . . . ," Donnel began.

"If you had a trumpet, what?" my mother interrupted.

Suddenly, police sirens burned the night; broke us from below.

"Jesus," my mother sighed. "Why they always got to be fuck'n everything up."

Never had I been so still, so weightless; never had I been in a pool on the roof of Ever. I looked at the moon one last time and then I closed my eyes. I was surrounded, floating in darkness. The wail of the sirens faded, disappeared, and I waited for someone to speak, to say anything, to overcome the silence, to speak before police sirens arrived again.

"So," my grandma finally said. "What're you gonna do with your trumpet?"

"If I had a trumpet," Donnel answered, his voice soft and longing. "If I had a trumpet I don't know."

II

It didn't happen every Sunday, nor did it occur with enough regularity to be considered an occasional occasion, but when my grandma went to church, dragging with her anyone in our apartment who didn't have a legitimate reason why he or she could not join her, it was not because she was a churchgoing type of woman who believed she needed to be in church to be saved by Jesus and heard by God. Rather, on the mornings when my grandma went to church it was because she awoke with an irrepressible longing, a hurt so great no other place but a place where brothers and sisters came together could salve her wound. Sometimes the wound was born from recollection, a dream, a memory she went to bed with at night. Sometimes it was a product of the television, the five, six, and eleven o'clock news and the reports of brothers killing brothers in Los Angeles, brothers killing brothers in Texas, brothers killing brothers in Africa, in Liberia, Nigeria, and Sierra Leone. And sometimes this hurt was born from one thing, a murder in Ever, a thievery. But no matter how much she hurt, no matter how sick or tired she was, my grandma never once allowed herself to be defeated. Her will, her determination to live was too great. But I am skipping ahead.

Born in 1952 to a single teenage girl, my grandma was orphaned in Harlem at the age of five when her mother fell in love with heroin. For the next seven years, my grandma was a ward of the state. She lived in children's homes. She lived in foster care, where she was fed only oatmeal, water, and eggs. By the time she was twelve, my grandma had fought off three rape attempts, kicking and biting and tearing at the eyes of each of her attackers. By fourteen, she'd had two miscarriages, given birth to my Aunt Rhonda, and dropped out of school. She was tired, she said, too damn tired to do anything with her head. At fifteen, she fell in love for the first time. Like her, he was young, a hard-knock brother, a dreamer who, five years later, left her with not only my Aunt Rhonda, but his daughter, my three-year old mother, as well. It was 1972. My grandma was twenty. She said she considered the world, considered where she was in it, where she might go, and she could only conclude: nowhere, nothing. Martin Luther King was dead. Malcolm X was dead. Brothers were dying in Vietnam. Black power, black nationalism, black hope was, quite simply, losing. Brothers and sisters needed more than revolution. My grandma was alone, jobless. Her babies needed more than diapers, more than food. Rent went unpaid. The electricity and the gas were shut off. For six months, my grandmother, my Aunt Rhonda, and my mother lived in the cold and dark. They ate one meal a day, lunch in a soup kitchen. For dinner, they prayed a local bakery would throw out stale bread. Yet and still, every night, my grandma told my aunt and mother it was going to be OK. And then, only after she was sure her children were sound asleep, she cried until the morning, when with dry, red eyes, and before my mother and aunt woke, she would consider a way out, an escape. Sometimes, pitying herself, desperate, my grandma thought about killing herself.

There were lives, she reasoned, that were simply impossible to live. She could die and no one would care; no one would notice. Her children might have a better life. But could she repeat the cycle that had created and produced her life? My mother or aunt would wake and call for her. She would take a deep breath and then, always, my grandma decided: no, she couldn't. She wouldn't let herself fail. There was no other option. No action that fostered any variation of genocide would be accepted. So she held her chin higher than heights unreachable. So she sashayed and strutted when she walked. So she laughed bigger laughs than could possibly fit in her body. And then, a week after my grandma turned twenty-one, she met, fell in love with, and married my grandfather, my Uncle Roosevelt's biological father, Sterling James Singleton, a man who fueled and fortified my grandma and taught her that she was not the only one who was determined to overcome, surpass, and leave a legacy that transcended the lengths men went to generate and fortify damnation.

Sterling was a good, solid forty-something-year-old brother with a head of salt and pepper and a sliver of space between his front teeth. He attended church regularly and played cards. Often, he announced he was a simple man, a brother who was just two things: a plumber and in love with my grandma. He bathed her. He kissed and massaged her feet. He planned for their future and the future of their children and their children's children, and quite possibly, if the world was still the world, the generations of children that would forever come. One day, God willing, he said, he would have his own business. Then two. Then three. He adopted my mother and my aunt and they took his last name. Everyone on the block called him Pop and at parties, he took my grandma by the hand and made her slow dance with him, first at the party, then as they walked home, in the middle of the street, with and without music playing, with him humming and whispering her a tune, rain or shine, in the light of the afternoon, at night, in the yellow circle the streetlight made on the black street. He was gallant, hardworking. Then while walking home alone one night, while my grandmother, my Aunt Rhonda, my mother, and my then two-year-old Uncle Roosevelt slept, he was shot dead by a man who knew Sterling Singleton had a wad of cash in his pocket when he walked home, whistling after gambling and drinking all night.

After his death, my grandma came to the decision that no man would sleep in her bed. So no matter how many times Lyndon Goines asked she swore she would not go on a single date with him. She said she didn't care if he had all the money in the world and a diamond heart because none of it could stop man's insanity. As for Mr. Goines, not only was he crazy, she said, but she didn't have the energy or the time for him and his damn foolishness, running around protesting and shouting and acting like his itty bitty voice was worth minding. *Lyndon,* she would say after he knocked on our door holding flowers or offering to take her to the movies and sometimes to herself after he called and she hung up on him, *I don't need no man; why is that so damn hard to understand?* She was a woman, no longer some scared and confused twenty-year-old child. She said she was beyond love, far past it like stars are farther than the moon. It wasn't absent from her life. When she wanted it, she said, she'd listen to the Whispers or watch a good movie. So it wasn't something that needed to be recovered. She had a family to worry about. She had her children. And her daughters had me and Eric and Donnel. But that wasn't the truth. The truth was that although my grandma loved us and we loved her, the courage to love someone new, someone she had no hand in creating had been razed from her, torn from its roots, burned and hacked from every follicle, every pore. So she was scared to love. Because she didn't think she could handle it. Because what would she do or become if love was stripped from her once more?

The answer was nothing. That is, because love had been ripped from her before, she would remain herself.

It was the end of April, the time of year when the temperature rose and the basketball court teemed with brothers the winter had kept inside for too long. I was nine. I walked down Columbus Avenue dribbling my basketball.

The buildings in the neighborhood, the streets, the telephone poles and their drooping wires, everything around me was barely hanging on. The sidewalk was crumbled. Street signs leaned at an array of angles less than ninety degrees. Some of the doors and windows of abandoned buildings were shuttered with rotting, warped, and splintered plywood. Others were sealed with corrugated steel or blocked off brick by brick. Stray dogs walked with their noses to the ground, only stopping to lift their legs and urinate in the spot where another dog or a man had urinated minutes before.

The previous winter, two things occurred in my life. First, like a biblical plague that had finally matured and now enveloped us, the quantity of crack in Ever infinitely multiplied, becoming not just a part of the landscape but the greatest cause and the defining characteristics of the neighborhood's dilapidation. And second, I had reached an age, a point of maturation where I not only saw crack's effects, how it hollowed and gutted brothers and sisters, both its users and those who loved its users, but I also understood the sight to be an indication of a devastation that was a particular infliction of my life. The books and stories I read in school never mentioned it. And nowhere, not even on cable or public access TV, was there a truthful depiction of my life, how we in Ever existed, however since crack came there wasn't a single being, not a bird, person, or rat in Ever who wasn't desperate to either change our predicament or get out, move to a quiet, safe place, to live and breathe freely. Of course, my family had a chance to get out. And of course that chance was my Uncle Roosevelt, Nice, he who was as proud to be a product of Ever Park as he was to be our family's savior.

I dribbled with my left hand. I dribbled the ball between my legs. I spun it on my finger. As I walked down Columbus Avenue, I said hello to people my mother and aunt and uncle were cool with. I smiled at my grandma's friends. I said hello to my friends. Everyone smiled back. They said I looked like a miniature version of my uncle then laughed at the shining smile of my face. How excited I was. I was going to the basketball court and I was sure my uncle would be there. I'd watch him slither, dance, prance, and groove to the basket. I would have held my basketball under my arm and sprinted to the court if I was not aware, not invested in being cool, being a basketball player like him.

When I came within eyesight of the basketball court, I saw no one was playing. Not a single brother shot or dribbled a ball. A crowd was gathered on the side of the court. I stopped dribbling and cradled the ball against my hip. Then I walked toward the court until I could hear what people were saying.

Elijah Treadwell, a three-hundred-pound maple-syrup-colored brother, talked with his hands, the perpetually lit Newport pinched between his finger and thumb swirling and darting like a flaming mosquito.

"They got that nigga!" he shouted, yanking his cigarette to the left, pointing it at the sky, then swinging it like a sword across his chest. "They snatched him! For nothing!"

"We was just standing here!" shouted Beany. "Talking! Doing nothing! Then they came and got him!"

"Motherfuckers didn't even have the dignity to say what he did," interjected Hector Mendez, a skinny Puerto Rican who could have passed for Caucasian if not for the manner in which he rolled his R's and the Puerto Rican pride paraphernalia he always wore—the bracelet, the pins, the many T-shirts, the gold necklace with a Puerto Rican flag inside a gold medallion.

"And when I asked those niggas," continued Beany, so angry he was choking on his words. "When I said: *What my nigga do?*"

"They told him to shut up, get back, before he got arrested too!" Hector interjected again.

"So I was like," said Beany. "So I was like, *What? This is my nigga, right here! This is my girl's brother! Shit, arrest me! You know? Take me! Just let my nigga Nice go free! Let my man Nice be.*"

"And you know if they arresting Nice then ain't no motherfucker safe!" said Hector. "Believe that! Not a single motherfucker!"

"Me and Nice have been like brothers since we was this big," Elijah exploded, his hand two feet from the ground, his eyes full of tears. "You can't be running up and cuffing a nigga like Nice for no reason. It's damn near the twenty-first motherfuck'n century. This ain't no South Africa or China or Cuba or some fucked-up place like Mississippi!"

"Shit, when we gonna be like Crown Heights?" shouted Alton Johnson, a light-skinned brother with fingers as thick as my neck and freckles the size of M&M's on his cheeks. "That's what I want to know. When we gonna riot?"

Elijah threw his cigarette on the concrete, crushed it out with his heel, snatched his pager from his hip, and looked at it. "An hour ago," he said, breathless and suddenly defeated. "Exactly fifty-three minutes. That's how long it's been."

"And Luscious don't know?" blurted Cherrie, one of the few women in the gathering.

Still my mother's best friend, Cherrie had become a big woman with big juicy arms, three chins, and a neck like melted Rolos. She was twenty-three and in the previous two years, Cherrie's mom had died from breast cancer and her big sister Candy joined the army so Cherrie lived alone. She loved anything and everything that distracted her from this fact and offered her familial belonging, like talk shows and playing Spades and dominoes, and basketball. Cherrie lived for basketball so she was always at the basketball court.

"Hell no, Luscious don't know," said Elijah. He tore his pack of

Newports from his pocket, jammed a new cigarette in his mouth, and lit it with a lighter. Then he took a deep slow drag, blew it at the sky, and added: "And I ain't gonna be the one to tell her neither."

"Me neither," agreed Hector. "I ain't saying shit."

"Cause you know Luscious ain't having it," surmised Cherrie. "Lord knows she ain't letting her man go down for nothing."

"Shit," said Alton, sadly kicking aside one of the crushed cigarettes on the ground. "What the fuck Luscious gonna do?"

"Start a war, that's what we should do," Beany decided.

"A war?" said Elijah, considering the option. "Nigga, what kind of war we gonna win? What you gonna do when niggas roll up in Ever in a tank?"

"Niggas dropped the bomb on those Japanese," added Alton. "So don't think for a minute, don't think for a second that they won't drop one of them on us."

I was stunned, shocked, battered and beaten and so speechless I was invisible. No one looked my way. No one recognized that it was my uncle, my Nice the police snatched and yanked away. I wanted to know what happened. I wanted to know why. But I did not cry or shout. No, my body boiled from the outside in, from my skin to my heart. I listened to everyone describe what the police did and what we needed to do; how we needed to take control of our own community, govern ourselves; move, get out of Ever; how we were so damn sick and tired; and slowly I understood what happened, and put recent events together, and so I knew that Nice had decided that he couldn't allow what our home had become. We could not lack so greatly. And he was not helpless. He was a star, Ever Park's hero, a young man who kept on rising and rising. And he was just about to decide on which college was for him. But his family could not go in the opposite direction. We could not fall into greater poverty, greater pain and suffering. He had been to church enough times with my grandma to know Moses didn't stand for it. So neither would he. But the problem was what a basketball could do for us would take years. And it was a maybe. And we needed something now and definite. Appetites were increasing, so food stamps were not enough to feed still-growing Nice, and three growing boys in addition to my mother, my aunt, and my grandma. And then the last time I had been to the doctor, the doctor told my mother I was anemic. It was nothing serious but when Nice found out he asked a hundred questions. Was I going to die? Would I need radiation and chemotherapy? Was it like sickle cell? How would I be treated? He couldn't believe that my ailment could be solved simply by eating more meat, drinking more milk. And of course there was Luscious, and how he wanted to provide her everything. So he had taken a job in the only booming economy in and around Ever. Meaning he asserted his Americanness, became a capitalist, and followed the tenets of supply and demand. He didn't deal drugs. He wasn't a hustler. He was a sherpa, a mule, a ferry. His plans were to only do it temporarily, just until he accepted his college scholarship and left Ever. So when he was not playing basketball, or in school, or spending his time with Luscious, he put crack in his gym bag and carried it from point A to B. No one wanted Nice to do such a thing, not my mother, not my aunt, and, of course, not my grandma. But they also didn't ask him where he was getting money from or demand that he stop if they knew. We needed, and our simple needs took precedence over adhering to a legal code and system that did not provide. And so he got the money to pay our bills. And our refrigerator was full of food. And he had bought me new basketball sneakers, Nikes, the same as his, the same ones players wore in the NBA. How proudly I wore them, how sweet they felt on my feet.

That Sunday we went to church, my grandma, my aunt and mother, my cousins and Luscious and me. We sat silently in a middle pew of the Holy Name, the storefront church with exposed brick walls and no windows that was founded, managed, and maintained by Pastor Ramsey and his musically inclined son Jeremiah and attended by no more than a handful of people unless there was a funeral. Standing behind the rickety lectern, Pastor Ramsey, a diminutive, militant man who wore wire-frame glasses and flamboyant floral ties, ranted and raged, read from a ragged leather-bound Bible and breathed a sermon that concluded with the choice between faith and ire.

"Cause it's with Jesus! It's through Jesus! It is Jesus who gives us peace! John fourteen, twenty-seven. *Peace I leave with you, my peace I give to you: not as the world gives, give I to you. Let not your heart be troubled, neither let it be afraid.*"

I didn't believe a word Pastor Ramsey said. Although just a child, *Fuck Jesus* is what I thought. What had that nigga ever done for me? For my aunt? My cousins? Luscious? Nice? What had Jesus done for my grandma, she who, dressed in a white floral print dress, sat to my left at the end of the pew; she who raised all known generations of my family, parented herself, my aunt, my mother, my uncle, and finally Donnel, Eric, and me without the sustained support of a single man or blood relative; she who possessed a heart that had been wrenched and bent; she who held her chin at an angle that proved her indestructibility; she who stared straight ahead and wrung her hands in her lap while tears as large as dimes skated down her cheeks and dripped from her chin; she who never once blinked while Pastor Ramsey pounded his fist on the lectern or while Jeremiah, an effeminate version of his pious father, held the microphone inches from his mouth, closed his eyes, swayed, and, with a voice like sustained notes of fragile bells, sung of an amazing grace, a savior who couldn't save us from Ever.

One week later, we visited Nice in the city jail. He talked on a phone on one side of the glass; we took turns talking on the phone on the other.

He had met with his Legal Aid lawyer and decided to plead guilty. It was simple. He did it was all he said. He didn't cry or apologize for what he'd done. He didn't excuse himself or offer reasons and justifications. He dropped his eyes when Luscious cried and told him she loved him with all of her heart. He dropped his eyes when my grandma said he'd lost weight. He thanked Eric for the picture he drew him. He told Donnel that he was in charge now, that he was the man of the house, that Eric and I were his responsibility. He wore the orange jumpsuit the prison issued him and one by one he told us to forget him, not to write to him, to never send mail or money. I was the last to speak to him.

"Imagine," he said. "Abraham, imagine I'm dead."

He raised his eyes and let them rest on each of us, on my mother, my Aunt Rhonda, on Donnel and Eric, on me, and finally on Luscious. Then he nodded once as if to bid us farewell and looked straight ahead, acted as if no one, nothing, not even he was there anymore. He put the phone down on the table, rose from the seat, and balletically turning around he put his hands in his pockets and slowly walked away. Luscious wept and wailed into my grandmother's chest. My aunt and mother cursed and wiped tears from their cheeks. Eric and Donnel were silent. I kept the phone pressed to my ear and listening to the fading drumbeat of Nice's footsteps on the concrete, I tried to shout his name, but instead I swallowed it, felt it lodge in the back of my throat like a sticky round stone until Nice was out of sight and his sound was gone and his name dropped into my gut, echoing, emanating until it became marrow.

III

Saturday morning. Crackheads were starving for breakfast outside. My cousins and I were watching cartoons in our apartment. No adults were home. Nice was to spend the next seven to ten years of his life in prison. My grandma had found work on the weekends in a Laundromat sweeping up, wiping spilled detergent, and using a butter knife to free jammed quarters from coin slots. My Aunt Rhonda had gone out the night before in a black miniskirt and with red lipstick thick on her lips and she had not made it back, which meant she'd return sometime in the afternoon with her high heels in her hands and her eyes puffed and muddy. She was still dating Beany. But she was still searching, still desperate for that holy, transporting, nonexistent type of love, so she was dating other men too. I had not seen my mother the previous day, so I didn't know where she was. She had picked up a habit of disappearing, of saying she would be right back and not following through. I worried but said nothing. Since my uncle had been locked up, I had assumed a steely disposition. I imagined not that he was dead, but that I was tougher than I was; fearless, untouchable. I was ten years old and already I wore the mask of a man in a mug shot. Donnel and Eric sat on the couch and I sat on the folding metal chair next to it. Donnel was fourteen and growing into the face that was going to make him a good-looking man. Eric was twelve and his two front teeth were too big for his mouth. On the couch next to him was one of the tattered spiral-bound notebooks he drew in and cherished and carried around until he either filled the pages or lost and replaced it with a new one he bought at the ninety-nine-cents store. He was eating Cocoa Krispies and his spoon clacked against the plastic bowl. Then when he finished eating all of the cereal, he raised the bowl to his face and slurped the milk, and because Donnel hated when his cartoons were interrupted, I knew trouble was coming.

"Go ahead and keep make'n noise," he warned, without taking his eyes from the TV.

Eric lowered the bowl from his face and looked at it. Then he looked at me. He was helpless and worried. His eyes hung from his face and his cheeks deflated and drooped like tired sacks. Eric knew that Donnel would warn him once, then swing. Donnel didn't have patience or sympathy for Eric's deficiencies. Eric was his little brother and Donnel wanted him to act right, so Eric's doom was inevitable because he didn't have the coordination to eat quietly or the willpower to stop eating, and, even if he did, what Eric did with food could never be defined as eating. Eric consumed. Everything flew, crashed, and splattered into his mouth. And there was something very wrong with his digestive system, the whole thing, from the way he crammed food into his mouth and the gnashing his teeth did to how, minutes after eating, he went to the bathroom and, moaning and groaning, let it all out.

Eric looked at the TV. Then he glanced down at the bowl again. The remaining milk taunted him. His face grew taut. His lips stretched. He was fighting to hold on, to not eat. Silently he begged himself. He pleaded. But he couldn't put the bowl down. He didn't have the fortitude to stop himself. He raised the bowl to his face, then tilted it to his lips. I didn't have time to pray for him or the chance to get out of the way. He slurped once. Then Donnel's hand slammed against the bottom of the bowl. Milk splattered everywhere, on the wall and couch, on Eric's shirt and face, on his notebook, on my right arm and leg.

"What I say?" Donnel exploded. "Now clean that shit up."

Eric's lips quivered. The bowl was upside down on the floor and milk dripped from his face. He bit his bottom lip. He gnawed on it. He slowly shook his head. Then he stopped and suddenly turned and looked at me. He had come to a conclusion. Although he was twelve, Eric didn't recognize anything other than his emotions. That is, how he felt was usually the only thing that was important to him. But because Eric could not cry, physiologically could not shed a single tear, how he felt was often too large to put into words, so it made him act out. This is why Eric drew, and why he fought you when he was angry and fought you when he was sad. His eyes narrowed and I knew the conclusion he had come to. It was all my fault. Eric was going to lash out at me. There was nothing I could do but close my eyes and defend myself. He lifted his fist, but then, just as he was about to swing at me, a door slammed and a man yelled outside, his voice echoing through the hallway.

"Come here!" he shouted. "I ain't done! This ain't over!"

It was Beany. Eric, Donnel, and I looked at the door, stared at it as if it were a window we could see through.

"Nigga! Don't walk away!" Beany shouted. "I know you hear me!"

Beany was harmless. He made noise. He puffed his chest out. He made empty threats. I'd seen him squirm and turn green when my Aunt Rhonda popped one of his pimples and showed him the pus on the tip of her finger.

"Nigga," he boomed. "I ain't through!"

Then, as if the world stood still to wish Beany well, there was silence. Then two gunshots, a pause, and a third pop knocked through the hall. The gunman took off down the stairs, and because our apartment was next to the stairwell, we heard him go all the way down, the rumble of his footsteps, interrupted by the silence when he jumped the last few stairs, followed by the boom when he landed on the landing. Rumble, silence, boom. Then the door at the bottom of the stairwell groaned open, slammed closed, and its echo shook the chain latch on our door.

It took a moment to recognize what had happened because at ten I was never exactly sure of everything I heard. There were too many sounds I didn't know, and even some of the ones I thought I knew I misnamed. But as soon as I realized that the sound I'd heard had come from a gun, I understood the silence meant that one of the men in the hall might be dead. Still I looked at Donnel and Eric hoping to find a different conclusion. Eric's face was a floppy brown sail sagged from his hairline, draped over his nose, cheekbones, and jaw. Donnel frowned pensively, his eyes narrowed, his upper lip crooked and bowed so its crest rested just beneath his nostrils. They knew what the sound was too. Gunshots were a sound, an intrinsic element of our lives, like shouting and laughter. There were gunshots on New Year's, the Fourth of July, around Christmas and on Valentine's Day. Sometimes, for weeks at a time, gunshots were nightly occurrences. Most brothers I knew had either fired a gun, aspired to fire a gun, or lied and said they had been struck by a bullet. I'd fired a gun. In fact, I'd fired Beany's gun just the week before. Donnel had found it under our couch, and we went up to the roof and shot at the planes flying over Ever as they arrived and departed from LaGuardia and Kennedy Airport until police sirens filled the air and we ran to hide in our apartment.

Donnel sighed deeply. Then he calmly stood, crossed the room, and put his ear against the door. I wished for a sound, any sound.

"You hear anything?" Eric asked loudly.

Donnel swung around and looked at Eric. "Nigga," he scolded through clenched teeth. "Lower your voice."

Eric sucked a breath of air. "D," he whimpered. "D, you think? I don't hear . . ."

"Nigga!" Donnel snapped. "What I say? Stop being a pussy."

Eric's head fell, his chin to his chest like a puppet whose neck string had been cut, and his face became a gnarled root of pain. Then his eyes opened wide and suddenly he turned and lunged at me. He knocked me to the floor and landed on top of me. He burrowed his head into my chest and threw a punch that connected with my shoulder. Then, from behind, Donnel swatted Eric in the back of the head with such force the blow knocked Eric from me.

"Nigga, what're you, crazy? What're you doing?" Donnel scolded, standing over us.

Eric lay on his back, his knees up to protect himself as he rubbed his head with both hands. "I didn't like his face," he said.

"Well, I don't like yours," said Donnel. "But you don't see me swinging at you."

"You just did!" Eric shouted.

"Nigga, shhh!" Donnel demanded.

He muttered something about Eric under his breath and looked over his shoulder at the door. Then he went to it and pressed his ear against it once more. We listened. Still, there was nothing. No click or clack. No moan. No whisper. Not even the sound of a breeze climbing the stairwell or pushing through the crack under the door. Donnel looked back at Eric and me, then an idea came crashing over his face and his eyes flashed with light.

"Eric," he said. "Go and get some knives from the kitchen."

Eric stared at Donnel. He blinked. He loved knives. He was always messing with them, always sawing and hacking through anything he could get his hands on. It was another way he dealt with his emotions, another way he acted out. Eric cut all the butter sticks in the refrigerator into pats. He hacked the soles from old sneakers. He sawed through soda cans, plastic bottles, and action figures. He was mesmerized by Ginsu infomercials. When he was eleven, he carved an E into his forearm with the blunt tip of a dried ballpoint pen. Quickly, he got up from the floor, ran into the kitchen, and when he came back, both of his hands were full of knives and his face was glowing. He had butter knives, steak knives, a cleaver, the chopping knife we used to break up the frost that coated the walls of the freezer.

Donnel laughed. "Damn," he said. "How many knives you think we need?"

"All of them," Eric said. "Just to be safe."

Donnel took the cleaver and the chopping knife; Eric took two steak knives; and I took a steak knife and two butter knives. Then Eric tossed the rest of the knives on the couch. Some of them landed softly on the cushions. Some fell on the floor.

Donnel was disgusted. "Nigga, go pick those up and put them where they belong. Shit, who the fuck just goes throwing knives like that?"

Eric gathered the knives, disappeared into the kitchen, and a moment later, the utensil drawer squeaked open and the clatter and clang of Eric throwing all of the knives in the drawer at once rang loudly. Then he slammed the drawer closed, opened the drawer, and slammed it closed again.

"Nigga," said Donnel. "Now what are you doing?"

"It won't close," Eric complained.

"Just leave it," Donnel said. "Damn."

Donnel looked at me and it seemed as if we were meeting each other for the first time. Until then, I had not taken account of the soft hair that had begun to darken above his lip. Of course, I'd seen him marvel over it in the bathroom mirror, and I was with him when he bought the black comb at the corner store to comb it, but I hadn't noticed how the moustache transformed his face, how it took what were once boyish expressions of anger and threats of immeasurable pain and suffering and made them factual. Donnel was eight inches taller than me, but he might as well have been a mountain of a man.

He touched the corner of the cleaver against my chest. "Stay," he said.

He slowly tiptoed to the door, paused, and listened. Still, there was silence. Eric came back into the room and Donnel shot his eyes at him and dared him to make a sound. He put the chopping knife in his back pocket and raised the cleaver chest high. He took a deep breath. Then he slowly unlocked all of the door's locks, except the extra chain latch my grandma had recently put on the door because after my uncle was locked up there was something inside of her that always felt unsafe. Donnel took another deep breath, turned the knob, and opened the door. Slowly. A half inch at a time. The smell of a gunshot, of gunpowder and heat mixed with urine and rancid shit wafted into the room.

"Eouww!" Eric cried out, covering his nose and mouth and pointing at me. "A farted!"

"No I didn't," I complained, forgetting Donnel's order of silence.

"Shut up!" Donnel demanded, his eyes aflame. "The both of you! Damn!"

Donnel gathered himself and opened the door an inch more. The stench invaded the room. Donnel shook his head and braved through it. He lifted the neck of his T-shirt over his nose. Then he opened the door as far as the chain latch let him, pressed his face into the six-inch space, and looked into the hall.

"Get the broom," he said, glancing at us over his shoulder.

Eager to please Donnel, Eric ran into the kitchen. A moment later, he returned with the broom. Donnel took it by the brush end, got down on his knees, and aimed the handle into the hallway like a pool cue.

Eric and I looked out into the hallway over his shoulder. It was 9:00 a.m., but the hallway carried the shade of late evening. Objects were silhouettes. Suddenly, I couldn't breathe. I thought I saw a rat. But I was wrong. It was a bare foot. That was all I could see, just a foot. Donnel scraped the broom handle along the floor toward it. Then, when the broom handle came within two feet of the foot, he stopped it and said: "Hey."

There was no answer. Donnel looked back at Eric and me and then inched the broom closer.

"Hey," he said again. "Pssst, nigga, hello?"

Again, there was no answer. Slowly, Donnel drew the broomstick back, then gently slid it forward and poked the foot. Eric and I jumped back like the foot was going to kick us. But it didn't. The foot didn't move.

"He dead?" Eric asked, peeking outside again.

"No shit," Donnel answered.

"Maybe he's breathing," I said, sounding so weak even I didn't believe what I said.

"Nigga ain't breath'n nothing," Donnel huffed.

"How you know?" I asked, always hopeful.

"Cause," Donnel said and left it at that.

He slid the broom back into the room and stood up. Then he closed the door and unhooked the extra chain latch in one sweeping motion. Eric looked at me. Then he looked back at Donnel.

"What you doing?" he asked.

"First," Donnel said, confidently, "we got to ID the body."

"Who?" Eric said.

"Us," Donnel declared. "All three of us are witnesses."

Donnel had a fascination with knowledge, with discovery, with being the first one to know. He took a moment to gather himself. He gripped the doorknob and turned it. Then he stopped, reached around his hip, and took the chopping knife out of his back pocket. He held both knives in his hands and raised them like a boxer with clenched fists.

"You ready?" he asked.

Eric's eyes were huge. He nodded.

Donnel darted his eyes to me. "Ready?" he asked.

I swallowed and gripped my knives as tightly as I could. Donnel turned the doorknob until it clicked, and my legs went weak. Donnel took a deep breath and slowly opened the door. The stench was so strong it bit through my nose and scorched the back of my throat.

"Fuck," Donnel said, putting his face back beneath the neck of his T-shirt.

Dipping his toe into the hall like he was testing the temperature of water, Donnel took a hesitant first step out of the door. Then he took a second step and Eric and I put our faces beneath the necks of our T-shirts and followed him. The first thing I saw was a dark purple pool on the floor. It was blood. And there were little white feathers in it. Some of the feathers sat on top of the blood like boats. Some were half soaked. Others were sunk and saturated. I looked at the foot and saw that it bloomed from a pair of jeans, but I wasn't ready to see the body and my eyes leapt to the wall, splashed with blood that was riddled with feathers and little clumps that looked like raisins.

"Damn," Donnel breathed. "It's Beany."

Beany lay on the floor like he'd fallen from the sky and broke, his head at an odd angle, one arm twisted awkwardly beneath his body, one leg splayed, the other bent. He wore a black down coat, and the sleeves and the front of the coat were blasted open and feathers spilled from the holes. I don't know why he had his winter coat on in the spring on a Saturday morning when he didn't even have shoes or socks on. But it didn't matter. Beany was mutilated. He had been shot twice in the stomach and once in the face and because he'd put his arms up to protect himself the bullet tore through his sleeves, his arms. Half of his face was missing. From the nose down: gone.

"Should we call the police?" Eric asked, so stunned by the sight he sounded calm.

"We ain't calling nobody," Donnel answered, his arms, his hands, the knives hanging limp at his sides.

I looked at Donnel. His nostrils flared. He rolled his lips in and out of his mouth. He was fighting fear, fighting nausea, fighting to be what he thought a man should be, and thinking harder than he'd ever thought before, scouring each and every one of his cells for what to do next.

"D?" I said.

His eyebrows lowered. "We got to pray," he decided. "Then we gonna go back inside and act like nothing."

I was shocked. What was he talking about? Without hesitating, Donnel lifted his eyes to the ceiling.

"Dear God," he said. "This is Beany. Please let him into Heaven so the nigga can rest in peace. Protect him. And protect us, and keep us strong. And next time make sure my mom listens to me. I told her this nigga was no good. You too, Jesus. Thank you. Amen."

He looked at Eric and me.

"Say it," he said.

"Amen," Eric mumbled.

"Amen," I said.

When the police arrived, they needed witnesses. But who heard? Who saw? Not us. The police and people from our hall and from the floors above and below talked in the hall. There was shouting and crying, and there was speculation. Mr. Bradford, the old man from down the hall who always wore a yellow cardigan, said, *This ain't right; I'm too old for this shit.* And Ulysses, the boiler man who could have been a world-class chess champion, said, *Something's got to be done;* and Ms. Brown, always dressed like she had somewhere holy to go, said, *When will these young boys do some good?* Smudge talked through his cleft lip and told the police Beany's parents were away for the weekend. On a church trip, he said, a church trip to Atlantic City. No one knew where Beany's sister Cecily was. Chamique said she might've slept over at her friend Audrey's, but she couldn't be sure because sometimes Cecily woke up early on Saturdays and went to one of the libraries in the city because there were so many libraries and so many books. Nobody knew where my Aunt Rhonda, Beany's girlfriend, the love of his life, was. Questions were raised. Maybe she knew who shot him. Or maybe it was over her. She was always running around with some other brother anyway. Or maybe it was her; maybe she pulled the trigger. Accusations, insinuations, condemnations were hurled like scrap metal and stones against our door. Voices crashed and boomed. Some brothers and sisters tried to defend my aunt, said she wasn't doing anything anyone else didn't do. She wasn't wrong. She wasn't immoral. The police knocked on our door, announced themselves, asked if anyone was home. Eric and I stood in the middle of the room, a few steps behind Donnel, and we all faced the door. Donnel glanced at us over his shoulder and put his finger to his lips, making sure we knew to be silent. Then he turned back around and faced the door, one fist balled at his side, the other clenching the chopping knife.

Outside, it sounded as if the police would burst into our apartment at any moment. And if they did, they'd have to face Donnel, fight him until either he or every last person outside was dead, and that's what Donnel seemed to be waiting for; for all of them, for the police and everyone else, and everything they said about his mother, to be brave enough to come into our apartment.

Suddenly, the hallway went silent. Had my Aunt Rhonda returned? No. It was Beany's sister, Cecily. And when she came upon the police tape and the fact that it was Beany, her brother, who was dead, she cursed and wailed and the hallway echoed her and everyone else, swaying apologies and grief.

"My brother," she screamed. "No! Not Beany! No, it can't be! Why God? No. Not my brother!"

BAR 4
Soldier

I

For weeks, my Aunt Rhonda was more exhausted, broken, and disheveled than a sober sister had ever been. Her face, her lips and eyes, her breasts, her shoulders, each follicle, kink, and strand of her hair, every part of her, even the parts no one had ever seen, the parts doctors have yet to discover, were dry and wilted. She didn't eat or bathe. When she had her period she stained her jeans and the couch and left her bloody panties on the bathroom floor for all to see. She was gutted, splayed. She was battered, beaten, but without bruises or abrasions. She wept. She moaned and shivered when she slept. Beany had told her that he loved her, that he always would, that he wanted her to have his child, that he wanted for them to get married. But she hadn't been able to bring herself to believe him, hadn't been able to accept that she was lovable for such an infinite amount of time. The most she had been able to muster was the hope to be loved; like a red coal-filled fire, her belly was swollen with the heat of this desire. Why did she need; why did she keep a stable of men, and move from man to man; why couldn't she just be with one? She mumbled to herself. Sometimes she shouted, asking no one in particular. Sometimes she looked at one of us and demanded answers. Why not Beany? What wasn't he? Why was she always seeking greater love? Now she doubted if she'd ever be properly loved again. The other brothers? They didn't love her. They couldn't. It was Beany, only Beany she loved. But only with his death did she realize it.

Once, when the phone rang and it was for her, she asked: "Is it him?"

"Who?" I said, holding my hand over the receiver.

"Him," she said, rising from the couch, heavy and limp.

"Who?" I said again, innocent but painfully ignorant.

Suddenly, my Aunt Rhonda realized how ridiculous both her hope and her assumption were and she swallowed. Her features drooped, made her face look like a saturated paper bag. But she couldn't stop herself from continuing, from uttering his name. "Beany," she said. "Beany."

"Aunt Rhonda," I said, softly offering her the nothing I knew to say, just naming what I saw.

She wrapped herself in her own arms and heaved. "Oh God," she moaned. "Oh my God, no!"

The pride my Aunt Rhonda had once carried herself with, how she walked with her chest out, always one foot in front of the other, her hips rocking like a chair, was stripped from her, her sexiness snuffed. She never wore more than house slippers on her feet. She could not bring herself to go outside, to face Ever, the gossip, the rumors, the venomous denunciations, or those who had the independent courage to console her. She was hated. When Beany's sister, wholesome, pious Cecily, walked down the hall she shouted *Bitch! Slut!* She pounded her fists on our door and called my aunt a whore. She hoped she'd burn in hell. Sometimes Cecily's friends joined her, creating a chorus of hatred in the hall. But when my grandma, Donnel, or my mother made a move to chase it away, to throw open the door and threaten the lives of all those outside, my Aunt Rhonda would say *No! Stop!* in such a guttural tone their momentum would cease and they would deflate in the middle of the room, swamped by my aunt's depression. My aunt wanted nothing for herself, not a drip of water, a gasp of air.

My grandma did everything in her power to free my Aunt Rhonda from misery. She demanded it of her. She championed. She begged. We all did. Every time Donnel came home and left he told my Aunt Rhonda he loved her, pushed his face through the stench that hovered around her, hugged her although her arms hung limp, kissed her forehead, and promised everything would be OK while she rambled on and on about him being careful, that they were out there, looking, waiting, ready to kill him too.

Like my grandma and Donnel, my mother, who knew what it meant to suffer the loss of love and hate herself in its absence, did and said everything she could imagine to say and do in order to shake my aunt from her state of perpetual self-hatred. Sometimes they kept me awake and I listened to their voices slip beneath the bedroom door or seep through the walls as I lay head to foot in the bed beside Donnel.

"He said we were gonna go to Mexico," my Aunt Rhonda might say. "That we were gonna live in a mansion on the beach."

"Well, shit," my mother would answer. "You don't need a man to do that. A sister like you can get that all by herself."

"How?" my Aunt Rhonda might respond.

"God damn it, how am I supposed to know!" my mother would plead. "Love yourself! Believe that you're worth it!"

Sometimes, Donnel lay awake beside me, listening to his mother and mine, dwelling in how their roles had reversed, and when he thought I was sleeping, he would pray for his mother and wish that he'd wake with the power to end her pain.

"Just give me the chance. I swear," he'd say. "Just something. Anything."

My mother pushed my Aunt Rhonda to get out of the apartment, to look fly. She took out old pictures of my aunt, smiling, dressed to the nines. At first she led by voice. She told my aunt all of the things she was missing, all of the things she could be doing if she got herself together. She told her about parties, DJs at clubs. She told her about who asked for her, how many fine men said: *Where is Rhonda; where she been; what she up to?* The world was waiting for her, said my mother. How much longer was she going to make it wait? She couldn't stay shut in forever. Eventually, my mother took her own advice. So in addition to her cajoling, she led by example. First, she went out with Cherrie on the weekends. They went to this party or that dance. Then she added going out to some bar or club without Cherrie a couple of days during the week. She wore increasingly sexier, more revealing clothes. First, a few of her shirts were tight; then they all were; then each shirt she wore was stretched to translucency and beneath it, the bra she wore was always red. Soon a plethora of brothers called for my mother and she spent hours on the phone, giggling, talking coy. There was Rodney with a deep, rumbling voice; Derrick who always said please when he asked to speak to my mother; and Tyrone who, despite never meeting me, always said *What's up my little nigga?* There was Marcus who sounded as if he just woke up, Samuel who slurred his R's and S's, Leviticus who enunciated each syllable, and Farooq who was quick to tell me that his name meant *he who distinguishes falsehood from truth*. Sometimes my mother came home with a rose. Sometimes she came home with new shoes. She got gold earrings. She got a gold necklace. She got pedicures and manicures every week. Sometimes she would only be home long enough to sleep and shower. Sometimes she'd pack a backpack with clothes and cosmetics and not come home for two or three days. Sometimes, it seemed as if I didn't exist. She'd walk past me as I watched TV with my Aunt Rhonda, or walk in and out of the kitchen as I ate; once, twice, three, or four times before she'd finally meet my eyes, say my name, tell me what I didn't do, what I needed to do, or something.

My mother's sudden determination to live and celebrate life, her hedonism, drove my grandma crazy. She tried to remind my mother that she was a mother, that she couldn't be coming and going and leaving me for her to take care of. I wasn't her responsibility. She'd raised three of her own children. She was my grandmother, not my mother. And she needed help with my Aunt Rhonda and help with Donnel and Eric. And she needed my mother to contribute some money to the upkeep of our apartment.

"Roosevelt's gone," my grandma would say. "And Rhonda ain't doing good. And you still thinking like you thirteen! You still thinking about only yourself!"

My mother shouted back. She said I could take care of myself, that I was damn near a man, and that sooner rather than later I had to depend on myself. She'd raised me as best she could, the only way she knew how, the same way she'd been raised. It was a hard world. There was no room for soft men. And she'd give my grandma money when she had it. But she didn't have it. In fact, she barely had enough money to get things she needed.

"Like what?" shouted my grandma.

"Like," said my mother. "Like things."

Back and forth they'd argue, their voices blowing and battling as if everyone in Ever was never there; as if the walls were not thin; as if no one was ever in earshot.

"Slow down!" my grandma ordered her. "You loose!"

"Momma, life is short!" my mother shouted. "This is my life! I'm a woman! Don't tell me what to do! I been going slow for too long!"

I was old enough. I was too young. I could take care of myself. I needed to be reminded, pushed. He couldn't. He could. He did. He didn't. He knew. He knew no such thing. My mother gave me money, ten dollars here, five dollars there. She tried to buy my love. She had Farooq pay for a pair of Jordans for me and this brother named Clayton paid for my new clothes. Sometimes my mother would come home late at night, wake me after I fell asleep on the couch waiting for her to come home, and cuddling with me, having me rest my head in her lap, stroking the side of my face, smelling of cigarettes or booze or cologne, she'd whisper that she loved me, that she'd go to war for me and only me, that nothing and no man meant more than me. I, Abraham, was her everything. I was her prince, her king, her little soldier. She swore to it.

She confused me. Who was she? Who was this woman who so loved me while I slept yet was so uninterested in me when I was awake? And which Abraham was I, the one my mother saw or the one my grandma knew; the one who needed to be scolded and coddled or the one who was deemed a man, albeit prematurely and without warrant? What had my mother done to the way we loved? And what had happened to my Aunt Rhonda? Was it irreversible? Would she be who she had become for the remainder of her life? And Donnel and Eric, who suffered the same affliction as me, who oscillated between despising my mother and my Aunt Rhonda and being desperate for them, what would they do? I waited. I hoped for their leadership. I followed them outside. I searched for answers. I looked for them on the sidewalk and the street corner. I looked for them in the park. I looked everywhere young brothers gathered for the solace and sanctuary we needed to fortify one another, to be one another's ancestry.

II

Roosevelt never answered any of the letters my grandma dictated to me because she was embarrassed about how poorly she wrote and spelled. My mother, in addition to all of her social activity, got a job working part-time in McDonald's, stocking the condiment station and napkin dispensers, microwaving fish fillet sandwiches, and putting the cheese on cheeseburgers, so she only stayed home long enough to unload soiled clothes and empty the contents of one pocketbook into another. My Aunt Rhonda slowly but steadily rose from the depths of her self-hatred and depression, surpassed her original capricious promiscuity, and came and went as she pleased. And Donnel, Eric, and I were preoccupied with missing our mothers, and the throes of our daily lives: what happened in school, what happened at the park or on the street, what bounced and banged in our hearts and heads and the hearts and heads of those who were of similar age and circumstances in Ever Park.

So my grandma was alone. Of course, she had friends. But life had taught her to keep people at arm's length, so those whom she would have called friends were really no more than casual acquaintances, people she talked to but never really opened up with. My grandma did not complain about any loneliness or ask for company. She did not request or beg for attention. She never so much as whimpered or asked for a hug and kiss. Instead, my grandma did her best to keep the apartment immaculate, hounded us to do the same, and maintained an indestructible disposition that would have been a prison if there were men inside of her. But then she finally found a full-time job as a porter in a shiny Manhattan building she called the real white castle and something inside of her bent. My grandma worked twelve-hour shifts. She worked overtime on the weekends. She returned home with barely enough energy and desire to drag her feet and keep her eyes open. And slowly, a little more each day, some perverse force, some invisible and unnatural disaster infected her, and the laughter I had always known her to fill our home with became infrequent. Then it stopped altogether.

Our apartment became a mess. Empty soda cans, paper cups, glasses, and plastic bags filled with wrappers and Styrofoam containers were left beside the couch. Sneakers and socks were left in random spots, and stains dappled the grey carpet as if sprung from some pulsing well below. In the kitchen, pans with crisps of food floating in used oil and pots with murky spaghetti water sat on the stove, spilled drinks and food made tacky spots on the linoleum floor, and birdseed was strewn around the edge of the lovebirds' cage.

Then late one evening I came home from playing basketball at the park with my ball on my hip and squiggling lines of dried sweat dancing down my cheeks. I was eleven and my childhood love of basketball as a game had grown into my great escape. While playing at the park, there was nothing else, no Ever, no wondering about the whereabouts of my mother or Donnel, no having to defend myself, no familial or emotional or communal pain, just running, jumping, leaping. I could channel everything into it. Playing basketball steeled me. It blinded me and made me deaf to truth.

All of the lights in the apartment were off. It was no surprise to me. Eric and Donnel could be with friends. My mother could be out. My aunt too. My grandma could have been working overtime or she could have come home early from work and gone to sleep. I did not turn on the living room light because I didn't want to see the mess around me. I walked slowly, never lifting my feet more than an inch in case a plate or bowl or a shoe might be waiting to trip me. I made it to the kitchen's threshold safely. I was hungry. The light switch was to my immediate left. I reached up and flicked the switch. As they did each time the light was turned on in the kitchen, the lovebirds chirped and tweeted.

But I didn't hear them. I didn't hear them because as soon as the kitchen lit up I gasped. It was a petrifying sight. My grandma stood on a kitchen chair in her underwear and a white T-shirt that only reached the uppermost part of her thighs. She held a near empty bottle of Boone's Farm wine in one hand and specks of blood were spattered on her feet and shins. On the floor was one of the red bricks Donnel ran with and a dead rat, smashed and leaking blood. My grandma had killed the rat, followed the sound of its pattering feet and squeaking as it walked about the kitchen then hurled the brick where she was sure the rat was. The thud she described as the sound of a dropped carton of milk hitting the floor. The rat's squeal she described as a nail on a chalkboard. The rat had then stumbled about, wheezing and moaning like an old man with emphysema as it dragged its busted body on the floor until it could drag its death no more. Then the rat breathed a few last heavy breaths and died. But until I turned on the light, my grandma didn't know where the rat had stopped, where it had crumpled and stiffened. And so she remained on the chair, drinking the wine she originally opened to fortify her against the rat and then continued to drink because she could not stand the thought that she had killed something so brutally, and because she was afraid if she climbed off the chair she'd step on the rat's bloody body.

"Abraham," she said, her voice full of sad breath.

Her eyes were only half opened, and she was too exhausted and drunk to be surprised to see me. She rubbed her face in a sloppy, forceful fashion, burrowing the heel of her hand into each eye then dragging her hand beneath her nose, over her lips and chin, and down her neck. She dropped her eyes to the floor and looked at the bloody tracks the rat had made and where its life ended, halfway between us in a pool of blood. Then she raised her bottle of wine level with her eyes, swirled its contents to see how much she had left, and swigged it down in one gulp. She studied the empty bottle for a moment. Then she lifted her eyes up the length of my body, ascending my legs and torso until she met my eyes. Although we were ten feet apart, I felt her weight lean on me. Her eyes drooped and seemed sure to burst. Her lips trembled. She slapped her free hand over them and this caused her eyes to close, which caused tears to flood her face. Suddenly, she was aware of our reality.

"Abraham," she said.

Then she stopped everything: speaking, breathing, and crying. She wiped her face with her hand again. Then she stood as tall as she could.

"Come," she said raising her chin, focusing, forcing her eyes wide and pressing a wobbled but determined look on me. "Help me get this mess cleaned up. Hurry. Before anyone else has got to see it."

III

A sodden soiled flag.

"Abraham! Abraham! Mister Man! Don't get on that bus!"

It was my mother. It was the winter and it was raining and it was early in the morning so the sky was a hue between black and blue with an undertone of pallid light. She was outside in her powder blue house slippers, an oversized red T-shirt, and a pair of dirty white leggings. I was waiting for the city bus to go to school with two dozen young brothers and sisters from Ever. My mother waved her hands over her head and ran through the parking lot. She was braless and her breasts bounced. She lifted her knees too high for the pace she was going. I was embarrassed, ashamed. What was she doing? What did she want? I glanced down the street. The bus was coming.

"Abraham!" she hollered. "Abraham! Wait!"

She came to the edge of the sidewalk across the street and stopped short, her momentum causing her to rise up on her toes as if everything but her feet wanted to leap into the street, the oncoming traffic. Between the fingers of her right hand was a cigarette. She jammed it between her lips, yanked it out, and jammed it in again. She looked left and right, threw the cigarette down, and wrapped her arms around her chest. The bus was almost there. She glared at me. She shivered. A car passed. She looked right again, saw the bus, and looked back at me with angry, begging eyes. She was frantic, but her franctiness was stuck beneath her skin, as if a great desperation was burning and pounding to get out of her body.

The bus pulled up, its steel body a wall between my mother and me. Brothers and sisters from Ever climbed onto the bus. One by one, they glanced back at me. I wondered what I should do. I wanted to get on the bus. I wanted to leave her, disappear from sight. It was January and I was in a foul mood. Things I loved, gifts I'd been given for Christmas and my birthdays were suddenly missing, lost, gone forever no matter how I scoured our apartment, no matter how many times I told on Donnel and Eric, no matter how I claimed they had taken my most precious possessions and ordered that they give them back. Although Donnel and Eric swore they didn't have them, although they even helped me look for my missing things, I called them liars and fought them. I criticized the way they looked, how they smelled, and I predicted what they were going to be, dumb niggas, criminals, fat, anything and everything that might damage them. I called them retarded, queer, and white. Someone stole my stuff. Like my Discman my grandma bought for me. And like my gold chain with my name on it that had gone missing the previous Friday, incredibly vanishing from my neck sometime between when I feel asleep on the couch and when I stood in the shower the next morning.

"Abraham!" my mother screamed. "Abraham!"

My friends watched me out of the bus windows. They waved and shook their heads and pointed at me. They laughed. They were sure

I'd done something wrong. The bus driver, a dark-skinned heavyset brother who wore leather driving gloves, leaned over his steering wheel and looked out of the door at me.

"Hey," he said. "You getting on or what?"

There was a jagged rock lodged in my throat, balanced on a precarious ledge. I closed my eyes, squeezed them tight, saw red, and then I swallowed, opened my eyes, and said, "Go. I'll get the next one," because if I didn't I would have climbed on the bus and looked at my mother out of the window and the rock in my throat would have plummeted, ripped a wound all the way to the soles of my feet instead of stopping in my stomach.

So the bus pulled away and it was just she and I, my mother and me. Only the width of the street separated us. She stepped off the sidewalk. A car was coming. It jammed on its brakes and honked and the driver angrily threw up his hands. My mother paid him no mind. I was sure she was going to get hit, if not by one car then by another. But my mother walked without fear. She crossed the street as if no cars were coming, her eyes fixed on me, like a ghost, like she was indestructible and made of gas. She wasn't working anymore. She didn't quit her job at McDonald's. She didn't get fired. She just stopped going, gave up waking herself. And when she did wake herself, she might disappear for days or sit on the couch, staring at the television, an emotional, combustible wreck who'd come after me with anything she could grab, shoes, plates, utensils, Donnel's bricks, Nice's trophies when I crossed her, when I asked her a question like where had she been or if she'd seen something, whatever thing of mine that had recently disappeared. But there was more, something else. My mother had lost weight and she did crazy things, like coming outside as she was, not caring what she looked like to the world, dressed as if it were an early Sunday summer morning and the only people outside were crackheads, men and women who worked early Sunday morning shifts, and those who needed one item, that milk, those eggs, that roll of toilet paper so they hastily made their way to the corner store dressed in what they'd slept in, as thrown together and disheveled as she was.

"Abraham," my mother said, stopping just short of me, standing on the street, the cold billows of breath tumbling from her mouth. "Where's that money Momma gave you?"

"What money?" I asked.

"Don't play with me," she scolded. "The money Momma gave you for lunch."

"The dollar?" I asked.

She screwed her eyes. "Is that all it was?"

"That's all it ever is."

She thrust her hand into the air between us and left it there, lying flat, collecting rain. "Give it to me."

"But it's for me to get something to eat."

"I don't care what it's for. I need it. Now give it here."

One dollar, that's all she wanted; all she was desperate for. I stared at her hand for a moment and then I lifted my eyes, put them even with hers. Her eyes were brown but her pupils were so large I could see my reflection in each black disc. I didn't have an umbrella. My coat was soaked. Water dripped down my face.

"Abraham," my mother screamed. "Stop looking at me like that! Give me that dollar!"

I hadn't been looking at her. That is, I was looking at a woman who used to be her, a woman who was so absent all that was left was the rain soaking a shirt and making it cling and stick to the sodden sacks that were her breasts. Her nipples were hard. She didn't even have the wherewithal to hide them, to fold her arms across her chest, to know she was cold. I was dumbed, numbed. I jammed my wet hand into my wet jeans and pulled out the dollar bill.

She snatched it from my fingers. "What about change?" she asked. "You got change from yesterday or the day before?"

Who was she? Who was this woman glaring at me? I stared at her, searched her face for the slightest intimation. Her lips were chapped. Her eyebrows were unkempt, misshapen. When was the last time she had plucked them? I never knew she had sprigs of hair between her eyes. And her fingers? Her nails were gnawed to nubs and her cuticles were dry. Some were even bloody. Mom? Mother? Ma? Ms. Singleton? Sister of Roosevelt and Rhonda? Aunt of Donnel and Eric? Daughter of Gloria? Hey? You? Angela? Jelly? Mother of Abraham? Lady from apartment 4C?

A surging hatred pulsed in her face, made the black bags beneath her eyes sink deeper, darker. Her nostrils flared. Suddenly she coughed, hacking three times with such force that her torso twisted and her chin slammed against her chest. I thought she was going to fall down. I was sure she would buckle and crumble. And then she stopped. She cleared her throat with a rumbling gargle and spit a wad of dark green phlegm on the wet black street. Then she lifted her eyes to me. What did she see? Who was I to her? She looked hungry, starved.

She rushed at me, grabbed me, and slammed her hands in my coat pockets. She wrenched out lint and threw it over her shoulder. She dug with her fingers and found a pen cap, a paperclip, a candy wrapper and threw them down on the wet street. She smashed her hands in the front pockets of my jeans, rooted around and yanked them out. Then she stepped back and smiled a smile that was sick because she was my mother and I was her son and her smile was selfish and insincere.

"I knew you was lying," she said. She laughed. She held a quarter and two pennies up for me to see. "What's this? Huh? Abraham? What's this? Nothing?"

My mother clenched her fist around the change and swung around. Cars were coming, passing left and right. She hesitated. She started, then stopped, then she walked like walking was something new to her, crossing the street in a spastic, teetering rush, oncoming cars slowing, stopping. She held her hand up, thanking them. She wobbled across the yellow lines. A car passed. She zigged, then zagged, then walked straight to the other sidewalk, and stepped up onto it. I could not believe what had happened. Then she stopped, turned around.

"Abraham," she shouted. "Get your ass to school! Go ahead. Get! You hear me? And do your work. I don't want to hear nothing from none of your teachers."

IV

The middle of May, not yet the beginning of summer, and already it was as hot as the very pit of hell, the type of hot that makes the street steam, the type of day one can't get out from under. In fact, it was so hot not even Lindbergh was moving. He sat beneath the lean-to he built by fastening cardboard and an old bedsheet to the fence at the baseline of the basketball court. He was shirtless and without shoes and socks on his feet, which were so dry his toes looked like crumbled concrete. He drank a sixteen-ounce can of Budweiser and ate a battered, almost rotten orange, peeling its skin with his dirty fingers and mumbling something to himself each time he spat a seed onto the court. I had on jeans because Eric took my shorts before I woke up. All day long, I played basketball with friends. We sprinted and leapt and wrestled for rebounds with our shirts off and only took breaks to laugh, argue a foul call, or speculate about Lindbergh. Who was that crazy old nigga talking to? What made him suddenly burst with laughter then cease laughing even more suddenly? What did he find so funny? Who cared?

We were indefatigable, the type of burgeoning young men who weren't fazed by heatstroke, dehydration, the violence and sufferings in Ever Park or the hallucinations each ailment caused. There was Tony Carter, "Kitchen" is what we called him, with a stocky build and a premature moustache and a lisp that made every word he said begin and end with an *s*. And bigheaded, grey-eyed, perpetually bubble gum chewing Yusef Lincoln, who never believed anything anyone ever said and shouted all declarations and hypotheses down with wild, rambling decrees that bored, exhausted, or confused you into agreeing with him. There was Jefferson Waters and his identical twin brother Cleveland, who, despite having witnessed the murder of their mother and grandmother, laughed as if they were mountains with lungs and throats of thunder. Precious Hayes was six inches taller than everyone our age and as gentle as a dove, and Ishmael Arthur, aka Titty, was forty pounds overweight, twenty pounds of which was equally divided between his breasts. Andre Grant loved to dance and would just break out dancing in the middle of a game. Leroy Madison needed glasses so bad he squinted to read his watch, and Xamir Clinton, a half-Dominican brother with skin that glowed like patent leather, was the Don Juan of brothers our age, a go-getter lover who made out with any girl, anytime, anyplace, and then made out with her sisters, her cousins, and her best friends. And there were others. And then there was me, the skinniest of us all, the quiet one with the long eyelashes and the gap between his front teeth; the one who did the homework not because I wanted to but so everyone could copy it; the one who devised master plans so we could all cheat and pass our tests, like the time I wrote the answers on a Post-It and stuck it to my back so Titty, who sat directly behind me, could get a hundred on a history exam.

Halfway through our last game, just before the older teenagers and fully matured men gathered on the sidelines and kicked us off the court so they could play, a butterfly fluttered over the court. We acted like it was an attack. Jefferson was dribbling the ball and he stopped and ducked and swatted and threw the ball at the butterfly, shouting: *Get it! Kill it! Get it!* Cleveland ran and leapt and tried to snatch the butterfly out of the sky. Precious pointed at it and announced: *We studied that shit in school! Watch out! It's a bat! Shit will eat a nigga alive!*

"It is not," Yusef called out, waving his hands above his head. "It's a butterfly! Let it be! I seen them on TV!"

Leroy squinted. "I don't see it. Where?" he said. "Where?"

I stood in the middle of the court with Xamir and Titty because Titty only ran for basketball and food, Xamir was too pretty to chase and shout about a beautiful thing, and I was more a watcher, a spectator of life, than an active participant. I absorbed my surroundings. I soaked.

The butterfly was black and orange and fazed by nothing, by no shout, no swat, and no great attempt to tear it from its flight. It flew like a plastic bag in the wind, sort of tumbling, sort of circling, sort of progressing indifferently on its way. It wandered toward Lindbergh. It stumbled down an invisible staircase. Lindbergh looked up from his orange. His battered leather-bag face became shiny and youthful. The butterfly rose and landed on the rim near where Lindbergh sat. We tiptoed across the court and stood beneath it, awed as it slowly opened and closed its wings. Lindbergh stood up, stepped out from beneath his lean-to, and joined us in watching the butterfly. He ate his orange, tearing sections from the whole, jamming them in his mouth, gumming them to pulp, and spitting the seeds out. He didn't take his eyes off of the butterfly. He tilted his head to the side as if he were holding one ear to whispered instructions.

"Fuck," whispered Jefferson, his face dappled with acne and wet with sweat.

"Damn," added Cleveland.

"It's tired," said Titty.

"It's not tired," Yusef whispered. He took the standard deep breath that preceded all of his infamous lectures. Then he continued. "Butterflies ain't never tired. They always flying. That's it. That's what they do. Like how fish is always swimming and trees is always growing. Things in nature ain't never tired. They always doing what they do."

"How you know?" said Xamir, his mother's Spanish accent always coming out when he asked a question.

"Cause that's how nature is," said Yusef. "It goes. Like your heart. Living don't stop."

"Abraham," said Leroy, squinting harder than he'd ever squinted before and standing on his tiptoes as if the few inches he rose actually gave him the chance to see. "What you think?"

Because I helped them cheat on tests, and my friends knew I wrote my grandma's letters to Roosevelt, and because Yusef had me write love letters to Beany's sister Cecily and Xamir relied on me for what to say when breaking up or wooing a new girl, I was considered the genius of our crew. Of course, I didn't believe in my intelligence. The ease with which I retained information and presented it was no more or less defining a characteristic than my outie belly button. I looked at the butterfly. I understood it was what Leroy was asking me about. But I could not help thinking about Lindbergh. I wondered what he thought, wished to say, or might mumble to himself about the butterfly later. In the years since he had come back to Ever, in the years since I first understood who and what he was, Lindbergh had descended further into degradation and madness. He was so thin his body appeared to be haphazardly pounded out of rusty tin. No rhyme or reason remained in his mind. And no longer were only his hands and feet calloused; his elbows were calloused and hard too. His cheeks were sunken. His ears were full of coarse hair. He no longer wore fatigues or had the mental stability to work for anyone else but himself. So he collected cans. Occasionally he built a helicopter here and there. But the helicopters he built were more desperate than they were previously, more ramshackle so not just without the chance, but also without a hope of flying. Lindbergh wore stained jeans many sizes too big for him that he cinched tight with a woman's lavender belt he must have found in some bag or pile of trash. The jeans hung low, revealing the crack of his ass. He pulled them up and cinched the belt tighter as if the act enhanced his hygiene and appearance. He watched the butterfly with all of his might and faculties. What did he see? What did I think? I thought many things, all of them a swirl in my head, each thought a wing, a fluttering body. I had never seen a butterfly before. I had never heard someone else say they saw a butterfly in Ever. I wanted to touch it, hold it. What did it smell like? What did it feel like to be so, to fly so free?

But before I spoke, the butterfly rose from the rim and flew away. We shielded our eyes from the sun and watched it become a black speck in the sky. Then Lindbergh reached his hand up, waved, and shrieked like one of the seagulls that picked through the Dumpsters behind Ever.

"Cawww! Caww!" he called out. He waved more vigorously. "Caww! Caww!"

First, they were stunned. Then my friends burst with laughter.

"Nigga's crazy!" howled Titty, holding his stomach. "I'm gonna piss. I swear this nigga is gonna make me shit myself!"

"Oh my god!" Kitchen exploded, twisting and turning with laughter and then grabbing on to both Cleveland and Jefferson so he wouldn't fall down. "Oh my god! Nigga thinks he can communicate with it!"

As if he were deaf, Lindbergh calmly returned to sitting beneath his lean-to.

"That's a butterfly!" Yusef shouted at him. "They don't speak bird!"

Truth be told I broke up with laughter too. But it wasn't just Lindbergh that made me laugh or the fact that the deep, wholehearted laughter of my friends was inescapably contagious. It was the whole scene and scenario. It was the previous impossibility of it. I would have never guessed. I would have never supposed. Not even in my wildest fantasy. What a relief, a butterfly had come and gone from Ever.

Of course, because we were still children, because we could be momentarily affected and then disaffected, we played basketball again as if nothing had happened. We banged and bumped. We chased and ran. The sound of the ball, its bounce and bump off the backboard and around the netless rim was our wind. It lifted us. It carried us away.

At four, the heat began to ease and young men began to gather on the sidelines. Then when there were ten, they kicked us off the court so they could play a full-court game. My friends and I hung around and watched them play for a while, marveling at the way Julius, a young dark-skinned man with veins rippling his calves and shins, handled the basketball like it was a yo-yo he threw around and between his legs and all over the place in front of himself; and the way Malik, his dreadlocks bundled in an old stocking and a tattoo of a horse across the span of his fan-shaped back, snatched rebounds from a foot above the rim. Eventually, one by one, and in small groups, my friends went home until I, the one who was never satisfied, the one who craved more as if there might not be another day, was the only one left.

I had nowhere to go and there was no set time I had to be in. My grandma was working the overnight shift and I was of the age and at a time in my life when I thought as long as I came home alive, my mother was satisfied. I sat against the fence on the side of the court and watched the game. I studied every move so later I could practice what I saw. Lindbergh broke down his lean-to, packed it into his shopping cart, and putting on his battered, mismatched shoes, he pushed his cart away. Then he stopped, looked up, and pointing at the sky, he scratched his face and mumbled something that made him look down and shake his head in disbelief. Then he started walking away again, the wheels of his shopping cart rattling and squeaking.

I grew hungry. Rather, my stomach realized I was no longer running and jumping and it began to churn and groan. I had not eaten since the pack of cookies I had for breakfast. I tied my shirt around my head like a turban, a style I was convinced looked good, and I rose to my feet. My left leg, from my hamstring to the tip of my big toe, was asleep, so I held on to the fence and waited for the feeling to come back to it.

"What's wrong with you?" said Alton Johnson, standing on the side of the court with the steadily increasing gathering of men, some of whom had been my uncle's friends.

"My leg's asleep," I said.

"Shit." Alton laughed, looking at the men standing to his right to make sure he had their attention. "That's cause you jerk off too much." He pointed at Elijah Treadwell, who was just about to light a cigarette. "Tell 'em, E., tell this little nigga how jerk'n off makes you addicted to cigarettes. Tell him to leave that shit alone. Just say no. Go get some young pussy or something."

"Jerk'n off don't make you addicted to cigarettes," Elijah countered, blowing the smoke of his first inhale into the air through the hole where a front tooth used to be. "It makes your hands hairy."

"Abraham," Alton said, swinging his eyes back to me. "Come here. Let me see your hands. Come on. Hold 'em out!"

The men laughed and continued to tell jokes about masturbating and me, but I didn't move or speak. Some men came to the court to play. Others came to laugh and tease. And some came because they wanted to disappear, to forget adulthood, to rekindle that carefree camaraderie they had when they were teenagers, to forget their job or lack of one, to avoid the nagging of their mothers if they still lived with their mothers, the ailments of their grandmothers if they still lived with their grandmothers, and the inherent responsibilities related to having a wife, a girlfriend, and kids. As for Alton, he had a daughter my age named Virginia who fucked twenty-year-olds and stripped for me and my friends just two days before for ten dollars. Of course, I knew better than to say anything about it. I'd seen Alton angry and the sight was violent enough to let me know Alton was not the type of brother who would deal well with his daughter's truths. Once, I'd seen him snatch a revolver out of the back of his pants, cock its hammer, and jam its barrel through a man's clenched teeth. I didn't want to die. And I sort of liked my smile. So, without so much as blinking, I stood there and took Alton's jokes, thinking, *Nigga, your daughter has got nice tits, nipples the size of dimes, and a constellation of freckles she must have inherited from you on her ass,* until my leg came around and I started walking.

"You better wrap your shit," Alton called out from behind me. "Use a condom. Shit, the last thing I need to see is another nigga catch AIDS and walk around Ever dying."

I dribbled my basketball along Columbus Avenue. It was crowded. But its crowd wasn't a crowd because it was a crowd I knew the moment I opened my eyes on the world. So everyone on the sidewalk; everyone talking in groups of twos, fews, and half dozens; everyone holding hands of little ones and leaning on walkers; everyone listening to headphones, sipping straws from beers in paper bags, and smoking cigarettes; those kissing; those reading books; the children drawing chalk rainbows between the litter and broken glass on the sidewalk; every man and woman and child was first and foremost my intimate environment. Some were just getting home from work. Children were just getting out of summer camp. Some had the stains of their lunch on their faces and shirts.

Traffic was heavy and I waited for it to break so I could cross the avenue. I looked across the street at where we lived, Ever Park. The two forty-two-floor redbrick buildings, tower A and tower B, were in an area of Queens where there was no commerce or train transportation, and all of the streets were named after dead presidents, New World discoverers, and trees that had never been seen in the neighborhood. Pine

Street, Locust Street, Maple and Dogwood Avenues. Willow Street
intersected with Eisenhower. Elm Street and Oak Street ran parallel
with Lewis and Clark. There were twelve apartments on each floor
of Ever Park, six on one side, six on the other. Five hundred and four
windows faced Columbus Avenue. From some windows, Puerto Rican,
Dominican, Haitian, and Jamaican flags clung limply, tied to the child
guard or the rusted fire escape, the summer heat strangling their wave.
From some windows curtains hung and drooped like sad sails; from a
few, air conditioners teetered. Between the towers was a concrete courtyard with concrete benches and a rusted jungle gym. Surrounding Ever
like a moat, running between the buildings and the avenue, was a large
parking lot with potholes, yellowed weeds bursting from cracks in the
concrete, and a collection of cars, some working, some not; some to be
proud of, some the dilapidated chariots of those who were just happy
to have a ride.

From my left came a group of girls, ranging in age from a five-year-
old to a thirteen-year-old with a woman's figure and the innocent disposition of a puppy. They weaved through the crowd and ran past me
laughing and shouting, "Go!" "Run!" "Hurry!" Behind them, plodding,
red faced and wheezing in failing hot pursuit, came Latricia Bowers,
a heavyset girl too knock-kneed to ever catch even the smallest and
slowest of the girls.

"Hey, Abraham," she gasped, greeting me with a flaccid wave as she
lumbered by.

"Hey," I said, wondering what determination possessed her to keep
running when she was so far behind.

Waiting for the bus and sucking on neon-colored Flavos, Arthur
Winfield, Laurence Matthews, and Delonte Henry, three fourteen-
year-olds who had played basketball with me earlier in the day, took
turns dribbling a ball, its hollow thud lending the evening a heartbeat.

"Good playing today, A," said Arthur, never quite sure of himself yet always speaking with the calm grace his father demanded of him.

"Damn, look how fine Carmela is," interrupted Delonte, taking his headphones from his ears, always weary eyed, always with shoulders held firmly back and straight, and always good for switching the topic of any conversation to the topic of a beautiful woman, be she thirty or ten.

Across the street, Hector Mendez, one my uncle's old friends, washed his white Toyota Camry, turquoise racing stripes on its sides, with a bucket of soapy water and a sponge while his wife, Carmela, cradled their newborn son and talked to Hector in half English and half Spanish, occasionally making him laugh and stop what he was doing to gaze adoringly at her, his wife carrying his son.

"Man, I'm telling you," Delonte continued. "That's exactly how my lady is gonna be. Sexy as shit."

"Nigga," cracked Arthur, "You ain't even kissed a girl."

"So what?" said Delonte. "Plus, I ain't talk'n about kissing."

"Then what you saying?" said Laurence.

"I'm saying love," said Delonte.

"Love?" laughed Arthur. "Nigga, what you know about love?"

"I know it's strong," Delonte said. He was serious. He stared straight ahead, studied Carmela and Hector. He held the basketball and bounced it once.

"That's it?" said Arthur. "That's all you got to say?"

"What else is there?" said Delonte.

Traffic ceased. I crossed the street. Hector saw me coming, tipped his chin, smiled wider than he was already smiling, and pointed the sponge at me.

"You was practicing?" he asked.

"We played all day," I said.

"That's good," Hector said. "Keep you out of trouble. Stop you from being like me when I was your age."

Hector laughed because shortly after my uncle got locked up Hector went upstate for forging a check to pay for his mother's medical bills, and he'd come home grateful for everything, for the fact that he hadn't had his gun on him when the cops picked him up so he only served three years; for his car and his beautiful Carmela; for his son Junior; for every morning, every night, and the chance to rectify his wrongs by offering advice and belief to young men like me. Hector worked as a youth counselor in an Alternatives to Incarceration program, and every evening he bought Carmela flowers on his way home. He plunged the sponge back into the bucket and began to wash the side of his car again. He was wearing a tank top and as his hand circled, the muscles in his arms and shoulders rolled beneath his skin.

"You know something?" he said. "One day you gonna make it all the way to the NBA and give me front row seats. I swear it. A star. I seen it in a dream."

Hector stood tall and pointed his sponge at Carmela and his son. "I'll bring Junior," he said. "And by then your uncle will be home and . . ."

"*Conio!*" Carmela snapped. "What about me? You ain't gonna bring me to the game?"

Hector smiled, his left eye tilting, his right opening slightly wider, both shining a playfulness that indicated Carmela's scolding tickled him. He opened his arms wide and stepped to her. She sucked her teeth. He gently wrapped his arms around her waist. He kissed her neck, then the wisps of hair on the crown of Junior's head.

"*Tranquilo,*" he said, soothing her in an easy, deep rumbling tone warmed and emanating from the base of his neck. "We all go. *Mi familia.* We take a family trip. Maybe we go see Abraham, then go to Paris. How 'bout that? Drink some of that good-ass white people wine. Anything you want. Anything for my wife and son."

Holding towels and wearing shorts and bathing suits, Taquanna

James and Kaya King, both my age and best friends with mothers who were best friends too, walked toward us.

"Abraham," Taquanna whined, stretching my name out and pointing at me just as she and Kaya reached us. "Why you got your shirt tied around your head?"

Taquanna was contentious, rail thin, with a mischievous grin and the disposition of a peeved middle-aged woman. She was always on the edge of something, be it finding out a secret or having sex with someone older than us. She talked with her hands, wagging them above heads and in faces, and when she laughed she clapped and stuck her tongue out and hollered about how she couldn't take it anymore.

"What, you think you got a good body?" she cracked. "Cause you don't."

I glanced at Hector, hoping to convey the sense that he need not worry; I had the situation in control, which was, of course, not the truth. Then I looked back at Taquanna.

"Don't play yourself," I said.

"Play myself?" Taquanna shot back. "Shit, you the nigga with a shirt on his head and the body of a piece of paper."

"Just last week you said I was fine," I countered because it was the truth, or at least that was what Titty told me.

"That was before I saw you with your shirt off." She pointed at my belly button and went in for the kill. "Kaya," she said. "Don't you think Abraham should get that thing cut off? It looks like he got a nose in the middle of his stomach!"

I had so hoped Taquanna wouldn't drag Kaya into the conversation that I'd blocked out the fact that she was there, as beautiful as she was the day before, the day to come, forever. I glanced at her. Then my eyes fell to the concrete. No matter if a girl was fat and ugly or so beautiful she was too beautiful, I was quiet around her. My grandma said it was because I was shy. But the truth is I was quiet around girls for two reasons. First, I believed my uncle—both the man who had been in my life until I was nine and the even more fantastical version of him his absence and time built in my head—was the only way one could and should be a man and such a thing felt impossible for me. Second, I had witnessed the damage other men caused and I didn't want any part of being like the others, not their presence or absence. So it was not that I was shy and quiet around girls. Rather, I was insufficient and apologetic because I wished to be great but had come to a place in my life where I was sure that my mother would have found greatness and joy if it had not been for my father and what he begat. That is, me.

Yet, there was something different, something more about Kaya. So I was more than just quiet around her. I lost all sense of self. I became nothing but breath. Kaya was a diminutive brown girl with copper tones in her cheeks and forehead and with eyes so gentle they made even the loudest, most caustic man whisper. She was soft-spoken. She did well in school. She possessed a strength that was an inherent fact so it did not need to be demonstrated, bragged about, or manifested in defiance. If I'd had the courage I would've done what I imagined dozens of men had already done and asked Kaya to spend the rest of her life with me, right there and then, beginning that evening, or, at least, first thing the following morning. But I couldn't do that. And not just because I was twelve and unable to confront how I felt about her. Because I could. I just couldn't speak it, deal with it face to face. I could write it though. Lord, how I'd spent hours writing about Kaya. In my room, on the floor, on my bed, in the kitchen at the kitchen table, even in the bathroom while I sat on the toilet, writing. Of course, I didn't give her anything I wrote and my loving her didn't make me unique. Everyone either loved Kaya or planned to. So she was flooded with smiles and hellos, and men, ranging in age from eight to forty and riding fleeting surges of courage and testosterone, always stepped to her, telling her not just that she was beautiful but so beautiful she was that thing they had to possess.

"Where you headed?" Kaya asked me, saving me from Taquanna's attack on my belly button as well as the potential heartbreak her own judgment could cause.

"Huh?" I said, so enamored and thankful, so in awe of her, and yet so soothed by the tone of her voice that all I could do was grunt.

"Ahh," laughed Taquanna, pointing at me. "Look at you. Nigga can't even talk to Kaya!"

"He can speak," said Hector, coming to my defense. "Go ahead, Abraham. *Vamos.* Tell the lady what you think."

"Nothing," burst Taquanna. "Nigga's got nothing to say."

I focused my attention on Kaya's question. It was like a rite of passage, a test of my budding manhood. *Where was I headed?* she asked. I took a great big gulp of breath. Suddenly, two bleats from the siren of a police car shattered the air and a cruiser with two white cops in it stopped and flashed their lights. From the loudspeaker they addressed the young man doing chin-ups from the crosswalk sign affixed to the lamppost at the far corner of the street.

"Get down!" said the cop in the passenger seat. He held the microphone to his mouth with his left hand while his right arm hung out of the open window. "You!" he added. "Let go! Fall right now!"

It was Donnel. *Ah dear God,* I thought, *fuck Lord what the hell?* Donnel hung with his arms straight. Then he dropped to the sidewalk, his long, strong arms falling slack, his shoulders, neck, and face following, becoming so limp the only part of him that was not flaccid was the frail, pained expression in his eyes. He was sixteen going on disengaged and destitute. He looked down. Then he set his eyes on the police car and the two cops in it. He could have killed them. That thought, that want, the very antithesis of who he was, he put it on his face for them to see. I wanted to shout and run to him. I wanted to tell him about my day playing basketball, the shots I made, the around-the-back pass I threw. But there was something too great between us: the police. I feared for him, for what the cops might do. How would they remind him not to look like he looked, not to do what he had done, that which was nothing until they had come? The back brake lights shone bright red and the police car came to a stop.

"Abraham," Hector said. "Abraham, quick. Call your cousin."

"D!" I shouted. "Yo, D!"

Donnel's eyes jumped across the street and landed on me. He read my face. He understood what I feared. Then the rancid glare he had fixed for the police softened.

"I'll be home in a minute," he shouted. He pointed over his shoulder at the tiny corner store that rarely had eggs or gallons of milk that were good for more than just a few more days. "I got to get something for grandma."

I knew Donnel was lying and that my grandma was at work, and I was so thankful he had been able to see the fear on my face. But I was also afraid that it wouldn't be enough, that the police had determined that Donnel needed to be taught. So I didn't smile or wave. I thought only about saving Donnel more.

"Can you get me some peanut butter?" I called out to him.

"Chunky, right?" he asked.

The back brake lights lost their red electric glow. Slowly the police car drove away. I watched it until it was just another car in the distance. Then I raised my arm, made my hand into an imaginary gun, and aimed my index finger down Columbus Avenue in the direction the police car went.

"Abraham," scolded Hector. "Don't give them no reason to turn around."

I heard Hector, glanced out of the corner of my eye at Kaya, and considered if I should drop my hand. I looked across the street to see what Donnel wanted. But he wasn't there. I shifted my eyes to the corner store and saw that the door was just closing. I assumed Donnel had just walked in but I couldn't be sure. Every day Donnel was becoming more furtive, so much so that his disappearances approached being indistinguishable from the commonplace of the day. Donnel ran with one of the crews that sold crack not in Ever but on the other side of Queens. I couldn't say he was selling crack at the time. There seemed to be no additional money coming in. And he didn't have any new clothes or sneakers, and my grandma still complained about unpaid bills. But things happened so suddenly to men in Ever, be it how quickly death came, how fast a father vanished, or how swiftly a man was whisked off to prison I couldn't be sure. All I knew was Donnel carried himself with an intensity and distance meant to guard against such suddenness and the timeless nature of his life. A life in which there was no more attending school, no hobbies, no job or potential vocational pursuit, nowhere he had to be that might provide even the glimpse of a worthwhile opportunity. I worried about him. Slowly, I dropped my arm, unfurled my fingers, and let go of my imaginary gun.

V

The front of my building had a heavy steel door beneath a rusted overhang only large enough for two people to stand beneath when it rained. The bricks around the door were written on with markers and pens. And initials, profanity, and hearts were scratched into the building's bricks with keys. The door was propped open with a cinder block that had trash stuffed in its holes. In front of it, laughing, and acting in an intimately affectionate fashion, Luscious and her best friend, Qadisha Smith, discussed virtues and existence.

"There ain't no doubt I'm beautiful," Qadisha said, folding her arms across her chest and cocking her head and body to the right. "Cause God made me."

"God made everyone," said Luscious. "But some of us is easier on the eyes than the rest."

They didn't see me coming. Luscious leaned against the doorframe, her feet a little more than shoulder width apart, one leg in the building, one leg out. She stroked the back of Qadisha's arm with the tips of her fingers. Qadisha slid her hand along Luscious's side and left it to rest on her hip. Luscious was just as beautiful, just as holy and praised as she was the day Nice got locked away. But there was something different about her too, something in the way she shunned men's cooing and advances, something self-assured and aloof, something so utterly uninterested and uninvolved. I had heard rumors that Luscious was a lesbian. And word was it was she and Qadisha. Word was they loved each other, that they shared the same bed, and that Nice was out of the picture, no longer in Luscious's heart. But I didn't understand it. Love like theirs, love I had revered, love everyone in the world hoped for; how could it be diluted, interrupted, aimed at another? How could it be trumped, even equaled? And what would Nice say? What would he do if he knew? Or did he already know? Had he been broken by the news in his cell? Had he raged? Or had he lain down and wept?

Luscious hooked her finger in the top of Qadisha's jeans and pulled her close. Qadisha's hip fit between Luscious's splayed legs. Her shoulder pressed against Luscious's cleavage. Closing her eyes, Luscious kissed Qadisha's forehead, left her lips pressed there until Qadisha smiled and playfully pushed away from her.

"And that's why," Qadisha said, leaning back and putting her hands on her hips. "We one hundred percent almighty! We more than just beautiful. We heaven and holy. OK?"

"Sure," smiled Luscious.

"Just like Jesus," Qadisha concluded. "Cause we all is made of flesh and blood."

Suddenly, Luscious saw me out of the corner of her eye. She stiffened. "Abraham," she said. "How long you been standing there?"

I had no idea, not even an inkling. I looked at Luscious. I thought *traitor, backstabber, bitch*. I dropped my eyes, then lifted them and laid them upon Qadisha. Contrary to her delicate features, Qadisha was a warrior with a sometimes clumsy grace. But she was not reckless or righteous. She raised her two nephews because her sister was addicted to crack. The oldest one was in an academically gifted and talented program. The youngest was three, always said please, and he could already tie his own shoes. I was struck by her face, by how comprehensive and thus powerful Qadisha's surety was.

"Where's your cousin?" she asked.

I shifted my eyes to Luscious and thought about my uncle. I hoped that she'd see him in my face, see in me what she first fell in love with, a skinny boy and his basketball. I bounced my ball twice as if, in addition to the sight of me, the sound of a ball bouncing might jog her memory.

"Which one?" I said.

"Donnel," Qadisha said. Then she smacked the side of my head. "What you looking at Luscious like that for?"

"Like what?" I said.

"Like you thinking something but too scared to say it."

"I ain't thinking nothing," I said.

"So where is he?"

"Who?"

"Donnel," said Qadisha. "Who you think I'm talking about?"

If my eyes were knives then I would have been guilty of stabbing Qadisha in the throat, then standing there, silent, thinking about my uncle as I watched her bleed.

"Ain't you supposed to be smart?" she continued. "I heard you the only nigga in your house that can write. That ain't true?"

It wasn't true. My grandma's penmanship was that of a ten-year-old, but she could write basic sentences. And Eric said he hated writing but, although he couldn't spell well, he could write too. And although my Aunt Rhonda rarely spelled polysyllabic words correctly, my Aunt Rhonda could write also. And I knew my mother could write because she liked to write poems and songs, lyrics never sung nor put to music. And Donnel could write, albeit always crammed with commas and never with a single period. But I didn't say anything to Qadisha. Even if it was just knowledge, I didn't want her to have anything else integral to my family.

Qadisha thought for a moment, then suddenly realized what my looking at Luscious meant, and her face became molten chocolate, sweet, gooey brown with a blaze beneath.

"So what good are you?" she scolded.

I sucked in, pulling my cheeks in hard like they were rags I was wringing dry with my back teeth. I refused to lash out. I would not give her anything. I thought about my uncle. Then I thought about Donnel. What would he say? Why was he always on the move, always going here and there, always on the way out of our apartment? And when he returned, why did he claim he was nowhere only to soon be going again, and later coming from nowhere once more? I saw Donnel only like this, only in passing. Just like I just saw him on the street. He was there. Then he wasn't.

As if thinking that by keeping their hands waist high and at her side I would not see, Luscious reached out and took Qadisha's hand, wrapping her index finger around Qadisha's. She gave it a gentle tug.

"So tell him we looking for him," she said, pressing loving yet imploring eyes on me and clearly hoping that I would go away. "Tell him Luscious needs him when you see him."

I studied Luscious for a moment. I understood the pain of my uncle's absence. And I saw how she had moved on, how when she looked at Qadisha there was no sadness. I looked down. I saw how tenderly she held Qadisha's hand.

"OK," I said, raising my eyes to meet Luscious's. "I'll tell him."

VI

Perhaps I was mistaken. No, I had to be wrong. I stood in front of our apartment door, cursing myself in the hallway's dimness. I couldn't find my keys. I searched my pockets. I turned them inside out. I tried to recall when I last saw them. On the kitchen table? On the couch? On the side of the basketball court? When was the last time I heard them rattle? Had I put them in my socks, tied them to my shoelaces? I checked. No, no, not there. I had no idea. I couldn't recall taking them with me or if I had them during the course of the day. I gave up on finding them. I knocked on the door and listened for any sound, the TV, the radio, someone talking, my mother, my Aunt Rhonda, Eric. I sniffed the air. Maybe someone was in the kitchen cooking? But there was nothing. I knocked on the door again. Still there was only silence. No one was home. I put my back against the door, slid down until I was sitting, and thought about what I should do. I didn't want to go back outside. I was exhausted. And I didn't want to see Qadisha and Luscious again. And although I wanted to see her, I also didn't want to see Kaya either. Because what would I say? And besides, hadn't Donnel said he would be home in a minute, just after he got whatever he needed from the store? I decided to wait. I believed him not because it was easy, but because it was what I most wanted.

A few minutes passed. Then a few more. Then ten. Then twenty. I scolded myself. What was wrong with me? Cherrie, my mother's best friend, had our spare key. I didn't have to wait. I walked down the flight of stairs and knocked on Cherrie's door. Her television was on. An audience cheered.

"Who is it!" Cherrie shouted.

"Abraham," I called back.

"Hold on," she said. "I'm coming."

Cherrie unlocked the locks from the inside of the door. Then she opened the door and pressed her plump, oily face in the six inches afforded by the chain latch.

"Abraham," she said. "You know you interrupting my show."

"I lost my keys," I said.

"What do you mean you lost them?"

"I mean I can't find them," I said. "And you got the spare."

Suddenly, Cherrie's hand flew out from the six inches of space between the door and the doorframe and she snatched my T-shirt from my head. "You stretching it all out like that," she scolded. "Either put it on right or don't put it on at all."

Just as quickly as Cherrie took my T-shirt, she threw it back at me and I caught it against my chest.

"You sure I got them?" she asked. "Cause I could swear I gave them to Eric just last week. I guess we can check. Come on. Come in."

Cherrie closed the door and in the moment it took her to unhook the chain latch I pulled my T-shirt on over my head and realized that I had not seen Cherrie and my mother together for a few weeks. Cherrie had not been to our apartment nor had I seen them together outside, nor had I answered the phone and heard Cherrie and the familiar, syrupy yet percussive salutation—*Abraham, what's going on, where your ma at?*—she chanted when looking for my mother.

The door opened and Cherrie stepped aside so I could walk in. All of the lights in her apartment were off and the ivory shades were drawn over the windows so the only light in the apartment came from the TV. It laid a stream of pale green across the room and onto the small glass coffee table and the couch. On the walls, there was an old poster of Harriet Tubman, a painting of Jesus, and a cross hammered above the TV. Even in near darkness it was clear that Cherrie's apartment was pristine. She kept all of her windows down so the dirty air and gray street dust couldn't come in but that also made it feel as if there was no air in the apartment. I didn't understand how she could breathe. But it was Cherrie's place and she never had a problem making it clear that it was her apartment and you could get out if you didn't like it so I didn't say anything.

The theme song for the *Ricki Lake* show filled the apartment. Cherrie closed the door and locked the chain latch, the door, and the deadbolt. Then she pushed me out of the way, ran past me, and planted herself in the middle of the pale green light on the couch. Cherrie was a boulder of a woman with a boulder for a head, boulders for legs, boulders for arms, and two boulders for breasts.

"Check the jar on top of the fridge," she said, pointing to the kitchen, her eyes trained to the TV. "This one's too good. It's a repeat. The guests is crazy as all hell."

Cherrie shifted her weight to one side and pulled something from beneath her rear. It was a small Bible. Cherrie put it on her lap. Then, without taking her eyes from the TV, she searched the couch for something else. She ran her hands over the cushions and between them. Reluctant and frustrated, she stood up, stepped away from the couch, and glared at the floor, the coarse grey carpet a deep, black pool. She huffed, then she dropped to her knees. She slid her hands beneath the couch, dragged and rubbed in circles. The sound was grating, as if her hands were as hard as the carpet was. I stood a step inside the door and watched her. What was she searching so feverishly for? Cherrie stopped. Then she looked at me over her shoulder.

"Abraham," she scolded, "I ain't the TV. Don't just watch. Come and help me."

I crossed the room and looked down. "What you looking for?"

"It's black and silver," said Cherrie. "My pen. It's one of those that has a bunch of different colors that you can click down."

Cherrie ran her hands through the couch cushions once more and found what she wanted.

"It's just a pen," she said, holding it up for me to see. "But it was my mother's lucky one. Pastor Ramsey gave it to her with the Bible."

Something clicked in Cherrie's head and she looked at me, her face a sad, round stone in the TV's green stream of light. "Abraham," she said. "How's Jelly doing?"

Although I had just thought about the changed relationship between Cherrie and my mother, I was stunned by the question, by the expression on Cherrie's face and the fact that here was Cherrie, my mother's lifetime best friend, asking me, a son who rarely saw his mother, how she was. Yet I answered her automatically.

"She's good," I said.

Cherrie considered my answer. Was I right? Was it just a wish? Would she believe me? Cherrie put her free hand on her knee and with a sigh and soft groan, she pushed herself up from the floor. Then she looked at me and tried to make a smile out of distress.

"Come," she said, motioning for me to follow her into the kitchen. "Even if we can't find the keys then at least let me make you something to eat. You Abraham, so I know you must be hungry."

BAR 5
Holidays

I

My mother was nowhere to be found, not at the park, not at anyone's barbeque or picnic, not with friends in front of our building, not sitting on one of the benches in the concrete courtyard, not anywhere along Columbus or Washington avenues. It was the beginning of summer and I had just completed the seventh grade. My mother was missing for three days going on four. Then it was after midnight and my grandma and Rhonda were in the kitchen talking about my mother. They argued. They shouted. I was in bed. Donnel lay next to me. Eric was on the mattress on the floor. Everything could be heard through the walls. They didn't hold opposing opinions. They were in agreement. So they argued because they didn't want to agree, because they hoped that the other might say something that was more true than the truth they knew. No my mother couldn't be. No, not her. Not crack.

"What else could it be?" demanded my grandma.

"And the way her arms is all clawed up," my Aunt Rhonda yelled. "What kind of rash is that?"

"She told me she caught an allergy!" my grandma shouted. "And she ain't never had no allergy in all her life so what she suddenly allergic to?"

"She looks like she been eaten alive!" burst my Aunt Rhonda.

"And what would eat her in the first place?" asked my grandma. "Jelly has become nothing but some bones and a whole heap of lies!"

Who could sleep with all of their shouting? I wished I could. But I was not even tired. I was only anger, a silent rage with ears in bed.

"A," Donnel whispered. "You awake?"

I didn't answer. I hated him. Where had he been all day? And if my mother was a crackhead what had or hadn't he done to make it so? Lord help me if she got the crack from him. So I couldn't speak. Because I was afraid to. Because inside my throat was a rope that pulled my toes to my nose each time I breathed. And if I opened my mouth, I was sure that all of my insides would fall out and I would break wide open and weep. And I refused to weep. I would not. At least not in the blue darkness of the bedroom with Donnel and Eric present. If I was to cry I would cry alone. Maybe in the morning as I walked to school. But then again maybe not. I had begun to set decrees upon myself, rules that I believed would quicken my maturity, hasten my manhood, make any sensation related to pain and loss vanish with the rest of childish wants, things, and feelings.

Donnel propped himself up and looked over my shoulder. He put his face close to mine. His warm breath pushed on my neck and cheek.

"A," he said. "You really sleeping?"

Again, I didn't answer. I kept my eyes closed, and although I felt them quivering I tried to keep my lips as still as possible.

Suddenly she was home and my grandma and my Aunt Rhonda were shouting at her.

"Jelly!" said my Aunt Rhonda. "Where you been?"

"Tell us now!" shouted my grandma. "What's going on? What you got yourself into?"

My mother denied everything. And she was professional about it. She didn't stutter, hem and haw. She never circled back and reconstructed her previous position. She made everything sound simple and plain. She'd lost weight because the summer was coming and who didn't want to look good. And the rash was a rash. And she was no doctor. So how was she supposed to know what the rash was from? And her hair? Well, shit, she just hadn't had the time. With all the running around for the last few days. Did they know she was working? Yeah, she got her old job back at the McDonald's. In fact, that's where she was coming from.

"My work clothes?" she said. "I leave them at work. I ain't trying to walk around dressed like Ronald McDonald."

"Look at yourself," my Aunt Rhonda hammered. "Jelly, God damn, you look like one of those crackheads you used to make fun of!"

"Think of Abraham!" shouted my grandma. "He don't deserve no mother like this!"

In a swirl and rush, Donnel threw the sheet off and stormed out of our room, opening the door, then slamming it behind himself.

"Abraham's sleeping!" he shouted. "Fuck! Can't you all respect that!"

"Who you talking to?" my grandma exploded. "Who you cursing at like that?"

"I'm cursing you!" Donnel countered, his voice not the voice of a teenager but the sure, huge booms of bombs and big brick buildings slamming to the ground. "I'm saying you all need to shut the fuck up!"

"Get out! God damn it! Get out!" burst my grandma.

Then I heard slapping, a hand slamming against the bare skin of a flat back and chest, a muscular neck, the hard bones of a face. Who was hitting whom? Was it my mother? Was Donnel hitting my Aunt Rhonda? Had they ganged up on my grandma? Suddenly, the door swung open. I played dead. I was afraid the fight, the war was coming for me. I lay on my side, my hands knotted between my neck and chin. I focused on keeping my eyes closed in a way that they would look like eyes look when people are really asleep. I felt light on my face, saw red on the back of my eyelids. I heard someone open a drawer and slam the drawer closed. I heard someone snatch something else, a sweat jacket. I recognized the sound of its zipper smacking against the armoire. It was Donnel.

"Fuck you!" he shouted. "Jelly's a crackhead! Why you even asking her about it? And you all crazy! You all go fuck yourselves!"

"D," begged Eric. "D, don't go."

Donnel leapt onto the bed and kneeled behind me. He planted his hand on my shoulder. Then he leaned forward over me.

"A," he whispered, his breath a warm thump on my neck. "I know you ain't sleeping."

There was a second of nothing, a second of tranquility, a silence so utter and complete I felt my heart beating in my chest and the blood pumping through my arms and legs. Then Donnel slammed his lips against the side of my face. He kissed.

"I'll be back," he said. "Don't worry."

I squeezed my eyes tight. He's lying, I thought, lying like my mother; lying like everyone else. They're all liars, I thought. Every single one. Even me, I thought. Even if I don't know it.

II

My mother and I sat on the couch, saying nothing to each other and with a foot of space between us. On the television, a chorus sang *the rockets' red glare, the bombs bursting in air, gave proof through the night that our flag was still there* while fireworks exploded above New York City's skyline. Outside, bottle rockets, firecrackers, and sporadic gunshots whistled and popped, and a tangle of many songs from numerous stereos climbed high into the sky and fell into our apartment, stumbling, smashing, wielding cacophony. It was as hot and steamy in our apartment as it was outside, and the rotten stench of the hot garbage overflowing from the Dumpsters behind our building was joined by the smell of barbeque. My mother was sweating. Her once rich brown skin was moist, taut, and sickly, rife with olive undertones and mauve stains beneath her eyes and in the barren valleys that were once her cheeks. She sat like a boxer, exhausted in a corner. Her arms were flaccid in her lap. Her torso was concave. She blinked once, real slow and real hard, as if it took all of her focus to close her eyelids and then all of her strength to open them again. Regardless of what my mother did and who she was, I loved her. But that is not why only she and I were home on the Fourth of July. We were stuck. That is, my grandma was at work, Donnel and Eric and my Aunt Rhonda were somewhere celebrating independence, and my mother was approaching being clean for one week. So in addition to lacking the fortitude to refuse the temptations that were certainly outside, she had promised my grandma and my aunt that she was going to stay in. As for me, I promised my grandma that I would stay with her. Yet that is not the only reason I was stuck on the couch. No, I was also stuck because I was caught between wanting to barge into my mother's brain and rearrange what she craved and wanting her to get away from me forever. So I was paralyzed by the impossibility of one feat and the guilt created by the hate that made me desire the other. How could she have become who she was? How could she be so vicious to herself?

She wiped her hand down the side of her gaunt face. "Abraham," she said.

I couldn't bring myself to look at her.

She put her hand on my leg and shook it just a bit. "Abraham," she repeated. "Get some ice from the freezer."

We weren't drinking anything but I didn't ask why she wanted ice. I looked down and noted the contrast between her bony hand and my brown leg, and I considered if I should leave her, if when I stood and turned my back she would bolt for the door. Because of hope, I quickly decided that she wouldn't, and if she did in fact try to flee I surmised that she was too weak to get to the door and out of the apartment before I stopped her. So I stood and walked into the kitchen. The light switch was to my left and I turned it on. Dishes were in the sink. A few rapidly rotting bananas were on the counter. Fruit flies hovered above and landed on them. My grandma's birds chirped. Their feathers were slicked. To combat the heat, they bathed themselves in their drinking water. I opened the freezer and took out a plastic tray of ice. Then I turned off the kitchen light and returned to the couch, putting the tray between us. My mother took a deep breath, grabbed the ice tray, and twisted it with both hands. An ice cube popped out, bounced off the couch, and landed on the floor.

"Get that," she said.

I got the ice cube from the floor and my mother twisted the ice tray again. She was so weak her arms shook before another cube popped out and landed on the floor just like the first.

"Shit," she said, frustrated by her weakness. "Why don't they make it easier to get out?"

I wished I had an answer, but nothing came to mind. I got the second ice cube off the floor and held both in one hand. Where I could put them? If it had been any other day and I had been with any other person I would have either taken the ice cubes into the kitchen and put them in the sink or left them on the floor to melt. But because I felt as if I could not trust my mother, and because I had given her one opportunity to flee but I would not give her two, and because I was shocked by the fact that she barely had the strength to twist the plastic ice tray, I remained on the couch. Finally, my mother was able to dislodge then pick an ice cube out of the tray with her fingers.

"Here," she said, holding the ice cube out to me. "Rub it on my neck."

I took the ice cube and my mother tilted her head down. Then I touched the ice cube to the back of her skeletal neck and she shivered.

"Shit's cold," she said. "Go slow."

I slipped the ice cube up and down and back and forth, making figure eights around the crest and trough of her vertebrae. I still did not look at her. But as I watched the TV, the bursting of fireworks, their iridescent and luminescent rain, I thought about her. How had she become so shrunken and trapped inside the shell beside me? She took deep breaths through her nose and sighed softly. Tears filled my eyes. I began to cry silently and the flashes of fireworks on the TV became neon streams falling before me. I still held the ice cubes in my other hand. Their cold made my palm ache. As they melted, water seeped between my fingers and dripped on the couch, still one of my grandma's most prized possessions. The ice cube I slid along my mother's neck melted quickly as well. Water ran in rivulets over her skin and it soaked the collar of her shirt.

As if she'd heard a voice, my mother lifted her head and stared at the TV. Then she looked at me. Her eyes were magnets. Mine were metal filings. There was nothing I could do, nowhere to go, no way I could thwart their pull. Finally, I looked at her too.

"Abraham," she whispered. "You crying?"

The question made me empty. I was speechless. I didn't move. I couldn't even blink or twitch.

"Oh, Mister Man," she sighed.

My mother cupped her hand against the side of my face and gently pulled me toward her. I fell like an ember, slow and steady until my head landed in her lap. I closed my eyes. Could I sleep and dream everything away? I heard the fireworks' finale on the TV, the pops, booms, and bangs. The ice cubes melted in my hands. The ache they created dissipated until it became a faint throb, then the silent flapping of wings in the distance. My mother stroked my head. She massaged my earlobe between her thumb and index finger. How could we explain our pains to each other?

"We gonna be all right," she whispered. She let her hand rest on the side of my face. "Promise. Just don't never give up."

I placed my hand on top of my mother's hand. "I won't," I said. "I swear it."

III

There were bodies stricken with a rampant, devastating emptiness; lovers and beloveds; I knew them, all of them, if not by name then by face; if they didn't live in Ever then they lived around; they had children in my school, children in my class, children who played at the park with me; they were everywhere, like gore splattered around the wreckage of the room, naked and fully clothed, tangled and strewn about, trounced upon, torn and tussled and turned inside out; to my right, to my left, all over the floor; mashed and mangled in the narrow halls; leaning, lonely shadows on the wall, crying and muttering to themselves; hollering, bleating like battered sheep; brothers and sisters and mothers and aunts and uncles and grandmas and sons and daughters. It was the day before my thirteenth birthday. I was in the crackhouse on the corner of Columbus and Pine, but I could have been in any of the crackhouses that riddled Ever Park and its surroundings. Rats and roaches and militias of dumb, stumbling maggots the size of Tic Tacs and pinky toes; broken bottles, crushed aluminum cans, gaping holes in all of the walls; candles, melted to nubs, seeping and sagging on the floor, singed slivers and shards of wood, cardboard, makeshift campfires were here, there, everywhere. The windows were boarded. The door was bolted, soldered shut. There were holes large enough for a person to squeeze through in the ceiling. I'd squeezed through. Reluctantly, street light did the same, falling through the room, splintering and bathing my brown skin a muddy, blood red. I was on a mission, governed by an irrefutable responsibility. My mother had relapsed. I hadn't seen her for a week; not outside, not inside, not far off in the distance, stumbling or dragging herself in circles like a bird with a broken wing.

I breathed because I had to, because it was an involuntary bodily function, not because I had the strength. I covered my nose and gasped through my mouth, the rancid stench, a taste of fetid diesel that scraped across my teeth, burned my tongue, and planted a viscous phlegm in my throat that hung from my tonsils and dripped an imminent devastation into my lungs one splatter at a time.

"Mom," I shouted. "Mom! You here?"

She smoked crack as if the smoke were a rope to rapture. Unapologetically, greedily, with an unabashed determination, she smoked it wherever oxygen reached. Rain, sleet, or snow. Morning, noon, and night. Had she sold her body for crack? Would someone knock out her front teeth or tear her earring from her ear, leaving the lobe cleaved and floppy? All of these things happened to crackheads. All of my mother, including the parts neither she nor God had ever dreamed, was gone.

We had fought with her. We had told her no more, not now, never, not one more time. We cried. We hollered. We begged. My grandma took me to church. We held hands and prayed for my mother. We called upon Jesus and Mary Magdalene. We looked to Psalms for guidance. We looked to Proverbs. My grandma Scotch-taped inspirational quotes on the refrigerator to give her, to give us strength. But did it matter? When Donnel was around he said it wouldn't. I stayed silent and thought against him. My mind kicked and punched and screamed for him to stop. I thought everything, including it, was his fault, an idea too sick to say, too ghastly to put my breath into. He swore my mother was a fiend and she was a fiend for good. He said he'd seen it before, a thousand times over, she was not my mother, but just like the rest of them, a crack whore whose sole goal was death no matter if she knew it or not, no matter if it came quick or slow. Of course Eric had agreed with him. Of course he just repeated what Donnel said when Donnel was not around. And my Aunt Rhonda had said as far as she was concerned she didn't have a sister anymore and sought sanctuary in the arms of this and that man to keep her from changing her mind.

As for me, I had done three things. One: I went to school. I sat like a piece of furniture in class. I stared out of the window, put my head down on the desk. I did my work when I felt like it. I passed it in rarely and most often never. I didn't raise my hand, not once. My mother, she whose sole responsibility was to love me unconditionally, proved I held less value than a small chunk of baking soda and cocaine. So what did I have to ask or contribute? So I had stopped talking. I had become mute. Two: I played basketball. Up and down the court I went. I practiced for hours. I pounded and shot until my fingernails split from their beds and bled my fingerprints all over the ball. And three: I searched for my mother. And I refused to give up. I scoured Ever. I swept and memorized every inch. I walked every desire line a crackhead could travel. Each time I found her, I dragged her home. Once, I carried her over my shoulders like a sack of wet cement. She had crack. But seeking was my addiction.

So I was relentless, tireless. And I swore I would always be.

"Mom," I shouted. "Ma, where you at?"

To my left there was a couch, soiled and pocked with burn holes. To my right there was a broken wooden chair covered with a bloody pillow. On the carpet there were spots that had been burned away and dark stains the shape of countries and continents. I wanted to disappear, blink and vanish. Just somewhere, anywhere was everywhere I wanted to be. But I couldn't. I promised. And what would happen to her if I broke the promise? The question was projection. That is, my real fear was: what would happen to me if I let go?

There was moaning. Suddenly, I became hopeful. Was it her? Could it be? I looked to my left. A boil-faced, gaunt man had his hands on his hips, his eyes closed, and his head tilted back as he proudly accepted a blow job from another man. But it wasn't he who was moaning. Breathing hard, sighing *Oh Lord . . . Mmmm. Oh don't stop!* was what he said. I shifted my eyes farther to my left. There it was. A woman. She was on the floor. She moaned louder.

"Mom?" I said.

The woman shot me a look. It wasn't my mother.

Some kids go to the zoo. Some get to blow out candles on birthday cakes. Some get money from tooth fairies. I was where I was and I had been there before. I had been propositioned in that house, begged from, spat upon. I had been prayed to, pointed and laughed at, ordered to leave. I had been clung from. I had been pushed. I had been stared at, devoured. Once, I was attacked by a fat man with three teeth who was so weak his blows were no more than the last gasps of faint wind, and there, in that room, with one swipe, I sent him sprawling to the floor.

I planted my left foot between splayed legs. I stepped on an old soda can and it crunched. I called her name. I said my grandma wanted her home. I said Rhonda was crying. I told her Nice had written her a letter and we were waiting for her to come home, open it, and read it aloud. Over and over again, I lied. I said Donnel had won the Lotto, that Eric was in the hospital, that my father, her first and only love, had come back for her; it was amazing, crazy, as if he fell from the sky. I didn't know how. I didn't ask him where he'd been, why he'd gone. That was for her to do. All I knew was that he said he was back because he loved her. He loved us. He always had. I shouted everything, anything she might want, wish, and need to hear. Come on, I pleaded. It was me, Abraham, her only.

"Mom," I shouted. "Mom!"

Never did I think I wouldn't find her. I was never too tired, never too afraid. Never was I without the unwavering belief that, as if by some great holy, unbreakable connection, like a divining rod finding water, I knew where she was. I walked down a narrow hallway. There was a door to my right. I stopped. I remembered that once I found her there, her legs pulled to her chest, her chin tucked between them, rocking left and right as if teetering upon an invisible edge. I gripped the handle, but before I opened the door, I considered calling her name again. Then I decided not to. Sometimes I called "Mom!" and ten women answered in different tones and manners. Some cried and thanked God a son had come for them. Some cursed and threatened me. Others laughed, cackled, and shouted "yeah" over and over again.

I turned the handle. I pushed the door in. Garbage was piled around the edges of the room, moldy clothes, tangles of brass, wires, and bent copper pipes. A dozen candles were in the middle of the floor. A few were lit. I took one step into the room and stopped. Suddenly, every pore on my body released a flood of sweat. Then I vomited. Not all of me, but something specific, some kind of invisible line that ran from me to my mother broke. Suddenly, I only hated.

Numb, I turned around and left, climbing out of the same hole in the ceiling that I dropped in through. This was the last time I searched for her, the last time I shouted, "Mom! Mom! It's me, Mister Man, Abraham."

Before dawn the next morning, Donnel woke me by whispering my name and shaking my shoulder.

"A," he said. "Wake up." He tapped my head with his finger. He pulled on my ear. "Come on," he said. "Meet me in the kitchen."

I was annoyed and groggy. I didn't want to speak to him, let alone look at him. Just like I hadn't found my mother, I hadn't seen him the previous day. So I'd gone to sleep cursing him just as much as I cursed her.

"What?" I complained.

"Just come," he said, his voice childish and impatient. He shook me once more. He got out of the bed and headed for the bedroom door. Then he stopped and turned around.

"Come on," he begged. "I got something for you."

Donnel left the room and I lay in bed and despised him for a few moments more. Why couldn't he just leave me alone, I wondered. Why couldn't he just disappear and stay disappeared? And why couldn't my mother do the same? But then, that was not what I really wanted him or her to do. I wanted them always near. So I sighed, rolled out of bed, and dragged my sleepy and forsaken-feeling self from the darkness of our bedroom to the kitchen, squinting in the flourescent light until my sight was no longer covered by a bright white blur.

Donnel stood with his back to me and he leaned over the birdcage, whistling, clicking his tongue and talking to my grandma's birds. He poked his finger into their cage. His back was fan shaped, as if beneath his skin were not muscles but folded wings. On the kitchen table was a black backpack with a big red bow on it. He turned around and pointed at it.

"Happy birthday," he smiled. "I bet you thought I forgot. Go ahead. Open it."

"Open what?" I said.

"The backpack," he whispered. "Unzip it. Look inside."

Inside the backpack was a dictionary, a thesaurus, and a small white box. I pulled the box out of the backpack and Donnel quickly came to the table.

"What's this?" I said.

Donnel smiled, then shrugged.

I opened the box. Inside was a thin gold chain with my name on it just like the gold chain that my grandma had bought me and my mother stole and sold.

"Where you get it?" I asked.

Donnel thought for a moment. Then he zipped the backpack closed and slid it across the table to me.

"You always asking questions," he said, his face and voice tight like the skin of a brown drum that does not beat or pulse but hums no matter how quick and hard it is pounded. "Just take it. Put it on. And if grandma asks, tell her you found the old one under the bed or something."

IV

A perpetual tidal of tumbling, his shoulders rising, his knees bending, his back bowed, his face unfurled, a tattered sail anchored to the sidewalk, Titty wept like a battered woman in Yusef's arms.

"It's all right, big man," said Yusef, stroking the nape of Titty's neck. "Let it out. Let it go."

Without Yusef, Titty would have crashed to the concrete, splashed on our feet.

"Like a angel," he sobbed. "Like a angel, that nigga could sing."

It was the first day of February. In winter coats and white shirts with collars and cuffs that were too big for our necks and wrists, my friends and I stood outside the Holy Name. We were in the eighth grade, at a time in our lives when our heads and feet were big, incongruous balloons affixed to our bodies. We were growing into ourselves or so we were told. We had pimples and wisps of hair above our lips and, if we angled our heads and stood in the light just right, wisps of hair could also be seen on our chins. The sun was bright. The sky was an electric, ethereal blue. There was no wind, and it was so cold no scent had the fortitude to hang in the air. A few church vans from other churches sat double parked behind a hearse on Columbus Avenue, and a steady stream of people gathered on the sidewalk, swelled with sadness, that steaming heat that made the coldness of the day inconsequential. Three days earlier, Titty's cousin, Pastor Ramsey's son Jeremiah, was killed for everything he had: five crumpled dollar bills, a nickel, two dimes, three sticks of Big Red, a book of matches, a condom, a bad joke with a punch line he could never get right, a head full of hymns, and a half-smoked cigarette, the habit he kept from his father. It was his funeral. Those who refused to let the public see them with anything other than unflappable stoicism, or at the very least indifference on any other day, wore true faces. Wrenched and twisted by grief, they held one another. They kept one another standing. They blinked slowly, holding themselves apart from the world, fighting back tears, regrouping so they could fortify one another again. Dappled about the congestion, shining, emanating the sweet of cocoa butter and knockoff bourgeois perfumes when hugged and leaned upon, women cradled small children to their chests. Some whispered secrets to distract others from their pain. Old men who had known this sort of death too many times to count wore black and blue suits. Some men's ties and shirts were spotted with faded stains of dripped coffee and food from previous services. Some men talked intermittently about current events and sports because the sin of Jeremiah's death was a theme they had hashed and rehashed so many times before that their sadness could now only be demonstrated by how their favorite player and team made them feel.

Wearing a black leather overcoat and a black Kangol driving cap pulled crookedly over his right eye, Mr. Goines walked through the crowd passing out flyers for a peace march and homemade buttons with Jeremiah's likeness on them.

"Put it on!" he shouted, holding a button over his head, spittle vaulting from his lips. "Pin them to your skin! Never forget young Jeremiah!"

With his spongelike brown eyes, Precious watched Mr. Goines and couldn't stop shaking his head no. But he didn't shake his head out of disgust. He shook it out of familiarity. Precious was raised by his father and his father was an old Black Panther, so Precious knew the sight of a man as the embodiment of paternal strength and maternal love. He sensed something. He lay his heartbroken eyes on me. He was still my most gentle friend.

"You all right?" he asked.

"Yeah," I said. "I'm good."

What a lie. Because who was? But then my greatest pain was not related to Jeremiah's passing. That is, I was saddened, perhaps even devastated by Jeremiah's death. But what Precious saw on my face was panic. Before Mr. Goines had come near us I had seen my mother across the street, like a skittish rat scampering between cars, scratching herself and darting from one car to the next, eyes glued to the ground. She scoured the parking lot, bending over and scratching the dried tufts of scrub grass that bloomed through the cracks in its concrete, kicking patches of gravel, and circling parking blocks in search of the nothing she thought she dropped or that something some other crackhead might have abandoned mistakenly, a few last crystals in a vial, a crumpled ball of tinfoil, a tiny Ziploc baggie. She had come home in the fall then left and came home and left on a binge again just after New Year's Eve. The arrival of Mr. Goines had distracted me for a moment and when I looked back my mother was nowhere to be seen. So I feared she was somewhere nearer and that everyone might soon see the teetering, spastic slow motion that was the collision and ensuing grapple between her emptiness and her craving.

I looked back across the street and lost myself in prayer and scanning the parking lot for my mother. I hoped that she had wandered off to parts unknown. I hoped she would remain unseen, deceased if need be, at least until Jeremiah could be buried in peace, at least until everyone entered the church and the devastation that would be her public appearance passed.

Suddenly, from down the street came my grandma. She wore a black dress, a black hat, and black sunglasses that not only hid her eyes but made her look like a train. She aimed herself at me. She leaned forward, swung her arms, accelerated. Every time a young man was killed in or around Ever, she made rules and demands that made our home a penitentiary. We couldn't go out. No visitors. I couldn't be at the basketball court by myself. No one was going to die unnecessarily. Not on her watch. Over her dead body. But things had changed drastically. That is, her watch had proven to be insufficient. She couldn't keep Donnel in. And Eric followed Donnel's lead. And my mother, wherever she was, was a lost cause. And my Aunt Rhonda was a grown woman, so my grandma's rules didn't apply to her. So it was just me. I was the only one she could capture. She ignored my friends. She brushed past them. She kissed me on the cheek. Then she grabbed my shirt in her fist.

"You coming right home after all this," she said. "Understand?"

I blinked. She tore her sunglasses from her face with her free hand.

"Answer me," she demanded. Then, with my shirt still in her grip, she lifted her fist against my chin and shook me. "Abraham, I'm talking to you."

"Gloria!" Mr. Goines shouted from behind us. He came up on our left, and swiftly putting the buttons in his pocket, he grabbed my grandma's wrist with both hands, crushing his black and white flyers around it.

"Let go of the boy," he said, trying to pry her grip from me. "Abraham ain't done nothing. Gloria, let go."

There was an awkward pause in which my grandma and Mr. Goines looked at each other. Then she looked back at me and I saw it there, how it filled the dark depths of her brown eyes with smoke and ash. My grandma had seen my mother just as I had seen her. And then she saw that I had seen her as well and she froze, her fist still balled around my shirt.

"Gloria," said Mr. Goines, his voice gentle, pleading. "Gloria. Come on now. We at a funeral. Let Abraham be."

My grandma's face changed from the determination she pressed on me to a weariness that was the stalemate between rage and helplessness. Her furrowed brow quivered. Her shoulders slackened. Peeling back one finger at a time, Mr. Goines unclenched my grandma's fist. With one delicate tug, he pulled her from me. Then, as if my grandma's grasp of me was all that had kept her standing, she wilted and folded into Mr. Goines's chest.

"Let it on out," he said. "Don't worry now. We gonna go on. Lyndon has got you."

"You a fool," said my grandma, weakly scolding him as she cried into his neck and halfheartedly pounded her fist on his chest. "You ain't no good."

"Not now," he said. "Not now, Gloria. Everything gonna be all right. Everything gonna be OK."

Inside the church, I sat with my friends, Mr. Goines sat with my grandma, and Pastor Ramsey stepped behind the lectern, welcomed everyone, and fought through tears and the continuous constriction of suffering in his throat to explain how he had never imagined he would be where he was, doing what he was doing, presiding over the funeral of his son Jeremiah.

"But, I am obligated to be here," he reasoned, his voice hovering at the threshold of devastation. "Not obligated by the Lord. Not obligated by paycheck. Not obligated because I wouldn't have food, or shelter, or clothing if I didn't stand before you today. But obligated by life. By my very existence. I watched this young gentleman grow up. I witnessed who he was in entirety. I know his truth; that he wasn't just some hellion from the projects. This is my son. Jeremiah. In a different time, in a different place, in a different country and city and century, he would have been David with a harp for a voice."

Pastor Ramsey paused. He fought hard not to break down and cry. He held on to the lectern and rocked back and forth.

"So," he said, his voice weak. "What are the living supposed to do? What am I, his father, supposed to do?"

Suddenly Pastor Ramsey filled with strength and pounded his hand on the lectern. "Should I cry out?" He pounded the lectern again. "Should I demand to know why? Do I plead for justice and peace?"

That was it. Pastor Ramsey deflated. He sighed and shook his head.

"I don't know," he continued. "No, I have no idea. I know only one thing. There is only one thing I am sure of."

Slowly Pastor Ramsey raised his hand in the air. He closed his eyes.

"Jesus," he said, his voice becoming louder. "Psalm Twenty-three, verse four. *He causes me to lie down in green pastures! He leads me beside still waters! He restores my soul! He leads me in paths of righteousness for His name's sake! Even when I walk in the valley of darkness, I will fear no evil! For He is with me! Thy rod and Thy staff—they comfort me! You set a table before me in the presence of my adversaries! You anoint my head with oil; my cup overflows! May only goodness and kindness pursue me all the days of my life, and I will dwell in the house of the Lord for length of days.* And let us say . . ."

"Amen," said everyone in the small church, even those who questioned their belief, even those who doubted God like me.

"Amen," Pastor Ramsey breathed. "In the name of Jesus. Amen."

Then it was Valentine's Day and there were flowers from Mr. Goines in a glass vase on top of the TV. Reruns of the old *Cosby Show* were

on. Thirteen years old and I was already thinking, already determined
to live in Brooklyn with a beautiful wife who was a lawyer and five
well-meaning, well-behaved children. I would be Heathcliff, a doctor, a
sweater wearer, a jazz fiend without an instrument, a humorist, a drop-
per of knowledge, a reveler in the bliss of life. I sat on the couch. With
the card that had come with the flowers in her purse so she could read
it once more on her way to work, my grandma had just left. She was
thinking about the things Mr. Goines said. Maybe she would take him
up on that offer of one dinner, one trip to the movies.

Suddenly, there was a clack. Then there was the click of keys at the
door and then the door swung open and Eric launched himself into
the apartment, out of breath, sucking in air and heaving it out of his
mouth.

"Abraham!" he shouted.

"Nigga, shhh!" I scolded, swinging my index finger at the TV. "*The
Cosby Show* is on."

"Fuck the Huxtables!" he said. "Bill Cosby ain't shit!"

Eric was fifteen, and so enraged he was quaking, his arms shivering, the vein that ran through his temple and down the side of his neck
pounding. Snot trickled from his nose, slid across his top lip, dripped at
the corners of his mouth. Without turning around, he swung his arm
and slammed the door closed. Its crash echoed down the hall, bounced
back and forth from one side of the narrow corridor to the other. Eric
stood in the middle of the room, waiting for me to either scold him for
slamming the door or look at him. He was of average height for his age
and although he was not fat he also was not thin. His body was soft, as
if he had no muscles, as if between his skin and bones there was only all
of the French fries and pork lo mein he bought from the hole-in-the-
wall Chinese food spot. His eyes darted between me and the TV. Then
he sighed. He would have refused this truth, but Eric loved *The Cosby
Show* just as much as me.

"It just start?" he asked, seemingly forgetting why he'd stormed into the apartment, as if hoping that the Huxtables might offer him some salve for his wounds, some special elixir, a placebo, an absolution.

"Shh," I said.

Bill Cosby was in the kitchen and Theo came in, pushing open the door that led to their living room and the rest of their house. They talked about this and that. Bill Cosby made a joke, a funny face, and rolled his eyes. Theo laughed and pointed at him. A half-hearted but all-he-could-muster smile stayed on Eric's face until a commercial came on. Not because he was good-looking; not because he was a good athlete or smart or had a good smile or game with girls or was the least bit chill, the least bit smooth, but secretly, Eric and I wished to be Theo. Why? The reason was simple. He had a father, a man who scolded and, most importantly, embraced him; a man who knew what he was thinking, who had caused the ways of his thoughts; who infused his demeanor with a fine soldierly pride just as much as he'd taught him patience and humor, whose shoulders were broader than his, shoulders he'd sat on when he was a kid, shoulders he could imagine having and using as a pedestal to plant his own children upon one day.

Suddenly, Eric remembered why he'd come home, why he'd launched himself into the apartment, and he rushed into the kitchen. I heard him tear open a drawer. Utensils and cutlery rattled and clanked off the floor. In their cage, my grandma's lovebirds squawked and screeched. Eric ripped out what he wanted and threw aside everything else. He slammed the drawer closed. It didn't close. He punched it, kicked it, yelled at it to shut. Then he shouted *Fuck!* kicked the cutlery that was on the floor, sending it clattering along the linoleum until it crashed against the wall, and came back into the room, the cleaver, his favorite knife, clenched in his hand and held at eye level. One of Eric's fingers was cut. Blood dripped down his arm and fell on the floor from the point of his elbow, speckling the already stained grey carpet. He glared at me, daring me to say something, ask him what he was doing. Go ahead, his eyes said, go ahead and try to stop me.

Because just moments before I was living with Clair and Heathcliff and a crazed young man with a knife was nowhere to be found, I stared at Eric but uttered nothing. I was shocked and he waited. Then, inch by inch, body part by body part, he quit. His shoulders stooped. His chest heaved. His legs bowed. He was stripped of everything, even the free time he spent sketching cartoonish evildoers and superheroes in his spiral-bound notebooks. Then, no longer carrying the fury that had fueled his actions just moments earlier, Eric did the only thing he could do to maintain the meager amount of dignity he had left. He shuffled to the door. But when he grabbed the knob, he stopped and dropped his head.

"I wasn't doing nothing," he said.

He sucked a deep wet breath and shook his head. Then he slowly turned around and laid his twisted, should have been wet with tears but dry as bone eyes on me.

"I was just walking," he continued, his voice dropping to a near whisper. "Niggas came out of nowhere and robbed me. They stole everything I had. They even took my notebook out of my back pocket and ran."

Eric turned halfway around and showed me his empty back pocket. "It was here," he said. "Right here."

Suddenly there was the click of keys being put in the lock of our door and the squeak of the lock being turned when it was already unlocked. Eric stepped back. The door swung open. Then Donnel walked in, seventeen, six feet tall and strong, every inch of him hard, electric. Donnel was muscular, seemingly in possession of boundless energy, but his face revealed that he was exhausted. The bags under his eyes were so deep they seemed greasy, streaks of tar, oil slicks. He looked at me, the TV, and then he looked at Eric and saw the knife in his hand.

"Why you looking like that?" he scolded. "And I know you ain't holding no knife to Abraham."

Eric shook his head. "I chased them," he muttered. "I chased them for as long as I could."

"Who?" asked Donnel.

Eric was destitute. And just as I knew, Eric knew his plan of vengeance was thwarted. Donnel would never allow him outside with a kitchen knife. He knew Eric wouldn't be able to handle himself, to fight with the viciousness he needed, to be as inexhaustible and fearless as a young man in Ever bent on waging war for what he wanted, what he deserved, was required to be. Chances were if Eric went outside with a knife and found the young men who robbed him, they'd strip him of his weapon and gore him with it. Eric was not a fighter. And when he did fight, he wasted all of his energy hurling himself, throwing his weight into one swing that never connected and left him gravely exposed. And he was not fast enough to run from a fight. So if he fought he'd get pummeled, beaten, and battered, eyes blackened, his jaw so sore and swollen he wouldn't be able to whistle or brush his teeth let alone chew solid food. Eric knew this about himself. So he swallowed and showed Donnel his back pocket and then his coat pocket hoping to gain Donnel's sympathy and therefore his strength, his ability to fight.

"Niggas took my new notebook," said Eric, his entire body heavy and limp. "And they took the new Discman and headphones you got me. And the new pencils, they took them too. D, I ain't never been robbed so bad in all my life."

Donnel looked down and shook his head. How were he and Eric from the same womb?

"What I tell you about going around flaunting shit?" he asked.

"But—," began Eric.

"Nigga," Donnel scolded. "What I tell you?"

"You said not to do it," Eric mumbled.

"Stupid," Donnel whispered.

He shifted his tired eyes to the knife, thought of something, and lifted his eyes to the TV. I glanced at the TV; *The Cosby Show* was on again. In their kitchen, Heathcliff told Clair what Theo said and swore he didn't understand his son's thinking as he cut himself a piece of cake. Why couldn't our lives be like that? I watched Donnel. I saw his anger build, his eyes narrowing, his nostrils flaring larger with each breath. He rolled his tongue over his bottom lip. Then he bit his lip and pulled it into his mouth and held it there, pinched beneath his front teeth, squeezing it until it finally popped free. Donnel took a breath and opened his mouth to speak but just before he said anything, there was a thump and a moan, and a moment later my grandma's bedroom door opened. Out walked my mother, the woman who gave me life, dragging herself, stinking like dank wool and vomit, her face so gaunt her cheekbones seemed to be outside instead of beneath her skin. Once again, swearing she wanted to get clean, she had come home three days earlier. Fear and the feeling of need, the gnawing of neglect swelled into all parts of my body. I tried to act as if she were not there. But she was. So I put my eyes on Donnel and did what Eric had just done. Silently, I begged him to make everything all right.

Donnel looked back at me. There was no longer the slightest doubt that he was selling drugs. He had new sneakers on, new jeans. He looked at my mother. Then he took one determined step toward the door. I feared he was leaving, disappearing again. But he didn't. He stopped and locked the door, the two chain latches, the knob, and the deadbolts. Then he turned back around, put his eyes on my mother, and, aiming his arm and index finger straight ahead, he pointed at my grandma's room.

"Get back in there," he said. "Go lay down. You ain't going no-where."

My mother stopped walking. Her eyes were bloodshot, shocked and worried, like she'd lost something precious a long time ago and had spent every night since thinking about where it might be. She wore one of Grandma's dresses and she held one of my grandma's purses, the white leather one my grandma often took to church. My mother had lost so much of herself she didn't even recognize which clothes were hers. She slipped the purse up her bony arm and balanced it on her bony shoulder. Then she planted her hand on her skeletal hip.

"Well happy Valentine's Day to you too," she said, her tone and face laced with disdain.

The purse slipped down her arm and its descent to the crook of her elbow wobbled her, nearly knocked her to the floor. She gathered herself and slid the purse up her arm again. Then she returned her hand to her hip and looked at me.

"Abraham," she said, her voice feigning vitality just as much as every other part of her body, "Go open the door for your momma."

Donnel shot his eyes at me. Then he calmly crossed the room and stopped at Eric. "Give me that," he said, gesturing at the knife Eric held.

Dumbly, Eric handed Donnel the cleaver. Donnel looked at me. For a moment, I feared he was suddenly feeling murderous and about to act on it. Then I realized that what he was feeling was not murder-ous but resolute. His face was blank. His eyes were blank. His body was stiff. He was a wall, a dam. Only that which he allowed would pass him.

"Go and play ball," he told me.

"I don't want to," I said without thinking.

"Then go to the library," he snapped. He put his eyes on me in a fashion that was gentler than his tone. He looked at Eric. "Take him. Make sure he goes and reads or something."

"Abraham," my mother interrupted. "Mister Man. Listen to your mother. Open the door for me."

"Go," Donnel said, ignoring my mother, his eyes planted back on me. "Now."

"Nigga, fuck you!" my mother shouted at Donnel.

"A," Donnel said calmly.

"You ain't shit!" my mother screamed. "You nothing!"

"Nigga," Donnel said, his voice rising, his eyes never once shifting from me. "Do what I told you."

Suddenly, my mother snatched my grandmother's purse from her arm and, wielding it like a stone, she held it over her head. "You think you gonna cut me? Huh? That it? You think you gonna stop me!"

"E," Donnel said, shifting his eyes to Eric. "What I say? Take him. Get A off the couch."

"You think you got me scared?" screamed my mother. "Abraham! Don't you leave! Don't you go nowhere!"

Gently, Eric patted me on the shoulder. "A, c'mon. Let's go."

Eric hooked his hand under my arm and pulled me up until, like a zombie, I rose from the couch. I stared at Donnel. I could not believe who my mother was. I could not believe what Donnel might do. He raised the cleaver shoulder high and took two steps toward her. She took two steps back.

"Abraham!" she screamed. "Abraham!"

"Abraham, go," Donnel said, glaring at my mother. "Go and don't come back until I come for you."

"No," my mother screamed. "No! You can't leave!"

What crushed me most was that I could not disagree with whatever Donnel decided my mother deserved. So without making a sound, without breathing heavy or crying, I thought it was the last time I was going to see my mother, and looking at her, at the sad, ashen bag of bones she'd become, I took a moment to love her more than hate who she'd become. Then Eric put his arm around my shoulder, led me to the door, unlocked the locks, and we walked out of our apartment, down the stairs, outside. There weren't any other mothers, any other truths but this one for me.

V

The hate I gained was simple and pure, the water of all hate, a level of hatred only accessible to a child abandoned by his creator, a hatred that after it is formed doesn't need fuel or reasons to remain and grow. Maybe my mother first turned to crack because I was getting older and my maturity and independence caused her to feel useless and discarded, or maybe she was just looking for something other than me to give her a reason to breathe. Or maybe she began by simply looking for some fun, or perhaps, just once, she gave in to a grave craving for a momentary escape. I don't know. But whatever the reason was it didn't matter to me. That is, what most mattered to me is three weeks after Donnel didn't let her leave our apartment, she was back at it again, smoking crack, claiming she was clean. My grandmother was the one who most believed her lies. Admittedly, I, for some time, believed them too. But then, there are only so many times I could come home and find my mother sitting on the couch, hurrying to hide a pipe beneath her leg or under the cushions or tightly gripped

in her fist, those fumbling, hasty attempts followed by my mother looking up, smiling at me like a little girl posing for a picture or solemnly
pretending she was watching the TV. How could I not know the diesel
smell hovering in the room? Did she think I didn't know the difference between a lie and the truth? My mother stopped taking care of
her hair. She gnawed her fingernails to nubs of blood. And each feature
of her face from her eyes and eyebrows to her nostrils and the shallow
dimple on her left cheek was destitute. So I knew who she was. And
my grandma knew. And when my grandma stopped denying it and my
mother disappeared one day and did not return the following morning,
my grandma changed the deadbolt lock on the door. I came home from
school and had to knock to be let in.

"Who is it?" shouted my grandma from the other side.

"It's me, Abraham," I said. "My key ain't working."

My grandmother unlocked and opened the door but she didn't say
hello or explain what she had done. She pressed her eyes on me then
ordered me to join her in the kitchen. Mr. Goines was there, sitting
at the table, drinking a cup of coffee, a couple of screwdrivers, some
screws, and the door's previous deadbolt in front of him. We said hello.
Then he shifted his eyes to my grandma and said, "Let me get going. I
got some things to do."

He finished his last swallow of coffee and stood.

"I'll walk you to the door," my grandma said.

Then she looked at me. In the minute I'd come home her eyes had
grown from the heat she pressed on me to a gaze that pulled me in,
even kissed me on the cheek and breathed in my ears.

"Abraham," she said. "Do me a favor and finish washing these dishes."

There was too much weight in the room, too much grief for me to
possess the capacity to sigh, let alone protest. So I said good-bye to Mr.
Goines and when they walked out of the kitchen, I went to the sink,

turned on the faucet, and began washing dishes with the old green sponge. When my grandma returned she did not speak right away, so I assumed the disposition of a good soldier, washing the dishes because she had given me an order and continuing until she told me to do otherwise.

"Abraham," she finally said, her voice a trumpet steadily rising over the sound of running water. "Your mother ain't coming home. No more. Not until she gets herself together forever." She paused. "Abraham, look at me. Stop washing those dishes. Turn around."

Here was her order. Without hesitating, I turned off the water and turned around. As if she tore her tears out and held her crying in her fists, my grandma's hands were balled at her sides. And her eyebrows were crooked stiches. Clearly, inside she was aflame, bleeding.

"So when she comes back," she continued. "Don't go opening that door. Don't even think about it. Let her bang until her fists bleed. This is my home and I'm the one who decides who's in and who's out. Do you hear me? Abraham, you listening?"

I swallowed. I had never heard words so clearly in my life. "Grans," I said. "Do what you gotta do."

"I'm gonna pray, Abraham," she said. "That's it. That's all there's left to do."

Suddenly, struck by some clap of intestinal, maternal pain, my grandma winced. Then she shook her head, took a deep breath, and, as if building herself taller cell by cell, vertebra by vertebra, she pushed her shoulders back and lifted her chin.

"And do you want to know why I'm gonna pray?" she asked, her eyes aglow. "I'm gonna pray cause your mother ought to be able to see the man you're gonna be. And your mother's a fool if she can't do good so she can be there. And I ain't got to watch her be a fool. She's my daughter and I ain't got to see that."

On the morning of the last Sunday in March, just as my grandma was about to leave for church, my mother returned home, pounded on the door, and begged to be let in. Donnel was not home and my grandmother refused to let me, my Aunt Rhonda, or Eric near the door. She stood in the middle of the room, her arms out at her sides as if she were halting everything behind her. My mother banged all morning. Then she left, only to return and bang in the middle of the day, and then again, late into the night. She cried and screamed and swore to Jesus she wanted to be clean. And she called my name. *Abraham,* she shouted. *Please, baby. Please let your mother in.* But my grandma made sure no one moved to open the door. She reminded us who was in charge. She responded to none of my mother's pleas no matter how her begging and pounding tortured us.

"Momma, Jesus," complained my Aunt Rhonda. "Please. I can't take it! Just give her one more chance."

"Shut your mouth!" my grandma ordered. "This place ain't no coffin! And it ain't no hospital for people who're set on killing themselves. No. Not me. That's not what I'm gonna let this home be!"

VI

It was April, spring break, and I had a week off from school. The sun was out. The sky was perfectly blue and perfectly clear. Seagulls honked, pigeons cooed; a few birds I'd never heard sang like frolicking children in a city pool. With my basketball, I walked out of my building. A small brown bird with a red chest was perched on the nearest telephone wire. A robin, *Turdus migratorius.* Mr. Goines had told me about them. I stopped and watched the robin for a few moments. Then I picked up a piece of gravel and threw it at the bird, missing it but causing it to fly away.

I continued walking. It was 7:00 a.m., early enough for me to be sure that there wasn't going to be anyone at the basketball court. I walked along the avenue dribbling my basketball, bouncing it from my left hand to my right, between my legs, and around my back. I passed the liquor store, the bodega, and the Holy Name, Pastor Ramsey's dilapidated storefront church that had not held a service since Jeremiah's funeral. It's doors and windows were covered by a rusted steel gate. I made moves, spin moves and crossovers to get past the world around me. I went around the garbage can overflowing with garbage, a sodden cardboard box of discarded housewares, rusted pots, pans, and a toaster sitting in the middle of the sidewalk. I dribbled around shadows, faked out broken glass, and pounded the ball between cracks in the concrete. I imagined I was on my way to a championship game. I created the entire scenario, fantasized about the season that had led to that imagined game. My team? We were the underdogs. But I possessed a particular conviction, an imagined fact that let me know my team would win the game. It was our time to rise up. Nothing, not even fate could stop us.

Just behind Ever there were railroad tracks, and a train heading into Manhattan from Long Island rumbled by. I stopped dribbling and watched it. All of my life, trains had been coming and going, interrupting Ever's daily life with their loud disregard. Sometimes I counted the cars. Sometimes I wondered who was on the other side of the glinting windows. But on that morning, I did something that I don't recall ever doing, although I might have done it when I was a very small child. I waved. I don't know why, but I felt a sudden urge to be recognized. So I raised my hand over my head and wagged it back and forth, and only when the train was no longer in sight did I lower it and start walking and dribbling my basketball again.

When I got close to the basketball court, I saw that there was someone sitting against the inside of the fence. I stopped. I planted the ball on my hip. I squinted. But I couldn't make out the person. So, slowly, I walked forward until I crossed the line between blurry vision and clarity. The person sitting against the fence was a woman. I took two more steps. Then, although I couldn't see all of her features, although I couldn't make out the exact beginnings and endings of her nose or her lips and mouth, I knew that the woman, the body slumped against the fence, was my mother because I knew her shapes, how those shapes rested, and the body inside of her body, that body I spent nine months inside and grew up grabbing and clinging to. It was a miracle. I had not seen her all summer and through the fall, seven months. It was grief. And seeing her was also finding out that seven months meant nothing when compared to the pain of seeing her right then.

My mother's arms were spread and her fingers were hooked in the fence. Her head was tilted. The sun shone on her. And she was soaking it in, bathing in the warmth and light as if it were a lover kissing her neck and the underside of her chin. I took a few more steps. Then I stopped. I didn't want to believe it was her, but I had no doubt. She loved the sun and the summer. She loved wearing tank tops and looking in the mirror at how brown her shoulders got after a day of being outside. She had a soiled grey coat on that I'd never seen before and it was unzipped. Suddenly, I remembered how, when I was young, my mother never let me go outside with my coat open, how she used to say *Ain't no one gonna think I'm sending my baby out to catch a cold and die.* For a fleeting moment, I wanted to go to her, zip her coat, and carry her home. Then I thought about my grandma, and what she might say or do; how would she handle the sudden discovery of my mother? I dribbled my ball once. Then I returned my ball to its station on my hip. Why was my mother on my court on a morning that was mine?

I considered throwing my ball at her, hurling it into the fence so the impact, the rattle of the ball crashing into the rusted fence would scare her, cause her to leap to her feet and run for her life. And then, there was the part of me that wanted to press the basketball against my stomach, curl over the ball like a shell and squeeze it until everything, even me, disappeared. But I didn't move. The shock of seeing my mother paralyzed me. I stood with the ball on my hip for a long time. I stared, glared; my eyes burned before I blinked.

She didn't feel my gaze. She didn't glance over her shoulders with the sense that someone was there. All my mother knew was the sun. She rolled her head from one side of the coat's thick collar to the other. She dragged her arm under her nose. She hooked her fingers in the fence again and tilted her head back, her arms spread. Yet, because she was either at the end of a high or in the slow syrup before the rush of its beginning, there was nothing wanting about her pose. All of her wishes were sated. All of her wounds were tended to. I thought about going over and talking to her, sitting beside her, resting my head in her lap like I did when I was a little kid because although she was a crackhead and desperate, although I could muster no more love than numb hate, she was my mother, the sanctuary and savior I knew before I knew life, and she, in birthing me, had presented me with my first essential freedom. Outside of the womb, a baby could be heard. She had given me voice. I wanted to shout. I wanted to weep, wail, testify. I wanted to call down the sky, turn off the sun. With my voice, I wanted to lift Ever up, shake it free, then lay it back down, carefully place it where and how it should be. I wanted to run to her, sing to her, whisper *I love you* in her ear.

But I couldn't. I had nothing to say, no song to sing. I owned not a single word, not a guttural syllable. No matter what I claimed, what I learned in school, how I loved to jump and run, how I played basketball for hours with friends, and alone in the dark of night against imaginary defenders, no matter how I watched TV for hours: I was not free. The absence of my creators enslaved me. And not just me; there were armies of brothers, so many children, like me. So I did what I had to do. I did what plenty of other brothers did too. I looked down, spit on the ground, and stopped myself from crying. Hell no; Lord knows, I would not break. From then on, I would be a dam; a dam that dammed a dam. Nothing would leak from me. Nothing would slip in.

VII

On December 18th, 1996, a week shy of Christmas, my mother was found dead behind my building, stabbed three times, once in the chest, once in the neck, and once in the soft spot at the back of her head. She was twenty-seven and it happened late at night, and her body wasn't found until early in the morning, just when the sun was lifting the cold off Queens. I was fourteen, a freshman, and I was on my way to school. I came out of my building and saw the police cars and the first and only thing I thought was: here we go again; once more, they're giving someone a hard time. So I cursed them. Then I jammed my hands into my coat pockets and followed the puffs of my breath to school. My mother was found facedown, stuck in a frozen pool of her own blood, and the police had to pour hot water on her so they could peel her from the concrete. They never caught who killed her. If asked, I would have bet they didn't even try. She was a crackhead. So they probably thought the world was better off without her.

My grandma was the one to go down to the morgue and identify my mother's body and when she came home, she turned the TV off, stood in the middle of the room, and calmly told me where she'd been.

"Abraham," she said. "Your mother's gone to join Jesus. May God have mercy on her soul."

My grandma turned on the TV again, slowly walked to her room, and closed the door. I sat silent on the couch. The five o'clock news was on and the meteorologist was giving the weather report. The next day was going to be a beautiful day, not a cloud in the sky over the entire East Coast from Florida to Maine. Suddenly, my grandma began to wail as if all of her organs were squeezing through her pores, fighting, clawing, and jamming their way through holes too small for anything other than a bead of sweat to slip through. I couldn't take the sound, the grinding howl of a hymn incongruously interrupted by coughs and gasps for air. Without thinking of anything, I stood up and walked the four steps across the room to my grandma's door. I didn't knock on the door when I got there. I didn't pause or hesitate. I gripped the knob, turned it, and walked in.

My grandma was on the floor in the fetal position by the foot of the bed. Her red, ankle-length winter coat was still on. She looked like a lump of clotted blood. She shivered and buckled. She choked. She heaved. She wheezed. She didn't notice I was there. I looked down at her and thought: my mother is dead.

I was an orphan. And there was my grandma: broken on the floor. I lay down behind her and wrapped my arm around her, spooned her as if she were my wife, the woman I loved, the woman I would forever die for. I held my grandma as best as I could. I held her so she knew I was there, so she knew I wasn't leaving.

"Shhh," I whispered. "Shhh."

"My baby," my grandma wept. "My little girl."

She punched the floor with the side of her fist.

"Why?" she screamed. "Why?"

She wrenched her body as if she were trying to bore herself into the floor. I strained to keep my arm over her. I refused to let her go. In her crying, everything my grandma had in her body, everything she'd ever swallowed and held in, everything that had ever plagued her and abused her and offered her only silence when she demanded justifications and answers broke out.

The door opened. I glanced over my shoulder. Donnel came into the apartment. He walked toward us. Then he stopped behind me, a step from the doorway of my grandma's room.

"Nigga," he whispered sadly.

Donnel knew what happened. He knew my mother was dead. Never in my life had I seen him look so feeble. His firm, full lips bent. Donnel was headstrong, arrogant in his assumption of immortality and defiant when confronted with talk of death, but there, looking over my grandmother and me, he was not just confronted by death, he was absorbed by it. My grandma quaked. She erupted. She screamed in tongues. Once again, she was overtaken by wretchedness and rage. Her crying was the siren of a woman drowning in fire, gulping for air, kicking, flailing, so damn desperate. Donnel looked left, then right. I feared he was going to leave. I couldn't watch him. I turned my face and pressed it into my grandma's back. I clenched my eyes and squeezed her as tightly as I could. Then Donnel was on his knees behind me. Then he lay across my grandma and me, wrapped us, enveloped us, held us in his arms.

"I got you," he said. "Don't worry. I got you."

BAR 6
Timbuktu

I

The alarm clock blared rap music, but its off button was broken so I fought out of sleep and pulled its plug from the wall. Then, as if gathered by a hopeless breeze determined to be hopeful, I sat up, put my feet on the floor, rubbed my eyes and face, and mentally prepared myself to rise from bed. It was Tuesday, January 21, 1997, the day after Martin Luther King Day. Behind me, Donnel slept with his back to me. And on the floor on the other side of the bed, just feet from the white wall, Eric slept on the kid-sized mattress. They breathed deeply. Their sound balanced between snoring and the wind of last breaths. It was 6:00 a.m. Eric was still officially enrolled in school but never attended. Donnel and the notion of school were as foreign to each other as snow and fire. Then there was me. I was getting up. And even if I stood and collapsed, I'd stand again. I had to go to school. It was inexplicable. I would have sworn I never learned anything. And I would have passed a polygraph when saying I hated it, despised everything about school from the way the broken bell didn't ring but rattled between periods to the teachers, all of them, from the exuberant, white neophytes who came to save every brown child in the room to the black ones, those whose conviction swelled when confronted by the tumultuous brown sea that could be their children and those whose frustration seemed to drown them. Yet there was something inside of me, some dogged compulsion that made it a moral imperative for me to be in school. Was it my subconscious, those promises I made my grandma and my mother? Was it the memories of those nights I sat up with my mother doing my homework? Or was it the absence of Nice? Was it because I wanted to be a basketball star just like him? I didn't know. Maybe that's why I was going. Because I was full of questions and voids, and wasn't school the place one went to discover?

So I took a deep breath. I stood. And then that sound hit me, that thumping of a helicopter flying over Ever and the neighborhood. It was a familiar and hated sound. The police were looking for someone. Suddenly, I was a nail and that thumping was a hammer on my head. Then its spotlight crashed through the window, trampled across the floor, stomped on the bed and up the walls and left me wilted. All of my life, every whisper of my breath, the strength in my muscles, the rigidity of my bones, even the potency of my morning breath was stripped from me. I wanted to lie back down, curl into a ball, and pull the covers over my head. I wanted to bury myself. Because that thumping and spotlight caused me to recall that afternoon when Lindbergh gave my mother and me one of his helicopters while we waited for the bus when I was six and so sick I coughed and spit green mud. Once again, as if it were a fact I didn't already own, I knew my mother was dead. And my grandma had her shift changed at work so I also knew that she had left for work an hour earlier. And my Aunt Rhonda had gotten a job working the overnight shift for the city cleaning buses so I knew that she was not home either. So it was just us, Donnel, Eric, me, and that police helicopter and spotlight thumping us, three young men who had no say in when they had to be men. And perhaps there it was, the reason why I had to go. I wasn't fearless like Donnel. And I didn't have Eric's imagination so I couldn't lose myself in fantastical cartoons and superheroes scribbled in a notebook. I needed a say, a voice. And maybe school was where I'd find it. So school it was. But then I didn't think that my attendance might change anything. It was simpler, more basic and naïve than that. There was a basketball team and a chair for me, a place to sit near a window to look out of. So for periods of forty-eight minutes I could get away. I could be. And I could want. And I could open my notebook and write about each one and it would look like I was taking copious notes, like I really wanted to be there, like I was some hungry student, which, in the end, in my heart of hearts, beneath all of my sadness and frustration and any of the refusing I might have hurled and claimed, is what I really was.

I dragged my feet across the cold floor. I took the clothes I was to wear that day from the dresser, my towel from the nail on the wall, and left the room, quietly closing the door as if my slight sound might disturb my cousins.

All of the lights in the apartment were off but the approaching dawn lay blue through the room so I saw them and knew I had been mistaken. Donnel, Eric, and I were not the only ones home. Two bodies lay beneath a bedsheet on the couch. I studied the bodies. Who were they? One looked like my Aunt Rhonda. I wondered why she wasn't at work. Had she gotten off early? Had she been fired? Or had she quit? And the body beside her? All I could see was that it was the body of a man whom she had welcomed into our home like he was worthy of sleeping where we lived. I couldn't believe it, but then I could. It was not the first time I had met one of my Aunt Rhonda's newest lovers this way. Still, I stared at them. Despite my mother's death, life had not changed. It had grown no greater or worse. But because I was fourteen and caught in the throes of growing from a childish, self-centered perspective to the recognition that I was one of billions, a speck in a world of specks, the fact that everything was status quo hurt. If my mother was dead, shouldn't something have occurred? Shouldn't I at least have had an angel?

I don't know how long I stood there. And no description can describe how deeply I buried my grieving. But when the pale light of the day's first sun eased into the room and Nice's golden trophies came into view, I stared at them for a moment, then stepped toward the bathroom. Then I stopped again. Two black garbage bags and a few shoeboxes of my mother's belongings sat against the wall to the left of the front door. It had been a little more than a month since she'd died. While we slept, my grandma must have filled the bags, tied them off, then left them for someone else to muster the courage to take out. I considered the bags, then all of it, my Aunt Rhonda and the unknown man on the couch, Nice's trophies, and how my grandma must have looked filling and tying the bags and dragging them to the door. I thought nothing and everything at precisely the same time. I breathed the room in. My heart was in those bags. I looked at the trophies. It was in them too. I had to be something, somebody. But who?

I started across the room again. I shuffled my bare feet across the hard carpet and stepped onto the cold of the bathroom's linoleum floor. I turned on the light and closed the door, and squinting through the bathroom's white brightness, I pushed the opaque white plastic shower curtain out of the way and turned on the shower. Then, holding one hand beneath the water, I turned to my left, kicked the black toilet seat up, and urinated in the white porcelain bowl as I waited for the shower to get warm. In the morning cold, the shower always took too long to heat up. I stopped urinating, took my hand from beneath the shower, and looked at my reflection in the mirror above the white sink. I studied my face, scrutinized my blemishes, sought out any new pimples that had arrived on my cheeks overnight. Then I leaned back a bit. For the first time in my life, I was shocked with the sudden recognition of my own appearance. I looked at myself good and long. My face was simple, but not plain. My features were equal with each other but not necessarily balanced. My nose was not the nose of a Roman king nor was it squat, flat and rounded. Its bridge was wide; its end was a triangular drip angled slightly downward, as if casually pointing to my lips, full and thick with a subtle crest in the middle. I took a moment more to look at my lips. The top and bottom lip shared an equal weight and significance that made it seem one could not exist without the other. Gently, I pinched them together with my index finger and thumb. I tried to blow. My cheeks filled with air. Then I let my lips go and the breath rushed out. I touched my cheeks, then my cheekbones and the angle of my jaw. I looked at the reflection of my eyes, first one, then the other, each brown bulb boxed in by the fan of upper and lower eyelashes. Sometimes I was mistaken for Dominican or half Puerto Rican. Once, someone told me I must be Guyanese. Sometimes I let people's pronouncements of my ancestry become my identity. *Yeah*, I'd say, *that's it, that's exactly what I am.* What did I know? My father's sperm could have held DNA from anywhere. So if someone said I looked Haitian then maybe my father was related to Toussaint Louverture and I had revolution in my blood. And if someone said I looked Nigerian then maybe my father's father or mother or maybe his great-great-grandparents were from Lagos, the descendants of tribal leaders. And if a sister swore I had Cherokee in me because she had a grandfather who was half Cherokee so she knew the look then maybe my father's father was a full-blooded chief. All of this is to say that my ignorance made me a specific type of young man. That is, I could either see myself as a nonentity, or I could see myself as whatever I wished to be, like a star, born from the bang of nothing or a dream.

Finally, the water was warm. I stepped beneath the shower, closed my eyes, and let the water run over my head. I lifted my chin and the water ran down my face, neck, chest, and the rest of my body. I breathed. I soaped. Then there was a knock on the bathroom door. It was Donnel.

"Nigga," he said, "you in?"

I was surprised to hear him but I tried to speak as if I weren't surprised at all. "Yeah," I said, "I'm in."

The door opened. Cold air swelled into the bathroom. Then Donnel closed the door.

"I got to go," he said, peeing in the toilet.

I looked around the edge of the shower curtain. Donnel had his back to me. He was fully clothed. He wore a hooded sweatshirt, a pair of jeans. I wondered why he was awake and dressed so early in the morning. Where was he going? What did he need? He finished urinating and flushed the toilet.

"D," I scolded. "Nigga, damn!"

"Shit," he said. "Sorry. My bad."

Water pressure dissappeared and the shower became nothing more than a trickle of water. Without turning around, Donnel turned on the sink to brush his teeth, wetting his toothbrush beneath the dribble of water from the faucet. I positioned myself beneath the weak drip from the showerhead, my futile but only source of heat.

"Where you going?" I asked.

"Nowhere," he said.

"Then why you dressed?" I pressed.

"Cause," he said.

His answer wasn't good enough. I wavered on the edge of frustration. "Cause why?"

"Cause," he began. Then he erupted. His voice was loud. But it was not anger. He was demanding, ordering. He was leaving no room for me to think of anything to contradict him with. He threw the shower curtain open. He was fully clothed. I was naked.

"Cause that's it! Shit!" he shouted. "Cause what's with the questions? Cause I could walk out of here and—"

I heard the word *die* before he said it and interrupted him. "Nigga, you ain't going nowhere," I said.

"Says who?" he asked.

"Says me."

"Ain't that what Beany's sister would've said?" he asked angrily. "And what Pastor Ramsey would've told Jeremiah? Shit, ain't that what Grans would've said about Nice? And you too? Nigga, it could happen anytime."

"I'm talking about right now," I said. "You ain't going. Get back in bed. Go to sleep."

There was a moment of silence and I realized I was naked. But my nudity was not why I was silent. I could not believe I gave Donnel an order. Suddenly, I was nervous. What was he going to do? How would he respond? He was silent. Was he preparing to lash out at me, strike me? I snatched my towel from its place draped over the top of the curtain rod and wrapped it around my waist. The bathroom wasn't big enough for two people to stand in unless one's ass was pressed against the sink while the other stood with his calves pressed against the side of the bathtub and they were kissing passionately, clearly on their way to making love.

"Move," I ordered.

A thin veil of steam hung in the air between Donnel and me. He reached his hand up and tried to touch my face but I flinched and pulled my head back. He responded calmly. A short breath of laughter fell from him. Then he placed his hand on the side of my neck.

"Always," he whispered. "Always remember, you loved."

II

I put on my black winter coat, my Yankee cap, and shouldered my backpack. I felt exhausted. Leaving our apartment, my hands jammed in the pockets of my coat, my chin tucked behind the zipped collar, my Yankee cap pulled down tight and twisted a bit to the right, my bones were water, my muscles, air. I walked along Columbus Avenue, kept my eyes on the few feet of concrete directly before me. I could not look up. I did not meet a face, a pair of eyes, my reflection in a window, or the distance before me. By the time I had come out of the bathroom, Donnel was gone.

I came to a line, a river of teenagers against a fence, determinations waiting, deserving; wonders, marvels, freaks, virtuosos. It was cold. Some made fists and blew their breath through them. Some bounced on their toes to stay warm. Others laughed and talked and breathed flowers of breath. Some took drags off cigarettes. There were young men smacked with too much cologne and young women sharing cups of hot chocolate, tea, and coffee. Some were huddled together, others stood a step away from the crowd.

Before us stood our high school, a three-story redbrick building with windows that were covered by metal grates, ceilings that leaked, rats and roaches that went where they pleased, and textbooks that were torn, scribbled upon, and populated by references and innuendos that implied our ancestral history was not worth being studied until Africans were "discovered." To our right, walking past us along the edge of the sidewalk, went our teachers, one by one and in small groups, those whose hopeless idealism made them romantic and slightly delusional, those who gave passionate rants against right-wing politics, those who empathized too much and not enough, those who believed our attendance was necessary no matter how improperly guided and ill provided our education was, and those who came solely for the paycheck and their beloved, unequaled vacation time. As for how we, the students, felt about our school, the general sentiment was: who were we to complain? School had always been this way, even worse for our parents and grandparents. So the injustice was not just what our generation got. It was our culture; that is, it was the only history we were exposed to.

Titty, Yusef, and Precious stood at the back of the line. I greeted them and then traced my eyes along the length of students.

"What's this about?" I asked.

For a moment, they said nothing. Then, working chewing gum with his back teeth and looking straight ahead, Yusef said: "Metal detectors ain't working."

"They searching niggas by hand," added Titty.

Yusef spit his gum out. "Slavery," he huffed. "That's what this shit is."

"How long you all been waiting?" I asked.

"Forever," said Yusef. "For far too fucking long."

III

With the thirty-five other students in my third period World History class, I was jammed in, squeezed beside, and confined by walls of cinderblock painted pale green. We had a total of fourteen incongruous textbooks. All were published before we were born, so some of the maps, country names, and truths were wrong. They remained stacked on our teacher's bowed metal desk. There were twenty desks. I was one of the privileged who got to sit by himself at one. I sat in the back left corner, the seat closest to the soot-streaked, metal-grate-covered window that fractured but did not thwart the near noon sun beaming across the warped wood floor. At the front of the room stood our teacher, Mr. Cullen, a heavyset, ruddy-faced fifty-something-year-old Irish man who addressed each student in class by his or her surname and savored junk food like every Oreo was a purveyor of perpetual strength, each M&M a capsule of the fountain of youth, every potato chip an endless oral orgasm that didn't leave him drowsy. He leaned against the dusty chalkboard and read from the handout he had passed around the room. It was a photocopy of a newspaper article from the previous Friday. Bill Cosby's son, Ennis, had been murdered on the side of a Los Angeles highway.

"You mean some white nigga killed Theo?" exploded Taquanna, who was even louder and more caustic than she was when we were children, and whose body and disposition had become a stack of broken bass speakers: a big square body, a big square head with square eyes, and a square mouth that radiated squelchy pounding.

"You stupid," sighed Precious, sitting beside Titty at the desk in front of me.

"What you mean I'm stupid?" snapped Taquanna, swiveling around in her seat beside Kaya at the front of the room. "You the nigga who's dumb! Ain't Theo Bill Cosby's son?"

"This is his real son," said Mr. Cullen.

"Why niggas always got to get shot?" Kitchen asked from the last seat in the row next to me.

"Cause that's the way it is," announced Yusef.

"It's racist," Kitchen decided, settling on the label he assigned everything that was either inhumane or difficult to explain.

"Bill Cosby's son?" asked Titty, returning from a daydream so just realizing the topic of conversation. He swigged from a bottle of orange soda, his face the same round baby face of his youth, still flabby and fat but adorned with a faint moustache. "I thought the Huxtables was rich."

"Nigga, ain't no money protect no niggas from getting killed," said Yusef. "Look at Tupac. Ain't none of us safe."

"He in a gang or something?" asked Taquanna.

"Theo wasn't in no gang," Titty dismissed, his brow and eyes folded like fabric.

"Ennis," corrected Mr. Cullen. "This is Bill Cosby's real son."

"So you saying only *real* niggas get killed?" Precious asked. "Like Martin Luther King?"

"No," said Mr. Cullen. "I'm saying—"

"Like Jeremiah?" burst Titty.

"Who?" said Mr. Cullen.

"My cousin," said Titty. "That nigga was a angel."

There was a moment of silence in which we were not students in a classroom but witnesses, survivors of perpetual funeral processions. Who would survive that day, that year? Who would live to twenty, twenty-five, fifty? How many of us would be blessed with death by natural causes? Mr. Cullen took his always present can of diet soda from the blackboard's chalk shelf and sipped its plastic straw.

"So why we reading this?" Taquanna demanded, waving her handout in the air as if desperate to surrender. "Why I got to care?"

"We surrounded by enemies," Yusef sadly surmised. "A nigga can't even be rich and not get killed."

"Even Cosby's real son," said Precious, shaking his head. "I thought white people loved Bill Cosby. He's on TV and everything."

"So what's the solution?" Mr. Cullen asked, his voice tinged with apathy.

"Solution?" Taquanna crashed. "There ain't no solution to people acting stupid."

"You tell us," Yusef told Mr. Cullen in an accusatorial tone, scoffing at the possibility that a man from Long Island who always smelled like fresh-cut grass could grasp what murder meant. "You the one who's white. Ain't none of you getting shot."

Mr. Cullen glanced at Yusef then decided to ignore his provocation. "Come on," he begged everyone in the room. "Are you just going to say people kill each other? That's it? No, there's got to be a way. Take a second. Imagine you're the mayor of a city where there is a high murder rate. Better yet, imagine you're the president. Tell me. How do we stop young men from killing each other?"

"We don't," said Taquanna. "I mean please, shit. It ain't like you can teach someone not to do it."

"Why not?" Mr. Cullen asked.

"Cause you just can't," Taquanna said. "I mean everyone knows it ain't right. But that don't stop them."

"You got to teach people who they are," announced Kaya from her seat at the front of the room. "Like Timbuktu."

"That ain't no real place," said Kitchen.

"Yeah it is," said Kaya. She looked at our teacher. "Mr. Cullen, ain't Timbuktu real?"

Suddenly, the bell rang and everyone leapt from his or her seat, the squeak and screech of our desks and chairs trumpeting our rush to exit.

"Wait! Wait!" Mr. Cullen shouted, waving his hands over his head, his voice swallowed by our sound, the sound of students exiting other classes, and our collective echo pouring through the hallway. "You tell me! Ladies! Gentlemen! For homework! Timbuktu! Tomorrow, be prepared to tell me if Timbuktu is true."

IV

Without a doubt, our table was the loudest, most dramatic table in the cafeteria. Sure, other tables had their rumblings, their occasional disputes, their celebrations. But our explosions were a daily happening. We exploded in political, cultural, and economic discussion. And in irrelevant ones. We clashed over who was the most beautiful sister. We boomed about rap music. Some accused while others denied. The salacious happenings at school, who breathed heavy on who, who was humbled by a cold shoulder, and who mistook five minutes of unsatisfying sex in the school boiler room or topmost stairwell plateau for making slow and sweaty love all night long: we made it all a jubilee. We were the rowdiest waltzers at the dance. We spoke with tongues of Christmases and Fourth of Julys. We were Ever Park brothers, revolutions in the name of an imperative cause. We sat jammed together. Elbows, plastic trays, and the remnants of eaten food, wrappers, tinfoil, balled napkins, and plastic utensils covered the table. We ate. We talked. We breathed. Precious sat at the outside corner of the table. Titty sat across from him. Yusef sat to Titty's left. I sat to his.

Titty reached in front of Yusef's face and snatched a handful of French fries from my Styrofoam tray.

"No ketchup?" he asked.

"Nigga," scolded Precious, ignoring Titty's thievery, his shining brown eyes pinned on me. "Who eats fries with no ketchup?"

"I do," I said.

"Shut your face!" Precious said, his eyes wide. "You don't eat no fries with no ketchup."

"How do you know?" asked Yusef, coming to my defense.

"Because I seen him," Precious said.

"When?" said Yusef, pushing his glasses back on his nose then folding his arms across his chest.

"McDonald's," Titty mumbled, his mouth full of food.

"McDonald's?" Yusef said, his voice shrill with surprise. "That big imperial bitch? Nigga, I've never eaten McDonald's in my life!"

"Not you," said Titty. "Abraham."

"Liar!" bellowed Kitchen, sitting to my left, his face weathered, pimpled and pocked from having to shave against the grain of the thick, rough beard that covered his face in order to earn the smooth skin everyone our age owned.

"Who's a liar?" said Yusef.

"You!" said Precious. "You just ate McDonald's yesterday."

"Nigga," said Yusef. "If there are two things I don't eat, it's fast food and pussy!"

"Liar!" said Kitchen again, pounding his thick hand on the table. "Liar!"

Suddenly I recalled that I didn't do the homework for math class and I looked at Yusef.

"What?" he asked.

"You got the math?" I asked.

A mischievous smile seeped across Yusef's face. "Kaya's got it," he said.

Everyone at our table went silent. Kaya King had become my month of March, lion and lamb, the cusp of spring and its irrepressible birthing; that is, whatever she wanted to do to me she did. She was my girlfriend but not my girlfriend. She liked me but didn't need me. Some days we'd have conversations that lasted for hours. Some days she wouldn't so much as sigh in my direction. Sometimes I'd smile at her. Others I couldn't stop looking at her, staring, my face blank. Kaya needed nothing to fortify her, not a single compliment nor sweet whisper, not a boyfriend, man-friend, nor child of her own. And she never had a problem making such things clear to me. She said it, walked it, and sat in class with it, the flag of a correct answer, her right hand, always primed to burst into the sky. Kaya made my tongue butter and my wants attach themselves to her wildest dreams. She was no longer that little girl I had a crush on. She was a woman. That is, she owned being. She didn't just participate, carry, or control it. Every time she settled her eyes on me a warm and deep river rose up from my soul and consumed me. My friends perceived this tension to be sexual. But what it was was the confrontation and contemplation of two determined forces weighing and measuring each other.

"You know," said Precious. "I'm getting real tired of your ass sitting back and just looking. Nigga, you need to step up and put it to Kaya. No more fucking around. It's damn near the twenty-first century. What the fuck you waiting for?"

"I ain't waiting on nothing," I shrugged.

"Nigga's scared," said Titty. "He was scared when we was little and nigga's scared now. Don't even waste your breath on him. Abraham ain't never gonna do shit. Nigga nuts in his pants just from knowing Kaya lives in Ever too."

"See," I said, shooting my eyes at Titty. "You always talking shit. But what about you?"

Titty erupted. "I tear pussies up. I beat on them like my first name's Jack and my last name's Hammer. You feel me?"

"Then tell me three parts," I laughed. "Go ahead. Name three parts of a vagina."

"Vagina?" laughed Yusef, his eyes squeezed closed and shaking his head as if trying to rid the smile from his face. "Nigga, only you would call that shit a vagina."

"Name three parts," I demanded.

"Lips," said Yusef.

"Titty," I said, making it clear my challenge was only meant for him.

Titty thought as hard as he could. He furrowed his brow then pursed his lips. "Eyes, ears, and mouth, I don't know," he listed. "Shit, what does it matter? I know what to do with the shit."

We laughed. Then, to cap off my victory and to prove I wasn't scared, and as if my mind weren't spinning, I stood up and walked toward the table where Kaya and her friends sat. Unlike our table, theirs was always clean and organized. There was never any trash, never an empty tray or wrapper or a drip of dropped food. The floor around them and beneath their feet shined. Their space was immaculate. They were immaculate. Their hair, their clothing, the gleam in their eyes; all of it was in its perfectly proper place. They were the same age as us, but there was no doubt Kaya and her friends were light years ahead. That is, we were certainly young men, but although some of us were intelligent, and some of us were physically attractive, and some of us were charming, we were immature, spontaneously unruly, brash and disorganized. And they were never afraid to let us know, highlight each of our shortcomings and identify the traits we had to aim for. Of course, we were guilty. But in defense of ourselves, we surmised that any girl and/or woman who didn't revere us was either a lesbian or an elitist. It was a weak defense, the weakest of weak defenses, but even if we were not sure we were right, we never let ourselves be wrong. We couldn't be. It was impossible. We were still alive, weren't we? And we were in school. So we were loud because we could be loud; because we had time to be loud; because it was our table and we were what the whole upcoming Black History Month was about; young, free, getting our equal education. Weren't we?

Kaya and her friends didn't see me coming, or at least it didn't seem like they did, although they might have known I was coming all along. Either way, they didn't look up or stop talking when I came near.

"You go to war," Kaya said, making eye contact with everyone at the table, "for love."

They might have been discussing something from the news or a movie, a book, or TV show. They might have been discussing a song, a ballad, Homer's *Iliad* and *Odyssey,* the creation of Islam, the spread of Christianity, patriotism, or the lyrics of a collaboration between a gruff-voiced rapper and a velvet-throated soulstress who clenched her fists and stomped her feet every time she reached deep into her chest for a high note. Or maybe they were discussing two people we knew.

"Abraham," Kaya said, suddenly looking at me and speaking with the same level of passion she'd just spoken with. "What you doing?"

I smiled, tried to play cool. "What you mean what am I doing?" I asked.

"After school," Kaya stressed. "You gonna go look up Timbuktu?"

"I don't know," I said. "You?"

"I already know it. Besides I got to read for English."

"You gonna go to the library?" I asked.

Kaya screwed her eyes at me. "What you think?"

Kaya was always at the library. She sat in the farthest cubicle from the front door and stayed there, hunched over, headphones pulsing music into her ears until all of her homework was not only finished, but written without smudge marks, crossouts, or crinkles in the page. How could I have forgotten such a thing? Suddenly, I froze. I was off balance. I stuttered. I shrugged. I feared someone, maybe Taquanna, would demand to know why I wanted to know if Kaya was going to be at the library. What did I care? And what was I doing there anyway?

Behind me, my friends exploded. They slapped the table with their hands, threw their chins in the air, laughed so hard some fell out of their chairs.

"A damn shame," Yusef called out.

"I told you nigga's scared," added Titty.

Scared? I thought. *I ain't scared of nothing.*

V

Keep your eyes closed," said our science teacher, Ms. Hakim, a young, exuberant clay color woman originally from California who once brought in her college diploma to prove to us that she graduated from Harvard. "OK. Open them."

Except for the slivers of white light cutting past the edges of the drawn window shades, everything in the class was black.

"Nightfall," said Ms. Hakim. "Now look up."

Nothing had prepared us for the sight. Some students laughed. Some giggled. Others gasped and sighed things like *damn* and *shit*. On the black ceiling there was a galaxy of glow-in-the-dark star stickers.

"Abraham," said Ms. Hakim. "Tell us. What do you see?"

I was fascinated by the sky, with stars, moons, and planets, and the far away. "To tell you the truth," I said, "I don't know what I see."

"What do you mean you don't know?" she scolded, refusing to let me off easy. "You quitting on yourself just like that? I thought you were somebody. And every somebody has an opinion! Try again."

I loved Ms. Hakim. "I mean," I said, "I don't know nothing about astronomy."

"But what do you see?" she urged. "Use your imagination! You're standing in the middle of outer space!"

"Well," I said. "If I'm in the middle of outer space then I'm a star too."

"Good," said Ms. Hakim. "Good. I hadn't thought of that. That's good. So we're all stars. Taquanna, what about you?"

"Well, first of all it's astrology, not astronomy," said Taquanna.

"OK," said Ms. Hakim. "Is it astronomy or astrology?"

"Which one is the one with the signs?" asked Yusef.

"You tell me," said Ms. Hakim.

"Astronomy is what we're looking at," decided Precious. "And astrology is the shit girls read in the paper to find out if a nigga loves them."

"Choose another word," scolded Ms. Hakim.

"Shit," Precious said. "I mean, sorry. Astrology is what girls read in the paper to find out if their nigga loves them."

"*Shit* ain't the word I was talking about," said Ms. Hakim. "Try again."

"Oh," said Precious. "My bad. Astrology is what girls read in the paper to find out if their man loves them or not."

"Thank you," said Ms. Hakim. Then she raised her voice and spoke slowly and clearly, as if she were reading the accomplishments of an award recipient. "For the next two weeks, we're going to surf celestial bodies and ethereal drift. How's that sound? Deep, right? Well it's outer space, the universe. Who thinks life is out there?"

"Definitely," said Titty. "You seen that movie *ET*?"

"If you do," continued Ms. Hakim, "then what kind of life? Is it life that we know? Or is it an alternative, extraordinary form? If yes, what do these beings endure to survive? What do they breathe? Hydrogen?

Carbon monoxide? Oxygen, like us? Are there trees in outer space? And how about if there is life on other planets, what is their capacity when it comes to love? Will they hate or love us if and when we meet? Do they even have the capacity to hate? Or are humans the only ones in this vast universe who do? And do you know that some stars, some of the biggest and brightest we see, actually died thousands of years ago? Almost like they are burning on the hope that they might be seen. Look up. Think. Tell me about the stars. Tell me. What do you see?"

VI

In front of my building, a brigade of brothers stood against the exhausted red bricks with hours to kill and breath smoking from their noses and mouths. It was late in the afternoon. The sun was just about to set. The coming evening soaked Ever in a fresh bruise. Some stood with a foot cocked behind them, the soles of their shoes pressed flat against the brick. Others stood with their arms folded across their chests. Alton Johnson stood with one foot on an old orange milk crate. Elijah had his hands jammed in his pockets. Heads were cocked to the right, tilted to the left. Ennui was postures, dispositions, faces, and fact. I said hello, slapped hands, and was teased a bit, then I hung around, eavesdropped. Talk spanned from women and no woman to jobs and no job, the government and the basketball games on TV the previous night. What happened to who? And what couldn't be believed. And what was going to be done about it. Nearly every time and no matter what the initial conversation had been about, talk always shifted into a relationship with revolution, personal revolution, familial revolution, community revolution; city; state; revolutions in other countries; monumental comebacks and reversals; last-second shots and touchdown passes; Muhammad Ali, Tommie Smith and John Carlos in the 1968 Olympics; Watts riots; Rodney King riots; the riots that should be happening in Detroit, St. Louis, New Orleans, Kings County, and Queens.

"Imagine," Elijah announced. "If a nigga became president."

"They'd kill him," said Alton. "Before a nigga even steps foot in the Oval Office, they'd shoot him in the head."

So the topic of discussion shifted to the notion that a brother might one day be president, a fantastical social leap our minds could not make without having to silence self-doubt, and the facts of our history, both as brothers in Ever and brothers in greater America.

"Shit," said Mo, a tall, slender brother in his late twenties with smooth russet skin who said everything as an exclamation. "All I know is one day rap music is gonna boom from the White House stereo! And whether or not it's a nigga or some white boy from the suburbs shit is gonna happen! America has got a hard-on for niggas! We're like the apple in Eden! First niggas hang us in trees! Then Eve plucks us. And all Adam wants is to be just like us!"

"One day Ever is gonna be historic," Elijah announced.

"Is that what you call this?" asked a short, fat, jovial brother who went by the name Moochie. "Is that what niggas are? History? Like we just standing around waiting to join the dinosaurs? Like one day some Indiana Jones is gonna come and dig up our bones and say *Wow, so this is how niggas lived?*"

Suddenly, someone came from behind and snatched me in a headlock, then wrenched and squeezed and bent me over. Brothers stopped talking. They laughed and called for me to fight back and fight back more. I fought with all of my might to get out of the clutch. I was yanked up. I was pushed down. I was a dinghy lost amidst a violent sea.

I was being drowned then saved by the same force. I flailed. I kicked. The arm around my neck tightened.

"C'mon Abraham!" shouted Alton. "Free yourself! Get out of that grip!"

I was turning blue. My lips were cold and wet and my tongue was bone dry. The strangler's wrist dug into my windpipe. I wheezed. My eyes throbbed, then swelled and sizzled. Snot leaked from my nose. The world was crusty purple and red. Brothers' faces melted into burgundy puddles during each sporadic moment I could see. I owned nothing, not even a sliver of my five senses. I smelled nothing. I tasted it. Then I felt it and saw it and heard nothing and all at once I stopped fighting and my entire body, from my eyelashes to my toes went limp.

"Who's your daddy?" the assailant asked.

I knew the voice as if it were my own. Donnel. Why was he choking me? He eased his grip. Then he shook me and squeezed his grip again.

"Nigga," he said, "I'm talking to you."

Digging deep, I uncovered a pocket of oxygen in my chest and gasped.

"I," I said.

"Nigga, what?" Donnel exploded. "Huh? Tell me. Shout it to the world! Who loves you?"

Who loved me? My grandma. My Aunt Rhonda. My Uncle Nice. Eric, I supposed. But him, Donnel? I thought so. But at that moment I wasn't sure. And the doubt caused my body to burst with rage. So I tore at Donnel's grip. I clawed at his arm. I wanted to breathe and I wanted to breathe now. I had to. Because I had to turn around and look Donnel in the eyes to see whether or not he loved me. I was desperate for that holy confirmation. But Donnel didn't give in. He didn't relax his grip or release me. He fought back and squeezed tighter. Then he leaned all of his weight on my shoulders. He was trying to buckle me, to make me succumb and crumble. I refused. I fought to remain on my feet. My legs burned. My knees quivered. I could stand. I would stand. Then I couldn't. I collapsed to the concrete. Only then did Donnel let go.

"Nigga, what you got?" he asked, bouncing back on his toes like a boxer, his fists up. "Huh? Get up. Stand and fight. Let's go."

I had nothing. He was relentless. I was too exhausted, too hurt to even look up. I remained on my hands and knees, burning and aching. My throat ablaze, crushed. I breathed deeply, filling my body with air. But I didn't rub my neck or let myself grimace. I wouldn't allow anyone the satisfaction of witnessing pain as a part of me. I looked down at the concrete and considered all of the ways I could respond; the things I could but shouldn't say, how I could charge at Donnel and swing. I could have cried if I were someone else, someone not Abraham from Ever. I cleared my throat and spit a wad of bloody phlegm on the ground. Somewhere I was bleeding. Slowly, I lifted my eyes and laid them on Donnel, hoping that it had not been him who attacked me. But it was. Why? I wondered.

I took one great deep breath and pushed myself up to my feet. Then I stared at Donnel blankly, my hands hanging at my sides, the sound of brothers teasing me a washed-out drone. Donnel wore a black hooded sweatshirt, a black winter coat, and a black baseball hat. I was hot, sweating. He bounced forward and snapped a jab that came within an inch of my face. Then he bounced back on his toes. What had he come for? Why had he chosen to arrive in the manner he did?

"Throw your hands," he demanded. "Didn't I teach you to fight?"

Donnel stood still and waited for me, his fists up. A mischievous grin creased his face. Then he dropped his hands and his smile unfolded into a soft tumble of laughter.

"What's wrong?" he asked.

He reached his hand out and waited for me to slap it. I stared at

Donnel's hand and thought about leaving it there, hovering between us until it rotted and stank, or dried and turned to dust, or he ran out of the strength it took to keep it aloft. But Donnel didn't give me the time to make a decision. He looked at brothers. Then he snatched his hand away. I thought about punching him with all of my might, blasting his head open with one ferocious blow. How could he do what he'd done? How could he attack, offer peace, then leave me with nothing?

He breathed, smirked, and shook his head no. "Where you coming from?" he asked.

"Nowhere," I said.

Quickly, Donnel swung at me and his open hand clapped off the top of my head.

"Nigga," he scolded. "Be specific."

I wanted to swing back. "The library," I said.

"The library? What you doing there?"

"Reading," I said.

"Reading?" he said, smugly glancing at the others as if to prove or at least question whether or not reading was a valid answer. "About what?"

"Timbuktu," I said.

He laughed. "Timbuk-what?"

I glared at Donnel.

"Timbuktu," I said. "Where everything, everyone, even salt was pre-cious."

BAR 7

Reconstruction

I

The older I got the more difficult it became to navigate my feelings about love and loss. From one moment to the next, I never knew what I might long for or hurt inside about. My mother or Donnel. My grandma. My uncle. And then there was Kaya. All through the spring I found ways to coincidentally meet her in the library. Then I would walk her home in the evening, sometimes in silence, sometimes dribbling my basketball around her as we walked, and sometimes pouring forth a succession of bad jokes and anecdotes to make her laugh as much as to keep the subject of our conversation far from what I was thinking and feeling. But then I never knew what I needed to express. I had suppressed my core, and in response, what was most imperative went without an identity. So my emotions were colorless and weightless. They had no scent or relationship to nature. I could not describe them in concrete terms, embodied by a metaphor or simile. My emotions were arrivals and departures, nonstop insignificances speeding through a station. In other words, I felt just some things because I didn't know nor did I have the capacity to verbalize and thus understand what I most lacked. So my emotions rose inexplicably, then split and fell in separate ways. I might be enraged. I might be solemn. Then I might be thankful. I might be sincere, honest with myself when thinking about potentials and predicaments. Then I might lie; say something was unbelievable although I believed. I might blaspheme and then suddenly be righteous. I might doubt and then know everything. I was like a plastic bag caught in the air, suspended by the battering of opposing winds. My grandma said it was my hormones, that they were making me real impossible; a motherfucker, a son of a bitch, just like one of those lunatics they lock up. "Abraham," she said. "What's gotten into you?"

The same question was applicable to her. That is, if I had lost my mind then so had she. Because Mr. Goines had become a sudden fixture in our apartment. He sat on the couch and talked at the TV during sitcoms and Knicks games. He ate at the kitchen table with a newspaper open before him and criticized the news to anyone who was near. He wrote ideas out on legal pads, page after page, his faux tortoiseshell glasses crooked. Everything, all of their seemingly heavenly and holy love affair, all of the perfect excitement my grandma swelled with over Mr. Goines's visits and overnight stays, how he slept in her bed and he and she would kiss, gently, like fish, made my stomach twist. Because I feared for my grandma but I also wanted her to be loved and happy. So I watched Mr. Goines's every move. And when she and he were near each other, I made sure to see if he loved her enough. It seemed he did. Even when they argued, he was respectful, calling her *Honey, Sweet lady, Baby* when he addressed her accusations.

But that didn't mean I trusted Mr. Goines, or, for that matter, wanted him in our home. Because I didn't. And because more than my mistrust of him, his presence poked holes in and deflated Donnel. I saw it in his face and all over his body. Of course, he said nothing about it. He didn't tell me or Eric or my Aunt Rhonda that he didn't want Mr. Goines coming around. He didn't talk to Mr. Goines more than a mumbled yes or no. Sometimes when Mr. Goines was there before Donnel came home, Donnel kept his head down and left within an hour. And when he disappeared, his absences were longer. And so no longer was it only that I rarely saw Donnel, but when I did see him, he didn't look me in the face nor let his eyes rest on anything too long. He was nineteen and he had considered himself to be the man of our home for a long time. But now it seemed a man had come to take his place. So he must have felt as if he was being pushed out. So he responded by acting as if he was running away. But not running to something; running as if he was chased, hunted and hounded, preyed upon by everything from the sun to the night, from the air he breathed to everyone, even me.

I didn't know how to handle it. I didn't know what to do, whom to align myself with. And then one October evening my grandma and I argued about nothing important, something as insignificant as whether or not it had rained on a Monday weeks before, and then Mr. Goines inserted himself into the argument, so I argued with him. Then I argued with my aunt and my grandma and Mr. Goines at the same time and punched the wall in my room, goring a six-inch wound in the drywall. Then I stormed out of the apartment, stomping down the stairs, each step echoing through the stairwell, my hand throbbing, my knuckles bloodied.

So I had been out since the evening, walking up and down blocks without stopping. And it was near midnight, drizzling after raining all day. I was tired and my feet hurt. The small of my back was tight and sore. But, as if the sound were the Morse code of me, I was still pounding my feet. I was on Columbus Avenue, my hands jammed in the pockets of my coat, my hat pulled low over my eyes. I kept my eyes on the concrete in front of me. I believed I would never stop. I would walk forever. I would follow the streets until they reached a sea that I would storm across too.

Then I heard the drumming of a ball and I stopped. I looked up. I was a half block from the basketball court. I walked to it. There, two little brothers played one-on-one at the far side. The rain made the concrete court gleam. The little brothers dribbled the ball. The sound was wet slaps. They shouted at each other. They laughed and shot at a rusted rim they could barely see. The cuffs of their too-long jeans and coat sleeves were soaked. They pushed their sleeves up their arms, past their elbows. Moments later, the cuffs gave in, slipped down over their hands again.

I crossed the street, walked around the fence, and sat on top of the back of the bench farthest from them. Water soaked through my jeans and sent a shiver along my spine. I hadn't been to school in a week. It was coming up on a year since my mother had died. My ability to rise from bed and shower was intact. But walking to school and sitting in classrooms were gone. I spent my days in the library, at the park, and when my grandma and my Aunt Rhonda were at work, in our apartment. I wondered what did a year since my mother died mean. Titty, Precious, and Yusef tried to talk to me. And Ms. Hakim called and made me promise to be in school on Monday. I hadn't made the decision to drop out. I thought I would eventually go back. So it was not my absence from school, nor the argument I had with my grandma, nor the throbbing of my fist that consumed me. It was thinking about my mother and one question: What about Donnel? *What about him?* Was he next?—the question caused me to drift about in a state of incendiary disarray and ignorance. That is, I had come to a mortal decision, a crossroads, the end of a plank. I was fifteen, at the start of my sophomore year. Was I thinking about Donnel because I was to follow him? Or was I thinking about Donnel the way I thought about my mother? Was his absence causing me to hate him? And was it all making me feel helpless and abandoned?

I watched the young brothers playing basketball, leaping and twisting about each other like tails of fighting kites, their sneakers slapping and skidding against the wet concrete. The larger boy stopped dribbling the ball and told the smaller one to tie his shoelaces. Suddenly, a particular variation of staggering longing landed in my head and a new question engulfed me. Could my mother see me? Right then, right there; suddenly that was all I wanted to know. Since her death, had she been watching me from above? Did she know what type of young man I'd become?

"Abraham," came a woman's voice from behind me. "Abraham, that you?"

I turned to see a silhouette, but I could make out nothing more. Not even the voice gave me a clue. The woman walked from the darkness and when she came near enough, I saw that it was Luscious, her arms folded across her chest, holding a waist-length black leather coat closed.

"Abraham," she said, her face inches from the fence that separated the basketball court from the sidewalk, she from me. "What're you doing out here all by yourself?"

I shrugged. Then I tipped my head toward the young brothers playing basketball and said: "Just watching."

Luscious brought with her the smell of menthol cigarettes and perfume of a seductive yet humble nature, lavender with kick and heat. She lifted her eyes from me and watched the young brothers play for a moment.

"No matter the time, life don't change," she sighed.

"What you mean?" I asked.

As beautiful as she had always been, but with her lips parted in a sad halfhearted smile, Luscious shook her head slowly, then softly said: "I got a letter from your uncle."

I was paused with the thought. My uncle? Never once had my family heard from him since he was stripped from Ever and locked away.

Luscious's eyes welled and she whipped them away from me, from the young brothers on the basketball court, from Ever, and she aimed them as high as she could, looking into the sky without lifting her chin. A tear slipped down her face, dripped from her chin. She wiped her face with the back of her hand and laughed gently, one tumble of breath when what she clearly wanted to do was weep. The rumors about Luscious had been true. She had been with Qadisha and when they broke up, she was with other women. She held their hands. She made love to them. But what did he write? What could she possibly say? And who was she to him now? I couldn't believe he had written to her. He had never once written to us, never even a note or card for Christmas or birthdays.

Luscious lowered her gaze, lay her sodden sight on the young brothers playing basketball again. "Seven years," she said, her tense tone blurring the distinctions between anger, longing, and defeat. "I ain't heard from that man in seven years. And even after all this, after all that's happened: I still love him."

II

For weeks, my grandma and my Aunt Rhonda talked about it. For weeks, they woke up and went to bed with the fact hot on their lips. For weeks, they planned a celebration so celebratory it was not a celebration but the birth of fireworks born from a Big Bang; a universe had come to the end of its infinite patience. They discussed DJs and songs that had to be played. They argued over where the furniture should be moved so there would be room for everyone to whirl and grind and dance the way they really wished to, with their eyes closed, as if they were alone in the dark and they had sadness and evilness to whip from their limbs. Who would cook what dish? What color should the plastic forks, cups, and plates be? These were major debates and decisions. And the napkins? The tablecloths? The streamers? How about what they would wear? They argued about the colors late into the night. What about red? White would show stains. What about blue? No. This was not Valentine's Day, a wedding, or the Fourth of July. This was greater; a holier celebration of love and independence. They had to match. It all had to match; the entire festival was to be color coordinated. For weeks, there was no news on TV; no weather outside; no America, Ever, or Queens. No world beyond the joy of our home existed. Old family stories were recalled, old family photographs passed around. My grandma and my Aunt Rhonda predicted what would happen; how joyous the occasion would be; this man would certainly dance with this woman and then this other woman would certainly guzzle all of the punch and eat all of the cake and dance with all of the other men, rub her sweaty body against each and every one. And what about him and her? She and he? Thousands; that's how many would attend. Like teenage girls high on cotton candy, Coca Cola, and coffee, they couldn't contain themselves. There was no pause or slowdown. They didn't speak. They didn't enunciate. They didn't talk or discuss. They scatted; like *be-de-be-bo-bo rin-tin-tin hi-d-hi-d-ho*. They swung their hips, arms, and eyes when they moved. They cooked and washed dishes and scrubbed and mopped and dusted and wiped and cleaned the apartment from crack to crevice back to crack. They did everything, multitasked multitasking awake and asleep, simultaneously. Finally, my grandma's son, my aunt's brother, finally my uncle, lord have mercy, Nice was coming home.

Nothing could hurt us. Nothing could touch us. Nothing could take. And nothing was owed. Thanksgiving, Christmas, and New Year's passed. Then it was the spring and no bills were paid. And rent was skipped. Mr. Goines fixed the showerhead. He spackled the cracks in the walls and ceilings. He bought the lovebirds a new cage. And he gave me money so I could go to the hardware store and buy as many gallons of white paint, paintbrushes, and rollers as I could carry. Then when I came back with it all, straining to carry the gallons and plastic bags up the stairs, Mr. Goines, Donnel, Eric, and I painted the apartment. The walls, the ceilings, the doorframes; the bathroom, the bedrooms, the front room, the kitchen, he made everything shine with white.

"You see how we didn't go dripping nothing on the floor," he said pushing a firm gaze and countenance upon us and pointing at the carpet when he was done. "You all got to learn how to live like that. Responsible. Respectful. Your grandma don't got to be living with no stains no more."

That was a Thursday, and the next day Donnel vanished. He was nowhere to be found. No one, not any of his friends nor anyone else in Ever knew where he went. He was just gone. On Saturday, my grandma and my aunt asked me if I had seen him, and because I so hoped he was somewhere near and because I didn't want to disturb the incredible bliss of my uncle's pending homecoming, I said I saw him on Friday walking with some girl.

"What chick?" said my Aunt Rhonda, saying *chick* with a severity meant to emphasize that whomever he was with was not worthy of her son. "He ain't never said nothing about having no girl."

"I never seen her before," I said.

My Aunt Rhonda screwed her face. She didn't believe me. "She ain't from Ever?"

"He'll turn up," my grandma decided. "Don't worry. Sooner or later he's gonna have to change his drawers."

Compared to the incredible bliss of my uncle's pending homecoming, Donnel's absence seemed minor. In fact, after I told them that I saw him they seemed not to care. After all, Donnel was twenty, old enough to vote and fight in a war. So it was as if Donnel were some trivial, lost trinket that would turn up when and where they least expected. Maybe on Sunday, or maybe Monday. But if not on Monday, then Tuesday, and if not Tuesday then Wednesday. But if not by Wednesday then they'd call the police precinct to see if any black twenty-year-old male named Donnel Singleton had been apprehended or admitted to a nearby hospital because he had to be home by Thursday. Because Friday was the day my uncle was coming home.

But it didn't get that far. In the middle of Sunday night, Donnel shook me awake and demanded that I go to the roof with him.

"D," I said, my voice loud, my eyes blinking like he was a cloudy apparition. "Where you been?"

"Shh," he scolded. "Shut up. Just meet me on the roof."

Donnel turned and walked out of our room, leaving the door open behind himself. My heart pounded. As fast and as quietly as I could, I put on my jeans and grabbed my sweatshirt. Then I jammed my feet into my sneakers and hurried out of the room. But when I walked out of the room, he was already gone. Something made me stop before running. My keys. What if we got locked out? I couldn't let that happen. I slapped my hands on the front of my jeans to make sure my keys were in my pocket. They were. So I left too, making sure to close the door as quietly as I could.

I went to the elevator. The faint green L in the black circle by the buttons indicated that the elevator was at the lobby. I pushed the button. A second passed. I heard the elevator begin to move. But it was always too slow. And I had no patience. I could not stand there and wait to begin my ascent. And I thought that Donnel must have taken the stairs because the elevator was already below us and it never traveled that fast. So I ran to the stairwell, opened the door, and began to climb. The stairwell was so dark I might as well have been sinking in ink. My mind was electric, awake, but my body was still half asleep so I misstepped, tripped, and smashed my shins on the edge of the stairs. At another time, I would have paid attention to the pain. I would have lifted my jeans and checked for bleeding or how big the bumps had already bloomed. But nothing would stop me from catching up with Donnel. So I rushed to my feet and hurried faster up the stairs. I went all the way up without stopping. I never once put my hand on a railing. And when there were no stairs left to climb, I pushed open the roof's steel door.

Donnel stood at the edge of the roof. His back to me, his hands planted on the ledge, he looked down at the street. The first thing I thought was that he was going to jump.

"D," I shouted. "What're you doing?"

Donnel didn't move. So I ran to him. But after three strides, he turned around and laughed, and the sound of his laughter stopped me in my tracks.

"What's so funny?" I asked.

"You," he said.

"Me? Nigga, where you been?"

Donnel smiled the wide, all encompassing, and limitless smile of a child. Then he turned around and pointed at the night sky. "There," he said.

I looked over his shoulder, traced my eyes along his arm to the tip of his finger, and then followed his finger to what he pointed at. In the distance were the moon and the stars, and the lights from a few planes moseying across the black sky.

"Outer space?" I said. "Nigga, I'm serious."

He dropped his arm, turned around, and set his eyes on me. "Me too," he said. "I flew."

I shifted my eyes from him back to the sky.

"In a plane," he added. "First class too. Niggas thought I was some sort of rap star and everything. Gave me free drinks. Leather seats damn near big as our bed."

"Get the fuck out of here," I said.

I didn't believe him. I looked at him hard. In one of those steel birds that went silent and smooth thousands of feet above Ever? No way. Impossible.

He put his right hand over his heart and raised his left hand in the air. "Swear on Jelly," he said. "Swear on Grans, on my moms, on Eric, on any unborn kids that I might one day make."

I still didn't believe him. "Then where'd you go?"

Suddenly, he was sick of my incredulity. He made a face like he was going to eat me. He sucked his teeth and shook his head no. Then, in a rush, he reached behind himself, lifted up his shirt, and pulled out a crumpled gold-colored folder that had been rolled, folded, and crammed between the top of his jeans and the small of his back.

He unfolded the folder. He walked across the roof to me.

"Atlanta," he said. He jammed the folder in my hands. "Century Twenty-one. We getting out of this motherfucker. We ain't staying in Ever forever."

I looked at the front of the folder. He huffed a gust of irritation, snatched the folder from my hands, opened it, and handed it back to me. Then he stabbed his finger at a picture of some big white house.

"Nigga," he said. "I got half that easy."

It was too dark for me to see how much the house cost, but I stared at the picture of the house, refined white columns, front porch, seemingly palatial.

"What was it like?" I asked.

"Real nice," he said. "And hot too. And the girls, nigga . . . Even the real skinny ones is sexy, bodies like melting Fudgsicles, Pudding Pops, chocolate all curvy and dripping down my hands. God damn it was beautiful!"

"No," I said. I pointed at the sky. "The plane. Flying."

Donnel dropped his eyes and thought for a few moments. Then he looked up at me. "You a virgin still?"

"What?" I said.

"You a virgin?"

"Nigga," I scolded. "What's that got to do with anything?"

"Cause if you wasn't then you'd know what flying was like," he said. "Weightless. And the only reason you know you're alive is cause your dick is half hard and your heart is bumping in your throat."

There was a moment of silence that Donnel seemed to deem dangerous, and he grabbed the folder from me, jammed it back into the back of his jeans, and put his face an inch from mine.

"Say some shit," he whispered. "Tell anyone, and I swear to God I'll kill you."

III

Eric made the invitation for the party. I wrote what needed to be said. It was a welcome home Ever Park party. My uncle was coming home; another man was going to be released. I photocopied the invitations and delivered them, slipped them under doors, passed them out on Columbus Avenue, at the basketball court, on any bus, any corner, any street I put my feet on.

"Give them to anyone you see fit," said my grandma. "And don't be too choosy. The more people the better."

I gave the invitations to Titty, Yusef, and Precious, extended members of our crew and every fine girl regardless of her religion, social ability, and whether or not I knew her name or if she already had a man. I left a stack of them in all the barbershops, the recreation center, all the liquor stores, the Chinese food hole-in-the-wall, and all churches, corner stores, and hair salons.

Then there were four days left. Then three days. Then two. I wondered who Nice would be. Certainly not the same brother who'd left. Certainly he didn't have the same wants and needs. And what did he look like? He'd left on the cusp of adulthood. What sort of man was he now? Did he and could he know? What had the seven years done to him? What were his habits, his idiosyncrasies? Would anything he'd do, anything he was be familiar? What developments, emotionally, physically, intellectually, and socially; what state of affairs, what of the world, and what of his perspectives and convictions, and what conditions; whose death; whose life; whose maturity would surprise, possibly overwhelm him? And what about Luscious? How would they take to each other? Would they tell each other who they were while absent from each other's lives, how they lived, and what pains and joys they'd had? And whom she longed for, whispered to, and loved? And me and Donnel and Eric; how would my uncle deal with us? Would he see us as men or children?

Finally, the morning of his return came. Mr. Goines arrived with the cake and flowers for my grandma. Then Luscious knocked on our door, came in, and declared her baby was coming home. Although it was not yet summer she wore a white dress and a thin white shirt that exposed her shoulders and white open-toed shoes and through the windows the sky was blue and the sun was a cymbal, crashing its golden shine off the new white of our apartment and Luscious's freshly lotioned, lustrous skin.

"Luscious, baby," said my grandma. She hugged her and then holding Luscious's hands, she looked Luscious over, sized up her gorgeousness. "Oh," she said. "Don't you look just so fine."

My grandma and my Aunt Rhonda wore matching purple dresses and purple shoes and they carried purple purses with yellow stitching and accents. There were purple and yellow streamers Scotch-taped to the walls, purple and yellow balloons pressed against the ceiling. The tablecloth was purple. The napkins were yellow. The plastic plates were gold. The plastic utensils were silver.

"Abraham," said my grandma, "I almost forgot! In the kitchen. Get the sign. Hurry up. Put it on the door. I feel it in my chest. My son is close by."

The sign was multicolored, metallic letters strung together to spell *Welcome Home.* Standing in the hallway, I taped it to the door. I made sure it hung just right, that its curve was centered. Then I stepped back and looked at it and, although where I might go I didn't know, it struck me that one day soon such a sign might be befitting of me. Then I reentered the apartment, paused, and stared at my grandma and my Aunt Rhonda and Eric and Mr. Goines and Luscious. Then I looked at the white walls of our apartment, the family photos and school pictures of us above our couch, the television, and the purple and yellow pageantry. Yet I felt empty.

"You want me to see if I can find D?" I asked.

Donnel had left first thing in the morning, before my grandma and my Aunt Rhonda had gone to the beauty salon and had their hair done and their fingernails and toenails painted yellow and purple. They wore red lipstick and makeup and perfume and since they'd come home they'd gone everywhere in the apartment, into and out of the kitchen, into the living room, their room, and the bathroom. They couldn't stand, sit, or think still. And after Luscious arrived she joined them. But my question caused them to cease, forced their flittering to stop. My grandma looked out of the window. My Aunt Rhonda looked at the floor. Then she looked back at me, her eyes full of ire.

"And what you think he's gonna say?" she scolded. "You think he's gonna come? You think he wants to be here?"

"Let him be, Abraham," my grandma instructed. "He's too grown to go chasing after."

"One thing's for sure," burst Luscious, valiantly attempting to combat the sadness that I had introduced to the room. "Me and Nice are gonna have us some kids, a whole lot of them. We gonna make ourselves a family."

I sat on the couch with Eric and watched music videos. Of course, I thought about Donnel. And, of course, the waiting for Nice to arrive and my impatience made me think about him. But the product of my thinking about them was not just the conflict of one man's return and another's flight. Rather, it was one thing, one word, and that word was *free*. What did it mean? How could one be? Nice had insisted that no one pick him up. He was to walk out of prison like a man: free. He was to take a bus to the city, the train, the bus to Ever: free. He had twenty-four hours to report to parole. He had no job, no work history, no accreditation but the GED he'd earned the first year he was locked up. He had no relationship with the nineteen-nineties, with the last decade of the twentieth century, with all of the changes, developments, and new technologies. He did not know of my mother's death in a manner in which he could fully realize the loss, in which he could grieve. What was he going to do? Where was he going to go? And Donnel? Atlanta? Was that what free was, how he disappeared in order to provide?

Suddenly, there was a thunderous knock on the door.

"Oh God," my grandma whispered. "Oh, thank you, oh sweet Jesus, thank you."

"Look at me," Luscious announced. She held her hands out. They quivered. "Look how I'm shaking."

"It's him," said my Aunt Rhonda. "My baby brother is home!"

In a rush, my Aunt Rhonda turned the TV off. Then she clapped and ordered Eric and me to stand.

"Let's go," she said. "Get up. Get ready! And Eric, Jesus, wipe that toothpaste from your face!"

"Go ahead," said my grandma. "Rhonda. Go ahead. Get the door."

"Why me?" said my Aunt Rhonda.

"This ain't no time to argue," scolded my grandma. "Go."

My Aunt Rhonda took one deep breath and then she walked across the room, grabbed the doorknob, and looked over her shoulder.

"Go ahead," said my grandma. "Open it."

"God, fuck, Jesus," listed Luscious, wringing her hands, desperate to calm herself.

My Aunt Rhonda unlocked the locks. She unhitched the chain latch. She opened the door. After years of being buckled, boxed in, and constrained in all aspects of his life and then suddenly, uneventfully being handed freedom back, albeit a warped version, there stood my uncle with a face of stone, a countenance of awe and exhaustion, beset by incomparable relief and confusion, the crashing of joy and self-doubt raging in his chest, the numbing tumult and paralysis of freedom after being cleaved from it. Roosevelt. Nice. No longer a young lithesome brother, but a full-grown, hard-looking, bearded brother with strain in his face.

"Oh Roosevelt," said my grandma, tears streaming mascara through her rouge and foundation. "Oh thank God!"

He wore a simple white T-shirt, a pair of dark blue jeans, white prison issued canvas sneakers, and his head was crowned with a black kufi. His biceps, shoulders, chest, and neck were so muscular his brown skin simultaneously stretched to the point of bursting and possessed a glow that was the amalgamation of pain and meditation. My Aunt Rhonda wrapped her arms around his muscular neck and hugged him, and she kissed his cheek, repeatedly mashing her face into the side of his.

"My brother," she said. "Oh my baby brother!"

With one thick arm, and staring blankly ahead, he, stunned by where he was, disaffectedly hugged my Aunt Rhonda back. Then when she let go, he let go and there was a moment when everyone just stood there, in silence, he looking at us, we looking at him. Seven years of incarceration had made his beauty the type of beautiful you had to commit yourself to, the type of beautiful you had to study to understand. He was no longer good-looking, no longer handsome. Rather, he was greater. He was kingly, indefinitely regal, in possession of a strength so vast it is only available to those who've overcome banishment. His nose was square. His lips lay on a plane of unwavering indifference, as if no longer possessing the capability to smile or frown. He looked at my grandma, at Eric, at me.

"You all got so big," he breathed.

His eyes were deep set, staid, oval, dark hallways that led to extensive contemplation, the pondering of things his five senses did not have the chance to confirm or refute; scents and sights, the way that exact moment would feel. Seven years of thinking and constant wanting, of longing and silencing the begging for time to speed by in the blink of an eye had not prepared him for where he was nor what was before him.

He scanned the room: the same TV, the same couch he sat on the day I was born, the trophies he'd won along the base of the wall. In his right hand, he held a small plastic bag of his belongings. Veins rippled and splintered into a web of rivulets along his forearm. He put the bag on the floor. He looked at Luscious. Then he stood as tall and as proudly as he could.

But what to do next? He took a deep breath through his nose, sucking our apartment and Luscious and his freedom in. His huge chest expanded. He closed his eyes. We waited and watched him. Dappling the straight, hard lines of his cheekbones and cheeks and scattered on his forehead were shallow pockmarks and small scars from the pimples he'd picked out of having too much time to scrutinize blemishes and mistakes. There was a scar on his forehead that was dotted with marks from stitches and a three-inch scar on his neck and his left eyebrow was cleaved with another. He had been battered and abused and he had battered and abused himself.

Luscious stood in the middle of the room, her hands over her mouth, her entire being shaking. My uncle opened his eyes and studied her. How had he awaited this? How had he dreamed? How had he acquiesced to what might come, to the defeat that she might no longer be his? He breathed slow and inconsistent breaths, breaths only taken to suppress the swell of tears born in one's throat and chest. Then he raised his arms and opened them like doors.

"Come," he said, his voice soft and deep, the echo of a bottomless vessel. "Come and let me feel you."

IV

That night there was a party, a celebration so incredibly grand every brother and sister in America had at least one cousin there. Wonderful Ever Park people. Chocolate City. That's what it was. It was sweet and it was thick and it was beautiful; a melting, a divine amalgamation. Angels stood along the walls and in the corners of the room, brown skin shining, perspiration above their upper lip and at the cusp of their hairline, smelling of Egyptian musk, French vanilla, and sun-warmed tropical fruit so swelled with juice that with one bite their insides would leak all over, saturate, and leave a mane of pulp on a face. There were artists with photographic memories and stutterers with cerebral files on every player in the NBA. There were doves who were breakers of school chairs and reckless pugilists who had been dating the same girl since the sixth grade. Prophets and martyrs, writers of love letters, apostles. Some girls giggled like candied lambs. Some men had voices so deep their tones were drums of testosterone rumbling in their necks. There were heroes who were convicts and criminals who shouted the loudest every Sunday in church. We were jammed in the apartment. We flooded the hallways. We spilled down the stairwell. Dares and stories were bestowed. Explanations and smatterings of lyrics were lofted by liquor-loosened tongues. If there was ever a more august gathering, a more majestic parade, if there was ever anything more essential and dignified it was only because confronted by a sudden apocalypse, the world had learned its existence would never end. We danced. We sweated. We reveled in the refuge of one another, in the need for release. We were highlights and hallelujahs. Mr. Goines took pictures with an old camera. Young women shook what their mothers gave them and what their fathers wished they didn't have and every lover of a woman's shape suffered palpitations. Everyone elucidated their laughter with more laughter. Hope had arrived. No one, no matter how starved or exhausted or battered by the previous days, suffered from the slightest wavering or weakness.

The couch, the TV, and the coffee table went in my grandmother's bedroom. Quentin McKnight, DJ Q, set up his turntables and spun everything from Madonna to Wu-Tang. Bass bumped so loudly the windows of cars in California rattled. Jewelry, our necklaces, earrings, rings, and bracelets shivered on our sweat-shining skin. Plastic cups and bottles of liquor and beer were held above heads, spilling and foaming over their edge. Aluminum trays, piled high with food, with chicken wings and potato salad and macaroni and cheese and salad and ham and peas and rice and spaghetti crowded the kitchen counter, spilled onto the floor, and when emptied, crowded the kitchen sink and garbage along with plastic utensils and plates and soiled napkins. A variety of beers—Coronas, Heinekens, Budweisers, and Bud Light, Red Stripe, Amstel Light, name it and it was there—packed the ice that filled the bathtub. There were bottles of champagne and bottles of malt liquor and bottles of cheap red wine and cheaper sparkling white, and the sweet scent of the kindest, greenest marijuana ever, harvested from the West Indies to hydroponic Amsterdam, wobbled its smoky hips through the air. Gallons of rum punch and piña coladas and every alcoholic beverage that could be swallowed without permanently blinding and burning was emptied, saturating tongues, livers, lungs, and kidneys. By 10:00 p.m. the apartment was so crowded and hot all of Ever Park was dressed in fog.

"Abraham," said my grandma. "Go and get the fan from my closet."

I went into her room, came back out, and using the only string I could reach, I pulled one of the laces from my sneakers and hung the old, rickety box fan in the kitchen doorway. Then I stretched the cord as far as it would go, plugged it in, turned it on high, and left the fan swaying and blowing a faint breeze as if whispering might cool us down.

Good old Doo-Doo Dave, who used to live on the third floor but had since moved to the Poconos, arrived saying his twin brother Jamel sent his regards. Then he and his big, round belly seemed to attach themselves to my Aunt Rhonda's hip and for the rest of the night he played the straight man to her raucous celebration. My Aunt Rhonda was never without a drink. She danced. She hooted and hollered. Her lipstick dripped and slid from her lips.

Then after midnight, from across the mash of bodies in the room, my Aunt Rhonda held on to Doo-Doo and set her crossed, heavy-lidded eyes on me. She blinked hard. She wiped her face, dragged her sweaty hand down her sweaty cheek to pretty herself up. Then she leaned forward, pushed herself away from Doo-Doo, wobbled, steadied herself, and teetered through the crowd toward me, swimming through bodies with her elbows because she had a plastic cup in each hand. When she reached me, she slurred every word, even those without an *s* or *r*. She told me my mother would be proud, so God-damn, motherfucking proud of me. She repeated it three times. I had to know. *Abraham you got to know.* I needed to understand. She closed her eyes, slung her arm over my shoulder, and pressed a plastic cup against the left side of her chest.

"Cause deep inside," she sighed, shaking her head left and right. "Because that shit, Abraham, that crack, baby, that crack can't touch this."

V

There was only one wrong committed all night, only two wrongdoers: Donnel and Nice. Their wrong was neither a simple gaffe nor was it a misdemeanor or felony. The crime they committed was nothing punishable. It was worse. It was too great.

Neither laughed or smiled more than halfheartedly. Neither danced. Nice shrugged away Luscious's attempts to get him to join her for slow songs and stood against the wall, awkwardly greeting brothers and sisters he had once seamlessly loved, mechanically embracing those who embraced him, and stiffly refusing helpings of food, things to drink, and even the slightest taste of the marijuana sweetening the room. And when Luscious was not at his side, whispering in his ear, pointing out who was who and who was whose child and setting him at ease as much as she could, he scoured the room, dissected every brother and sister with an otherworldly, infernal mistrust, and followed Luscious's every move, his eyes twisted with suspicion and jealousy. Who was she talking to? Who was that brother, that sister to her? How intimately did they know her? Why were they touching her the way they did? Were they lovers? Had they seen her naked, smelled her secret scents? And did they know who he was, or rather, who he had been? And who was he? In that room; at that party; amidst all of the brothers and sisters he had once awed and been worshipped by, he seemed lost.

And worse, throughout every moment of the celebration, he was scrutinized, scoured by the hateful glare of Donnel, seeming always to be leaning against the wall opposing Nice, nodding and shrugging when people joined him, darkly smoking blunts and drinking the same warm forty-ounce all night while measuring Nice, his musculature and failed attempt at a disaffected disposition. Not once did Nice and Donnel speak. Not once did they make eye contact. Matter-of-factly, but not specifically, Luscious had told Nice. She said Donnel was doing, you know, things; running, you know, the streets. Early in the night, Nice came to me for verification. And I said: "D? You know, he's good. He's all right." And that's all I said. I took the Fifth against everything else Nice asked, against the very idea that Donnel was headed down the same path Nice had previously traveled and, just hours before, returned from.

So all night, Nice and Donnel shared just two things: nothing and critical judgment. And yet, my grandma wasn't having it. No. Such divisions would not exist in her home. And so, when the party's population finally dwindled to a few dozen exhausted brothers and sisters and the only people dancing were a handful of couples, my grandma, drunk herself, stormed over to DJ Q, pulled the headphone from his ear, and told him what she needed to hear. Then she marched across the room, snatched Donnel by the hand, and dragged him into the middle of the floor.

"Go ahead and leave this spot," she blasted, her eyes and face ablaze with a murderous level of sincerity. "And you don't never come back! As God is my witness, just keep on vanishing!"

Then my grandma left Donnel, crossed the room, and snatched the hands of my Aunt Rhonda, Doo-Doo, and Eric, and led them into the middle of the room to stand with Donnel.

"Luscious baby, Roosevelt," she shouted, holding my Aunt Rhonda and Donnel by their wrists. "Let's go! Both of you! Come on over here."

It took a moment, and something she whispered in his ear, and a gentle tug of his hand, but Luscious led my uncle into the middle of the room where my grandma and Eric and my Aunt Rhonda and Doo-Doo, and Donnel, slouching to demonstrate his defiance, stood.

I stood by the window with Kaya and I had been telling her things I could only say because that night was a celebration of my family, of whom I was born loving, and I had the courage of malt liquor and marijuana swelling my chest. She was beautiful. I had dreams about her. And I told her the secrets, how I had written her love letters when we were in middle school and written her letters apologizing for not giving her the letters; how I struggled with seeing her because of how deeply just the sight of her meant to me. I didn't know why. It just was what it was. Maybe because seeing her made me forget myself, forget the sadness I harbored. I wanted to take her to a movie. Did she want to go to a movie with me? How about to dinner? What about dinner and a movie and maybe some ice cream? What was her favorite flavor? Butter pecan. Wow. Me too. But not really though. So what type of cone, sugar or wafer?

"Abraham!" my grandma shouted. "Abraham, what you think you're special? Get over here!"

With a smile sweeter than anything a horn made of sugarcane could play, and with eyes shining her own inebriation, and although I couldn't quite believe I saw it there, some level of infatuation too, Kaya said: "Go. Your family needs you."

I hesitated. Kaya took the beer I was nursing then gave my shoulder a gentle push.

"Go on," she smiled. "You can come back."

I crossed the room and joined my family. Stevie Wonder singing "Ribbon in the Sky" filled the apartment, everything and everyone in Ever. Then Mr. Goines tried to join us. He let his camera rest on his chest and approached. But my grandma held her hand up and stopped him.

"No," she said. "Take a picture. What else you got that camera for? We taking it back to the beginning, back to how it should have always been."

Mr. Goines's shining eyes went dull and wide, spread like ink seeping into a tissue. She'd hurt him, knocked the wind from his chest. His knees buckled. He rocked back on his heels. Desperately, he grabbed his camera with both hands and lifted it in front of his face, his hands fists around the camera's sides.

As if her body were suddenly made of rubber bands, my grandma stretched herself as far as she could and lashed her arms over our shoulders. She reined us in and she held us strong, and we breathed on, in, and with one another, and on my forehead and cheeks, and on the front and sides of my neck, the silent harmony of our breathing fell, following the rhythm my grandma made, the slow swaying of us left and right like she was a gentle ocean and we were the small boat it coaxed homeward.

"It's good," she said. "Lord, ain't it so good."

VI

His name was Abdul Jalaal Najeeb, "the servant of the glory of the faith of noble descent." He didn't want to be called Nice or Roosevelt any longer. Every morning he woke before dawn, unfurled himself from the couch, causing the groan and whine of its old springs to echo through our apartment. He folded the bedsheets and the blanket he used in perfect squares, washed his hands, mouth, face, and feet in the sink. Then he dressed in a salwar kameez, slid his feet into slippers, walked out of our apartment, and climbed the misery of the stairwell, the rank ascent of our building, a prayer mat under his arm. On the roof, he faced east and prayed. He touched his ears and knees and prostrated. On Fridays, he attended the mosque for jummah. He talked about one day going to Mecca, making hajj. He spoke about unity, brotherhood. He said he had no interest, no desire to touch a basketball. It was a white man's game: white lines around the edge of a court; a fence surrounding concrete; a cement yard; a crude contest where one put a ball through a rim. It imprisoned us, glorious brothers and sisters such as we were.

Wherever he went, to parole, to find work, for long walks around Ever Park and its surroundings, he repeated the passage of the Qur'an he aimed to memorize or rememorize for that day. At night he quizzed himself, writing passages in both Arabic and English, underlining already highlighted passages, and crowding the already crowded edges of the pages with more notations, more considerations, more insights and questions. He didn't watch television. He didn't listen to hip hop stations on the radio. He said *As-salāmu 'alaykum*, "Peace be upon you," and reported to parole, gave them urine when they demanded it, and attended the drug and alcohol counseling program and anger management therapy, group, and one-on-one sessions that were the conditions of his release. He did it all with a self-assured humility, as if such subjugation paled in comparison to his manhood. He said freedom was not physical. It was cerebral and spiritual. No matter where his body may have been, no matter what walls or bars or confinements he was forced behind, no matter what sense of self-nothingness he was force-fed and ordered to abide by, he had been free ever since Islam came into his life.

"Because here," he told me, touching his temple with a finger. "And here," he added, touching his chest with the flat of his free hand. "No man can limit the vastness of Allah, peace and blessings be upon Him."

And because he believed this with an incomparable degree of faith, he also believed that he had been free since he pronounced the Shahadah, his pledge of faith, two years to the day after being first locked down. And because he believed this, when his parole officer showed up at our apartment, my uncle welcomed him, introducing the stranger to me and Eric and my Aunt Rhonda as if a found member of our extended family had suddenly wandered into our home. Fellow Muslims, men with similar but not so severely humble dispositions who he had befriended in prison, brothers his age who he had educated and older men who had enlightened and counseled him, visited our apartment and sat with him in the kitchen, dissecting ethics, politics, and the particulars of the sermons they heard at the mosque.

He listened and spoke softly and I couldn't believe him. He was too holy, too devout, so devoid of emotions and detached that I feared what might happen when something, someone, some fact slipped past his shield, the shroud and armor of his unwavering faith, and struck his foundation, piercing not Nice, but the heart of Roosevelt, that which was too soft and too huge, too much like a swollen red balloon inflated to capacity not to explode. Of course, I knew the truth that would do this. And so I feared the revelation, feared when I saw him talking to brothers and sisters he was close with before he was locked away, and feared when Luscious wanted to hold his hand, kiss him, sit on his lap, love him, envelop him with the affection he had once initiated, reciprocated, and basked in. He held her off, kept her love at a distance; never revealing a sliver of intimacy while they were in public. She would sit on the couch and he'd sit not fully beside her, maintaining a few inches of space between their thighs. She'd reach for his hand and he'd sneak it from her reach, slip it into his pocket or bury it by folding his arms across his chest. She teased him, poked and pushed him the way an awkwardly coy middle school girl might mess with the high school boy she liked. But he didn't respond, barely smiled. Instead, he laid awkward, uncomfortable, and somewhat disapproving eyes on her. His detachment wore at her patience. He frustrated her. Shortly after his return, they argued like an old tired couple who had grown sick of each other. She shouted, slammed her hand on her hip, and barked at him. He pretended to listen, nodding at inopportune times that proved he had heard nothing, and then he attempted to rationalize his thinking, his behavior with circuitous, unsubstantiated statements about Islam and love and respect. He was not the same young brother who'd left

Ever. He had faith, he said, guidance from Allah (peace and blessings be upon Him).

"Don't mistake me for just some brother in some ghetto thinking things that amount to all of nothing," he said.

"Nigga," scolded Luscious. "What you think, your shit don't stink?"

"No," he said. "On the contrary. I know my stench."

She left him, said it was over, and came back a few days later to try again. Then they fought and she said she couldn't take him again, that he was impossible, that loving him was killing her.

Then one day I was playing basketball at the basketball court and Luscious was standing on the sidelines talking to friends. My uncle marched down Columbus Avenue, marched up to her, and glared through her smile and hello.

"Baby, what?" she said, laughing uncomfortably. "Why you looking at me like that?"

He had found out whom Luscious had loved and who had loved her, and as if his arm were a sword he swung it through the air, clamped his grip around Luscious's neck, and thrust her against the chain-link fence, sending a rattle through the rusted metal. He pinned her there. Then, ignoring shouts and pleadings, ignoring everyone regardless of whether or not they called him Roosevelt or Nice or Jalaal or Nigga or Brother or Cousin or Son, or they cursed him like the devil, he raised his fist to batter her. I stood on the basketball court, frozen, suddenly out of breath. I had never once seen my uncle angry, never once seen him raise his voice. And there he was; his fist raised; paused; prepared to smash Luscious. But then, as if my silence were the world's loudest shout, my uncle glanced over his shoulder, made eye contact with me, and dropped his fist.

"You're dead to me," he said, turning back to Luscious, giving one last squeeze to her throat and pushing her against the fence before letting go, marching away, leaving Luscious to fall into a heap of weeping.

"Roosevelt!" she shouted through the chain-link fence as he walked away. "Roosevelt, no!"

She was a shunned pile of shivering and crying, and although he said nothing of it, my uncle was heartbroken. His true foundation was shattered. Luscious, the real hope that had maintained him for seven years, was not fantasy but human, imperfect and impure just like him. He gave up on finding a job. He gave up on going outside. He gave up on Ever and himself, and for weeks, when he was not praying, and until all hours of the night, fueled by the thick black coffee he brewed, he sat in the kitchen, two feet back from the table, his legs crossed, his elbow balanced on the arm of the chair, looking out of the kitchen's small square window, drifting far off in thought, the Qur'an open on his lap, a pen sitting in the furrow between the left and right page.

Birth of a Nation

I

What did I know about love, about being in love and loving? What had I seen between a man and woman that was not forced to wrestle with perilous social predicaments? What love had time not devolved into pain and violence? Where was love undeterred, indestructible, and pure? And of such relationships around me, which were not infected by Ever Park, by the sight of failed and devalued brethren and the abject conditions of our public schools and nearest hospitals, the institutions we placed our children and infirm in the care of? Nowhere else in America did love have to navigate so many emotional, intellectual, and spiritual obstacles.

And yet, although I wasn't mature enough to understand what declaring love meant; although I didn't know love could start wars and end wars and keep fruitlessness battling for years; and although I understood love could be abandoned, just as my father had done to my mother and she had done to me, I said it. I looked Kaya dead in the face and told her. I loved her. Then we stood in silence. It was dawn, the beginning of November, there was a chill in the air. We were juniors in high school and we were on the roof of our building. I watched her, studied how she digested my declaration aglow in the nearly nonexistent light that buffed the blackness from an Ever Park night and made it day.

"So," she said, holding the word for a moment. "I mean, now what are we supposed to do?"

She stopped short. I jammed my hands in my pockets and tried to feign as much nonchalance as I could. We had already kissed. We had already held hands. We had already tickled and teased and tested each other. I had already tasted her and she had already tasted me and we had already had sex; that is, we had both thumb wrestled condoms, and I had poked and stabbed and pushed myself through her taut anxiety and into her in the dark of her mother's bedroom, in the dark of the room I shared with Donnel, Eric, and my uncle when no one was home, and once in the dark of the bathroom in Yusef's apartment.

"Cause you can't just be saying shit," she scolded. "Because I ain't the type of sister to be bullshitting. And besides, you ain't ever even seen me."

"Seen you?" I said.

"I mean seen me for real. Like I ain't ever seen you."

"I see you right now."

"Naked," she said. "Nude, nigga. That's what I'm saying. I mean we never even seen each other's whole bodies in the light before."

A swell of emotions grabbed me by the neck. For a moment, I couldn't breathe. Everyone whom I loved was linked with abandonment. So a precipice was my life. That is, it was just one foot in front of the other; Monday to Tuesday; Tuesday to Wednesday. But one step too far to the left or right, one friendship, one heartbreak and I might be dead. Truthfully. As dramatic as it sounds. As twisted and perverse as it seems. It was not just my pride, but my survival skills that were on the line. That is, what Kaya said was a test to see how I handled being vulnerable, something that could affect me for days, weeks, years to come. Naked, I thought. Like a baby?

But then I looked at Kaya and she smiled a smile so disarming it severed my bonds with toughness and posturing. Such a cleaving caused parts of me not to lose sensation but to gain it. Coming upon me was a swell of contentment, completion. I gave in. And then, just as doctors and scientists can't explain why one's chest swells or aches when falling in or cut off from love, I don't know how or why but I felt stilled, as if I would never be hungry or thirsty or in need again. Without taking my eyes from Kaya, I lifted my left foot and took off my sneaker. She didn't believe me.

"Stop playing," she said.

I took off my other sneaker. Then I took off my socks.

"OK," I said. "Your turn."

After a moment of hesitation, Kaya took off her sneakers and socks. I took off my coat. She took off hers. I took off my sweatshirt. She unfastened her belt, pulled it free, and dropped it on her shoes. I took my T-shirt off, stood shivering. She smiled.

"It's cold," I said.

"Look at all your little muscles," she said.

I was lean and my muscles were well defined. I was becoming a man. Every day a different hair above my upper lip seemed to darken and thicken. Kaya paused to consider which article of clothing to take off next, her shirt or pants. Then she stripped her shirt off over her head. She wore a black bra, and shivering like me, she folded her arms across her breasts.

"That's cheating," I said.

"Cheating?" she said. "Nigga, stop stalling. Go."

I unfastened my pants, let them fall around my feet, and stepped out of them. As was the style of brothers in Ever Park, beneath my jeans I wore both basketball shorts and boxers.

"Your turn," I said.

Holding one arm across her breasts, Kaya unfastened the button and zipper of her pants and pushed them down her legs. Then, a bit awkwardly, hopping slightly on one foot, seemingly about to lose her balance and fall, she took them off. She wore red panties. Still hugging herself, she stood tall. I took off my shorts. Kaya took a deep breath. Then, keeping her eyes affixed to me, she reached her arms behind her back, unclasped her bra, slipped it off, and let her arms fall to her sides. Her breasts sat still, like swollen drops of rusty dew suspended from her clavicles. This was it. I had only one article of clothing left.

"You scared?" she asked.

"Of what?" I said.

"Of letting me see you."

Before that dawn, I would have lied. I would have shouted or laughed or smiled smugly and trumpeted no. I would have used her question, manipulated and molded it until it was an accusation I could use to maneuver from the whole disclosure of myself. But I didn't then.

"Yeah," I said. "I mean, you?"

Kaya considered what I said, dawn parading upon her body, sunlight rising around her, from her, through her thighs, honeying the gentle mounds of her hips and shoulders.

"We can look up," she said. "Then go at the same time."

"OK," I said. "On the count of three."

We looked up. Above there were three tiers of flight. The first were the birds, fifty to one hundred feet above Ever and Queens, seagulls and pigeons, and small silhouettes that I couldn't name darted, soared in circles, and fluttered through the near morning. And thousands of feet above the birds there were a few planes in the distance, gliding, lights blinking on their wingtips. And then above the birds and the planes there was the moon, growing fainter by the moment as if it were floating farther and farther away.

Without taking our eyes from above, we counted to three. Then we took off our remaining article of clothing. She slipped her panties off one leg at a time. I slid my boxers down my legs. A naked young woman stood before me. But I kept my eyes on the sky. I was not afraid to look. I was frozen by the thought of what Kaya might see.

"You're beautiful," she whispered.

I didn't believe her, so I laughed a breath of mistrust. Then, inch by inch, I lowered my eyes from the sky. I expected to find Kaya looking at my body, at my penis, or maybe my outie belly button. But she wasn't. She stared at my eyes. She absorbed how nakedness dressed me, how fear and discomfort came to my face from deep beneath.

"What?" she said. "You don't believe me?"

My eyes fell from hers, tracing her body until they reached her feet. Then I quickly lifted them and looked at her again.

"No," I said. "It's just—"

"Just what?" she interrupted.

"It's just," I said. "It's just that I am not as beautiful as you."

She smiled, rolled her eyes. "Nigga," she said. "Don't be thinking you're all slick. You're Abraham. It took you years just to ask me out."

She was right. I wasn't slick. And it did take me years to ask her out. And I also didn't believe her that I was beautiful. Thus, what mattered most was not the shape or sight of Kaya's nudity, nor was it what we did afterward, how we made love with incomparable heat. Nor did it matter most that I was naked or that I had given myself over to fear and thus bared my complete self, not the defense, parceling, or demonstration of it. And what mattered most was not that I needed to see and hear that I was beautiful. No, what mattered most was that I was in love with a young woman whose love for me introduced me to the vastness of the universe, the infinite and the finite, from Timbuktu to me, the young Ever Park brother who played basketball and wrote secret letters, and who sometimes just happened to, you know, stumble in and find Kaya in the library after school.

II

pring, and it was like I was awakened from a deep sleep. Some teachers and students in my classes talked about college. We could take a free SAT test if we wanted. Some were taking it. Too many were not. It was our chance, Kaya said, and she studied at the library for it. And she'd sit there with an old Peterson's college guide and look up colleges and their students' average SAT scores. And she would read the description about the campuses, the student to faculty ratios, and how difficult it was to be accepted. She developed an encyclopedic knowledge of colleges and universities. She knew their locations, their mascots, their fight songs.

"There's got to be like a hundred colleges in New York," she said. "There's Fordham and NYU, and all the city colleges, and St. John's, and FIT, where, you know, aspiring clothing designers go. There ain't no historically black colleges though. Ain't that strange? You'd think with all those rich people, like the Cosbys and Puff Daddy, they might have started one."

Through and through, Kaya was sure she was going to college. Someplace. Somewhere.

"College, Abraham," she said. "That's what I'm about. I don't got to go to Harvard like Ms. Hakim. There must be a bunch of colleges that'll accept me. But maybe Harvard? You never know. If I score real high on the SAT. I got good grades. Like Mandela said, it ain't who am I to be brilliant? It's who am I not to be, you know?"

Kaya was so about college and that SAT that the window to kiss and make love with her was so small it might as well have been a pinhole in an all black sky. No matter how or what I whispered in her ear, no matter how smooth I tried to move and ease into foreplay, all she wanted to do was talk positive and negative integers, binomials, vocabulary words, and college majors.

"What you think about psychology?" she'd ask me in the middle of my sweetest, gentlest kissing on her neck. "Or sociology? You know Ms. Hakim majored in religion?"

Kaya told everyone within earshot about colleges. My grandma loved it. She listened to Kaya like everything she said was a drip of honey on the tip of her tongue, so sweet its savoring was not to be rushed.

"College," she'd say to me after Kaya left. "Abraham, you know, you smart enough."

My Aunt Rhonda humored Kaya, but she mocked her when she was not around.

"That chick talks more white every day," she'd say. "What the fuck does intrepid mean anyway? And loquacious? Abraham, if I didn't know she loved your ass, I'd swear she was cursing you."

On the rare occasion when Kaya spoke about college and Donnel was present, he'd look at me and his gaze would grow harder, more exacting, as if he were trying to dissect a delicate insect, a butterfly steeped in fog. His mind was the perfect fit for higher education, precise in its movements, associative. And he wanted to go to college. I saw it on his face. And once he swore he could do it.

And when Kaya spoke about college my uncle watched her the way a man ponders an old picture of himself, a plain and simple expression on his face as if he was not just hearing and seeing Kaya but soaking in the recollections of that time in his life, the many events, and the feelings that swelled in his chest about who he had been and where he could have gone—college. Sometimes my uncle wondered aloud about what it would be like. And sometimes he said he was going to take classes as soon as he got some money in his pocket. But he was also scared of it, as if sitting in an institution of higher education was more difficult than sitting in prison, an institution meant to limit men, even rot them away.

Eric didn't have a job or a social life, and when he wasn't drawing the only things he did were sleep, eat, watch TV, and spend any money he had on scratch tickets. But when Kaya talked about college Eric stopped and listened like a piece of lint being sucked into a vacuum, all up in Kaya's mouth, leaning into everything she said. Once, he got so close to her he repeated her declaration verbatim, with the exact intonation and pronunciation.

"I am going to college," he announced, launching to his feet from the couch. "Make no mistake about it!"

"Eric," said my Aunt Rhonda. "All you do is sit in front of that TV. And you ain't even got your GED. Ain't no college gonna want you. You got to get that piece of paper first."

So Eric said he was going to get his GED. When? Soon, he said. And my grandma and my Aunt Rhonda told him to take Donnel with him. But no one pushed him on it because no one believed he would do it. Not because Eric was slow minded. But because Donnel wasn't leading and Eric had only liked learning once, when he was in art class in elementary school. So he procrastinated and delayed investigating

GED classes. He lied and said he called some schools but the ones that called him back didn't have any room for him.

As for me, I didn't think about college. Rather, I considered it. I paid attention in the school assembly about college that our guidance department held for the entire eleventh grade. I heard them talk about the college admissions process, the applications, preparing for the SAT test. And deep inside, I wanted it. But I neither acted on nor seriously considered my consideration of college. It wasn't ignorance or laziness. It was that I didn't believe I should leave Ever; or that I could. I was just as afraid as my uncle. No, I was more. So, no matter what Kaya said, that free SAT test came and went without me.

III

Although I was at the park, on a concrete basketball court, the scent was of an old recreation center's gymnasium; sweet; sweat; old warped wood that had been wet, then dried, then wet and dried again. It was humid and tropical, a bastion of physicality. A half-dozen police cars were parked along Columbus Avenue. Police officers leaned against them. A few folded their arms across their chests. The others stood with one hand propped on their holstered gun. It was the middle of August, the summer of 1999, a little more than four months before the twentieth century came to an end, a new millenium. Some people talked about an apocalypse. The sun was just beginning to set. The lights around the court were beginning to flicker and hum. The day, like all days in Ever, was a day of wanting. I was warming up with my team, dribbling, going through layup lines, shooting jump shots, preparing to play in the championship game of the summer league sponsored by the Police Athletic League. Everyone from Ever, every Lotto player and scratch-ticket junkie, clairvoyant and hellion, temptress and trickster, every calliope and manifesto and sage confounded by the world was gathered around the court. They debated and elated. They established reasons based on historical precedence why they shouldn't pay taxes and bills. They recalled previous championships and inflated the points they scored in the game. Some sat on milk crates and folding metal chairs. Others stood. Some young brothers climbed and clung from the fence to get a better view.

Sucking on a lollipop and wearing white shorts so small and tight they might as well have been a stain on her thirty-three-year-old body, my Aunt Rhonda walked through the crowd, flirting and meandering like a cat, aloof yet hopeful.

"Hey," she said, waving, winking, pointing her lollipop here and there. "How you doing? Look good? Huh? You want to know me? Shoot, nigga, get a library card. Look up Nefertiti. Then maybe we can talk."

Outside the fence, two crackheads, their brown faces gaunt and green, solicited a revolution, declaring and arguing over the fact that they would fight and pummel each other for the sake of our enjoyment while a handful of young, truculent men mocked them, because they could and because they were not as separate from the men as they hoped to be.

"Time for . . . ," one crackhead shouted, holding his fists up like a boxer, priming us for their self-loathing.

" . . . the war of all wars!" said the other brother.

"Who cares about basketball? We gonna go at it!" responded the first. "Me and him! We gonna beat each other down!"

"For a dollar."

"Who got a dollar? You got a dollar? For one dollar we'll make each other bleed!"

"One dollar, that's all it takes!"

Donnel and Eric were in the crowd. And Kaya was there. And my grandma had taken the day off from work so she was there too. But she was supposed to be coming to the game with Mr. Goines, and he was nowhere to be found. So she stood in the crowd with the expression of a barren island surrounded by a sea of people. Her face did not move. She kept her eyes on me. It was as if only I existed, as if she were impatiently demanding yet waiting patiently for me to do that anything, that something she just knew I could do. Ever since my uncle's coming-home party, Mr. Goines and my grandma had been fighting, arguing about anything and everything. What made it happen was that he kept moving to be a part of our family and my grandma kept pushing him away, keeping him at arm's length, crushing him just enough that he came back swinging, not physically, but with frustration and fear. He questioned her loyalty. He said he deserved a woman who supported and welcomed him. He told her that she projected all of the blame of her past heartbreaks onto him. Yet they stayed together.

Because she had hope. Because she always had hope. And so did he.

My grandma clapped. She called my name. "C'mon, Abraham," she said. "Let's go, baby. Bring that trophy home. We always got room for more."

My uncle's fervent piety had relaxed since he had come home. Wearing an almond-colored linen shirt and pants set, he stood on the sidelines with old friends like Elijah and Hector Mendez, whose five-year-old son, Junior, stood beside them, looking up, studying their expressions and dispositions, a miniature replica of Hector learning what it took to be big.

"You remember that time you killed those niggas from Bed Stuy?" Elijah asked my uncle. "Dropped fifty on them, sent them back to Brooklyn like bitches."

"And you remember when we was like Junior's age and you was dunking?" Hector asked my uncle.

"Nigga," scolded Elijah. "Ain't no one dunking when they was five! Not even Jordan could do that!"

"Who's talking about Jordan?" Hector defended. "I'm talking about Nice, nigga. The king of Ever Park."

A ball hit hard off of the rim and bounced to my uncle.

"See," laughed Hector. "Just like a baby to its mama. Junior be going to Carmela just like that. Go ahead, shoot."

Holding the ball in both hands, my uncle looked down at it like it was a tome, an entire encyclopedia set, an almanac.

"That's a basketball," teased Elijah. "In case you forgot."

"Forgot?" said my uncle. "Brother, a man ain't never forget what he bleeds."

My uncle took two dribbles with his right hand, then two dribbles with his left. Then he pointed at the closest rim, which was some twenty-five feet away.

"Ten bucks says you can't make it," Elijah challenged.

My uncle took one more dribble. Then he raised the ball over his head, flicked his wrist, and shot . . . an air ball. His friends broke out in raucous laughter. My uncle considered them. Then, as if letting go of a weight, he smiled a sheepish smile that was the first easy smile I'd seen on his face since he'd come home. So it was relief, an expression of the notion that all he had to be was a man, not some immortal, unconquerable hero. But then the smile was not just the product of the air ball, the joy of old friends, or self-acceptance. Luscious was at the court too. She stood on the other side, as far from my uncle as she could stand. But when he missed that shot, he looked across the court and caught her looking at him. Thus, as much as his smile was the product of his missed shot and his friends' laughter, it was an apology, an admission of smallness in the presence of the beauty he still longed for.

"Let's go, A," Donnel shouted. "Get your head in the game!"

Donnel stood on the baseline with friends. He glared at me. He knew I was nervous. And he knew all of the reasons, how first I was nervous because I was always nervous before a game. And how I was also nervous because it was a championship game and everyone from Ever was there so people would be talking about the game until the championship game next summer. And Donnel also knew I was nervous because Kaya was there. But more than anything Donnel knew I was nervous because he was nervous, because here was a chance for him to show my uncle how, despite everything, we were great without him; great without Mr. Goines too. Because he, Donnel, was the man of the house; because he had protected me; because he had taught me how to be a man. So I was not just a basketball player who utilized a layman's version of my uncle's style of play, that untouchable nonchalance that he had once carried himself with, but I was also fierce and strong.

"Focus," Donnel demanded. But he wasn't satisfied. So he walked out onto the court. "Come here."

I stopped warming up and waited for him. When Donnel reached me, he clamped his hand around the back of my neck and pulled my ear to his mouth.

"We got this," he said. "Understand?" He pointed at the concrete. "You leave it here. Everything. All the blood, sweat, tears. Ain't nothing can stop you."

The referee blew the whistle. The game began. And we, the ten young brothers on the court, touched hands, embraced, and wished one another luck. Then there was the jump ball. We competed. We defended and offended. We slammed our hands on the small of one another's backs. We grabbed one another's jerseys and shorts. We grappled for rebounds and loose balls. We patted one another's asses, slung our arms over one another's shoulders, uttered words of love and encouragement. We slipped and skidded on one another's skin. In any other place, in a dark room, a bright room, the boiler room of the school, a stairwell, a motel on the highway, or in a Jacuzzi on the threshold of Niagara Falls, what we did would have been foreplay, making love minus disrobing and penetration. We sprinted and permeated. We pressed and squeezed one another. We clutched and tore free. And when our lungs were hungry for oxygen, we breathed deeper, harder. We only rested momentarily. When there was a break in the action we put our hands on our knees, blinked, licked the sweat off of our lips or let it fall, watched it spot the concrete.

All around the court, people rooted and cheered. They shouted our names and nicknames. They ooohed and ahhed. Some hooted. Others hollered. Older men commented on our skills. Younger men shook the fence and banged on it to celebrate our moves. Women delighted over our idiosyncrasies, our musculature, our haircuts, fashion sense, and tattoos.

"Look at Abraham," Taquanna shouted into Kaya's ear. "Nigga still thinks he's too cute. Walking with that swagger."

"Taquanna, shhh!" scolded Kaya, so focused and wanting for me her brow was coated with a sheen of sweat.

At halftime the game was tied and both of my knees were bleeding from diving on the court. DJ Q spun records, and little sisters, adorned in candy ring pops and candy necklaces, faces stained from ice pops, danced the sugar-fueled synchronized routines they'd choreographed earlier. After my coach told my team what we needed to do, Donnel stormed across the court wielding a towel and a bottle of water like a sword and shield.

"Keep working," he said. He straddled my legs as I sat on the court. He bent over, poured water on my knees, and dabbed at my wounds with the towel. "You wearing those niggas down."

He studied my injuries. "Ain't so bad," he said. Then he looked down at me and smiled. "But A," he said. "Be smart. Stay on your feet. This is concrete you playing on, not a pillow."

He handed me the bottle of water. "Twenty more minutes," he said. "That's nothing. So don't stop fighting. Don't quit for nothing."

Q stopped playing music. The referees blew their whistle for the game to resume. Wesley Timmons, the small, skinny, perpetually starving boy whose responsibility it was to watch the ball for the referees, and who stuffed his loose socks with candy and junk food from the corner store so he could feed his little sister before they fell asleep on the bathroom floor of their aunt's apartment, tossed the ball to them. Then we, ten young, strong men, walked, ambled, moseyed, and sashayed onto the court.

I glanced at my uncle. His face was stone, but his eyebrows were crooked, and he bit his bottom lip so he looked proud yet struggling to understand what he'd seen. I didn't play anything like him. No colleges recruited me. I was not even a starter on my high school basketball team. My coach said I didn't listen, that I couldn't listen, that I didn't know how. *Singleton,* he'd shout, *you got your own agenda, a personal modus fucking operandi. You don't execute. You're not organized. You don't move with purpose!* Straight lines, right angles; there were plays I had to abide by, rules for movement, established responsibilities and regulations meant to create and maintain harmony. I was to go from point A to point B at this specific time, when this specific thing happened, this many times. But how? All my life I moved when deemed necessary, not as movement was construed. Dart here. Wait there. Try and tell a brother who built his own horn, wrote his own song, and taught himself how to play when to make music: it wasn't happening. I couldn't do it. But it wasn't because I was unruly or disrespectful, or defiant and arrogant in my belief that I knew better than my coach did. I didn't have the ego of a celebrity or an NBA star. Rather, my style of play wasn't governable because basketball was the way I lived, so personal every action, every dribble, every pass, every move to the basket, every defensive stance was essential, notes in a song.

My whole soul went into playing. I fought for position beneath the basket with players twice my size and strength. I swerved. I juked. I loped and jogged and sprinted and I gritted my teeth and swooped. I flipped the ball underhand, hooked it over my shoulder, floated it high off the backboard. I dribbled to the hoop without the consideration of ever being stopped. I threw blind passes around my back. I played with my mind but I was fueled by burning guts. I warred. I smashed. And I talked trash with a wounding precision. With an omnipotent hate, with the knowledge of what hurt most gained only through projection, I told you what your mother was and what your father was and what that made you no matter how determined you were, how hard you tried not to be. I said such things because I had heard them all before, because although I was able to fight through them, I knew their weight, how the steady procession of derisions could knock even the greatest man down, chisel his stone pedestal and armor away.

And I did it all, moved as I moved and said what I said, for one reason and one reason alone. That reason was I had to win. And I did so any way I could, legal or illegal, whatever I could enact between white lines painted on concrete and hardwood. I was vicious. I'd rip your face off if need be. I'd hammer you with elbows, forearms, and knees. And you couldn't hurt me back. No matter how much you tried, you could do nothing to me. There was no attack, no elbow, no bruise or blood or pain that you could inflict that fazed me. Talk about my mother, talk about my uncle, tell me my aunt was a whore, say whatever and still nothing. My body, my mind, and soul were not composed of precious, fragile parts. I threw myself after loose balls. I collided. I clawed. I wrestled. My knees and elbows and the palms of my hands were so scarred and bruised, so toughened it seemed I'd crawled across mountains of rocks and broken glass since the moment of my conception. I could shoot through crippling hunger. I could dribble with tears in my eyes. I could play through the pain of blood blisters as big as quarters bulging from my heels, the balls of my feet, and in between my toes.

The game resumed. The second half was a carbon copy of the first. Then with a minute left, a shot went up and every brother on the court fought for position, leapt and reached for the rebound. Twenty hands, one hundred wanting fingers. I leapt and reached and wanted it more. I landed and passed the ball to Yusef, our point guard, chewing a huge wad of gum, and I drifted up the court with the others playing in the game.

We were down one point. Yusef passed the ball back to me. I took a deep breath and held it against my hip. Out of the corner of my eyes, I found Kaya in the crowd. Maybe the holiness I perceived her to emanate was not real, but like hands holding me upright, as tall and proudly as she stood, I felt the force of her gaze.

"Right now!" someone shouted. "Right here! One time, Abraham. Take him!"

This demand was not a shouting or a calling out. It wasn't an asking to be heard or testifying. It was Donnel.

"Let's go!" he shouted. "Let's go!"

Donnel was full of hope, betting everything on me. So because he called my name, because Kaya believed, because my uncle was there and my grandma was alone when she no longer wished to be, and despite how tired and sore my legs were, I swore I was not going to let us lose.

Then everything went silent. I surveyed the action in front of me. Lorenzo Davis, a skinny, perpetually angry-faced, unpredictable brother with his two self-proclaimed penchants, basketball and guns, announced by the tattoos on his arms, guarded me. I took a deep breath and looked over his head. How to describe the movement before me? Run your lips over every inch of your lover's body. There were no obstacles, no impossibilities. A calm came over me, dressed me with omnipotence.

On the sidelines, Alton Johnson reached into his pocket and pulled out a thick wad of cash. He licked his fingers, plucked two fifties out of the stack, and held them in the air for everyone to see. Then he smacked them down on the concrete.

"A hundred," he called out. "A hundred dollars says Abraham ain't got shit."

From his spot on the baseline, Donnel looked at Alton and his money. Then he pushed a smug smile through his lips, like smoke, billowed and fattened on nothing. He jammed his hand in his pocket and yanked out a folded stack of cash so thick it could have been a brick if it wasn't green and made of paper.

"A, what you want?" he shouted to me. He licked his finger and counted out twenties. "Huh, nigga? You want CDs? New Jordans? Fuck it. You want an airplane? C'mon. Which hand you gonna do this nigga with, left or right?"

Titty, who in a matter of six months had become chiseled and squared jawed and the tallest, strongest brother I knew, planted himself in the paint and raised his hand shoulder high.

"A," he said, calling on me to pass to him, his defender pinned behind his back. "Here. A!"

Who doesn't possess the potential to be a hero? I took one last look at Donnel. Then I glanced at my grandma and Kaya. I looked at my uncle. His arms were folded. He unfolded them, clapped twice, and bending over, he planted his hands on his knees and looked as if he just might join me for the last moments of the game. I took a deep breath. And then I looked into Lorenzo's eyes and took a quick glimpse at the halo of the rim. I hunched over, slowly dribbled the ball with my left hand, then I bounced the ball between my legs to my right hand. There were an infinite number of ways I could go, an infinite number of actions; pass, drive, shoot. I sliced my arm through the air.

"Move!" I called out, ordering Titty and everyone on my team to get out of the way. "Watch out!"

Donnel dropped to his knees and pounded his hand on the concrete. "Let's go, nigga! Let's go!"

I licked my lips, tasting the sweat, my flavor dripping down my face. Then I turned my back to Lorenzo and used my hip to back him down. He planted his forearm across the small of my back and pushed with all of his strength.

"You ain't shit," he muttered. "You nothing."

I talked to myself, told myself it was over, we were going to win. The only sound became my breathing, my voice, the drum of the ball on the court. I wiped the sweat from my forehead with my free hand, then dragged my hand down my cheek. Then I suddenly wondered what would happen if we lost. What would Donnel say? What would we do? And I lost my concentration and dribbled the ball off my foot and it rolled away, toward the other team's basket. I couldn't believe what I had done. For a moment, I deflated and my arms hung at my sides. Lorenzo raced for the ball. Out of the corner of my eye I saw Donnel. All of him had fallen forward so he was not just on his knees but on his hands and knees. And his mouth was open. And his eyes were on the edge of brokenness. No, I thought, no. It couldn't be. I wouldn't let it be. I clenched my fists, turned, and chased Lorenzo.

I caught him, and like starved men hot on the trail of the world's last morsel of food, we grabbed and pulled on each other's jerseys to keep the other from getting to the ball. The referee didn't blow his whistle. We ripped and tore more. Then Lorenzo lowered his shoulder and swung his arm like a club and the blow knocked me to the concrete and all I saw was him scooping up the ball and taking off down the court, the echo of dribbling, the hammering of a nail. It was over. We were going to lose.

But Donnel refused. He wouldn't let it be. He leapt to his feet and charged after Lorenzo. His fists and knees punching holes in the air, Donnel tripled Lorenzo's stride. Lorenzo reached the foul line. One dribble later, he was eight feet from the basket. He picked up his dribble, took the two allowed steps, and leapt. And then, from ten feet behind, Donnel launched himself through the air and a moment later, he exploded into Lorenzo's back, thrusting his forearm through Lorenzo's spine as if he were trying to cleave him in two. Lorenzo flew through the air and landed on the concrete, tumbling into the legs and feet of the people standing on the baseline.

The ball trickled away from his lifeless body. There was silence; a vacuum. No one, not even me, could believe what had just happened. Donnel lay on the concrete for a moment. Then he picked himself up and began to walk away, flicking gravel out of the bloody wound his crash landing had made of his elbow.

"Hell no," he muttered. "We ain't losing. Hell motherfucking no. We ain't going out like that."

Suddenly swirling to his feet, Lorenzo retrieved the ball and threw it at Donnel as hard as he could, and the ball slammed against the back of Donnel's head, and then, between the moment of impact and the moment the sound of the impact registered in everyone's ears, Donnel's eyes exploded wide with rage and he swung around and went at Lorenzo without thinking, with all of the helplessness he refused but was consumed with.

"No!" shouted my grandma from the sidelines. "Donnel! No!"

But it was too late. Donnel ran at Lorenzo. He lifted his knees high. He brought his arms back like wings. He was an eagle descending, accelerating toward its prey. When he reached Lorenzo, the collision was the sound of raw meat pounded by a sledgehammer, wet coupled with the crack of ribs, and because Lorenzo had not had the time to put his hands up and protect himself, his arms and legs and head flapped like wet flags each time Donnel pummeled him. Donnel was merciless. He pounded with his forearms and he pounded with his fists. Lorenzo groaned a horrendous tearing groan. Donnel kneed him in the stomach. He was desperate, reckless, endless.

As if pulled by an incredible gravitational force, I rushed toward the mangle of Lorenzo and Donnel. So did Eric. And so did my Aunt Rhonda and my grandma. And my uncle ran at them too. And so did the police, one with his gun raised above his head, fighting and pulling their way through the crowd. Then, just before I reached the mangle of Donnel and Lorenzo, their flying legs and fists, just as I reached to take hold of Donnel and pull him away, Lorenzo unfurled and swung wildly and hit Donnel so hard his head whipped to the side and a spray of sweat and blood splattered across my shirt. But the blow didn't stop Donnel or even cause him to pause. He was from Ever, a Singleton. He hooked his hand in Lorenzo's mouth and, holding Lorenzo'a face still with his grip,

Donnel threw a punch that caught Lorenzo on the side of his nose and blood splashed everywhere; blood on the concrete; blood on the basketball; blood all over me.

They kept fighting, no matter how hard we tried to stop them, grab them, pull them apart, keep them from killing each other, killing us. Donnel flailed. Lorenzo thrashed. Then, tangled in the crowd trying to stop the fight, lashed by the swirling whirl of arms, I lost my balance. I went backward then fought against the movement and lunged forward, and then I tumbled. I slid, slipped, and bounced. I was pulled and pushed, held and thrown aside. Everything rose over my head. Everything swallowed me. I was drowning. I reached out. I grabbed at shirts and legs. I clung to someone's arm, but I lost my grip and because I felt as if I would fall forever, because there was nothing else I could do, I swung with all of my might. I hit someone, something fleshy and soft. Then I hit the concrete and I got hit back; in the back of the head, the side of the neck, between the shoulder blades. I was stomped on and pummeled. I was sure I was going to die. But who hit me? I swung more. I beat oxygen and light out of the air. I punched ankles and calves and knees. Hands came toward me. I didn't know if they were fists or hands offering help. I didn't know if brothers were trying to lift me up or beat me down. I swung and kicked and swung. For how long? Time was of no importance. I was battered, trampled.

And then I was pinned on the concrete, three cops on top of me, a knee like a dull guillotine jammed on but not cutting through the back of my neck, drilling my chin into the concrete. The police cuffed me, ripped me to my feet. My hands behind my back, my chin and nose leaking blood, they led me through the crowd, everyone's shirts torn, collars stretched, sweating, so confused and so used to such confusion their faces were the heartbreak of the already heartbroken. My grandma pushed through people. A cop stood in her way and told her to stop.

"Back up," he said. "Get back or you'll be arrested too."

"That's my grandson," she shouted. "No! Let him go!"

Then I was outside of the fence. I was being led to the police cars. There were sirens. More police cars were coming, speeding down Columbus Avenue. Behind me, my Aunt Rhonda screeched *No!* over and over again. Some people shouted my name. Others cursed the police. The cops opened the back door of their car, slammed a hand on top of my head, and stuffed me in. Then they slammed the door closed. I looked out of the window. I saw my uncle grab my aunt, restrain her, and pull her away as she screamed for me, then screamed for Donnel.

All I could think of was him. Why had Donnel done what he did? Why was it necessary? And where was he? Had he been been arrested too? Or had he gotten away, taken off running so fast he flew?

Suddenly, my grandma shoved the police officer aside. She took one fierce step forward, her face a tangled brown jungle, so baffled, so hurt it was without any identifiable feature other than her eyes, demanding as always. We made eye contact. Bloody and battered, I glared at her out of the window of the police car. I threatened her. Without a word, with just my eyes, I warned her. I ordered her to cease. Didn't she see? I was nothing, and right where I was supposed to be, in the back of a police car, my hands yanked and cuffed tight behind my back. Blood trickled from the steel biting into my wrists. It dripped down my thumb. I made hate my face. I breathed deeply. My chest rose and fell. My grandma stopped walking. She glared back at me. Slowly, she shook her head no. I read her face. *Didn't I see?* she begged. No, Abraham, baby. That's not the case.

IV

For six hours the police held Donnel and I in the precinct's small holding cell with a dozen other brown men. Occasionally, the police came and took a man away. Sometimes he returned. Sometimes a few new men were introduced to the lot of captives. Some of us sat on the floor. Others sat on one of the steel benches affixed to the left and right walls. Some stood. Some men slept, their breath a dragged pot through the rubble of their drunkenness. Others talked to one another as if the holding cell were a barbershop or a park bench warmed by the sun because they'd found a common subject to discuss, or they knew one another from the neighborhood or a previous stay upstate, or because if they remained silent humiliation and hurt would fill their throats and kill them. Some men were disheveled and seemingly eviscerated, their souls and faces raisins. Others were dressed in slick suits with matching patent leather shoes. Some men feigned satisfaction, as if they were finally a step closer to their real life, their truest true love, that perverse institutional wife who clothed, fed, and never complained about being wed to them. Then there were those who shouted and screamed their innocence, who snatched the steel bars by the throat and, in a range of tones from litigious to irate, expressed the details of alibis and constitutional rights. Other men laughed about everything as if the possibility of innocence in this world was so preposterous even the shouters, the screamers, and the bars were telling jokes. Then there were the handful of men, those who were the youngest and brashest and whose pride was so misguided they were righteous and pompous about what they had been accused of. These men whispered and bragged about how much dope they sold, how many times they shot and stabbed, how much money they had stacked and hidden so they were not worried about making bail. There were drunks, and junkies who were so high that whatever they said was meaningless and difficult to listen to. And then there were the men crying in their hands, worrying about what they would tell their lovers, mothers, daughters, and sons. Seeing that I was wearing basketball shorts and a bloody summer league jersey, and that my face was battered, some of the men wanted to talk to me about the game. Others wanted to challenge me.

"You in here like you nice," said one man. "Look at this nigga. Michael Jordan finally got done did."

I responded to nothing, no one. With my legs bent and my arms draped over my knees, I sat in the back corner of the cell with my back against the concrete wall. I stared at the concrete floor between my feet. I hadn't ignored the fact that being arrested and held in a cell was one of the inherent possibilities of being from Ever. Police took us like groceries; eggs, milk, honey, whatever was on their list that day or night. But I also wasn't sitting the way I was, like a crushed thinker, because of subjugation or oppression. It was how and why, and who had caused me to be where I was. No matter how many times Donnel tried to talk to me, I couldn't look at him.

He stood over me. "Come on, nigga," he said. "It ain't that deep."

But it was also not just that Donnel had caused everything because it was also that the cell was a choose your own adventure book. That is, each and every one of the men in that cell was a man I could one day be. Who knew? One could have even been my father. So I was in a cage of mirrors, confronted by the possibilities of what my life seemed destined to be. And there were no doctors or lawyers. No bookish teachers or wild-haired scientists. There were no Wall Street professionals, physics professors, politicians, or philanthropists. Of course, there were artists. There were poets and painters and great saxophone players in that cell. Some had an idea about who they were. Some didn't. But we all knew it was just Ever Park men in that cell, hardworking, resourceful men who before they committed a single crime were confronted by limited opportunity; men who adapted to it, men who refused to give in to it; men who had heard about limited opportunity so quit before they were forced to confront it; men who began being men at nine, ten, and eleven years old, when emotions most govern us; and men who used substances as if they were magic carpets, hot air balloons that rose over walls and aided their escape. Although my body no longer ached, and inside of me there was not a single throb or burn, I was full of pain, for I struggled with two notions. The first was that I was simultaneously fortified and destroyed by my nation, by those I loved and who loved me. The second was the insidious question: what chance do I have?

"It was just a fight," Donnel said. "Niggas get into fights all the time and they back home the next day. Don't worry."

He was lying to me. I heard how his voice struggled with the act, how it creaked like an old wooden bridge at the peak of a roller coaster, how behind it were screams, eyes closed, hands in the air surrender. Donnel said that he'd solve everything. But more, he'd never let anything hurt me. He'd never let anything stand in my way. He couldn't. He never had. He never would.

"Nothing," he said. "You know what I mean. Not nothing."

Donnel tried to convince me that he did what needed to be done, that he couldn't let someone take something from us like that. And the referee should have blown his whistle.

"They was cheating," he said. "You and Titty got fouled like two hundred times. And they didn't call a thing. A, look at me."

Donnel's legs straddled my feet. He reached down, grabbed me by the chin, and lifted my face up.

"Nigga," he said, his face inches from mine. "I'm right here with you."

I grabbed his wrist and yanked his hand from my chin. "Get off of me," I said.

He was stunned. "A," he breathed.

"I wish it was you," I said.

Donnel looked left and right as if there might be another man I was talking to or someone who might translate the foreign tongue I spoke in. There wasn't. He wobbled. Then he planted his confused eyes on me and smiled what he had left, that trickling hope that I was making a joke.

"What you mean?" he said.

A thousand thoughts raced through my head, a thousand songs, a thousand shouts, a thousand cries. If Donnel aimed to save me then where was the man who was supposed to save him? And if he was trying to be my hero, who had missed the call to be his? And what was I going to do? Shit, what could I do?

Nothing. The last thing in the world, the very last thing I wanted, was to be nothing, was to know myself as nothing, as powerless. But there I was. It seemed, once again. Just like I was when I searched for my mother and could not find her. Just like I was when she left me for crack and my grandma didn't let her come back. And just like I had been when my father left.

I looked at Donnel harder, with more hate than I knew I could muster, and said: "I wish you was dead."

Donnel raised his hand as if he was going to hit me with all of his might. Then, he stopped. What I inflicted on Donnel was neither a physical nor a psychological injury. It was worse than a spiritual attack. I know because I saw Donnel's face speed through a range of expressions and then he was crying. Not aloud or cut off by gasps. And not stymied by swallows. But as if he were melting; that last trickle of hope, that smile leaking from his eyes.

Simultaneously, I couldn't believe what I'd done to him and I was embarrassed by it. I sucked my teeth and looked down at the floor.

"Damn, D," I said. "Nigga, shit."

Then I wanted a knife. Not so I could stab myself until I didn't see it, or so I could stab, slice, and hack away Donnel. I wanted a knife to kill everything around us. Then we could be something else instead of young men waiting to stand before a judge. But how ridiculous an idea. So, I suddenly wanted a ledge. And I wanted the courage to stand up and jump. I was suspended between rage and sadness, hanging, dangling. So I didn't just want a knife and a ledge. I wanted a gun. I wanted to end Donnel's crying quick. I wanted a knife and a gun and a tank. I wanted soldiers. I was vulnerable and violated by everything surrounding me, the sounds and sights of impounded men, men locked in. Because I was locked in. And Donnel was doing the one thing I needed to do, that which I had refused myself since that last moment I saw my mother alive made me feel as if I'd been caught doing something not even God was allowed to do.

I was jealous. I couldn't cry. I had convinced myself that crying was nothing. Even more than nothing. Because I was nothing. Empty and numb. And crying wasn't freeing or healing. Or was it? And it didn't get a man heard. Or did it? And I was a man. Wasn't I? That is, had I not been one since I was too young? Because isn't that what my mother called me? Mister Man, Mister Abraham.

Hearing Donnel cry, seeing how his lips quivered while his countenance remained unflinching, made me hate myself. Because no matter how much I felt like I hated Donnel I first knew I loved him. And he loved me. That was all we ever did. So I knew I was wrong. But I had too much pride to apologize. I was scared, angry.

Donnel wiped his face in the crook of his elbow. Then he grabbed me by the chin again and lifted my face so high I felt the skin of my neck burn from the stretch.

"Don't never say that," he said. "You understand? No matter what you think. Don't never say that to me again."

Donnel let go of my chin, and leaned against the wall beside me, his arms folded across his chest as if he was there to protect me. I looked down at the concrete floor. All I could think about was writing a letter. To whom, I didn't care. Dear Sir, I thought. Madam; Miss; Brother: My Nigga; Kaya, My Love; Excuse Me; Hey God; To Whom It May Concern; Mom; Dear Father: Was this who I was destined to be? Captive, confined? Just like my uncle, just like so many Ever Park men?

V

I sat with my grandma on the Columbus Avenue bus. We headed home. I faced a litany of misdemeanor charges, rioting, disorderly conduct, and things I didn't even know how to do like endangering the welfare of a child. The court-appointed lawyer said there were so many charges it didn't matter. Some might get dropped. New ones might come up. I was a minor. I was given a court date and released. The key for me, said my lawyer, was to focus on myself, to focus on the positives. Go to school, he said. Stay out of trouble. Enjoy being with your family. Donnel was an adult. And he faced more charges than me. Assault, battery, criminal anarchy, resisting arrest. He had fought with the police, broke one's nose in addition to breaking Lorenzo's. And he was not legally employed. And he was not in school. And my grandma said he looked at the judge with a face like broken bricks, hard and sharp, his eyes accusatorial, as if it were not he who needed mercy but he who dispensed it. The judge took offense and set bail at seventy-five thousand dollars, and Donnel went to jail.

"He is guilty of something," my grandma said. "But all that? He ain't never been in no trouble."

She sat straight and stiff, more rigid than the plastic bus seat, and trying to avoid the reality of Donnel's situation, she told me that her relationship with Mr. Goines was over.

"Forever," she said, staring straight ahead, her hands holding her purse in her lap, her face taut. "I ain't taking no more flowers and things. He's a fool. That's all he is."

I stared out of the window and did not speak. I was so tired, empty, and hungry my lips and eyelashes were too heavy to bear. We were silent for a few minutes. My mind wandered to Mr. Goines. So that was it, he and my grandma's love was done?

"But that judge," said my grandma. "That judge took it like Donnel was some whole army of men that just up and started acting crazy."

It was the last day of summer camp. Each time the bus stopped it filled with the antithesis of us, the carefree relief and release of children in the bright colors of parks and recreation camp T-shirts. High on candy and soda, eyes bloodshot from city pools, lanyards adorning wrists and ankles and hanging from the keys in their pockets, their final arts and crafts projects jammed in backpacks and wrinkled in their hands, some children had first-place ribbons. Others had seconds and thirds. They laughed and disputed and championed frivolous ideas, enlightening one another, professing fates and favorite songs, each voice bursting above and ducking below others.

"Seventy-five thousand?" my grandma continued. "Who got that kind of money? What are we going to do?"

Outside on Columbus Avenue, the sidewalk was peppered with people making their way through the rigors of the day, walking over patches of heaved and crumbled concrete, past plastic bags, newspaper pages, broken glass, and tampon applicators. The bus passed the corner store and the decrepit Laundromat, its windows steamed and filled with the rainbows and suns and simple faces children too young for camp carved into the fogged glass. It passed Pastor Ramsey's church, the Holy Name, its metal gates lowered over its door and windows. It passed the liquor store, still glowing yellow from the new coat of paint it received that summer.

The bus stopped at a red light and I saw Lindbergh pulling his shopping cart by a rope. The cart was piled high with plastic bags of cans and bottles, a broomstick and a tattered square suitcase. It was heavy and Lindbergh leaned so far forward to pull it, his body hovered above the sidewalk at a forty-five-degree angle, just between falling and standing. Suddenly, he slipped and fell to his knees. But he didn't let go of the rope. He put one hand down to break his fall and held the rope that was tied to the cart with the other. Then he stayed on his knees and looked down the street like he was seeing something holy, something once promised long ago, something that was still promising.

The light turned green and the bus continued forward. On the horizon, looming at the very end of the avenue, Ever Park's towers rose upon us floor by floor. Donnel's money was somewhere inside. Or it was somewhere near. And even if it wasn't, it was findable. It had to be. Because I was determined to find it. I was going to free him. Not just because I felt guilty for saying what I said to him and I wished to apologize. But for brotherhood. That is, wouldn't Donnel have done the same for me?

VI

I followed my grandma off the bus. Although Ever was the same as it always was—the same tired red bricks covered with grit and grime, the same scrawls and scribbles, the pleadings and preaching of teenagers with markers and cans of spray paint doing everything to prove they were alive, nicknames and gang names, the same phrases with the same words misspelled, killer with an *a*, fuck without a *c*, *Rest in Peace* written with the peace symbol instead of the word—it felt unknown to me. No longer did I see it as a residence. Rather, it was a vault, a lockbox. Maybe Donnel's money was beneath our bed. Maybe it was hidden in a sneaker box in the closet. Maybe it was in a safe. If so, I would find the safe and the key. Nothing would stop me.

In front of my building stood Kaya. She babysat Nakita Webb's four children, Valentine, Mercedes, Shavon, and infant Asia, sitting on Kaya's cocked hip as she watched the others play tag. My grandma said hello to Kaya. Then she said that she'd leave us alone to talk and she continued inside. I had talked to Kaya on the phone from the holding cell. I had told her I was fine, that things were all right. But everything was different now. She could see that. She smiled a soft smile composed mostly of sadness. She shifted Asia higher on her hip. Neither of us could find words to say. So when Valentine stopped playing, it was he who spoke first.

"Abraham?" he said, studying me with round, gentle eyes as if I were an apparition he had never imagined. "What happened to your face?"

"I got in a fight," I said.

"I got a boyfriend," interrupted Mercedes, eight years old and already full of sass.

Suddenly, Shavon, who because she just turned three did not know how to question my wounds or brag, latched on to my leg. She looked up the length of my body.

"Hungry," she said. "Me hungry."

I touched her head, looked at Valentine and Mercedes, then I lifted my eyes to Kaya.

"Their mom's working," she said.

"She bringing us McDonald's," said Mercedes.

"She's a pilot," said Valentine, already a hoper of such a colossal degree that he was also a pathological liar.

"She ain't no pilot," scolded Mercedes, a liar herself. "She builds the planes."

"She cleans them," Kaya whispered because she couldn't bring herself to announce something that might disappoint the children.

She looked down the length of Columbus Avenue, sighed, and shifted her eyes to me.

"You OK?" she asked.

It took all of my strength to shake my head yes.

Kaya sighed. "You know, that was the worst thing I ever seen."

She stopped herself. Then she forced herself to smile.

"And you," she added. She shook her head, took a deep breath, and then she let the words and a small laugh out at the same time. "You the worst damn fighter I ever seen."

"Nah," I said. "Nah, I'm good. I got caught off guard. I didn't see it coming."

"See what?" she said.

"How I got hit."

"It was Eric."

"Eric hit me?"

"No, stupid," she scolded. "He was pulling on you from behind. He was trying to pull you out of the fight."

VII

I climbed the stairs, rose like smoke. If there was shouting, the sounds of televisions and radios coming from the hallways, I didn't hear them. If there was laughter or crying, I didn't recognize it as sound. The stench that hovered around Ever, the stench I had not fully been aware of until that day, the day of my return, was multiplied by the stairwell's confinement. Thus, although I ascended the stairs, it seemed as if I burrowed deeper into the stink, closed in on its awful core.

I reached my floor, I opened the stairwell door with the flat of my hand and stepped into the hallway's dimness. As it was in the lobby, because only a few of the fluorescent lights in the hallway worked, humming and flickering through their long dying, the hall was dusk. The apartment doors were black. In front of a few, there were welcome mats. I was home. I took the two steps to my door. There was only silence. The welcome home sign that had greeted my uncle was still taped to the door. I felt choked, as if two invisible hands were clamped around my neck.

I knocked. The door opened an inch, then two. Then my grandma opened the door all the way. I walked in. Eric sat on the couch, his arms wrapped around his chest, his sketchbook open on his lap. He turned his head and looked at me.

"D ain't coming back," he said in a manner that could have been either a question or statement.

He swallowed something round and huge the way someone who is drowning seizes and clings to a gulp of air. Then he shook his head no.

"I'm sorry," he said.

"Sorry?" I said. "For what?"

"I got to get stronger."

Suddenly, my Aunt Rhonda ran across the room. Her face was torn leather. She raised her arms high. Then she dropped them with a thump around my shoulders.

"Oh Abraham," she cried into me. "Oh Abraham, why?"

My uncle stood alone at the window, his muscular arms folded across his chest. He turned and looked at me bracing my aunt, bearing all her weight. He studied the sight. Was this how it was when he left? Were we wounded by his absence just as much? He closed his eyes and held them closed. He was a man privy to the aftermath of his own absence, how, no matter how he prayed that it didn't, it had victimized us, his family, at least as much as it victimized him. He turned and looked back out of the window. He looked left, down the length of Columbus Avenue, as if he would wait right there and never move, not until he saw Donnel walking his clip-clop stride home.

I opened and closed every door in my head, searching for a portal, some avenue of chance that led to a different reality. Where could Donnel's money be? The failure of not being harder on Donnel; for not demanding that he want more for himself; for allowing him to assume the familial responsibilities that his nature predetermined him to assume; for resting silent and still in his arms when he held me the moment I was born into this world, then letting him carry me, bathe me, whisper to and defend and soothe me: for all of this and more, I reasoned his imprisonment was my fault. If only I had not dribbled the ball off of my foot. If only I had refused to be knocked down. How could I love someone so much and say I wished he was dead?

I couldn't take the television. I couldn't take not knowing right then and there where the money was. I couldn't take my family. I couldn't take myself. So I left. I didn't bother to excuse myself. I didn't say where I was going or when I would be back. No one called out. No one tried to stop me. I turned around. I opened the door. I ran out and slammed the door closed behind me. Then I ran down the stairs, skipping the last three steps of each flight with a leap to the landing. I sprinted across the lobby. I slammed my hand against the steel door. I ran past Kaya and Nakita Webb's children and I had no plans of stopping. I was going to run until I reached the edge of the world or the air I split wore me away, rubbed my skin, bones, and organs to ash and left my soul to the whim of the subsequent wind. But then I heard my name and my legs refused to churn and go.

"Abraham!" Kaya shouted. "Abraham!"

I slowed to a jog, then walked a few more feet with my hands on my hips. Slowly, the urge to blame Kaya for everything, starting way back when we were children, devoured me. Because she wasn't family. Because we didn't share blood. I had so much hurt I needed a target. I stopped walking and turned around.

Kaya walked toward me, her face twisted as if she had read my mind and her heart was broken.

"I ain't going," was all I could compose, surprising myself with the declaration.

I was talking about school. Somehow, she knew it. She absorbed everything I hurled at her with those three words. But she would not stand for it.

"You got no choice," she said, her voice forceful yet no louder than a whisper.

I looked down. I looked left and right. I searched for a reason, for some sight that provided me the proper words to respond with. In a week, we would begin our senior year. I could be the first Singleton in history to graduate from high school. But I was afraid. I was suffering, buckling. I closed my eyes. Where was that money?

"Abraham," Kaya said. "Promise me. On the count of three. Swear to me."

BAR 9

If We Must Die

I

onnel wouldn't tell me where the money was. He wouldn't write about it in a letter. He wouldn't talk about it on the phone.

"That's for Atlanta," he said. "That ain't got nothing to do with this. I worked too hard to blow it."

Still I searched for it. It wasn't beneath the bed, in the closet, or behind the refrigerator in the kitchen. It wasn't beneath the sink in the bathroom. It wasn't hidden in any sneakers or shoes. Where does one put so much money? No, that was not the question whose answer I was seeking. It was more. It was where does one hide freedom? I asked every inanimate object we lived with. The showerhead, the floor, the toilet. *Where was it?* I thought. I whispered. I shouted. But it was as if everywhere I looked, from the black night to the first morning sky, had sworn to secrecy.

"So what you want is bigger than being locked up?" I asked Donnel when we talked on the phone.

"That's it," he said. "That's exactly how it is."

I became enraged. This motherfucker, I thought. Who does he think he is sitting in jail for the sake of what? Us? His nobility? His martyrdom? He made me so mad I started thinking about selling drugs myself. How many nickel and dime bags would it take to get to seventy-five thousand? How much time would it take me? I was confounded by brotherhood. I was confronted by the question of whether or not I should be more tied to what Donnel wanted or what I wanted for him. In the end, I couldn't sell drugs. I was scared of standing on the street. Scared of the police. Scared of being seen by Lorenzo at the wrong place and time because he told my friends and Eric that what happened at the park wasn't over, that if he caught me alone or without Kaya it was on. So I rarely walked alone and when I did I avoided him, ducking into a store, turning around, or cutting down a different street whenever I saw him or any of his friends. But more than anything else, I was scared about one thing: not doing what Donnel told me. He would never let me follow him, never let me do what he did.

Still, I kept looking for the money. Finders keepers: if I found the money then the rule clearly stated that it was mine to use as I pleased. So I looked even more than everywhere, which led me to look in places I had no business looking in, like my grandma and my aunt's panty drawers. I prayed to God. *Lord, where is it? Tell me where one hides such a thing.* I kept faith that I would find it.

And I kept my promise to Kaya and went to school. There, I did only three things. I thought about the money. I loved Kaya. And I wrote Donnel letters. But not just hello, how are you letters. I constructed petitions, pleas, and demands. I created rationales and arguments meant to confuse him and bend his heart into telling me where the money was. But it was fruitless. Donnel told me it was useless.

He said, "What do you think, just because a nigga is behind bars he don't have principles?" He breathed a breath that I knew so well I could see he was smiling. Then he added: "But don't stop writing. Shit is entertaining, at least."

Still I kept searching. And I lay awake and thought about being free. But I couldn't find the money. On the phone it became a back and forth between Donnel and me, cat and mouse, Abbott and Costello. Who's on first? What's on second?

"So, where is it?"

"I don't know."

"You don't know where it is?"

"Exactly."

"But it's yours?"

"Yup."

"So where is it?"

"I already told you."

"Nigga, you said you don't know."

"Exactly."

Somehow, and despite the fact that he was incarcerated, the conversation between Donnel and me always ended with him laughing. Which always made me laugh. And so I continued asking Donnel where the money was. Because I hoped he would tell me. But if not then at least I could hear him laugh. And so he could hear me. And without going into emotions and details, we could assure each other we were forgiven; and he could tell me he loved me; and I could prove the truth was I loved him.

II

I sat on the couch watching *The Simpsons* with Eric, who was eating the pork lo mein and French fries he'd bought at the Chinese food hole-in-the-wall down the block. A bottle of pineapple soda and a bottle of hot sauce were at his feet. He slurped and chewed loudly. He had headphones on and the volume of the Discman Donnel bought him to replace the stolen one was as loud as it would go. I don't know how Eric heard the TV, but he watched it with a level of intensity that demonstrated he not only heard, but his whole soul was in it. He laughed at opportune times and nodded to the rhythm of his music. He shoveled some lo mein into his mouth, chewed, and, following the rhythm of a song's bass line, he tapped the plastic fork on some invisible drum above his head.

The phone rang. And because there was no sense asking Eric to do anything when he was eating or watching TV, I went to the kitchen and answered the call.

"Good evening," said the voice on the other end. "I'm looking to speak with a Mr. Abraham Singleton."

"Speaking," I said. "Who's this?"

"Abraham, this is Coach Rivers from Brandeis University," said the man, his voice heavy with authority. "I was wondering if you have a few moments to speak."

I doubted Rivers was real. I thought a friend was playing a joke on me . . . maybe it was Cleveland. I listened closely. Hold on, I thought. What was that noise? Was that Jefferson giggling in the background? Maybe it was Titty. No. Could it be Precious? Yusef? Maybe it was a scam, I thought. Maybe it was one of the fulsome Army recruiters who called once a week luring with lies about serving my country.

"I know your uncle," he said.

"You from Ever?" I asked.

"Brooklyn," he said. "Brownsville. But I used to coach in the summer leagues out in Ever Park. We were the only team that ever had a player block one of your uncle's shots. You know you're a hard man to find?"

"Why's that?" I asked.

"You tell me."

I was silent. I leaned back against our brown refrigerator and waited for Rivers to continue talking. For a variety of reasons, messages weren't passed in my home. Sometimes it was simple innocence; sometimes forgetfulness; sometimes it was spite; other times it was worry. I didn't take it personally.

"You know," said Rivers, awkwardly filling the silence, "I spoke to your uncle. I've heard a lot about you, a lot of good things."

"Yeah?" I said, still not trusting Rivers was who he claimed to be.

"Your uncle said you're a hard worker; a warrior; a determined, head-strong, smart kid. That not true?"

"If that's what you heard," I said, shrugging as if Rivers were standing before me.

"How're your grades?" he asked.

"All right," I said.

"What's all right? You got A's? B's?"

"Some," I said, still doubting he was who he said he was.

"What's some? You don't know?" he asked. "What you got in English? How 'bout science?"

"I got a B on my last test."

There was another long moment of silence. Again, Rivers was the one to break it.

"Listen," he announced, hoping to infuse me with some excitement, "I'm gonna be straight with you. Students come to Brandeis with straight A's. Maybe a B in gym or something like that. What's wrong? The work too hard for you?"

"Nah, it's all right," I said. "It's just."

"I might be able to help you out," Rivers interrupted. "I can't say you'll be a starter or even play on my team. You'll have to try out. I don't even know if you can make it. I've never even seen you play. So don't go thinking you'll be some kind of college superstar. Brandeis ain't like that. But you'll get a damn good education."

Rivers told me about Brandeis. He said it was a small division-three university where athletics were hardly the most important thing.

"But," he said, "I can't make any promises."

But he'd try. He'd advocate for me. He would write a letter to the admissions office, stand before the admissions panel and say that I was worth whatever the risk was. As long as I kept passing my classes. And if I took the SAT.

"You take it?"

"No," I said.

"Then sign up," he said. "What you waiting for? There's got to be only one, maybe two more times you can take it before it's too late. You owe it to yourself. And your family. You understand what I am saying?"

"You think I got a chance?" I asked.

"It ain't about what I think. What do you think?"

"What did my uncle say?"

"He said you don't back down from nothing." Rivers paused. He softened his voice. "Think of it as opening a door. As giving you the key to a lock. What do you think? What do you have to say?"

Suddenly, I was sure Rivers was a liar. So sure, in fact, I had the urge to hang up the phone.

"Have you thought about what you want to be?" he asked. "What type of work are you going to do? What sort of career? If you could be anything?"

Anything? I thought.

"What about president?" I asked half sarcastically.

"Have you ever heard of Angela Davis?" he responded.

"No," I said.

"Well, look her up. Do you know where she went to school?"

"Where?"

"Brandeis."

Rivers talked about Brandeis like it was a new phone service or some kind of pyramid scheme he wanted me to sign up for. Then he told me Brandeis was a Jewish school and asked me if I thought that might be a problem.

"No," I said. "I don't think so."

Then Rivers's voice dropped to a serious tone. "Abraham, I know what I'm talking about. You got to trust me."

Trust him? I wondered what Rivers looked like. Was he tall or short? Thin? Fat? Fatherly in disposition? What was fatherly? And what would Donnel think? What would he want me to do?

"Son," Rivers said, "Do you know who Plato is?"

He called me son and a thick knot blossomed in my throat.

"No?" he asked. "Well, Plato was a Greek philosopher who said that all a man takes with himself when he dies is his culture and his education. That's it. Nothing else. Think about that. Ask yourself, what does it mean?"

I began to speak but Rivers cut me off.

"Don't answer," he said. "Just think about what I said."

When I got off the phone, I returned to the couch, watched *The Simpsons,* and thought about what Rivers said. I thought about Ever and what I had and I thought about my friends and family, Donnel and Eric and my uncle and my mom and my Aunt Rhonda and my grandma, all of us crammed in my grandma's two-bedroom apartment.

Eric shifted one of the earphones from his ear. "Army recruiter?" he asked.

"Air Force." I said.

He slammed a forkful of lo mein into his mouth. "Fuck those niggas," he said. He finished chewing. Then he added: "I seen Lorenzo just before."

"What he say?" I asked, trying to sound impervious.

Eric kept his eyes on the TV. He swigged from his bottle of soda. He swallowed. "Nothing. Same old shit."

We continued to watch *The Simpsons.* I thought about Lorenzo and the fight at the park and what Rivers said. I thought about what might happen if and when I ran into Lorenzo alone. And I thought about Kaya, about how she said going to college might mean being apart from each other. That thought made me feel empty. I thought about where Donnel was. I wondered how empty, how much nothingness he felt. And sitting on the couch, I knew I wanted more than such nothingness. I wanted more for him. And what I wanted was more than Ever; more than what my grandma had and what my mother had; I wanted more than dying. I wanted no more crackheads; no more brothers selling drugs; no more prisoners and parolees; no more prowling cops, truant officers, and social workers. No more brothers killing one another, inherently killing ourselves.

III

A week later, I came home from school and got the mail. In it was a manila envelope addressed to me. I walked across the lobby to the stairwell and opened it. Inside there was a glossy college bulletin, an application to Brandeis, and a short handwritten note on a Post-it that said *Did you think about it? Coach Rivers.* In the dim light of the stairwell, I studied all of it as best as I could. I walked slowly, pausing at each landing. I read Rivers's note over and over again. I devoured it. I didn't lift my foot high enough and tripped on a step. I fell, putting one hand down, holding the application against my chest. I stood and started walking again. *Did I think about it?* Of course, I thought about it. I thought about all of it, Ever Park, the charges pending against me, Donnel. What was in that bulletin was the antithesis of what was around me. How could I not think about it? I scrutinized the shiny pages of smiling faces amidst landscapes of green trees, kidney-shaped flowerbeds, brick buildings and walkways, and students sitting before disheveled professors in sport coats, shirts, and loosened ties. I read the text and studied the captions. I reviewed the table of contents and titles at the top of every page. I was mesmerized, awed entirely.

I scanned the application, its directions, what I was to write in each blank space, on each black line, what I was supposed to circle and check off and fill in. It was too dark to read in the stairwell. But somehow, I did.

At our apartment door, I stopped and looked through the bulletin more, slowly, all of it once again. I had never seen such a sight, never held such a prize.

I unlocked the door and walked into the apartment, still looking, scouring, picking apart everything, including the finest of fine print. Eric was sitting on the couch watching TV. I crossed between him and his electric lover.

"What's that?" he asked, intrigued by how serious I was, how much I ignored everything in our surroundings.

"Nothing," I mumbled, not stopping, not looking at him, my eyes planted in what my hands held.

Although I assumed my uncle knew, I hadn't told him about Rivers's phone call. And I hadn't told my aunt or my grandma about it either. I hadn't even told Kaya. The only thing of any importance was getting Donnel out of jail, getting him a decent lawyer, ensuring his freedom. I leaned against the kitchen counter and flipped the pages. I sat at the kitchen table. I went into the bathroom and sat on the toilet. I closed the bedroom door and sat on the floor. I lay on the bed. I took the bulletin, the application, and the note with me wherever I went.

Maybe Titty and Precious stood beneath the window and shouted my name. Maybe they said *Abraham, nigga! Yo, you deaf motherfucker! We know you're home!* Maybe someone was having sex in one of the apartments that surrounded ours. Maybe a sister was moaning and wheezing and the bed was bumping against the wall, squeaking as its legs scraped and skipped to the cadence of her lover's thrusting. Maybe there was the wail of police sirens, and the blue and red flash of police lights banging off the afternoon. But I wouldn't have known it. I was in Ever, but I was enveloped by Brandeis, encased by the wonderment of what it might be like to exist in a world so different from Ever. I studied the faces in the bulletin. Their eyes were eager. They seemed so innocent; so agape, so aglow with indomitable naïveté.

I heard the door open and my uncle come home and Eric tell him I was in our room. Quickly, I hid the application under the pillow and pretended I was sleeping. The bedroom door opened. My uncle came in.

"A," he said, shaking my foot. "You feeling all right?"

"Yeah," I said, putting sleepiness in my voice. "Just tired."

A short while later, my grandma came home, and some time after—I don't know how long it was. A half hour? An hour?—she shouted my name.

"Abraham," she said. "There's food out here! Abraham, I'm talking to you! Come and get something to eat!"

I couldn't go without it. I was a toddler with his favorite blanket, a little boy with his most favorite, invisible friend. I walked out of the room into the kitchen, my arms at my side, one hand clamped around the bulletin, the application, and the yellow Post-it. Dinner was spaghetti. Eric and my Aunt Rhonda were already sitting on the couch, their bowls in their hands, their eyes planted on the TV. My grandma and my uncle stood at the stove. She shoveled a heap of spaghetti from the pot and dropped it into the bowl he was holding. Then she saw me.

"What's wrong with you?" she asked. "You sick or something?"

She looked at what was in my hands then tried to read me, decode my expression, my lips, my eyes, the thoughts behind them.

"What you got?" she asked, tipping her chin at what I held. "That homework or something?"

"Nigga hasn't put that shit down since he got home!" Eric shouted.

"Ain't no one talking to you!" my grandma shouted back, her eyes burning on me.

I looked at my uncle. He studied me with a stoic yet slightly hurt expression, as if he knew what I held and wanted to know why I had not told him. My grandma wiped her hands on the dishtowel hanging from the handle on the oven door. Then she reached out and took the bulletin and application from me.

"Let me see," she said.

She studied Rivers's note for a moment. Then she peeled the Post-It back from the bulletin and studied the bulletin's glossy cover. She opened it, thumbed through the pages. She looked at its back cover. She looked at the front cover again. She read what she saw aloud and struggled with the pronunciation. The schools that recruited my uncle used to send bulletins. She had seen hundreds of bulletins before.

"Brandeeze, Broondise." She looked at my uncle. "What's this?"

"College," my uncle said, his eyes on me.

"No," said my grandma. "What's this note mean? *Did you think about it?*"

I wanted to speak. But I didn't know where to begin. My throat and tongue were lifeless, heavy. I did not know how to balance the excitement I felt over what Rivers said and Donnel, where he was and where that application meant I might go.

"You spoke to Rivers?" asked my uncle.

"He said I got to fill out the application," I said.

Thrust between joy and suspicion, and the realization that things were occurring in her home that she was not aware of, my grandma looked at me. Her eyes demanded clarification, specific details. She looked like she was reading, turning pages with her eyes, learning my face from left to right. What was I talking about? What kind of man was I becoming? She had just seen me in a police car for the first time. She had seen me handcuffed. But college? A student? How many times had she prayed for us, her children and grandchildren? How many times had she prayed for the capacity to fill the role of mother, father, grandfather, uncle, aunt, and a plethora of ethical family confidants? After everything that had happened, had she been able to imagine this?

My grandma brought the application and bulletin to her chest. She closed her eyes, took a deep, strained breath in through her nose.

"Oh dear God," she whispered. "I listened to her. I prayed and prayed on what Kaya said. But never once. Oh dear God, Abraham."

IV

Donnel called.

"So I got something to tell you," he said, sounding out of breath. "You there?"

"Yeah," I said.

"All right," he said. "So, I'm just gonna come out and say it."

"Go ahead," I said, fitting awkwardly into wonderment, my head spinning with questions. Was he coming home? Did the DA drop the charges? Had there been a settlement?

"OK," he said. He breathed. He started. He paused. "So, nigga. So, shit. So, I'm in love."

I laughed.

"Swear to God," he said.

"Who?"

"Me."

"No," I said. "I mean how?"

"You don't know her."

"How do you know who I know?"

"Cause she ain't from Ever."

"Nigga," I said. "How can you be in love?"

"Shit," he sighed. "You the last nigga who should be asking me that. Don't you know anything's possible?"

"So where did you meet her?" I asked.

"Waiting for the train. Before the fight. She makes me want to do things."

"Do things?"

"We're spiritually connected."

She was headed to classes at college. She was a student at Columbia, smart as shit, Donnel said, thick as a motherfucker.

"I mean, just the sound of her voice and I almost dropped to my knees and started praying. We've been writing every day since I got locked up. Now, you tell me what that means."

"What you say?" I asked.

"About what?"

"To get her to talk to you."

"Nothing."

"You said nothing and she just started talking to you?"

"No," Donnel snapped. "I asked her where she was going."

"And what she say?"

"Nigga," he scolded. "I just told you she was in school. She was going to class. Shit. I'm telling you. I swear to God. This woman is beautiful."

Donnel swore he was going to take her somewhere nice, somewhere in Manhattan, some five-star restaurant, then to the hottest club. Then he said, "Fuck that, fuck that. I'm gonna take her to the top of the Empire State Building. Then, I'm gonna take her to hear jazz. Maybe some nigga will be playing the trumpet."

"Since when do you like jazz?" I laughed.

"Nigga," he said, "I've always liked jazz. Shit, I might even love it."

Donnel told me what their lives would be like together, how they'd move down south. She could come to Atlanta if she wanted to. He described how she had a birthmark as big as a dime at the outside corner of her left eye and dimples too.

"And dimples that blink when she smiles," he said. "Her whole face: shining. You should see the picture she sent me. You can't even imagine how fine she is."

There wasn't the slightest degree of anger or restraint in Donnel's voice, not a hint of burning or sadness. He was simply testifying, announcing himself by identifying another's uniqueness and glory. He talked about getting his GED. So he could go to college like her. So he could help their kids with homework. Never in my life had I heard Donnel go into a tirade over his future. Never in my life had I heard him so convinced and so determined to convince someone of what he said without once raising his voice or threatening them.

"You want to hear something?" he asked.

"What?" I said.

"Hold on," he said. I heard a rustle of paper. "Never mind."

"Never mind what?"

"This shit I wrote," he said, then softly added: "This, I don't know, I guess, poem."

"She's got you writing poetry?" I laughed.

He laughed. "I told you. I'm done. I'm telling you: I'm gotten."

V

All night, I wrote. I put my headphones on. I listened to Eric's Discman until the batteries died. I scribbled and jotted and scratched out. I edited and unedited. I tore paper out of my notebook. I chewed the end of the pen. I gnawed. I gasped. I sighed; *Fuck.* I vacillated between believing I could do it and knowing I couldn't. I fell asleep with my head on the kitchen table, drool oozing from the corner of my mouth, soaking the corner of the page beneath my cheek. My Aunt Rhonda came home, shook me, slapped my face, and woke me up.

"What you doing?" she asked.

Barely awake, my eyes dry and heavy, I handed her the bulletin and application.

First, she flipped through it quickly. Then she turned the pages slowly, her face expressionless.

"College," she said.

"I got to write a personal statement," I said.

She skimmed through the application's last few pages, put it back on the table, and looked at me, her brown eyes swollen with the depths of too many thoughts, too many wants, too many declarations.

"Get some sleep," she said.

"But I got to write," I said.

"Tomorrow," she said, her voice stern. "You can take care of this tomorrow."

I skipped school the next day and my grandma called in sick and so did my Aunt Rhonda. And Eric was there. And my uncle was there until the middle of the morning when he left to go to parole. And when I grew frustrated and said I didn't think I could do it, my grandma told me I had to, that I had no choice. So I kept writing. I did so because I wasn't writing just for me. I thought if Donnel knew what I was doing he would kill me if I stopped. So his absence was also pulling the writing from me, compelling me to keep going. So I did. So I wrote.

The heat in our building was broken again and our apartment baked with a dry, desert heat that caused everything from my nostrils to my teeth to be chalky. The windows of the apartment steamed. I sat at the kitchen table in a white tank top and shorts. My grandma, my Aunt Rhonda, and Eric came in and out of the kitchen. Occasionally they called my name, shouted words of encouragement, argued over previous suggestions and edits they were convinced I had to make. I worked feverishly. Every word was a weight, a concrete block I pushed and pulled and dragged up a hill.

I wrote a paragraph, read it aloud, and my grandma and my Aunt Rhonda and even Eric offered their opinions.

"Let them feel you. Write like you mean it! You know what I'm saying?" said my Aunt Rhonda, relying on rhetoric to inspire me. "Stop telling them what you think they want to hear! And get your spelling right. You know how white people is about spelling!"

"Capitalize the first word of every sentence," said Eric, preaching one of the few grammar lessons he could recall. "And don't mix up your *b*'s and *d*'s."

"Go ahead!" my grandma said. "Go ahead and let those folks know who you is!"

What did I write? What did I finally compose? What song did I sing? Honestly, I kept it simple. I was not the type to fabricate details or go over the top concerning the facts of my life, my wants, my wishes. I delineated. I explained. I constructed an introduction that was simultaneously a whisper and slap in the face. I said my name is Abraham Singleton. I made my grandma and Aunt Rhonda cry. I stuck strictly to irrefutable evidence. I said my mother had me when she was thirteen, then she became a crackhead and then she was murdered but before even that she was dead to me. I didn't bother explaining what such a loss meant. I let the fact hang there on the page. I wrote four, five, six, seven; a total of ten pages. I told Brandeis I never knew my father; that my uncle, Nice, was incarcerated for two crimes, armed robbery and loving his family and a woman more than he loved himself, a crime against his own humanity, his essential potential. I explained how he isolated himself, disappeared himself from our lives. He didn't write letters. He didn't respond to ours. Put behind bars, he excised himself from the universe but not because he was selfish or deviant or vile, but because he wished for us not to be limited by his confinement. If this was my chance to be heard, to be free, then I was speaking. I wrote about Donnel, how he had bathed me, raised me, shielded me. I said Psalm Twenty-three, verse four: *Yea though I walk through the valley of the shadow of death, I will fear no evil: for Thou art with me; Thy rod and Thy staff they comfort me.*

"There you go," my Aunt Rhonda cheered. "Hit them with the biblical!"

Then I wrote about how it felt without Donnel. I didn't go into the details of his activities. Rather, I gave the details of his absence. I described the holes each day bored in my chest. Then I wrote about my grandma. I explained how she named me, built me, and demanded that I dream no matter how many nightmares sank their teeth in my head. I said as much as going to Brandeis was for me, it was for them, my family; Ever; every brother and sister I loved. I stole that line from the United Negro College Fund television commercial and told Brandeis that I was living proof that a mind is a terrible thing to waste. And I'd seen wasted minds. And I didn't want to waste mine. I refused to.

VI

The library was closing in an hour. It was dark outside. The fluorescent lights in the library only had the strength to make the library a grey dusk, so people had to get right up close to the books to read their Dewey Decimals. I sat at one of the rickety cubicles, my back to the door, reviewing my personal statement for the last time before Ms. Hakim would help me type it in school. Kaya sat to my right, pointing out when I misspelled words and suggesting last-minute adjustments. Cherrie stood over my left shoulder. We had already said hello and talked about what I was doing and how my family was.

"College," she said. "I always knew you was special."

Cherrie was singing in Pastor Ramsey's choir. Luscious had joined them. Cherrie was at the library to photocopy Song of Songs.

"Me and Luscious gonna put it to music," she said, her jowls jiggling with each hard syllable. "We gonna sing it for real. Do you know how good that girl can sing? She just closes her eyes and lets it go."

She put both of her hands on her big, round belly.

"You know from here; down deep. It's like . . . like the sound of *ain't afraid of nothing*. It's good, you know. To hear a voice like that. But you know that. You remember how your mother used to sing? Shit, Jelly used to kill it."

I stared at Cherrie. I had signed up for the SAT. I would take the examination in two weeks. I had met with my Legal Aid lawyer and he said things were still up in the air, my guess was as good as his. Who knew what the DA and the judge would do with me? I couldn't remember my mother ever singing louder than a whisper, or a time and place she sang to me. I suppose I was as close to crying as a cloudless sky could be to rain without raining. What do I mean? I was ten thousand feet high, sun shining, with unending visibility, but in my throat, an ocean swelled and heaved.

"You know I got a tape," said Cherrie.

"Huh?" I said.

"A tape," she said. "Me and Jelly used to tape each other singing. I know I got at least a couple of them."

The library door opened. Then the cold wind outside slammed it closed. In came my uncle, walking like the slamming door wounded him, dragging himself into the library like a sack of broken eggs, wrecked with exhaustion. He was getting off the job he just got swinging a twenty-pound sledgehammer working demolition for minimum wage. Beneath his arm were the books he finished reading. His eyes were down. He stopped and massaged his right knee. He flexed it, bending and straightening his leg. Then he saw me, walked toward Cherrie, Kaya, and me, and stopped when he reached us.

"What's that?" he asked.

"My personal statement," I said.

"It's finished?"

"I think so," I said.

"It's good," added Kaya. "Real good."

My uncle put his hand out. "Let me see it," he said.

I handed it to him. He read, his face six inches from the pages, intense, immersed in every word.

"Now, Roosevelt," Cherrie said, fearing my uncle's critical eye so using his given name to remind him we were in a public place. "He ain't got to be Shakespeare. Abraham just got to get the message across."

I glanced at Kaya. Then I looked back at my uncle. He finished reading. Dust from the drywall he'd leveled all day powdered his brown skin, speckled his eyelashes, eyebrows, and the edges of his ears. His lips were parched. He looked up and studied me. His eyes were the only part of him untouched, unsoiled. He must have read ten thousand books while locked up, maybe a hundred thousand. He closed his eyes and nodded yes slowly. Then he opened his eyes and they were soft, wet.

"There's a lot about Donnel," he said. He handed the papers back to me.

He looked away and thought for a moment. Then he held his books up. "I was just gonna return these and get the ones they got on hold for me," he said. "You almost finished?"

"Almost," I said.

He smiled. "I'll wait for you." He looked at Kaya. "If it's all right with you."

Cherrie left. At ten minutes before five, I finished, Kaya kissed me good-bye, and I said I would call her later. Not counting the librarians, only my uncle and I remained in the library. He stood at the back, flipping through a book he had taken from the shelf. I put my personal statement in my backpack, stood up, and walked to him.

"You ready?" I asked.

He closed the book he was reading and held it up for me to see. "*Moby Dick,*" he said. "Call me Ishmael. Man versus the sea."

He put the book back on the shelf.

"You should let D see it," he said. "You should send it to him."

BAR 10

Deliberation

I

Everything was waiting. I waited to hear from Brandeis. And we waited to hear from our Legal Aid lawyers, who waited to hear from the DA's office and the judge. Were we in or out; nay or yea? Would I be accepted to Brandeis? Would our cases go to trial? Would the DA be flexible, the judge lenient? Would they accept a plea? Because I would write one. I would have written ten thousand of them a day, every minute of every hour. Donnel would do anything, he said, any length of probation, any anger management therapy, any counseling, group sessions, or community service to get out of doing time.

"Nigga," he said. "I'll clean every subway station in Queens with a Q-tip if need be."

I checked the mailbox for the response from Brandeis every day. Sometimes three or four times, and even on Sunday. I asked people with mailboxes near our mailbox and those whose last names began with an *S* if they happened to get an envelope addressed to me. Nobody had.

The waiting was a plague, all encompassing, inundating. Everywhere I looked, I saw waiting. People at the bus stop: waiting. People at the barbershop, the beauty salon, outside on the street, the young men hustling: all waiting. And how about the nine men on the basketball court who were not shooting a foul shot, and the men and women in church thanking Jesus, praying that their children rise with pride, take every opportunity of a society deemed free: were they not waiting too?

When Donnel and I spoke all we talked about was waiting. But although he never said it, I knew the waiting hurt Donnel more than it pained me. Because waiting was his living. He had no escape from it. He was locked in with it. And everyone with him was waiting. And he couldn't be kissed or hugged, he couldn't be consoled or told an answer would come soon in the moments he most needed it. He had spent Thanksgiving waiting. And Christmas waiting. And New Year's. Then Valentine's Day passed. On the phone, he asked me what I did for Kaya.

"I wrote her a poem," I said.

"A poem," he laughed. "You trying to be me?"

Kaya was accepted to every city college and university she applied to. So she was deliberating, weighing the benefits of leaving Ever versus the costs. She could go to Queens College or Hunter; or she could go to Brooklyn College or City College; or she could go to Wellesley, or Temple in Philadelphia.

"I like the way that sounds," she said. "I go to Temple University. Makes it sound holy, doesn't it? Like I'm studying to be an angel or something. But what happens if I get homesick? Or what happens if I need something? You know, what if I want you to hold me, not just talk on the phone?"

March came and we were still waiting. I hadn't done my laundry in weeks. I hadn't cut my hair, gotten a shape-up, or tended to the fine hair that made a sparse tangle on my cheeks and chin. And no matter my age, no matter how my hormones raged, no matter how Kaya smelled or what she did or said, I did not think about sex or the shape and feel of her body.

"What's wrong with you?" she said, pouting when I didn't respond to her come-on and nuzzling. "You acting like someone died."

On March ninth, the judge sentenced me to two years of probation and fifty hours of community service, and Donnel plead guilty. He had to. Between the fight, and how he fought against the police when they arrested him he was facing anywhere between three to ten years depending on which charges stuck and which did not.

"I can't just give up that much," he said. "If I fight it and lose. Shit, they might try and keep me locked up until my hair goes white. There's things, nigga, things in life, that I want to do, you know?"

So they gave him three to five with the chance to be paroled anytime after thirty-six months. Every night I lay in bed, wide awake, too exhausted to sleep. I thought about Donnel. I wanted to blow up and extinguish where he was. I wanted to roll over, hit his shoulder, and say, *D, you snoring,* and hear him, still half asleep, say, *Then put a pillow over your head.* I couldn't leave him where he was. I wanted to call Rivers and tell him the whole thing was off, withdraw my application from the pile of applications sitting somewhere on some desk. And sometimes I wanted to pick up the phone and say: *Rivers, what's up? Yea or nay? Be honest. Tell me.* I couldn't take it. Nothing suppressed my hope for Donnel not to be where he was, that we'd wake up from it. Nothing eased my impatience. When was Brandeis's answer going to come?

I never called Rivers. Not at night. Not during the day. No matter how greatly I craved to. No matter how much I wanted to go to Brandeis. No matter how much I wanted to quit on it. Not ever. I could do no such thing. But it was never because of the hour it was, and it wasn't because of the cost. I didn't assume Rivers was sleeping or too busy to talk to me. Rather I couldn't call because I wouldn't. I was an indefatigably prideful brother. I refused to accept the possession of desperation, which, of course, was all I had become; desperate to learn; desperate to be educated; desperate for Donnel to be free; desperate for the opportunity to fully realize the most fundamental, the most basic element of my life, me. And desperate not to be afraid of leaving Ever, of Brandeis, of the unknown it might make me.

Another day came and went. And then another. And then Saturday, March 18th, the third Saturday in a four-Saturday month, came and by the end of the day my waiting was worse than any waiting I had ever known because not only had another day passed, but Donnel had cried on the phone when I spoke to him and he told me he just knew college was for me—he had dreamed it and written me a letter about his dream. Did I get it? But when I checked the mail nothing was there, not a single flyer or bill. Not at 10:00 a.m., not at noon, not at 4:00 p.m. or at six, not at eight, or ten, or midnight or a quarter after one in the morning when I finally accepted there would be nothing.

"Sometimes it don't come," said my grandma, hoping to console me. She was sitting on the couch, watching some infomercial because she couldn't sleep either. "Sometimes, Abraham, there just ain't none."

I mumbled good night and closed the bedroom door, and once again, I spent the night lying in bed, staring into the blackness of the room, feeling the way a boy on a timber raft in the middle of the ocean must feel, lost and isolated and fighting to maintain a sense of self, a sense of significance in the black vastness enveloping him. My uncle slept behind me. I listened to the night. The bed squeaked each time my uncle's lungs filled. Some pipes knocked. Eric slept on the mattress on the floor. He had a cold and his nose was stuffed, and he wheezed so deeply it sounded as if he might inhale all of Ever, its bricks and concrete through his one clear nostril. For hours, I lay there. But I didn't pity myself. I knew that whatever defeat I was near, Donnel was nearer.

Before dawn I got out of bed and went to the kitchen. I was not hungry. I was waiting. I opened the refrigerator. Then I closed it and stood in the blue dark. There was the sound of keys at the front door. Then the door flew open and my Aunt Rhonda, simultaneously turning on the light and slamming the door closed, rushed into the apartment like she had just won the Lotto, her chest leaned forward at a forty-five degree angle, her chin jutting out, her eyes aglow, her overstuffed purse with the broken zipper swinging from her shoulder, paper and envelopes and miscellany jutting from its top.

"Momma!" my Aunt Rhonda shouted. "Oh my god! Momma!"

She wagged her left hand over her head like it was on fire and failed to notice me standing in the kitchen or what time it was, that everyone was asleep or, in my case, should have been asleep. She breathed heavily and yet seemed unaffected by her shortness of breath. She crossed the room. She pounded on the door of the bedroom she shared with my grandma.

"Momma," she boomed. "Momma, wake up!"

She shouted like we lived down a hole instead of a two-bedroom Ever Park apartment shaped and as big as a lowercase *t*, the kitchen ten feet straight ahead from the door, the bedrooms abutting it, the bathroom just to the left of the couch. She stormed toward the kitchen then flicked on the light switch. She was shocked to see me, but her shock did little more than cause her to pause.

"Abraham!" she said. "What you standing in the kitchen for?"

My Aunt Rhonda was thirty-five and she had gained thirty pounds from her chin to her knees since Donnel had been arrested. She couldn't stop eating. She ate for comfort, company, and solutions, as if that box of Oreos, bag of Cheetos, and half gallon of Dolly Madison ice cream might bring Donnel home. She swung around, stepped over the threshold of the kitchen door, and planting her hands on the walls, she leaned forward and called for my uncle and Eric.

"Everybody!" she shouted. "Momma! Wake up!"

She turned and looked at me, a determined, joyous gleam banging from her eyes.

"Abraham," she announced, "you won't believe it!"

She held up her left hand for me to see. Around her chubby finger, the ring was a sliver of gold thread, the diamond like a chip of something, a crumb of crack, a flake of glass, one of the small glow in the dark stars children stick on a ceiling.

"I'm getting married," she said.

She ripped the ring off her finger, handed it to me, and told me to feel how heavy it was. I held it up to the light. The jewel was nearly opaque but not opaque enough to see anything but a blurry smudge where shine should have been.

"David," she said.

"What?" I said.

"Dave," she stressed. "Jamel's brother. We're getting married."

Still holding the ring up, I shifted my eyes to her. I could have laughed. I could have cried. I was shocked and amused and mildly wounded.

"Doo-Doo?" I said incredulously.

She snatched the ring from me and jammed it back on her finger.

"David," she said. "He hasn't been Doo-Doo since we was kids."

"Since when have you-all been together?" I asked.

She dismissed my question, sucking her teeth, flapping her hand in the air.

"Me and him have always had a thing. We just been too scared. You know, we've been dancing around each other for years."

Half asleep and holding her old bathrobe around herself, my grandma walked into the kitchen. "Rhonda, what the hell is you yelling about?" she asked, squinting in the kitchen's light.

My Aunt Rhonda held her hand out for my grandma to see. My grandma looked at the ring for a split second, then she left my Aunt

Rhonda's hand hanging in the air and shifted her eyes to me, her eyebrows buckled over her sleepy eyes, her face still asleep so drooping.

"Momma," my Aunt Rhonda said. "Can you believe it? For forever. That's what he said. Me? Rhonda? I ain't never thought no one would ask me to be with them like this."

"Who asked what?" said my grandma, snatching the tips of my Aunt Rhonda's fingers from the air and studying the ring.

"David," said my Aunt Rhonda.

My grandma shifted her eyes to me. She needed clarification.

"Doo-Doo," I said.

My grandma couldn't believe it. "Doo-Doo? Jamel's brother?"

My uncle walked into the kitchen, rubbing his eyes in the light.

"Look!" said my Aunt Rhonda, snatching her hand from my grandma's grip and thrusting it in front of him. "Its on my finger and I still can't believe it!"

My uncle looked at the ring.

"I'm getting married," said my Aunt Rhonda.

My uncle studied the whole scene, every inch of the ring and my Aunt Rhonda and my grandma and me. Rhonda was getting married? He could have said a thousand things. But he said nothing about the ring, nothing about what he thought. Instead, he pointed at my Aunt Rhonda's purse.

"What's that?" he asked.

He reached out, grabbed the envelopes jutting from the top of my Aunt Rhonda's purse, and held one up.

"It's here," he said, lifting his eyes to me. He handed the envelope to me. "Open it."

I studied the outside of the envelope for far too long. I read my name and our address and the stamp and the postage meter's faded red ink and the return address in the upper left corner: Brandeis University, Waltham, Massachusetts 02453.

"Abraham, shit!" burst my Aunt Rhonda.

She stomped her foot and snatched the envelope from me. Her excitement over her ring gave her no patience. She tore the envelope open with her teeth, spit the piece of paper on the floor, and tore the letter out. The envelope fell to the floor. She unfolded the letter. She read it silently.

"What?" begged my grandma. "What's it say?"

My Aunt Rhonda raised her hand over her head. "Oh my God, oh God," she said.

She bent over as if she'd been struck with cramps. Then she stood tall, clapped the letter against her chest and looked at me, her brown eyes wide and welled with something inexplicable, something she didn't know she'd come home with.

My uncle snatched the letter from my Aunt Rhonda and read the beginning to himself as quickly as he could, his eyes whipping left to right. I tried to read his face. I tried to understand.

"Roosevelt!" shouted my grandma. "Jesus! What's going on? What's it say?"

"All I got to say is you better not miss my wedding," said my Aunt Rhonda, laughing and crying, her voice swollen with exuberance.

"Oh Jesus," said my grandma, breathless in her shift from confusion to understanding, holding her hands to her cheeks. "Oh Lord have mercy, He heard me. He finally, finally heard me."

II

It was the first time I wore a suit. It was white with three black buttons. My shirt was black and it had black buttons too. Black were my patent leather shoes, black was my belt, black was my tie, and black was the cane my uncle called my "accoutrement" with a hint of a French accent.

"Accoutrement?" I laughed.

"Accoutrement," he smiled. "Look it up if you don't know what it means."

"Oh you owning the day, Abraham," said my grandma. "Every hour, minute, and second of it."

With a disposable camera, she took pictures of me doing everything. I tied my shoes: click. I brushed my teeth: click. I took the gallon of milk from the refrigerator. Click, wind, click. Like dapper naval men, my uncle, Eric, and Doo-Doo wore similar white suits. Click, wind, click: my grandma took pictures of them too.

Then like an eager student with the right answer, my grandma waved the disposable camera over her head. "Get together!" she shouted. "Get over there in front of the couch! Stand like you mean something!"

My grandma wore a white dress, bloodred shoes, and a bloodred shawl draped over her shoulders. Her hair was done, and the smoldering scent of her old hot comb lingered in the air longer than her perfume when she spoke or moved.

"Rhonda, baby!" she called out. "C'mon. We need you for a picture."

My Aunt Rhonda stood in the bathroom, her face inches from the mirror. She put on makeup, one hand planted on the edge of the sink.

"Coming!" she shouted. "Hold on!"

There was a knock on the door. I unfastened the chain latch and unlocked the locks. I opened the door and Luscious confidently walked into the room, perpetual sensuality beaming in her eyes. Eric, Doo-Doo, and I swallowed. I looked at my uncle. His face was patriotic, as if the anthem of his country was playing, its flag unfurled. Was she there to take him back? Was she there to open her arms and hold him? Or was she there to throw rejection in his face, tell him how dare he think how he thinks, do what he does, be who he was after being so far, so silent?

"Oh, Luscious," burst my grandma. She darted across the room and hugged Luscious hello. "Oh lord, it's good to see you."

Luscious hugged my grandma back. Then when they let each other go, she stepped forward and stood a foot in front of my uncle. He dropped his eyes. She waited. And when he finally mustered the courage to look her in the face, he lifted his head and said, "Hey," the single syllable the penitent purr of a bass's deepest string.

"I thought about what you said," she said, her tone fierce and strong.

My uncle waited for clarification. He tried to be patient. Then, lacking confidence, he guessed at what she meant and hesitantly raised his arms to embrace her.

"Don't get no ideas," Luscious said, pushing his arms down. "I'm here cause you said it was important to Abraham." She shot her eyes at me. "That ain't the case?"

I looked at my uncle. I knew damn well my uncle hadn't wanted her there for my sake. And I knew Luscious didn't really arrive just to support me. It would only be a matter of time, maybe fifteen or twenty minutes, before they smiled at each other, and the door that was their love would swing ajar.

"Yeah," I said. "It means a lot. For real. Thank you."

My Aunt Rhonda came out of the bathroom. She wore a white dress too.

"Let me get this picture!" shouted my grandma. "C'mon. Get together. We gonna be late! Get close! Everybody!"

We stood together and my grandma held the camera to her eye.

"On the count of three," she said. "One, two, three: say *Graduation!*"

"Graduation!" they said.

But I didn't say it. It was not because I didn't recognize the significance of the event. Rather, it was because I was struck by absence. The day, would forever be without Donnel. I breathed in my grandma's declaration and I stood shoulder to shoulder with my family, and we positioned ourselves to look historical, unconquerable. My uncle held his hands together, lifted his chin like he was keeping his face out of rising water and wore a countenance of tranquility. Luscious stood beside him, one foot slightly in front of the other, smiling like a queen loved by a king without a single failing. Eric squinted and clenched his jaw as if, for the sake of the world, he was holding back the power that filled him. Doo-Doo stood behind my Aunt Rhonda, his head peeking over her shoulder, his arms wrapped around her waist while she leaned against him. And me? I was the first person in the history of my family, in the hundreds and thousands of never-known generations, the millions of brothers and sisters sacrificed on shores, drowned in seas of water and concrete, to graduate high school. It was a new millennium, June of 2000. I put my left hand in my pants pocket and made a V with the index and middle finger of my right hand, a peace sign, and holding it over the left of my chest, I stared straight ahead, my countenance chiseled, a bedrock foundation.

"Just look at you," said my grandma. "You all so beautiful."

We walked down the dark stairs, out of the dim lobby, and into the gold and diamond light of midmorning. Then, with three dozen brothers and sisters in vibrant hues and matching shoes, hats, and clutch purses, blasting shine from gold necklaces and earrings and bracelets and rings; blasting shine from smiles and gold teeth; blasting shine from glossed lips and earthen-toned skin; blasting in finery; blasting the magnificent blasting that drummed in our chests, we waited for the bus to take us to graduation. On the opposite side of the crowd, Lorenzo Davis was there because his stepbrother was graduating. Lorenzo wore baggy black dress pants and a large, pressed, untucked white shirt with razor creases down the arms. He tilted his head and watched me and my family out of the corners of his eyes. When I felt sure that he wasn't watching us, I watched him. We took turns. Then I looked too soon and we made eye contact. My first instinct was to look away. But I couldn't be afraid just like I couldn't be afraid of college, of leaving Ever no matter how afraid I truly was. That is, as if being afraid was crying, I wouldn't let myself do it. For Donnel, I refused. So I didn't look away. And neither did Lorenzo. Then Lorenzo did something I still can't understand. He smiled a half smile, cool as he could be, nodded his head not out of ire or disrespect, but with appreciation, and gave me a lazy thumbs-up. With a level of zeal that I found embarrassing moments later, I reciprocated, nodding then giving him a strong thumbs-up and holding it there, before letting my hand drop slowly.

III

We filled the sun-soaked gymnasium, every shade of brown face, every age, every medical condition. It was a mass arrival into an inadequate space. Hundreds of people, two by two, four by four, siblings stretching as far as four generations back. Drug dealers, construction workers, line cooks, city employees; pastors and deacons; salesmen and administrative assistants, security guards, entrepreneurs, deliverymen. I put on the cap and gown that smelled of mothballs and past graduates. Ms. Hakim pinned a white carnation on my chest. A school administrator shouted through a bullhorn, demanding that all families and friends sit in the back while we, the few hundred who were to graduate, the few hundred who were just half of those I started ninth grade with, crammed into the front rows. Families and friends who did not get chairs stood in the back of the gym. Those who could not fit in the back stood along the walls. And those who could not be squeezed in, those who could not find a square foot of floor to stand on, streamed out of the heavy steel doors and spilled through my high school's hallways.

Names were hollered. Signs were held above heads. Cameras clicked. Flashes popped. It was hot. Two industrial fans hacked at the air, pushing the steam of our scents, our body odor and our perfumes, about the gymnasium. A scratchy rendition of the national anthem played over the loudspeakers. I stood beside Yusef, Titty, and Precious, the only other members of my crew to be graduating on time. I lowered my head and thought about my family, about my grandmother and uncle and aunt and Eric and Donnel. Then I was consumed by one thought: my mother. I had done everything in my power to eradicate her from my life. The pictures I had of us I had burned. The last gift she bought me for Christmas, the New York Knicks T-shirt, I had thrown in the trash. And I'd thanked God she was dead. Hundreds of times. Thousands of times. I'd walked to school with the thought and sat in class with the thought and went to sleep with the thought echoing in my head. But this was not what I thought about when the national anthem played. Instead, I imagined my mother singing, her mouth busted ajar by a rare, incredible, and uncontainable sound that could only be caused by the sudden collision of joy and triumph. Cherrie had let me listen to the tape of my mother singing, and I had listened to it over and over again. Chills spilled up and down my spine. I became aware of a lesson that had riddled and tormented my subconscious, a lesson that possessed the potential of guaranteeing my survival, that would perpetuate my ability to continue forth, to hope with even greater force, and to fight, to defend myself, my honor, my family when it was jeopardized. I knew then that regardless of what I did and regardless of time, I carried my mother just as I carried everything. That is, she was not a weight nor a thought, nor an object, a stone I lugged about or dragged and pushed. Rather, she was my composition, the integral integration of me, and, like Ever and all that occurred in Ever, no matter what I did or thought, no matter where I was or would go, I could not nor would I ever be able to strip or rip her being from me.

IV

I was in the prison's visiting room, encased by lifeless green walls and steel bars. Donnel walked in. I rose to my feet. I stood as tall as I could stand. I had stayed up all night writing him a letter, sitting at the kitchen table, scribbling and crossing out words and thoughts. The sheets of loose-leaf were in my back pocket. We embraced, said what's up. I was leaving for Brandeis in three days.

"You ready?" he asked me.

My mind went blank. My voice was gone, entirely stripped from me. Thank God, I had it all written down. I reached into my back pocket. Everything I wanted and needed to say was on those pages. I looked at them. I looked at Donnel. His eyes filled with wet.

"I wrote you a letter," I said, handing it to him.

He took it, looked at it, sniffed, dragged his arm under his nose, and blew a sigh from puckered lips. He fought against who he truly was. He would not let me see him cry. I hated the sight. He handed the letter back to me.

"Go on," he said. "Read it to me."

He was the one who carried me when I was weak, who cleaned, protected, and spoke on my behalf when he too was a child. He had been my father and grandfather. Without him, what would I be? An object? A ball? A brick? I inhaled and exhaled. I cleared my throat. I couldn't do it. My hands would not even open the letter.

Suddenly, Donnel lost all patience. "Put it there," he said, pointing at the chair.

"D," I said.

"Put it down," he demanded. "Drop it and go."

I put the letter on the chair. I turned around.

"Abraham," he said, his voice shivering like his throat was holding something he couldn't hold anymore.

It took all of my strength to stop. But I was too weak, too sad, too scared to turn around.

"You go up there and be some kind of doctor or lawyer or something," he said. "It's a beautiful thing. College, nigga. But write me, you know what I'm saying? And be strong, throw that motherfucking hand up when you got something to say. And don't never forget I got you, nigga. Understand?"

BAR II

Flight

I

My grandma woke me, shaking my shoulder, whispering, "Abraham, baby, Abraham. Open your eyes. It's time. I got to go."

She sat on the edge of the bed, the features of her face cloudy, a silhouette the only thing my groggy eyes could see, so it was not the sound of her voice but her scent, that amalgamation of cocoa butter and faint hot comb that made me know she was really there and I was not dreaming.

"Abraham," she said, whispering my name so as not to wake my uncle asleep beside me, or Eric asleep on the floor when she saw that my eyes were adjusting to being open.

Then as if she were blinder than I, so using her sense of touch to memorize the construction of my face, she laid the flat of her fingers on my lips, then gently pressed them against my cheek, my forehead, over my eyes, on my nose, my chin.

"Abraham," she whispered again. "I been waiting and praying and hoping so damn hard I don't know what to say. I don't know if I should hug you or kiss you or say don't never look back, don't never stop."

My sight cleared and I could see the struggle on her face, how she was tortured by my leaving, torn between feeling proud and feeling abandoned. She lived her life for me; for her children and her grandchildren; us, her family, we Singletons whom she loved unconditionally. And because the same was true for me, because the intensity of her hopes and prayers and her speechlessness were equaled by mine, and because what stood before me—college!—was nothing I could imagine, I took a deep breath.

"Grans," I began.

She held up her hand to stop me. "I don't want to hear it," she said. "Not now. Just don't go losing yourself. Man walked on the moon but he ain't never become no alien."

She would not let me see her cry. That morning had to be a celebration. She leaned over, and with all of her might, taking a deep breath and exhaling through her nose, consuming as much of my scent as possible, injecting herself, her boundless bravery into me, she kissed me not on the forehead or cheek or on my chin, but between my eyes.

She reached down and touched the side of my face once more. Then she stood.

"Now, stop holding me up. I got to get to work," she scolded.

She walked to the door. Quickly, I sat up in bed.

"Grans," I said.

She stopped, but she did not turn to face me. "Abraham, shhhh," she said. "Save it. And don't go forgetting your keys. But I ain't letting you in until Thanksgiving. So don't get no ideas about it being too hard, or that you're homesick. You in college now. I ain't taking no excuses."

II

I sat on the couch. A rap video was on TV. A young man talked about those who braved history by his side, those who trumpeted him and loved him like a brother no matter what he thought he had to be. I was nervous, scared. A part of me never wanted to get off that couch. A part of me wanted to leap and run so fast my velocity would propel me from the ground, lift me and keep me in flight. A collegial brother. A university student. What did it mean?

Above me, family photographs hung on the wall. Beneath me, the couch, battered and wobbly, had a phone book under its broken front leg. On the coffee table, there was some mail, flyers, and a plant in a clay pot, Sharry Baby, chocolate oncidium, those orchids that smelled like chocolate that my grandma loved most and that Mr. Goines brought over the previous night when he came to say good-bye to me and a quick, purportedly innocuous hello to my grandma. On one side of the couch were my uncle's basketball trophies. On the other side, a full garbage bag, my backpack, and my grandma's floral print suitcase,

fastened by a belt and two shoelaces tied end to end, were packed with
my belongings.

My grandma's bedroom door opened and my Aunt Rhonda, half
asleep and wearing a white bathrobe, shuffled into the room.

"Abraham," she said, sounding relieved. "What time's your bus?"

"Ten thirty," I said.

It was eight thirty.

"Ten thirty?" she said. "Well, you better get going. You know you
can't trust the trains. Anything can happen, and you can't miss it."

She dropped her eyes to the floor and thought about my departure.
I looked at the television and did the same. I was aimed in a polar opposite direction from Donnel, as if I were to live and he were to die. Or
maybe it was vice versa, I to die, he to live. I had no idea where I was
going. That is, everything I knew about Brandeis was two-dimensional,
in text and pictures, bulletins and brochures. So I was leaving not just
family and friends, but all I knew to be real and true about people and
the world. And I knew how my absence was affecting everyone, how it
amplified Donnel's absence.

My Aunt Rhonda lifted her eyes to the TV. She watched the rap
video for a moment.

"I wish you could take your cousin," she said. "Do Eric some good to
get out of Ever." She paused. "Shit, I wish you was taking me."

She took a deep breath and left the wish hanging between us. Then,
looking over her shoulder, she shouted: "Eric! Abraham's leaving! Come
say good-bye!"

She looked back at me. She took a deep breath. And with that breath
she pushed a weak smile onto her face.

"Quick," she said, opening her arms. "Come give your aunt some love."

I rose from the couch, crossed the room, and wrapped my arms
around her body.

"C'mon," she scolded. "Hug me like you mean it."

Taking another deep breath, my aunt hugged me the way she wished to be hugged, squeezing so tight my ribs bowed. I equaled her embrace.

"There you go," she said. "We so proud of you. I know Jelly is just shining up in heaven, bragging to anyone who'll listen, telling all those angels and saints to check you out, her little Mister Man. You gonna do great. I just know it."

The bedroom door opened and Eric, wearing a stretched-out wife-beater and mesh shorts, and still half asleep, walked into the room. My Aunt Rhonda stopped hugging me and stepped back.

"I'm gonna take a shower," she said. "Let you two have your good-byes."

She went into the bathroom. Eric rubbed his eyes and scratched his chest, and then he looked at me, slowly up from my feet to my face.

"You leaving right now?" he asked, his surprise and sleepiness making him sound disgruntled.

"Yeah," I said.

"You got money for the bus?"

"Grans gave me some."

"You got enough?"

"Yeah," I said. "I think so."

"You sure?"

"I'm sure." I said.

"So you going right now?" he asked.

"In a minute," I said.

Eric digested my answer. His eyes dropped to the floor. The shower turned on. He looked at the bathroom door. Then he swung his eyes to the television. I put my eyes on the TV too. For a few moments, we stared at it, exuding no emotions, making no facial expressions, never changing our postures.

Then Eric said, "Hold on."

He hurried back into our room. A drawer opened, slammed closed, and he came back out, holding something behind his back.

"D told me to give you this."

Eric's hand came from around his back. It was a wrinkled envelope. He held it out to me and waited for me to take it. So I did. The envelope was too thick and its contents were too heavy to be a letter.

"Open it," he said.

I held one side of the envelope between my index finger and thumb and shook it so the contents would shift to the other side. Then I tore the side of the envelope open and blew in it. Inside was a stack of money. I pulled it out. They were all one hundreds, five thousand dollars' worth. I looked at Eric. He smiled. Then the smile left his face and his eyes filled with a force, a piercing truth that couldn't be kept in.

"It's for books and stuff. And if you want to get Kaya something. But D don't want you wasting it on bullshit." The smile returned to Eric's face. "He said if he finds out you're fucking around he'll kill you."

III

I walked down the stairs. For no clear reason, I didn't think about taking the elevator. It was as if someplace deep wanted to discuss my progress with each step, each landing. I was going to live at Brandeis, in the North Quad, Scheffres Hall, on the first floor, in room 118, with a young man named Cole Monroe, a brother from Selma, Alabama, right where, he later bragged, Martin Luther King started walking to Montgomery, protected by federal troops and backed by twenty-five thousand followers. I was from a place where most didn't get a glimpse of their innate human potential. Yusef and Titty weren't going to college. Precious wasn't going either. And Cleveland and Jefferson were working in a warehouse stacking pallets in the back of flatbed trucks. This was the effect of Ever, that even the strongest and most courageous and most blessed of us, even the most confident and willful, even the most brilliant were infected with a dangerous degree of self-doubt, that damn dankness that infiltrated bones. In worst-case scenarios, it caused us to aim ourselves at self-destruction. In best cases, we fought and clawed and used that seed to fuel our refusal to fail.

I began to cry. And not just a little. And not just weeping. But silently, and with my head down so much water rushed out of my eyes and ran down my face it was as if I was an ocean, and my eyes were holes in my dam. I walked across the dim lobby this way. I shouldered open the steel door.

Outside, the morning was Eden, clear blue sky. I walked along the concrete path. My grandma's suitcase was in my left hand. The garbage bag of my other belongings was slung over my right shoulder. My backpack was on my back. Inside of it were pens, pencils, the cassette tape of my mother singing, her old diary, the Qur'an my uncle had given me before he left for work earlier that morning, and some family photographs. In one of my front pockets were my keys. In the other was the fat envelope of money. I'd said my good-byes to my friends the previous night, and after we talked about growing up together as we sat on the concrete bench by the basketball court, Kaya and I said our good-byes on the roof of my building. She cried. She had accepted a scholarship to Hunter. She was staying home. I kissed and whispered how much I loved her into every part of her body that my lips graced.

BAR 12

Reprise

I

I stood at the bus stop, the cusp of self-realization; the cusp of self-expansion. Behind me was a vacant lot surrounded by a rusted fence with black plastic bags snared along its top edge, where they'd been caught and now had to wait for the weather to beat them free. Across the street was Ever Park, our buildings, two towers looming, great brick beasts with my life in their bellies. Standing beside me were a few teenagers younger than me, and a young woman and her infant in a stroller. Cars drove past. I was the young, wiry, weary-looking brother standing on the side of Columbus Avenue, his back bowed with the weight of his belongings, his eyes wide with determination and shock.

Suddenly, as if he'd been dropped from a sky above mine, Lindbergh arrived, dragging his shopping cart full of miscellany. He stopped and studied us, we who waited for the bus. A car passed him. The driver honked and yelled out of the window for him to get out the way. Lindbergh didn't even flinch. He scratched his head. Then, as if recalling the initial thought that caused him to stop, he made a quizzical face, his brow furrowing with the cock of one eyebrow. I wondered what he saw. I wondered what he might mumble. I was a refugee, a child soldier, an asylum seeker who couldn't believe the pending bounty of his new life. Lindbergh stood tall, let his hand fall from his cart, then swung it to his forehead and saluted. He smiled, his few remaining teeth worn to nubs in his rose-colored gums. Then he laughed. He held his belly, leaned back, and laughed into the sky. He leaned forward and laughed at the street. He planted his hands on his hips. Then still laughing a little, he shook his head and turned to his shopping cart. He mumbled something to himself and dug through all that he owned, all of the bric-a-brac and gathered things and the items that reminded him of other items and selves, the courageous parts and the irreparable ones. He found what he was looking for, a solitary feather. Holding it between his finger and thumb, he admired it for a moment. Then he stuck it into his hair and with the feather jutting parallel to the street, Lindbergh took hold of his shopping cart and walked away, proud of his belongings, pulling them with him.

ACKNOWLEDGMENTS

I wish to thank my teachers and love, my wife, Nadia, all of whom are responsible for providing and supporting the privilege of my education in traditional institutions of higher education like schools, houses of worship, universities, and places that provided even greater lessons about humanity like bars, basketball courts, Greyhound buses, dance floors, 525 Gates Avenue, 8-Plus, 46 Beard Street, and the Leadership Alliance. I wish to thank my brothers: Joshua Goodman and David Goodman, Derek Hyra, John Wedges, Brian "Besus" Samuel, Gil Soltz, Adam Gerson, Ethan Field, and *The Nobodies*, Clintel "Steady" Steed, Michael "Big Mike" Dopp, and Jay Baron "Booms" Nicorvo. I wish to thank Thomas Perry, William Brown, Phil Jackson, Tony Isaacs, Eddie Batista, Ronald Willis, Tina Haluscka, Ronald Vanzant, Anthony McFadden, Felipe Vargas, and Bradley Solomon, men (and a woman) among men. I wish to thank Arisa White, Jessica Pressman (and my man Brad Lupian), Bill Knott, Martha Rhodes, Joseph Caldwell, Simon Ortiz, and Steven Kuchuk, all of whom prove poetry is more essential than dollars and bombs. I wish to thank Mark and Rochelle Jacobson, Gail and Bruce and the extended Leibowitz family, Chandra Williams, Eric Louis, Marquis Cothren, Benjamin Polo, Jae Cho, David Eustace, Uli Grueber, the 92nd Street Y, the Vermont Studio Center, Bread Loaf Writers' Conference, David Hagland, M. Mark, and the Pen Journal. I want to thank Victoria Sanders, Bennee Knauer, and asha bandele for believing, and Sulay Hernandez and Touchstone Fireside for believing too. I want to thank my mother, Arlene Goodman, who taught me the only way to love is with totality, and my father, Bernard Goodman, who taught me to think before speaking. Herein lies my heart, nothing more, nothing less.

Touchstone Reading Group Guide

Hold Love Strong

This reading group guide includes discussion questions, a Q & A with author Matthew Aaron Goodman, and ideas for enhancing your book club. The suggested questions are intended to help your reading group find new and interesting angles and topics for your discussion. We hope that these ideas will enrich your conversation and increase your enjoyment of the book.

FOR DISCUSSION

1. What is the significance of the title *Hold Love Strong*? From what scene in the book does it originate? What do you think its meaning is in the context of the book's message?

2. Abraham claims that "in Ever, we were three things: broken, desperate to leave, or soldiers in a war so impossible to win that everything we did, even blinking our eyes, even licking our lips, might be suicide" (p. 16). Discuss the following characters in the context of this statement: Abraham, Jelly, Rhonda, Nice, and Donnell. Into which of the three categories does each character fall? Do you think it's possible for them to move from one to another? Why?

3. Abraham's grandmother reasons that "there were lives that were simply impossible to live" (p. 75). Does the life that Abraham begins to want seem impossible? When does he realize that it is possible? What steps does he have to take to make it possible?

4. Abraham's grandmother forbids Abraham to allow his mother back

into the apartment once she succumbs again to her crack addiction. When he sees her on the basketball court, he refuses to approach her. How is this different from his earlier behavior? Was it just Abraham's grandmother who distanced them, or has Abraham himself changed? Do you think he would have handled it differently if he knew it was the last time he would see her alive?

5. When Nice returns from prison, Abraham claims that "seven years of incarceration had made his beauty the type of beautiful you had to commit yourself to, the type of beautiful you had to study to understand" (p. 235). What does Abraham mean by this? How is his uncle different from the man he knew?

6. Abraham constantly wants to be somebody. How does he handle the shortcomings of those he admires? What is the symbolism of the characters on *The Cosby Show*? At what point does he decide to be himself, to be "more than such nothingness" (p. 305)?

7. Why do you think that basketball is such an escape for Abraham? Discuss the statement, "Basketball was the way I lived, so personal every action, every dribble, every pass, every move to the basket, every defensive stance was essential, notes in a song" (p. 269).

8. Were you surprised when Abraham admitted that his mother "was my composition, the integral integration of me, and . . . I could not nor would I ever be able to strip or rip her being from me" (p. 340)?

9. What is the "effect of Ever" that Abraham mentions (p. 351)? Discuss both its positive and negative effects in terms of the main characters of the story. Who were the worst cases? Who were the best?

10. The author chooses to end *Hold Love Strong* with Abraham waiting for the bus to Brandeis University. Why do you think he decided to

do so? Would the story have benefited from chronicling Abraham's experiences at Brandeis? Why or why not?

11. In the beginning of the book, Abraham mentions that he "lived on a ladder, on one of the rungs between third and first world" (p. 15). Do you feel that is an accurate assessment of where he lived? Do you think he will ever move up the ladder? Why or why not?

A CONVERSATION WITH
MATTHEW AARON GOODMAN

Your ethnic, social, and academic background is very different from those of the characters about whom you've written. What served as the inspiration for you to write **Hold Love Strong?**

At the time when I began writing *Hold Love Strong*, I was teaching at an alternative school in the South Jamaica section of Queens while living at a boardinghouse. There were two hundred students with only fifty desks. We had no supplies. The kids had seen six or seven principals at the school within the span of a couple of months. There were no resources and very little stability in school and within their homes. I felt helpless, trying to figure out how to reach these kids. I was not functioning in a reality that most people experience.

Then our country was dealt another blow with September eleventh. As profoundly tragic as September eleventh had been, I was confronted with the reality that the kids I taught saw death and despair all around them every day. I wanted to find a way to tell the stories that we often don't hear—the bad as well as the good—and hopefully start a dialogue about what needs to be done to help kids and families like those you read about in the book.

How did you come to create and develop the characters?

Through my work with the students I taught and my work in the prison system as a case manager, I grew to know and love the people I worked with. Like anyone else who works on a job, the people you're working with is whom you talk about when you leave the office. They were my colleagues and coworkers. So I drew off the many people I had the honor of working with and helping, all of whom I came to love, respect, and care deeply about.

What was most challenging about writing Hold Love Strong?

It took eight years to complete the novel. To be honest, poetry had been my first love and I didn't truly know how to write a novel. So I had to learn how to govern myself in writing the story, really pacing the way I told the story. I also had to get out of my own way because it can be easy to convince yourself that you can't do something that you've not done before.

I also worked hard to make sure that I didn't overwhelm the reader. Abraham's story—and the stories of the people around him—are not easy to read. Not that we should run from them either. So I wanted to make them accessible and approachable without limiting the characters and their voices.

The voice throughout the book is that of the character Abraham, who is also at the center of the story. Abraham has a constant inner struggle with whom he believes he wants and deserves to be and what he sees all around him, including friends and family members. How were you able to strike a balance between the two sides of Abraham?

It really was not that difficult because I think we all struggle with balancing our lives. Take me, for instance. Although I didn't grow up in the same social environment as the character Abraham, I still struggled with the same sorts of issues. Where do I fit in? Is college really for me? What do I want to do with my life? I wasn't the greatest student but I grew up understanding that education is important, and I was obedient to that belief. I attended college at Brandeis, not always feeling like I fit in. I've lived in a number of different places, trying to make a home and life for myself. So I wanted to represent the inner struggles that Abraham was having, between what he wanted for himself and the realities of what he saw around him, based on my own experiences and what people go through every day, regardless of their circumstances.

Hold Love Strong *is a fictional account of an African American family, but how real do you feel these stories truly are?*
I know the stories in *Hold Love Strong* are based on real life because I've witnessed it through my work. I run a literacy group at present where I work with fifteen to twenty African American and Latino boys and girls who have been incarcerated themselves, on probation, or their parents have been incarcerated. Working with them gives me a front-row seat to a lot of what's happening in the world outside of what is considered the norm for many of us. And a lot of what I witness through my interaction with them is not fantasy or made up. It's real life for them, and as someone who works with them, it's real for me, too.

What made you decide to write the story from the perspective of the 1980s-to-early-1990s time period?
I wrote *Hold Love Strong* during this period because it bridged my own youth with that of the character Abraham. The eighties and nineties have their own respective histories, and I found a lot during that era to explore through the eyes of Abraham: the onset of the crack epidemic, the growth of hip hop, the colloquialisms of the day, what we were watching on television (e.g., *The Cosby Show*), while revisiting my own coming of age.

AIDS and the crack epidemic are front and center in **Hold Love Strong,** *particularly as it relates to Abraham's immediate family. What do you say to those critics who might say that you've written an unfairly stereotypical account of a black family in the 'hood?*

I don't feel that I've written an unfair or unflattering portrait at all. What's unflattering is reality. When we meet one another, we construct what we think to be one another's stories. Sure, you can get a short bio of where someone went to school, where they live, where they work. But only when we each look in the mirror do we see our own stories in its entirety. *Hold Love Strong,* while not representative of the whole story of any one community or family, is the story of countless Americans.

Teenage pregnancy and single motherhood are also at the forefront of the story. Abraham's grandmother is only thirty years old when he is born to his thirteen-year-old mother. There are no fathers in the household, only male nephews and cousins. How close to reality do you believe a story like this to be?

The truth is in the statistics. There are an overwhelming number of households, largely African American, being headed by single mothers. A lot of the kids I have worked with throughout the years speak to the high number of households where there is no father or father figure present. I chose to tell Abraham's story as such because it represents the positive that can and does come out of households headed by single women, particularly amid social adversity.

The "n" word is used throughout the book, which some may find offensive or difficult to digest, particularly coming from someone who is not African American. How do you explain its use and context in **Hold Love Strong?**

Claude Brown, author of *Manchild in the Promised Land,* once wrote, "Perhaps the most soulful word in the world is *nigger.*" I especially believe that our society's preoccupation with the word is also our way of avoiding the real issues that accompany the term. I personally have my own issues with the word and do not use it in my everyday life. However, I will say honestly that I've been called the "n" word in a loving way more times than my own name in some instances. I've also been referred to as the "n" word in not-so-desirable terms. My reason for using the term in *Hold Love Strong* is quite simply being true to Abraham's voice, not in any way, shape, or form condoning or glamorizing the word.

Tell me about who Matthew Aaron Goodman is.

I'm a boy who loved playing basketball, yet grew to be a man who strived to live his dream of being a writer. I've never pursued writing in the celebrity sense. My goal has been to write great, meaningful, thought-provoking stories that people can relate to, enjoy reading, and hopefully walk away having learned something from the experience. I'm also a person who loves my work with youth. I never walk away disappointed in my interactions with them. I learn from them as much as I hope they learn from me.

What do you hope readers will gain from reading Hold Love Strong? Are there any important lessons to be learned?

Mahatma Gandhi said, "A man is but the product of his thoughts; what he thinks, he becomes." I hope that *Hold Love Strong* is able to contribute to the discussion that proves our universal humanity. That is, if we can accept that we can build such destructive devices—the atomic bomb, weapons of war, et cetera—why is it that we struggle to believe that we can build constructive ones as well, ones that bring us together instead of destroying and dividing each other? I always find it amazing when someone says you can't understand someone else. Considering that human beings have the capacity to split two invisible atoms (nuclear energy), I think we have a much greater capacity to understand each other than we give each other credit for.

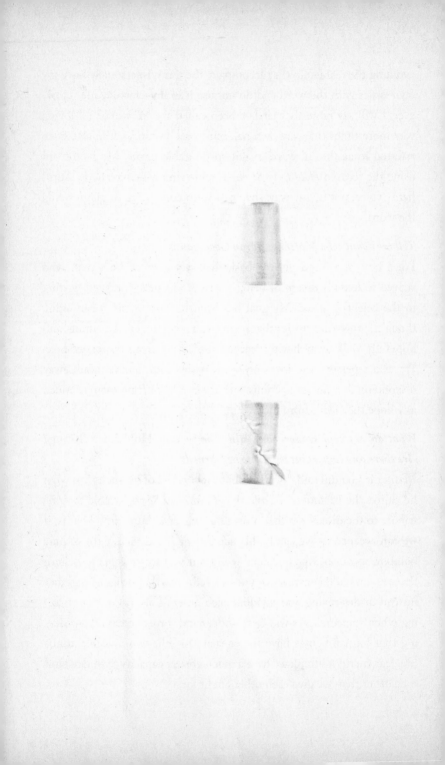

ENHANCE YOUR BOOK CLUB

1. Matthew Aaron Goodman currently leads a literacy program for a nonprofit organization that assists youth on the spectrum of criminal justice involvement. Visit their blog to learn more about their work: www.exaltscholars.wordpress.com.

2. Abraham plays basketball for the Police Athletic League. Visit www.nationalpal.org and find a chapter in your area. Then take your book club to one of their sporting events!

3. Idols, as you know, play a big part in the book. Discuss with your book club a few people who have been your idols. How have they helped you get where you are today? If you can, bring them to a meeting of your book club so everyone can meet them!